I0886098

The Argument of Stone:
Book II of The War of the Stone

The Argument of Stone
By Ben Stoddard
Map by Ciaran Morris

Zmok Books is an imprint of
Winged Hussar Publishing, LLC, 1525 Hulse Road, Unit 1, Point Pleasant, NJ 08742

This edition was published in 2025 Copyright ©Winged Hussar Publishing, LLC

PB ISBN 978-1-958872-85-7
EB ISBN 978-1-958872-95-6

Bibliographical references and index
1. Science Fiction 2. Space Opera 3. Action & Adventure

Mantic and Pannithor are the properties of Mantic Games
This book is published under license
Winged Hussar Publishing, LLC, All rights reserved

For more information on Winged Hussar Publishing, LLC, visit us at:
https://www.WHPSupplyroom.com
Instagram: WingedHussarPublishing
Facebook: Winged Hussar Publishing LLC

Except in the United States of America, this book is sold subject to the condition, that is shall not, by way of trade or otherwise, be lent, resold, hired out, or otherwise circulated without the publisher's prior consent in any form of binding or cover other than that in which it is published and without a similar condition including this condition being imposed on the subsequent purchaser.

The scanning, uploading, and distribution of this book via the Internet or via any other means without the permission of the publisher is illegal and punishable by law. Please purchase only authorized electronic editions, and do not participate in or encourage electronic piracy of copyrighted materials. Your support of the author's and publisher's rights is appreciated.

An Introduction to Pannithor

The world of Pannithor is a place of magic and adventure, but it is also beset by danger in this, the Age of Conflict. Legions of evil cast their shadow across the lands while the forces of good strive to hold back the darkness. Between both, the armies of nature fight to maintain the balance of the world, led by a demi-god from another time. Humanity is split into numerous provinces and kingdoms, each with their own allegiances and vendettas. Amongst the most powerful of all is the Hegemony of Basilea, with its devout army that marches to war with hymns in their hearts and the blessings of the Shining Ones, ready to smite those they deem as followers of the Wicked Ones.

Meanwhile, the Wicked Ones themselves toil endlessly in the depths of the Abyss to bring the lands of men to their knees. Demons, monsters, and other unspeakable creatures spill forth from its fiery pits to wreak havoc throughout Pannithor.

To the north of the Abyss, the Northern Alliance holds back the forces of evil in the icy depths of the Winterlands. Led by the mysterious Talannar, this alliance of races guards a great power to stop it from being grasped by the followers of the Wicked Ones. For if it ever did, Pannithor would fall under into darkness.

In the south, the secretive Ophidians remain neutral in the battles against the Abyss but work toward their own shadowy agenda. Their agents are always on-hand to make sure they whisper into the right ear or slit the right throat.

Amongst all this chaos, the other noble races – dwarfs, elves, salamanders and other ancient peoples – fight their own pitched battles against goblins, orcs, and chittering hordes of rat-men, while the terrifying Nightstalkers flit in and out of existence, preying on the nightmares of any foolish enough to face them. The world shakes as the armies of Pannithor march to war...

Pannithor Timeline

-1100: First contact with the Celestians

Rise of the Celestians

-170: The God War
0: Creation of the Abyss
2676: Birth of modern Basilea, and what is known as the Common Era.
3001: Free Dwarfs declare their independence
3558: Golloch comes to power
3850: The expansion of the Abyss

Ascent of the Goblin King
Tales of Pannithor: Edge of the Abyss

3854: The flooding of the Abyss, the splintering of the Brotherhood, and Lord Darvled completing part of the wall on the Ardovikian Plains.

Drowned Secrets
Nature's Knight
Claws on the Plain

Free Dwarfs expelled from their lands.
3865: Free Dwarfs begin the campaign to free Halpi – the opening of Halpi's Rift.
3865: The Battle of Andro;

Steps to Deliverance

Pious takes place six months before the events in *Steps to Deliverance.*

Through Thick and Thin takes place a few weeks after *Pious.*

Hero Falling and *Faith Aligned* take place several weeks after the events of *Steps to Deliverance.*

Honor's Price begins in early spring and ends in late August.

Pride of a King starts in the winter of 3865, but most of the events take place in 3866. The story continues in 3866 with *The Argument of Stone.*

3866: Halflings leave the League of Rhordia.

Broken Alliance

TRAGAR
Abyssal Wastes
Slazek-Don
Ezek-Mar
Tragazahk
Deigfell
Mount Ungar
Redgarakaz
Grunn' Keep
Duduach
The Redwalls
Helgarth
Tyr Gorfod
Ironhold
Fulgria's Shelf
Gatefort
Cwl Gen
Marn
Darthig
Gorric's Arch
Colledyg
The Lost Deep
Dandim
Atal Carreg
Crag Hudd
The Halpi Spine
Dynewrdd
Dragon Spite
West Halpi Ridge
Belyg'n Dam
Camuchel
Llyfanifeg
Creidd Aran
Deorm's Deep
Jarrun Bridge
Gars
Duhollt
Caer Eleud
Edrych Aros
Eastport
Cylmwyn
Pillars
Rhyn Dufaris
Golgamor
Shrew's Teeth Isles
Low Sea of Suan
The Halpi Mountains
Detailing the lands, Holds & passage ways of the region, including those areas Reclaimed by the Free Dwarfs & others still contested by their traitorous kin & other enemies.
TRAILS
KNOWN FACTIONS VYING FOR CONTROL
Free Dwarfs
Abyssal Dwarfs
Goblins
Ratkin
Undead

Prologue

The opening days of any great war are always important for study as to how the rest of the conflict might unfold. Here is the second volume in the continued study of The War of the Stone, or The Dwarf Civil War.

Our story picks up only weeks after the previous has concluded, with Golloch having been revealed to be in league with the Abyssal Dwarfs of Tragar, and the retaking of Cwl Gen with its new moniker of Hanner Brig, or the Broken Peak, by Sveri Egilax, the Berserker Lord. In the intervening weeks since then and the beginning of this particular volume, a few things have happened.

First, Banick Kholearm made contact with Golloch's nephew and heir apparent, Rordin, to whom he revealed the extent of Golloch's treachery. Aided by Garrek Heavyhand's testimony, Banick was able to convince Rordin of the veracity of his tale; and as such, Rordin began spreading the word amongst the rest of the clans. His efforts were met with a healthy amount of incredulity, thanks in no small part to the dwarfs' predilection to assuming that no dwarf of any kind of integrity would ever stoop to such depths – because of the belief that one cannot become king without some form of that integrity – as well as an inability to admit that they might have been tricked.

Meanwhile in Halpi, Sveri traveled down to the newly recaptured Eastport in order to rally the Free Clans to oppose Golloch. But the Free Clans find themselves hard-pressed with the logistics of trying to cement their hold in their former homeland and begin the transition from Estacarr back to Halpi. Further north, Herneas the Hunter and Grodgni the fallen stone priest have followed the traitorous Argoll to where he has rendezvoused with the Traitor King. This brings us to the place of particular note for this narrative, and the target for Golloch and his traitorous forces.

Crag Hudd is a place of importance within the world of Pannithor, not because of its connection to the dwarfs, but because of what the dwarfs uncovered beneath it. While the Abyssal Dwarfs of Tragar occupied this particular hold, an Iron-caster by the name of Dravak Dalken pushed his ratkin slaves to delve ever deeper in the earth until they uncovered the Rift. No one can say exactly what the Rift was, only that its discovery shook the foundations of the world. It can only be classified as a magical vortex of magical energies.

Any expeditions sent through the Rift were as likely to disappear entirely as it was to return, and those that did came back with tales of horror and wonder. Each expedition gave contradictory reports. Some said it was an elemental plane of fire, others declared it was a frozen world, still others claimed that the sky was choked with green clouds and the air was thick and barely breathable. The most common report, though, was of a world devoid of life on the other side. A quiet, dead world, but one that felt as though something was always watching, like that prickling sensation of unease one gets when alone late at night and there comes a sense of movement out of the corner of the eye.

As soon as it was discovered, it became a focal point for all the armies of the world. Forces marched to Crag Hudd in order to secure their claim on the Rift. The elves came to secure it so none other would try to use the dark magics that made it up. The goblins were drawn to the sensation of power which it emitted. The Hegemony of Basilea saw it as an abomination and sent their knights and battle sisters to try and destroy it, vain though that might be. The alliance of men, elves, and dwarfs from the frozen wastes of the North came with an even more dire directive to ensure that the Rift did not fall into the wrong hands. The dwarfs, sensing an opportunity, used this momentum to establish their foothold and reclaim Eastport before pushing further inland to fight at Crag Hudd.

In the end, the dwarfs reclaimed the lost hold, but it was decreed that all the allied forces that wished to see the Rift remain sealed off would need to help them in that endeavor. The Northern Alliance left a contingent of troops, including a few of their Ice Kin elves to help maintain the security of the magical gateway. It seemed as though a great victory had been won, but the power of the Rift had already been made known, and there are always those who will seek power to slake their lusts.

Crag Hudd plays a pivotal role in the story which you are about to read, so it is important that you are aware of its history. While this record is ostensibly about the dwarfs, they are but one race among the cavalcade of species that inhabits this world, and such things of the magnitude that this book speaks of are destined to affect all that live within this world.

This is a good bit of background and something to keep in mind as you proceed. Thus, without further preamble, here begins the second volume of the War of the Stone, which I have aptly dubbed: 'The Argument of Stone.'

Your respectful servant,

Jouer Brodenshod
Professor of Military History at
The College of Eowulf

1
Opening the Rift

> ***Golloch's reign was one of many firsts. It was the first time the Imperials saw someone rise to the throne through political means rather than through the weight of heroic deeds. It was the first time that the Free Dwarfs were forced to subjugate themselves to Imperial rule ever since their inception, and it was the first time one dwarf could slay another dwarf and be given the title of patriot rather than murderer.***
>
> ***–Kromoc Thrurnbeard***
> ***Imperial Archivist***

A heavy fist slammed against the door, waking Camwedd Ffydd from out of a deep slumber. He rubbed his eyes, washing away the dream he'd been having – a dream where he'd been in the dark and something had been stalking him, always behind him no matter where he turned. It had not been a comforting dream, and he was almost grateful for the knocking which had brought him back to the waking world. The hammering sound came again and he groaned as he pushed himself to his feet.

"Alright! Alright! I hear you! By the forge, what is it?!" he growled grumpily as he pulled the heavy wooden door open to reveal a younger dwarf staring nervously back at him. Camwedd could tell that something was off just by the nervous glances the young soldier kept giving over his shoulder. He gave several false starts before Camwedd finally barked at him to report.

"Sir! It's the high king! He's here!"

"Slow down, young'un, who is here?" Camwedd felt something prickling at the back of his mind, ghostly visages that echoed his dream, and part of him wondered if he'd really woken up.

"King Golloch is here, sir! He says he's come to inspect the Rift!"

This caused Camwedd to hesitate. The king was here? Why hadn't he been told of this sooner? Why had his scouts not reported that the Imps were sending up their blasted glob of a schemer to them?

Camwedd was the commander of the coalition forces that had been set over the freshly reclaimed Crag Hudd within the Halpi Mountains. Far more than just a simple dwarf hold, it housed an insidious magical rift in the bowels of its underground tunnels. Free Dwarfs, Imperial Dwarfs, elves, men, and even the combined forces of the Northern Alliance with their frozen counterparts had sent troops to ensure that the rift that was held inside the keep was kept out of Abyssal hands. The fact that an entire army could appear and catch them unawares, regardless of whether or not it was friendly, was a serious concern.

"How? Where did they come from? When did they arrive?"

"That's the odd thing, sir, they arrived from the north. Our scouts thought they were Abyssals coming to attack the keep. It wasn't until they got closer and the scouts saw their banners did they realize who it was."

"Why am I just now hearing about it?"

"They caught us by surprise, sir. Our rangers didn't find them until they were nearly on top of us."

"What about our far ranging scouts? What happened to them? Why didn't they see the Imps coming in?"

"We don't know, sir, they haven't reported in. Maybe the Abyssals or the greenskins got them?"

Camwedd closed his eyes and leaned back, letting a large sigh escape him. That would be his luck, that the enemy would have found his scouts or something else might have happened that would leave him blind to threats from the north.

"Get Braedul out of bed and have his regiment move out to try and find the missing scouts or discover how they let an entire army through without reporting back to us."

"Yes, sir. What should we do with Golloch and his troops?"

"Let the Imp King in, I will be down momentarily to greet him."

The younger dwarf nodded and moved off. Camwedd grumbled as he pulled on a quick pair of breeches and changed into a clean shirt. He would have put on more formal clothing, but the event had come unexpectedly, and besides, he felt a savage edge of pride at meeting the king with plain clothes on. Golloch had yet to really follow through on his promises to aid the Free Dwarfs in reclaiming their homeland in the Halpi Mountains. His only real efforts had been in sending troops to reclaim Crag Hudd because of the danger that lurked within the mountain hold's lowest levels. Beyond that, nothing had come from Caeryn Golloch besides edicts for heavier taxes on those Free Dwarfs who still remained in Estacarr.

Camwedd shivered as he pulled his shirt over his head and buckled on his belt. His mind involuntarily dipping down into the bowels of his keep where the Rift lay. A magical vortex that spiraled and pulsed with tendrils of dark magic, the Rift was a doorway to someplace dark and foreboding. It had come into being due to the greed of the Abyssal

Dwarfs delving deeper and seeking to further their power by employing forbidden magics. Its formation had shaken the very foundations of the world, and alliances across the breadth of Pannithor had rallied together to retake and contain its dark energies. Now it sat within the bones of the mountain, like a festering wound. The dwarfs and their allies had prevailed over their Abyssal cousins and forced them out, but none of the combined knowledge of all the races could determine how to completely close the Rift, and so it sat like an open sore, infecting the entirety of the Halpi Mountains with its energy.

The dwarfs and their allies had been able to construct some rudimentary contaminants to stopgap the Rift, but not enough was known to come up with a permanent solution. So now, a coalition made up mostly of Free Dwarfs, but including humans, halflings, and even some of the Ice Kin elves from the far north, had been left to guard it until that solution could be found.

Stuffing his foot into a boot, Camwedd stormed out of the door and hurried down the hallways. He had barely turned a corner when he was confronted by the tall, graceful figure of an elf. Her skin was a pale white tinged with the barest tint of light blue, as if she were carved from ice. Platinum hair fell about her face and framed sharp eyes that seemed to always be glaring out from beneath her brows.

"What is happening, Camwedd?" Her voice was sharp and crackled like ice breaking underfoot. Just looking at her made Camwedd feel cold.

"Inei! It's none of your concern, don't worry," he barked trying to step around her, but she moved to intercept and he stepped back, trying to match her glare with his own.

"A dwarf army shows up unannounced, and you say it is none of my concern? Remember why we are here, and do not waste my time with this posturing. Why did we not have any word of this force before it was on your doorstep?"

"As I said, it is none of your concern. They didn't come from the direction we would anticipate the Imps would use, that's all." Camwedd tried to keep the gruffness in his voice, but as he spoke, the ice elf's eyes widened.

"You didn't know either? But how...?" her voice trailed off, and Camwedd cursed her perceptiveness at seeing through his excuses.

"I don't know, it's the Imp King, though, so maybe that has something to do with it. Maybe he is moving in secret for security reasons."

"Golloch is here?!" Inei's face returned to its normal, disappointed glare, and Camwedd harrumphed, forcibly stepping around her and walking a few steps past.

"Again, it is not your concern, elf! You worry about your own soldiers, and I will deal with these new arrivals. If you want to be helpful, since you are so concerned, ready a few of your people and send them north. I have reason to believe that something has happened up that way, although we don't have any specifics, yet. That would be more useful than standing here and interrogating me!"

"Your scouts have gone missing, haven't they?" Inei's voice was still harsh, but there was something there that caused Camwedd to pause. Hidden beneath the frosty notes of disapproval in the elf's voice, so subtle that it was almost undetectable, there was something that he would grudgingly admit he had rarely seen the elf display. Inei was afraid.

"We don't know what this means," he said without turning, "all we know is that we're currently blind in that direction."

"And this new army just happens to appear marching out of that direction." While it was phrased as a question, the elf's voice made it a statement.

"Golloch is a lot of things: power-hungry, overly ambitious, and I would even go so far as to call him a liar. But I do not think that even he would be mad in the head enough to do what you are implying."

"I imply nothing, yet you knew without having to ask. That should reveal much."

"Even if he were that insane, his people would not allow him to do that. I dislike the Imps as much as any of my fellow clansmen, but they are not Abyssals."

"Who is it that you are trying to defend, Camwedd?"

He didn't respond to that, instead he stomped off down the hallway, leaving the elf looking after him. Anger warred with trepidation in his chest as he walked on. Was the Ice Kin captain right to suspect something from the Imps? Surely Golloch wouldn't try to take the Rift for his own gain? The whole of Pannithor united against the last person who tried to use the Rift for their own ends. How could Golloch hope to secure this, and what would he do with it even if he could?

He shook his head to dispel the thoughts. It was a massive leap to come to that conclusion. Golloch was a greedy git, and his honor was dubious at best, but even he wouldn't be so brash as that. His empire would rise up against him, wouldn't they? His mind drifted over the failed promises of the preceding decade, and the nagging sensation that Inei had stirred within him was still pulsing in the back of his mind as he rounded the last bend in the winding corridors. He arrived at the entrance to the keep and stepped out into the open air courtyard outside of the keep proper. The morning sun had yet to make its appearance, and the biting cold of a mid-spring high mountain dawn pierced the air. He was met by his attendant, Kalyth, after taking only a few steps.

"Are all of Golloch's forces inside the wall already?" he asked as the other dwarf fell in beside him.

"Yes my lord, they were invited in according to your instructions."

Camwedd cursed inwardly, but out loud, he kept his comments succinct.

"Let's keep them here in the courtyard, just in case. Have food and water brought to them. It's possible that Golloch won't be staying long, so we will try to delay him as little as we can."

"Yes sir, very good. I will pass the word along."

Camwedd was pleased to note that Kalyth did not seem perplexed by this order. He didn't want to start a panic based solely on a suspicion that was completely unfounded. It wouldn't do to offend the Imps; even if their support had been anything but impressive, it wouldn't help matters if he insulted them here.

"Where is the king?" he asked, and the attendant indicated one of the interior guardhouses that was generally used to greet messengers and such whose duties prevented them from staying long. Again, Camwedd was pleased to see this, as it indicated that Golloch didn't plan on hanging about, either. Maybe he had something that he needed to tell the troops here or, maybe he just wanted a report on the happenings at Crag Hudd. There were dozens of reasons he might have arrived here, all of them more plausible than the whispers of danger that Inei's words had planted in his mind.

Yet, even with this reason, the unease persisted. He had known Inei for a few years now, ever since they recaptured Crag Hudd, and she had been stationed here by the Northern Alliance to help guard the Rift. During that time, a grudging respect had grown within Camwedd for the pointy-eared frostling. He had fought alongside her and watched her stare down a full grown cave bear in the dark caverns below without flinching. She had stood her ground against endless waves of goblins and even withstood the withering fire of Abyssal Devastators without showing a single ounce of fear. Yet she had been afraid when Camwedd had told her that Golloch was here. Did she see something that he didn't? Or was she just being too paranoid? Perhaps he wasn't being paranoid enough?

His attendant stepped to the side as they approached the guardhouse. A sturdy wooden door was all that separated Camwedd from the Imp King now. He took a few deep breaths to calm himself before pushing the door open to step inside.

The room that greeted him was lit by a low crackling fire in a hearth that sent long, flickering shadows dancing along the walls. Two dwarf figures stood before the fire. One was turned away from Camwedd, a single hand extended toward the flames, a long beard typical of dwarfs regardless of breed spilled from his face and down his chest, his other hand was concealed under a long fur-lined cloak. Little else was discernible in the shadows of the dimly lit room. The other figure was a bit easier to see, as he stood facing the entrance and was the first to meet Camwedd's eye when he entered. This dwarf held himself rigidly, his hands clenched at his side. His beard was fiery red, although Camwedd couldn't tell if that was its real color or just a reflection of the ruddy light of the fireplace. A strange bald spot stared out from amidst his hair, a scar on his chin exposed to the open air; and above that, Camwedd had to stop himself from staring at an empty eye socket that gave the dwarf's visage that of a frowning skull. This dwarf seemed to be sneering at him, and Camwedd instantly felt his hackles rise.

"Your Excellency." He wasn't sure which one was Golloch, having never actually met the dwarf, but he'd heard descriptions of him and was fairly certain that he had both of his eyes in those reports.

"You will wait until you are spoken to, dwarf. The king does not wait upon your pleasure, it is the other way around," the one-eyed dwarf facing him growled. Camwedd nodded internally, his suspicions confirmed, and turned to square against the figure that was turned away from him.

"And I do not deal with upstart attendants who speak out of turn when their superiors are addressing each other," Camwedd replied. The other dwarf sneered and took a single step forward, but Golloch held up his hand from the fire and stopped him. The king turned, and Camwedd was greeted by an exceptionally handsome face that was marked with a few symmetrical scars that gave his visage a fierce quality that in no way detracted from his looks.

"Forgive Argoll, he has recently been chastised for failing me. He is anxious to make up for his mistake, and that sometimes leads him to make rash decisions in an effort to try and impress me. You are right to redress him. I will deal with him later, though, I assure you."

The one-eyed dwarf, Argoll, hesitated then stepped back, his face still a mask of fury. Camwedd released a breath he hadn't realized he had been holding and unclenched his fists. The uneasy whispers flared up in the back of his mind once more, and he forced them back down.

"I understand. To what do we owe the honor of your visit, Your Liege?" He was proud that his voice was solid, at least to his own ears.

"I have come to assess the strength of the Rift's defenses. I want to make sure our investment in reclaiming it is not being squandered." This caused Camwedd to bristle. The Imps had helped in the battle for the hold, but since then, they had sent token assistance when asked. The load was largely being carried by the already harried Free Dwarf clans. Yet this dwarf had the pompous attitude to demand a status update from him?

"I assure you that we are well-protected here. Our forces are adequate to the task, although Imperial aid in all of this would be appreciated. At present, a coalition of representatives from various Free Dwarf clans form the bulk of our troops. If you have come to discuss how you and your people might better assist us in this, I would be grateful for any that you could provide." Camwedd saw Golloch grimace at this statement.

"Gods but I hate those terms," he said, his face looking as if he wanted to spit something dreadful out of his mouth. "Imperials and Free Clans. Aren't we all dwarfs? Why do we have to segregate ourselves in such a base way? Are we like the humans who squabble over their little kingdoms all for the sake of distinction from their neighbors? When in reality there is little that is different from each tiny kingdom to the next."

"No, we aren't like the humans, we remember our heritage far better than they do. They fight to establish legacies that will not live past their children. We carve ours from the stones of the mountain, and they will weather the storms that tear the shallow roots of mankind's lives from the soil. We also do not forget the grievances that cause us to take strong actions, like separation between ourselves and our southern cousins." Camwedd tried to keep the fire out of his tone, but he failed. He was mostly proud of that failure.

"Do you indeed? What specific wrong brought about the sundering of our people? Can you name it?"

"In the dregs of the War with Winter, your lot left our ancestors to defend the north while you went off pursuing some mad king's desires for conquest. We were nearly destroyed outright, and it was only through our sheer determination that we held the lands that were our home, and saved your empire in the process. Yet we were branded as lazy and idle by your people. We do not forget such offenses. We may not be at blows now, but that doesn't mean that we are at peace with our ancestor's treatment. I know, it was my grandfather who told me tales of this separation. We are not so far removed that memory has grown brittle of that fact."

"You mean the orders of a king to march against an errant god who threatened to cover the whole world in ice? If your lot had followed his orders, then there might not have been the losses that led to the weakening of our people, and we could have reclaimed your lost holds once Winter had been dealt with."

"Forgive me, Your Majesty," Camwedd practically spat the honorific, "but if the support that your people have given mine lately is any indication of the aid our ancestors would have received, then I think they made the right choice. Estacarr is a lovely place to house your refugees, but it is no home like these halls of stones which we built."

"I know you are angry with me, your clans have not made this a secret. I had a reason for hesitating, though. Not that I need to explain myself to you, but would it help if I told you that I was working to have your holds returned to you? But doing so in a way that will not have such a high cost of dwarven blood being shed?"

This caused Camwedd to hesitate. He was angry, he knew this, and he knew he would regret his words later when he had calmed himself, but the arrogance of this dwarf astounded him!

"Words are useless with the Abyssals, they would rather spit you on a pike as soon as look at you."

"Maybe there's a reason for that!" Argoll took a step forward again, his hands were raised threateningly. Golloch restrained him with a wave of his arm. Camwedd was shocked by this outburst. Had Golloch's defendant actually just tried to defend the motives of the Abyssal Dwarfs?

"Again, Argoll is passionate about my mission, and he speaks out of turn because of this. We will have words later, I assure you."

"What is going on here?" Camwedd demanded, the creeping doubts in the back of his mind had blossomed into a slow sense of panic. Something was wrong here, but the only thing that he could think of as the cause for this was something so unthinkable that Camwedd struggled to even form the thought in a cohesive way.

"As I said, I have been seeking a more permanent solution to all of our problems. The dwarf people are a shattered lot. We have distrust and ruptures within our history that would have been fatal to any other society, yet we struggle on. The Free Clans have their grievances, the Imperials have theirs, and the Abyssals have their claim in this ongoing argument, too. They took your lands because of their own perceived slights. You have refused aid to the Imperials because of your own, and countless lives have been spent in these pointless and petty arguments. Are we not all children of Dianek, as your priests tell us?" Golloch's smile was charming, his eyes were wide. It all sent a cold chill down Camwedd's spine and he suddenly regretted that he had brought no weapon with him to this meeting, thinking it unnecessary.

"Are you saying...?" but he couldn't bring himself to voice the thought aloud, it was unimaginable.

"Yes, I was treating with our northern cousins to get your homelands given back to you. In doing this, I was required to make certain promises, as all good leaders will do when necessary. But this is all for a glorious purpose! Think of it! What could all the dwarfs accomplish if unified under one banner? Under *my* banner?! No other race on the face of Pannithor could stand against us! We would sweep across the land and secure our place as the dominant species. The humans are too disjointed and their loyalties are easily bought. The elves are treacherous and selfish in their actions and will be too slow. The Abyss would be our ally that we could use and discard at will! We can bring our people back to the glories of the past! We will rise again!"

Camwedd recoiled, stepping back so that his foot brushed against the door behind him. Some part of his mind vaguely registered that there were noises coming from the other side of the wall, but his focus was too swamped with the horror at what Golloch was saying to him.

"You are insane!" he said in something louder than a whisper but in a voice that was no longer tightly controlled. Golloch's expression wavered and then changed to one of sadness.

"I was afraid of that, which is why I won't try to convince you. I was telling you all of this so that you could see the vision that I hold and why I will do what I must. Argoll, take care of him and then go and see to the fight outside. Find me something decent to eat, too. Trail rations from Tragar are somewhat lacking in flavor, and I grow weary of them."

The one-eyed dwarf stepped forward, his vicious expression had changed from anger to anticipation and excitement. Camwedd grabbed the door handle behind him and turned to wrench it open. What he saw next stopped him cold.

The outer courtyard was filled with fighting. Bodies of his troops lay strewn across the ground, and to his dismay, the main doors to the keep were wide open. Golloch's forces were already inside. The warning bells were tolling, but it was a futile gesture. The enemy was already on top of them.

"Now you see that it is hopeless," Argoll's harsh whisper came at his ear, but Camwedd didn't have time to turn as he felt the sharp blade of a knife pass across his throat and warm blood bubbled up through the wound. He found that he couldn't breathe, and his vision was dimming. As he tumbled forward onto the ground, his thoughts turned inexplicably to the kitchens that were likely just putting out breakfast to his troops that would never eat it.

The shadow of Argoll stepping over him was the last thing his mind registered before darkness took him.

2
In Service to the Throne

> *Ostracization is an interesting concept among the dwarfs. In effect, it is the worst punishment, but it is oftentimes self-imposed. This contradictory way of social castigation is revelatory in the way the dwarfs view the individual versus the society in which that individual resides.*
>
> *–Jouer Brodenshod*
> *Professor of Military History*
> *The College of Eowulf*

The sun was already high overhead by the time that Garrek made his way through the center of camp. He walked with a restless purpose, and his eyes were fixed on a specific tent located on the edge of all the others where two other dwarfs sat casually to either side of the flaps. He gave them a cursory salute before ducking inside. Within the tent, the early spring temperatures made the air hot and sticky. The thick canvas prevented air from flowing, and because of the secret nature of its occupant, a wall couldn't be lowered to allow a breeze in.

Banick Kholearm sat at a camp desk in the middle of the area, his jet-black beard spilling across his chest as he sat with a pen poised above paper like he was preparing to write. The dry ink stains indicated that he was struggling from a mental block, however, as the page was otherwise blank. He looked up hopefully as Garrek entered, but his expression quickly fell after seeing the other dwarf's face.

"Still no word on anything," Garrek grumbled, walking over and grabbing a carafe of amber-colored liquor off another table in the room. He poured some into a horn cup and pulled a chair up beside his friend.

"I am going absolutely insane, Garrek! It's like I've traded one prison for another."

"As far as prisons go, this one is fairly swanky, you have to admit." Garrek raised his cup and took a swig. The drink tasted of cinnamon and other spices that burned along with the alcohol all the way down his throat.

"Yeah, except at least the dungeons were always cool." Banick wiped his brow which was practically dripping with sweat.

"Surprising lack of death and execution waiting for you in this one, though," Garrek pointed as he spoke.

"True. Part of me misses the straightforwardness of that aspect though." This elicited a raised eyebrow from Garrek. "It's just that I have no idea what Rordin wants from me. I've given him the information, I think he believes me, but he's forbidden me from telling anyone else or from even being seen! I can't even get a message to my friends at Cwl Gen to let them know what has happened! They think I'm dead!"

"All in good time, Banick," Garrek said solemnly, then chuckled. This time it was Banick who shot him a questioning look.

"It's just..." Garrek's chuckle threatened to turn into a full laugh, and he had to take a small breath before continuing. "Can you imagine their faces when you walk in, though? They'll think they've seen a ghost!"

Banick's face turned sad at this.

"I'd rather spare them the suspense. By now, word of my 'execution' has likely reached them, and what a horrible way to go about that. That's if they're even still alive. Who knows if the Ashtels didn't kill them all or took Cwl Gen. We haven't had any word from them."

Garrek stood up and filled another cup with the amber liquid, he walked over and set it before Banick and clapped the other dwarf on the shoulder.

"There's a purpose for all this though, isn't there? Right now, the Ashtels don't know where you are, or if you've contacted Rordin. It's all to keep you safe so that when Rordin has you share your story, it will be in a way that catches those bastards off guard and they won't have time to react. Rordin believes you, Banick, don't you worry about that. He's a good dwarf, that one, strong sense of duty about him, and surprisingly humble! After his disastrous traitor of an uncle's turn at the throne, the empire could do with a little bit more humility in it." Garrek spat on the ground as if he'd tasted something vile before continuing. "I still can't get over the fact that we had an Abyssal sitting as our king. Right under our noses. How did we not see it before?!"

Garrek slumped back in the chair he had been sitting in and drained his cup to punctuate his lament.

"We only see the things we want to see, and nobody wanted to see that they'd been tricked so soundly," Banick commiserated with his friend. "Even now, several Imperial clans are hesitant to believe Rordin from what you've told me. Even though he hasn't outright accused Golloch of his treachery."

"Be that as may be, it doesn't excuse us for hiding our heads in the dirt instead of facing up to the truth." Garrek shook his head and rose to his feet with anxious energy, causing him to bounce on his toes. "As for your friends, I'd say no news is good news. If their plan had worked, then it would have been published by Gruumen and his supporters as having uncovered a conspiracy going all the way to the top of your Free Dwarf leadership. With how long it has been and no news, it means that there was a fight, and a fight means that Sveri saw through his ruse, which means there is a good chance that they are still alive."

Banick nodded at this and took the cup that Garrek had poured him, downing it in one go.

"Like I said, how many dungeons have you stayed in where you get such excellent drink? Pretty swanky, right?" Garrek waggled his eyebrows and went to pour himself another cup.

"I'd still rather be able to move about as I please," Banick sighed and took a drink. "What is his plan, anyways? We've been sitting here for a couple of weeks now. It's almost like he wants Gruumen to find him and snuff us out."

"Rordin sent out messengers right after you showed up. They went out to all of the holds, all of the clans, saying that Rordin had dire news that he wished to share with the clan heads or one of their trusted advisors, said there would be a gathering soon to discuss it. The message was pretty veiled, didn't want anything that Gruumen or anyone loyal to Golloch being able to use against him before the word can get out. Not that it's stopped it from happening anyways. Rumors are flying that Rordin is campaigning to take the crown from Golloch, or that he's forged an alliance with the Basileans to take him out. There's tales that he found some ancient power in the ruins of Dolgarth and plans to use that to take over both Free and Imperial Dwarfs, and those are just the more believable stories blowing around the empire." Garrek took another sip and leaned back in his chair.

"You'd think the clans would have enough drama with my 'failed' assassination attempt and the declaration of war against the Free Clans in Halpi." Banick scowled, and Garrek felt the mood beginning to sour. News had spread of Banick's supposed execution after the sham assassination attempt on a fake Golloch that the Ashtels had pinned on him. Now there were talks of the Imperials preparing for war with the Free Clans to the north. It was all supposition at this point, but some of the louder clans were calling for blood with their northern cousins, others were claiming that the 'Free Loaders' in Estacarr, where many of the refugees of the Free Dwarfs still resided, should be subjugated and their clans dissolved. There were far more Imperial chieftains who remained undecided in their position; it was easy to see that something else was going on, but the misinformation was so thick that it was hard to make sense of it all. Garrek harrumphed to himself. He was privy to more information than most and even *he* wasn't sure what to make of it all.

"Well, the good news is that there are several clans already gathered." Garrek swished the contents of his cup around. "I saw the Afalans, the Flintbrows, the dwarfs from Anvil Mastery have come down with their Lord Thane, I even saw the Bwaroc Clan from clear over by

Caer Garric. More are showing up every day."

"Nice of them to hold off on condemning us 'Freeloaders' until after they've all discussed it first," Banick replied bitterly. Garrek shook his head in disapproval.

"Have a little faith in my fellow Imps," he said, wagging a finger at him. "The majority of your experience was with those dwarfs who lived in Caeryn Golloch. They don't represent the entirety of us Imperials. In fact, I daresay that the majority of the clans that reside there are friends of Golloch and have been the biggest victims of his propaganda campaign against your Free Clans. We do have the ability to think for ourselves, you know, and not all of us were okay with how your clans were treated. Think of Ithel! He was an Imperial chief! He supported you, didn't he?" Even as he said this last part, Garrek knew he had misspoke. Banick's scowl deepened.

"And look at what my friendship bought them," he said, his voice failing to mask a complicated mix of anger and regret.

"Ithel's death was not your fault."

"But he's still dead, nonetheless, and we haven't heard anything from Cerrig, either. It could be that the entire Ffionen line is dead."

"You don't know that."

"That's right, and we can add it to the rest of the things that I don't know right now."

Banick filled his cup again and drained it in one go, slamming the cup down after. Garrek sighed and tried to think of some way to respond when the sound of movement came from outside the tent. Agitated whispers and people walking toward the center of camp brought him up short.

"What in the Abyss…?" he queried, and Banick shrugged.

"I can't leave the tent, so you'd best go and investigate for the both of us."

Garrek smiled sadly and downed the dregs of his cup before standing and walking back out into the midday heat. He immediately saw that there was a crowd gathering and moving toward the command tent. Garrek caught a passerby and asked what was going on.

"The king's sent a messenger to talk with Rordin," the dwarf said and then turned to walk away, following the crowd.

Garrek stared after him, an uncomfortably familiar feeling of anxiety settling on his shoulders. He began making his way through the crowds, several dwarfs giving him sour looks as he brushed past them. It took him some time, but eventually he made his way to the command tent. That was as far as he was able to go, as a pair of Ironguard, Rordin's personal bodyguards in this case, stood with their axes barring the way.

"Good luck, Oathbreaker," a voice said behind him, and Garrek turned to look into the smirking face of Ddiangen Afalans, the chief of the Afalans clan. He had a long red beard tinged with strips of white running through it. He was dressed in his clan colors of blue and white, and had silver chains set with blue sapphires around his neck.

"Has there been any news, yet?" Garrek asked, trying to ignore Ddiangen's use of Garrek's family moniker that had been branded on them.

"Nothing so far, but they aren't letting anyone in."

"How long have they been in there?"

"Not long, I'd say less than half an hour." Even as the other dwarf said this, Garrek heard a murmur run through the crowd, and he turned back to look at the tent. What he saw there froze him where he stood. A dwarf stood with brown hair and beard tied into platelets with bright hazel eyes and wearing the blue robes of a stone priest.

"Ofn," Garrek breathed the name out loud. Ofn was flanked by two dwarfs in heavy armor bearing the Ashtel sigil of an anvil fashioned into a fist with a hammer crashing down on it. So this was the Imperial messenger from Golloch. Garrek's stomach twisted uncomfortably. As he watched, Ofn scanned the crowd. His eyes fell on him, and a small, sad smile spread across the stone priest's face before he nodded slowly and walked down the aisle of parted dwarfs before him prepared by his guards. Garrek watched him go, not taking his eyes off him until he was out of sight.

"It was smart of the king to send one of the *Athro* to parlay with Rordin," Ddiangen said behind him. "Many clans will see that as an olive branch, as he is a follower of Fulgria. Sending one of Dianek's servants to represent him sends the message that he is willing to listen to the views of those dwarfs that do not agree with his own beliefs. It will go a long way to placating those nobles that Rordin seeks to embolden."

"A clever ruse," Garrek agreed, "but it is just that. Golloch has no plans to share his power."

"Perhaps having his nephew and heir rise up against him has woken the old tyrant up to the precarious nature of his position."

"No, it isn't that," Garrek snorted, turning to face the Afalans chief. "Golloch's made his name and gained his power by keeping the clans divided. He sows confusion and division, and then uses the distraction to slip his blade in between your ribs."

"I suppose, as an Oathbreaker, you would know about sticking knives in peoples' backs, now wouldn't you? Family secret is it?" Ddiangen smiled coldly at Garrek, who tried and failed to ignore the comment.

"If you're not careful, you're going to end up getting yourself in trouble because you're watching me, when you should be keeping your wits about you for other threats."

He didn't wait for a response, for at that moment, he saw Rordin step out of the tent and scan the crowd, stopping when his eyes fell on Garrek. He motioned for him to join him in the command tent. Garrek stepped around Ddiangen and made his way to meet with Rordin, but not before he heard the other dwarf mutter under his breath, in a voice that he clearly wanted Garrek to hear.

"Rordin treats with an Oathbreaker before he addresses the rest of the clans. That doesn't bode well for his position." Garrek felt his shoulders tighten as he walked away but didn't look back or respond.

Stepping into the tent, he was met with a wave of stuffy, hot air from the enclosed space and the lamps used to light it. Rordin stood at the center of the tent, a large table in front of him with a map of the Abkhazla Mountains spread out on it. Rordin himself was an imposing figure. His flame-red hair and beard framed a set of hard features and a fierce gaze that caused many to think twice about what they would say in his presence. Garrek smiled at his friend. Rordin had a long and colorful history throughout the empire. He'd lived a life of drinking and adventuring before venturing beneath the bowels of the ancient capital of Dolgarth many years ago. Something had happened down there that had changed his perspective, and since returning, he had made it his mission to restore the ruins of that proud city to its former glory. Garrek had met him many times before this transformation, and it was sometimes hard to separate the hardened general before him from the drunken youth with a mug of ale in one hand and the bottom of a comely dwarven maid in the other.

"Well, Garrek, it seems our messages have gotten through to someone," Rordin said, throwing a rolled piece of parchment on the table. Garrek noticed that they bore Golloch's personal seal.

"What did they say?"

"A lot of flowery nothings, as is my uncle's wont. Or his patsy, whoever wrote this. It's a politician's response, and it makes me a little ill reading it."

"So we're back to where we started, then?"

"Not quite. Amidst the flowery bouquets of goat shit, there was a nugget of hope. They've agreed to summon a meeting of the clans."

"That sounds promising, when will it be?"

"That's the problem. It's supposed to be in a month's time. But it is in a location that I don't like the look of." Rordin stabbed his finger down on the map, and Garrek moved closer so that he could see.

"They want to have the meeting at Tyr Gurayd?" The hold was on the western side of the mountain range, close to the open plains that separated the mountains from Rordin's home base at Dolgarth, further west.

"Not exactly, a few leagues north of there is an old guard tower from the time of the Celestians. It's mostly in ruins, but they feel that this would be a suitable location and neutral enough that no one should feel threatened by it."

"But you think it's a trap?"

"I don't know what to think, Garrek." Rordin sighed and slumped down into a chair that was pushed up behind him. "Weeks ago, this Free Dwarf shows up looking for me right after an assassin tries to have me killed. I don't know that it was my uncle who ordered the attempt, but I can't discount it, either. Then Banick tells me that Golloch has gone over to the Abyss? What am I supposed to believe? How do I know that he isn't lying to me in order to turn me against him?"

"I can vouch for Banick, he's a good dwarf, and an honorable one. I would question why the Ashtels keep lying and saying that they have executed him, and yet here he sits in your camp. Or why he would risk his life to warn you instead of sneaking back to the Free Clans. I trust him. I've seen his character, and I've seen what lengths he is willing to go to for those he cares about."

"The messenger that just left said similar things about you." Rordin looked up at him. Garrek paused, momentarily thrown off his mental balance.

"Why would he…?" Garrek asked.

"I thought it was odd, too. He asked after you, specifically, right after he delivered the message. Said you were an old friend of his, and one of his misguided flock back in Caeryn Golloch. Said that he missed your talks and hopes that you can mend some bridges when next you meet, because you always made him think about hard questions."

"I…" Garrek started, but nothing else came out of his mouth.

"So who am I to trust, Garrek? Your friendship with Banick, or your friendship with this stone priest who speaks on my uncle's behalf? I trust you, we've been in enough battles and seen enough things together back before I came to appreciate my position in the world. You were always so smart, and brave, and loyal. But when I have two individuals who both claim you as their friend but offer me counsel where each contradicts the other, I am at a loss as to who to believe."

Garrek's memories played across his mind's eyes. He remembered his talks with Ofn, he'd thoroughly enjoyed the priest's company. In fact, in his entire time of knowing Ofn, there had never been anything that had led him to believe that he was capable of the things that Banick accused him of doing. Yet there was something that persisted in Garrek's gut, some intuition that told him that Banick was telling the truth. He couldn't directly identify it, perhaps it was because

Garrek had seen Banick actually sacrifice for his friends and for his beliefs. Beliefs that Garrek shared. Banick had come to a hostile city and demanded the respect for his friends and gained the aid that they needed through honest means. He'd sought the truth behind Queen Rhosyn's death and had never compromised himself in any way, even when it would have been convenient to do so. Ofn had interacted with Garrek only through conversations.

"I can't tell you what to do or who to believe. I can only tell you who I believe of those two, and I would stand by Banick any day."

Rordin nodded at this, then pushed himself to his feet.

"Thank you, that helps me make some choices, then," he said.

"So, what's the plan?"

"My troops will march for Tyr Gurayd. As for you and the other clans, I expect you will make up your own minds as to what you will do. I am not your king, nor your superior. But I will deliver my message to all who will listen there about my thoughts, and my response to Golloch's actions both on the Free Dwarfs as well as toward me. This gathering gives me the chance to do it to everyone at once, or at least as many as will respond to the summons."

Garrek smiled at this and caught himself bowing, hoping that it was before Rordin could notice. He quickly straightened and walked out of the tent.

"Oh, and Garrek," Rordin said behind him as he pushed the flap aside. Garrek turned to look back at him. "If I catch you bowing to me again, I'll shave your damn beard off, you hear me?"

Garrek chuckled and walked out into the sunlight. He moved quickly, his mind absorbed in his own thoughts. Ofn had shown up bearing the Ashtel colors. This was the first time Garrek had ever been confronted by that reality. Of course he'd heard what Banick had said to him about Ofn, but there was a difference between knowing something academically, and seeing it firsthand in front of you. Was Garrek wrong for trusting Banick so much? After all, he'd known Ofn for longer than Banick, and Banick was also a Free Dwarf, and Ofn was a citizen of the empire. But every time Garrek tried to ignore the things that Banick had told him, his stomach twisted and his mind drew a blank. Garrek had learned in his long life to trust that feeling. Any time he had pushed those warning signs aside, he had paid for it, or the dwarfs he commanded had paid for it.

His mind flashed to Ofn, and a strange sadness swelled inside. If Banick was right, then Ofn was the enemy. The worst kind of enemy at that. He was a liar, and a betrayer. In a near future time when they met, it would likely end with one or both of them dead.

He arrived at his destination, realizing he couldn't remember any of the path he had walked to get there. He braced himself and carefully pushed the tent flap to the side. Banick was still sitting at his small table, the carafe of amber liquid was significantly emptier than when Garrek had left.

"Good news! I think the waiting is almost at an end," he said as he stepped inside.

3
Concerning Fire and Stone

To an outsider, one might draw dark and light parallels between our society and that of our darker cousins of Tragar. But this is only a surface level comparison.

One of the most egregious comparisons is that of the earth elementals that we employ versus the obsidian golems that march with the Abyssal Dwarfs. Our elementals are the spirits of our Mother Earth coaxed gently from the rocks to take physical shape. There is no force employed in this process, and when whatever task that required the use of the elementals is completed, the spirits are released.

Whereas the obsidian monstrosities are the captured spirits, elemental and otherwise, that have been wrenched from their natural state and forcibly bound into the confines of volcanic glass. This is a hellish prison from which there is no escape except in their absolute destruction. I can think of no fate worse than being sealed away in such a coffin of fear, hate, and pain.

–Athro *Breas Gildwater*
Stone priest of Caer Galwyn

Argoll took a deep breath to steady his nerves before reaching up to knock on the door.

"Enter," a voice called from the other side, and he did as commanded. Inside was a small room with a large wooden throne and a sturdy stone table. Golloch sat on the throne, and another dwarf stood beside it in a whispered conference with the king. Argoll looked around the room and counted six Blacksouls standing around the edges, silent guardians in imposing sets of cruelly twisted armor. These were dwarfs who had sacrificed their bodies and minds to the point where there was little individuality left of them. In return for their sacrifice, they were granted incredible strength and near invulnerability in combat. They were the perfect killing machines, even if they were nothing more than automatons moving suits of armor around.

Golloch held up a finger before he could speak, and Argoll was forced to stew in his anger and resentment at being summoned in such a fashion. The whispering dwarf concluded his conference and stepped back, his black beard brushing the floor as he bowed deeply before the king and made his way out of the room.

"It's remarkable how unprotected they left this place," Golloch grunted. Standing and moving around the table, he grabbed a pitcher and a large flagon, and poured foamy liquid from the one into the other. "The Rift wasn't even closed, just contained. Breaking their seals was child's play for our Iron-casters. Everything has gone according to plan, has it not?"

"Yes, Your Majesty," Argoll tried and failed to keep his teeth from grinding as he responded, but Golloch didn't seem to notice. "Your tactical brilliance knows no bounds."

The dwarf king took a long pull from his flagon and placed it back on the table with a strangely loud click.

"You would be wrong in that," Golloch said in a quiet voice that made Argoll's hair stand on end. Golloch moved around the table until he was standing beside him. He reached up and placed a hand on Argoll's shoulder. "My tactical brilliance failed when I assigned you with the taking of Cwl Gen." Golloch growled and grabbed a fistful of Argoll's hair, wrenching his head backward.

"Your Majesty! It was not my fault, I told you that it was the fool Gwrthod who cost us our victory!" Argoll hated the pleading tone that crept into his voice. After all the times he had faced death and come out victorious, it still amazed him that another dwarf could create such fear in his chest.

"Do not excuse your weakness by blaming others!" Golloch sneered, bringing his face closer to Argoll's so that he could smell the sour scent of ale on his breath.

"I do not excuse myself, I simply tell you the truth."

"Who was the one in charge of the Imperial Garrison? I gave you enough troops to crush what was left of Sveri's forces ten times over!"

"But it was the Teirhammer's foolishness that let them on to our plan. They were not unprepared for us. It was his hubris that led to our defeat!"

"And what did you do to curb that pride of his? You gave him free reign to waste my warriors in a siege that you should have won by the second day!"

"How were we supposed to know that they would blow up half of their mountain on us?" Argoll grimaced in pain as Golloch's hand tightened its grip in his hair.

"Again with your excuses! How many warriors did we lose while taking this keep?"

"I don't..."

"How. Many?" Golloch enunciated each syllable.

"Less than a hundred warriors, my lord."

"Less than a hundred! The number of defenders here at Crag Hudd was almost ten times the warriors that Egilax had at Cwl Gen, and the force that we brought was half what we faced. Outnumbered two to one, and we lost less than a century of troops and took it in a day!"

He paused, as if waiting for Argoll to refute his response, but he wisely remained silent. Golloch released his hair with a disgusted grunt and moved over to take another drink from his flagon.

"I failed you, Your Majesty, I swear I will not do so again."

"You botched an assignment that should have been an easy victory. It was practically presented to you on a platter for you to enjoy at your leisure! By the Abyss!" Golloch shouted this last part and slammed his flagon down on the table, and the vessel exploded in a shower of stone pieces and frothy ale. "You know that the allegiances I possess from the lords of Tragar are tenuous *at best*! Dravak Dalken is salivating at the idea of me failing so that he can swoop in here and begin his dark experiments again! I can't have that! If my commanders cannot be successful, then I lose clout with them. If I cannot keep them in line, then we will all die, and they will march south practically unopposed and kill or enslave every dwarf they find. Then there will be no Free or Imperial Dwarfs, there will only be Masters and Slaves, and our race will die as we know it!"

Here, Argoll wisely kept his peace again. He cared nothing for the dwarfs of any creed. He would be more than content to watch the southern clans burn and their lands fall to ruin. If he was able to profit from it all then so much the better, but he just wanted the fire to burn all traces of dwarf from the land, even if it meant he was consumed alongside it. Golloch was quiet for several long moments after his tirade, then he turned toward Argoll again.

"We've come across another problem. The golems, they can't be controlled. Our Iron-casters are at their wits' end trying to figure it out. The spirits they tear from the Rift come through easily enough, and it seems as though they embrace the chance to bond with the bodies that we link them to, but then it's as if they go berserk! So far we've been able to contain them in what the casters are calling the Pens. But we need to be able to control them if we are to use them effectively against the Free Dwarfs!"

Argoll felt a sinking sense of anticipation steal over him. This had been the main reason for retaking Crag Hudd in order to gain access to the Rift. Dravak Dalken's research had shown that there were entities on the other side of the swirling energies of the Rift, strange intelligences or spirits, it was hard to say. Golloch had gathered several Iron-casters who were convinced that they could take these spirits and house them in golem bodies. Where they weren't twisted and broken elemental spirits, they would be easier to control and less likely to break down from the continuous use of the dark magic needed to sustain their existence. That was the theory, but it seemed that the reality was far more daunting.

"I am sorry to hear this, Your Majesty."

"Not as sorry as you will be if we don't find success, and soon. Because I am giving you your chance to redeem yourself, Argoll. Give me an army that we can use to crush any resistance to my rule."

"My lord, I am one of the least powerful of the Iron-casters, I am not worthy of such an honor."

"There are other qualities which you possess to supplement your lack of magical abilities, Argoll. Firstly, you are tenacious. You survived the slave pits and fought your way to freedom after you were captured from your Free Dwarf hold all those years ago. You have a strong will to survive, and that drives you to accomplish magnificent things." Golloch walked slowly back around the table and lowered himself back onto the throne as he spoke. "This will help you with your second quality: that of motivation. If you don't find a way to make these golems work, and you cannot produce results, then if you are lucky, I will kill you. If I am feeling less magnanimous, then I will send you back to the slave pits, and this time you will not escape. Am I understood?"

"Yes, Your Majesty."

"Good, now get out of my sight, and count your blessings that you aren't already being sent back to Tragar."

Argoll bowed and walked stiffly from the room. Once outside, his demeanor broke, and he slammed his fist into the stone wall of the passage. The gall of that dwarf! He was still a runt in his time with the goddess Ariagful. He'd spent less time in Tragar than the lifespan of a single ratkin slave! Who was he to demand and threaten him?!

He knew the answer to that question. Seniority had no meaning in the world of the Abyssal Dwarf – all that mattered was power, and Golloch had far more of that than him. Simply by virtue of being king of the Imperial Dwarfs, he trumped a large number of the warlords in either of the twin cities of Tragar. Even so, he was naive and foolish to believe that this power was secure in any way. Right now he held the cards, but that could quickly change in the shifting tides of Abyssal politics.

He stormed off down the passageways, passing deeper and deeper into the depths. The air became chilled, and the light of the torches seemed to become almost brittle as he drew closer to his goal. Finally, after he turned the last corner, he was greeted by the horrific visage of the Rift.

It appeared as a turbulent whirlpool of purple energy that stood easily thirty feet across. Tendrils of putrid white ricocheted across its spinning surface, and occasionally small bolts of energy attempted to escape from its edges. The Rift seemed to glow, but the image was flawed by the sense of creeping shadows that permeated the cavern where it sat like a fog of darkness that blurred everything it touched.

Possibly the most disturbing aspect of the Rift were the whispers. Long before he had rounded the final bend that led to this cavern, Argoll had known he was getting close because of the incoherent voices that began to prick at the back of his mind. It was like being in a crowded room where everyone was talking to their neighbor in hushed tones. He could never make out what any of the voices were actually saying, but he recognized the tone and cadence of a conversation and the form of words being spoken just out of earshot. It was maddening.

To his left as he entered the room, there was something resembling a laboratory set up – several large stone tables and chairs, along with racks of bottles and vials, and several bookshelves crammed with scrolls and ancient tomes. Three Iron-casters sat around one of the tables where the constructed form of an obsidian golem lay. They were attaching pieces together and pouring strange, glowing liquids over the volcanic glass. Another was standing a ways off, his hands scribbling notes furiously as he watched the others at work. Behind them lay the entrance to another passageway which led to the Pens where the feral golems were being housed until Argoll could figure out how to tame them.

Argoll sighed and began walking toward the Iron-casters, and as he did so, he saw two robed and hooded figures emerge from the direction of the Pens. They walked toward him, though one of the figures stopped and stared at him for a moment. In the difficult light of the cavern, Argoll wasn't able to make out the figure's features, except for his long blond beard. This caused Argoll to pause. Blond hair was not a common feature among the Abyssal Dwarfs, mostly their hair was some varying shade of darkness. There were some that dyed their hair other colors, such as one particular family of Abyssal Dwarfs that made their beards blue as a sign of nobility. But blond was irregular, and there was something that seemed familiar about this dwarf. Something that drew Argoll back to some distant memory that nagged at him from the depths of remembrance.

There came a spark and a small explosion from the direction of the Iron-casters. Argoll cursed and quickly turned his attention back to them, dismissing the robed figures as they walked past without another thought. His teeth grinded in his mouth as he stormed his way over to the stone table to begin his task of finding the impossible solution.

*****

Herneas kept his head down as they hurried from the chamber. His heart had leaped into his throat when he'd seen Argoll appear, and then when he'd stopped and stared at them as if he'd recognized them. This deep into enemy territory, and they wouldn't have had a prayer of escaping. He turned and gave a brief glance at his companion. Grodgni gave him a worried smile back in response. It didn't inspire much confidence, and Herneas didn't feel his heart settle until they were up into the surface levels of the keep. Even then he continued glancing around as if waiting for a troop of Abyssal Dwarfs to round the corner and yell at them to stop where they were.

Thankfully, they made it out into the relatively warm spring afternoon and hurried over to the stone wall on the western side of the keep. They followed it down until the wall connected with the side of the mountain that extended up about another hundred feet above them before coming to its peak. This part of the wall was not heavily guarded, as it was against the mountain and tucked away in such a manner that prevented anyone from approaching. At least, that was the thought.

Herneas and his scouts had followed Argoll and his troops as they had rendezvoused with Golloch's army further up north after the Battle of Cwl Gen, or the Battle of the Half Peak as many were starting to call it. When the enemy army had turned south, Herneas had feared the worst and sent word to Sveri that the enemy was possibly returning and in greater numbers than before. But when the enemy turned southwest and marched toward Crag Hudd, an even greater anxiety had crept in between his shoulder blades. He had realized their goal too late, and by that time, they had already taken the keep. His rangers had spent the following weeks trying to find a way to infiltrate the mountain hold and discover what it was that the enemy had planned. The only way in that they had discovered had been a steep climb that brought them up here along the western battlements.

Herneas swept his leg over the edge of the ramparts and forced himself not to look down at the dizzying drop of several hundred feet onto sharp rocks below. He gripped the security line around his waist and rappelled down beside Grodgni, who likewise was squinting his eyes shut and refusing to look away from the rock face in front of him.

"Damn but I hate this!" the disgraced stone priest muttered through gritted teeth.

"Nothing should be between a dwarf and the firm foundation of stone," Herneas agreed.

"Well, technically, there is nothing between us and the stones below. Unless you count open air."

"I suppose, but I don't think the rocks would be too welcoming if we were to take the quick way down to them."

They kept up the banter to try and distract them from the unpleasant descent. Herneas also kept his thoughts occupied by going over the things they had seen inside the keep. It had mostly been underwhelming, especially when he considered the dire results of the Abyssals taking the Rift those years ago. The first time it had seemed like the very fabric of reality was set to tear apart. Now, it was much more reserved. Much quieter. Perhaps Golloch didn't want to bring down all the sentient races on him like his predecessor, Dravak Dalkin, had.

Then there were the golem pens. That thought sent a shiver through Herneas's body, and he missed his footing, causing him to lurch sideways in a way that caused his head to spin as he inadvertently glanced down in an effort to regain his balance.

"Careful there, Master Hunter," Grodgni groaned. His face was paler than before, but Herneas was too concerned with his own progress, so he quickly looked away and didn't berate him for using that particular title.

Thankfully they didn't have to go the entire distance to the bottom. About halfway, there was a small cleft in the cliff face that led to a cave which would allow them to walk the rest of the way down the mountain. There, they could meet up with Herneas's rangers. The cleft was well-hidden, and for a moment, Herneas was worried that they had missed it until Grodgni seemed to disappear under a jutting rock. Herneas breathed a sigh of relief and followed quickly behind. As they finally touched down and moved inside the cave, Herneas felt his heart begin to relax in his chest. They permitted themselves a few moments to catch their breath before continuing.

"What about the ropes?" Grodgni asked as they started to walk away.

"I doubt anyone will discover them. Even if they do, what are they going to do with them? If they follow them down, it's likely that they won't be able to discover this cave. We only found it by chance. But suppose they do find it. What good would it do them? This approach isn't usable by an army. Any more than a dozen or so of us and we'd be risking detection coming this way. They can't really seal this entrance with any kind of demolitions, or else they might risk undercutting the strength of the mountain where the wall sits. The worst we can probably expect is that they cut the ropes down and include this part of the wall on their patrols more frequently."

Grodgni nodded, and they walked into the darkness of the cave. Herneas stopped and picked up a torch they had left when they'd first come this way. Quickly producing a flint, he scraped it against his knife until a spark ignited the dried cloth on the torch.

"What did you make of what we saw in there?" Herneas asked as he stood and made his way into the cave.

"Which part? Seeing Anobreth, or the feral golems?"

"You know his name is Argoll, now, right? The Anobreth you knew is long dead."

"Be that as it may," Herneas could hear Grodgni's shrug in his voice, "I'll keep referring to him as such until he comes to his senses or he kills me." This caused Herneas to stop and turn to face him.

"If the time comes, and you have the opportunity to kill him, will you be able to do it?" he asked, but the other dwarf wouldn't meet his eye.

"I don't know," Grodgni answered honestly. Herneas stared at him for a long moment before turning back.

"I wouldn't let the others know that," he said at length. "Tell me what you think about the golems that we saw."

"There was something wrong there," Grodgni responded, his voice taking on a strange tone. "Something... *unnatural...*"

"Unnatural how?"

"Nobody really knows how they are formed, but the theory that holds the most weight among the *Athro* is that obsidian golems are a perversion of the earth elementals that we are able to summon. We do this by calling up the spirits of the earth and guiding them into forming bodies capable of fighting or helping with other tasks. When the task is finished that we summoned them for, we will release them from their physical bonds, and they return back to the earth. The belief is that Abyssals corrupt this by omitting that last step. They take the elemental spirits and sever them from the earth. They imbue their golems with an unnatural power that forces the spirit to remain in its prison. It's a violent and terrifying process, from what I have heard, and it costs the person who does this a piece of their soul. It's essentially murder, only you are destroying a piece of our Earth Mother's spirit alongside your own."

"So how are these golems different, then?" Grodgni was silent for so long that Herneas thought that he was refusing to answer the question. "Grodgni?" he asked, and the name echoed through the rock passageway.

"I heard you, I'm just trying to find the words to respond. It isn't something that can be said really. I guess the best way to put it is to explain the difference between elemental spirits and our own consciousness. Elemental spirits experience things differently than ourselves. They do not have a spoken language like we do, instead they communicate through emotions, ideas conveyed through pictures, sometimes gestures that they mimic from us. But this is just the way that they communicate with us who *do* have a spoken language. Elemental spirits are different from us, they are not individuals. They are almost like broken up pieces of a greater consciousness. They speak to each other intuitively, and their voice is the sound of the cosmos, that general thrumming in the background that most will never recognize, but we stone priests can always hear it. It's almost like a song that is one continuous sound that has been going since the world was created. Perhaps one has to be stone-touched to perceive it."

"Interesting, but I'm not seeing how this compares to the golems."

"Well, when the Abyssals create a golem, they cut that elemental spirit off from that song. At least that's the theory, nobody really knows how it works exactly. The spirit inside the golem withers away into something akin to madness, and their song becomes discordant and unnatural. They can no longer connect to the rest of their elemental siblings, or rejoin the overall consciousness. Keep in mind that this is all my own theorizing as to how this all works. Even though I was a stone priest, there were still a lot of mysteries that are never explained. What I do know is that when I encountered obsidian golems on the battlefield, the usual thrum of that elemental music was reduced to an aggravated buzz, a muted tone that spoke to despair and anguish. Regular golems act like someone who has recently been blinded, or who has just lost both their legs in a battle. They are depressed at having lost some perspective, some extension of themselves that they have always known. Their despair gives way to rage and a type of grief that we likely cannot fathom in our mortal perspectives."

"So this process creates mad earth elementals, then?"

"No, the result is more nuanced than that. It is a sadness to make your bones ache, a longing for death that can never come, a desire for a return to an existence that has forever been shattered. It is terrible, and awe-inspiring, and completely unfathomable to our limited comprehension as creatures that are not eternal."

"That sounds like madness to me. So if all golems are mad, then why were these ones particularly feral? What makes them different from the others?"

"Typically, from what I understand, an Iron-caster will have the strength to make only a handful of golems at any given time. This is why you will rarely see entire armies made up of them. But this is different. There were more down there than I've ever seen in one place. That alone tells me that something is different about them. They must be using something from the Rift to craft these creatures. But that's not all…"

Grodgni's voice trailed off, and Herneas waited for him to continue. When he did, his voice was choked in a way that sent a chill down Herneas's spine.

"There was no song going between these golems. Not even the muted, depressed song that the regular ones sing. With them, I heard something..." Again Grodgni paused, as if searching for the words. This time Herneas stopped and turned back to look at him. His face was twisted up, and Herneas could see the fear in his eyes.

"What was it that you heard?" he asked in a hushed voice.

"Screams." Grodgni took a shaky breath. "They were terrified screams, like someone who had been locked inside a coffin and buried. I could feel the frantic edges of their voices, as if they were tearing their fingernails off in an effort to claw their way free, but knew that it was futile."

"What does that mean?" Herneas spoke quietly, Grodgni's fear beginning to become his own.

"I don't know, but there was something else. You remember how I said that elemental spirits were all linked to the same consciousness, you could say that there are no true individuals among them?"

"Yes?"

"Each of those golems had a unique voice. They were all individuals trapped in an obsidian tomb that they will never escape. And there were *thousands* of them!"

The cold feeling in Herneas's gut deepened, and he turned to continue walking down the sloping cave tunnel. Sveri needed to be told about this. They had to do something to stop the Abyssals from creating more of these abominations, but how? The silence stretched out between the two dwarfs as neither of them spoke while they descended further and further into the dark.

4
Treachery in Waiting

> *Desire is a trickster. It is desire that helps us get out of bed every day. Desire guides to our greatest loves, our greatest triumphs, and our greatest efforts. It was Dianek's desire for children which gave birth to our very race.*
>
> *Yet you must also remember that it was desire that drove Calisor to craft his cursed mirror, and the denial of that desire that brought its sundering. It was desire that fueled Winter's campaign on the world and plunged us into a second darkness.*
>
> *Desire is a fickle mistress. If we are denied it, we are nothing; yet if we do not deny it, then we are terrible.*
>
> *–Jiordyn Longbeard*
> *The Hermit of Rhyn Dufaris*

"So, Rordin has accepted our invitation, then?" Gruumen Ashtel leaned back in his chair with a wicked smile. Ofn suppressed an urge to pull out his knife and cut that little grin from his face.

"Yes, my lord. He said he will send out messengers of his own and will move to the assigned meeting place, just as you have designed."

"Excellent." Gruumen then turned to the other dwarfs in the tent with them. They stood in silence while the light of the brazier in the middle of the space filled the shadows with menace. These were the gathered chieftains who had sworn complete allegiance to Golloch, and by extension, to Gruumen.

"The would-be king has done exactly what I expected him to do," the Ashtel chieftain chuckled.

"What is it that you plan to do with that knowledge?" One of the dwarfs further back asked.

"We all know that it is custom to only bring a small entourage to a peaceful meeting such as this. Rordin would never break from that courtesy. He will come in good faith, and it is there that we will have him."

"You plan to march an army to the meeting? Won't they see that and flee before you can arrive? Wouldn't that just confirm what Rordin has been saying about you?"

"Oh no, I would never do that. Our army will be kept at the customary day and a half march from the site of the meeting." Gruumen's smile deepened, and the flickering light made the grin appear to stretch unnaturally until it became a horrifying mask. Gruumen waved a hand, beckoning one of the shadowy figures into the light.

"Helfather here, though, he commands the Fists of Golloch, an elite force of the Imperial Garrison. His presence will not be expected at the meeting, which is fine as he will be otherwise detained." The dwarf who stood before Gruumen was a hardened warrior, a fanatical glint in his eyes. "Since we control the underground tunnels in the area, he will be able to take a large contingent of troops through to come out a matter of miles from where the meeting will be taking place."

The rest of the dwarfs began nodding their heads in understanding. Ofn felt a sickly sense of worry rising in his stomach as the plan unfolded, though he couldn't quite put his finger on why he felt this way.

"When Helfather's troops descend on the reunion, the rest of us who *will* be there with our entourages will band together and try to seize Rordin and put this insipid rebellion down before it can solidify its hold on the kingdom!"

"How many clans are likely to attend?" Ofn couldn't see who asked the question, but Gruumen waved it away with his hand.

"Besides those that are in this tent, I assume that there will be perhaps a dozen other clans. Most of those will be small. Besides Rordin and his warriors, we'll need to watch that Heavyhand. He is sure to side with Rordin, and though they may be Oathbreakers, his dwarfs know how to fight. The majority of the other clans present will either be minor, or they will be traveling from such a great distance that they will not have had time to gather an army to accompany them in any case. The only unknown element that truly worries me is the Afalans Clan. They are large enough, and their hold is close enough to the meeting place that they will likely bring a significant force to it – if for no other reason than to show off their wealth, which they love to do."

"But don't the Afalans hate Garrek Heavyhand? Won't that put them against Rordin that he is so close with him?"

"They hate Golloch more than the Oathbreaker. They've always felt slighted by how Golloch rose to his throne. They feel as though they have a more legitimate claim to rule than him. Might have been true at the time, but their chance to object has long since passed." Gruumen snorted in derision before continuing. "The real question will be if they can see an opportunity in aiding Rordin or will consider him a lost cause and abandon him to us. Either way, it is an acceptable risk. If everything goes according to plan, their entourage guards won't be able to stop us whichever way that decision goes."

"What if Rordin escapes?"

"We won't let that happen. There's enough of us there that if it looks like things are going awry, just shoot the bastard and we'll be done with it. If Rordin dies, then the resistance will splinter. It will be a much bigger headache putting the empire back together if that happens, but there will be no unity. I'd much rather capture him and hold him hostage. Even if the other clans don't want to accept Golloch, their unifying factor will be Rordin, and they won't risk harm coming to him because of that. Ariagful only knows why Golloch never disowned him as the heir apparent, but here we are. So our first priority is to capture him, barring that, then we kill him."

"So, we have your permission to kill him if it seems as though we are losing control of the situation." This caused a nervous chuckle to ripple around the tent. Gruumen's response sent a chill down Ofn's spine and sobered the rest of them quickly.

"Use discretion, and only do it as a last resort," he said casually.

It was obvious that he was in high spirits, as he didn't berate the other speakers for asking too many questions. Ofn assumed it was because he saw the end to this whole situation coming about sooner rather than later. Gruumen had become angry and irritable since Banick had escaped earlier that spring. Ofn remembered reporting back about that escape. He'd been the one sent to escort Banick to his execution and had been surprised to find another in his place as a decoy. The dwarf who had died in Banick's place had been named Oedi. By now, his name was largely forgotten, his death explained away as some ignominious fate. But Ofn remembered him. He remembered a lot of faces that he'd watch as the lights flickered and died in their eyes.

"Ofn!" Gruumen practically shouted his name, and he looked up with a bewildered expression on his face. He realized that they were alone, all the chieftains and generals had left, and it was only Gruumen who remained.

"I'm sorry," he stumbled over the apology, shaking his head to try and clear it.

"Where did your imaginations take you this time?" Gruumen sneered, pouring something into a silver tankard and raising it to his lips.

"I was thinking of..." he scrambled to find an answer, the truth would only enrage the Ashtel chieftain. "I was thinking of how surprised Rordin will be when our forces sweep down on him. What will come after you've secured the throne for Golloch here?"

"I imagine that you'll be summoned back home. Your service here guarantees that the great warlords of Diew will have to give you deference, I'm sure that Golloch will be pleased with you."

"Ah." Ofn nodded, looking at the floor.

"Is that not what you wanted?"

"No. It is. If anything, I have grown to hate the Imperial Dwarfs even more than when I first arrived here. They are petty, small-minded, and arrogant. Their self-righteous nature makes me sick." But his words lacked any heat, and he could see Gruumen's eyebrows raise out of the corner of his eye.

"You aren't very convincing, *Athro.*" Gruumen threw the title at Ofn like a poisoned dart, and he winced at its use.

"You can say what you will, I don't care." This time his tone carried venom, and Gruumen smiled wickedly in response.

"You know, there are few who could have accomplished what you did here," the Ashtel chieftain said, setting his cup down with an audible click on the table. "You were able to infiltrate the priesthood of Dianek, gain the confidence of my sister, the queen, and then prepare her for sacrifice. Very cold-hearted of you. And you did it with such a convincing act that she went to her death without ever suspecting you. Even now, the wider society still thinks of you as a stone priest, you carry on your facade so well."

Ofn stiffened, and a sneer crept onto his lips.

"If there is nothing else, my lord." He went to bow, but Gruumen wasn't finished with his barbs, yet.

"Even Master Kholearm didn't realize you for what you are until it was too late. I think if he hadn't escaped, then Heavyhand might still trust you, even now. A shame, *that* would have been extremely useful in this situation."

Ofn froze mid bow. A cold sensation gripped the base of his gut, and he felt as if he might be sick. His heart quickened, and he forced himself to rise up and meet Gruumen's evil smile. He didn't say anything, but he stared into those contemptuous eyes for a long time before turning stiffly to walk out of the tent.

"I hope you don't think me rude, Ofn. You are cold and ruthless. A real credit to your ambition and an exemplary Abyssal Dwarf. I would not want to be your enemy. But then, we would have to be friends first, wouldn't we?"

Ofn stopped at the tent flap. He bit back a thousand responses that came to his mind and instead simply said over his shoulder.

"I would not worry about that, Lord Ashtel." *I would gladly put a blade between your ribs without a friendly smile*, he thought as he stormed out into the night.

The cold sensation in his gut did not abate as he put distance between himself and the wicked, smiling eyes that he could feel on the back of his neck even after leaving Gruumen behind. He walked until he reached the edge of the campground.

His breathing was heavy, and it threatened to mist in the cold, thin air of the mountains. He stared up into the sky. His heart thumped heavily in his chest, causing his temples to pulse in the same cadence, and he felt a headache coming on from it all.

"What is wrong with me?" he whispered huskily to the stars in the sky overhead. He saw Gruumen's face flash before his eyes. The mocking twist of his smile hovered in his imaginary vision, and he clenched his fists, grinding his teeth together as he did so. He wanted to scream. He wanted to wrap his hands around that stupid, smirking face and squeeze until the cruel laughter in his eyes was snuffed out like a candle. He wanted to watch while it happened.

He could almost hear Banick's voice in his head. It was easy to imagine his hand on his shoulder.

I think you know what the problem is.

Ofn smiled in spite of himself. He felt a lump rise in his throat as the thought formed in his mind. He remembered talking to Banick about the ghosts that he carried, and Banick had said that he sometimes talked with those memories that haunted him. Was this what that was like?

He thought back to that conversation. It had been about two months after Banick had come to Caeryn Golloch, and Banick had become one of the few regulars to visit the Temple of Dianek there. They had sat in the mostly empty chapel and simply talked. Ofn felt himself yearning for the memory, reaching out to it like someone dying of thirst grasps at a cup of water.

"Everyone who's seen war carries their ghosts with them. Regrets from the things that they've been forced to do, or have had to witness. Horror like that carries a toll with it." Ofn had said as he reclined back on one of the pews. Their whispers carried to the rafters in the vast chamber.

"Yeah, but I think I carry more than most," Banick replied with a heavy sigh. "I've made a lot of mistakes in my life. A lot of mistakes that have gotten a lot of people killed."

"But you've saved far more than have died from your mistakes. Surely that must balance the scales?"

"That's not how it works," Banick said, shaking his head. "We're a pragmatic people, and I think that's why we struggle with things like this. We want to think that there is some great cosmic scale somewhere in the heavens, or with our gods, where our good deeds will be stacked on one side, and our wicked ones on the other. We desperately want it to

be as simple as making sure that our good actions outweigh the bad we have done in this world. Gods, but our entire religion is made up of that concept in many ways. That's why people want commandments and societal systems, because it tells us when we're getting dangerously close to having our bad thoughts and actions outweigh our good ones. We want to know how far we can make mistakes and still be safe."

"Careful, you're starting to sound like a heretic, and in front of a priest no less. Have you no shame?" Ofn smiled, trying to lighten the mood of the conversation, but it didn't work. Instead, Banick sighed and scrubbed his fingers through his black hair. Silence descended, and finally Ofn could take it no longer.

"So what is the truth, then?" he asked. Banick shot him a confused look. "If there isn't a cosmic balance out there that needs to be maintained, then what is the better metaphor? What wisdom do you have that is superior to that of our gods?"

"The truth is… I don't know." Banick shrugged and looked at Ofn, who fixed him with a disappointed frown.

"I was expecting more than that. You poke holes in people's beliefs, but you don't offer any solutions? I thought better of you than being a simple critic, Banick."

"I know that I have done a lot of good in my life. And on some nights, that is enough to console me till I can sleep. On really good days, I don't even think about it. But I know that on bad nights, when the darkness seems to go on forever, that line of reason does absolutely nothing for me. The thought that I have saved more people than I have killed doesn't make the blood on my hands feel any lighter. It doesn't take the heat from the fires that burn beneath my eyelids whenever I close my eyes. It doesn't stop the dead eyes from staring at me accusingly from the shadows whenever I'm not looking. I try to think of the good things. People always tell me to focus on the good deeds, the happy moments of my life when those nights come on me. But you know how much that helps?"

Ofn only shook his head and shrugged.

"It doesn't." Banick stared at him with hard eyes for a long moment before he hung his head.

"This is the part where I'm supposed to say that there is a reason for your suffering. That your sacrifice makes it so others don't have to suffer the same way that you do," Ofn offered, but Banick simply gave a dry chuckle in response.

"I swear to Dianek that if you try to feed me this 'higher purpose' refuse that others have tried to use on me, I will walk out of here and never speak to you again." He brought his head up, and Ofn was surprised to see his eyes were rimmed with red. "My demons are my own. I am not haunted by the actions of others. I have seen terrible

things done to living beings, and not just by orcs and demons, either! I have seen atrocities committed by dwarfs, elves, and men alike! Those are not the things that keep me awake at night. Those are not the things that have had me take my knife from my belt and contemplate turning it on myself. No, those memories were brought about by my own actions, my own choices. My suffering is my own!"

Some part of Ofn reached out to him then. He felt Banick's words resonate with him. There had been so many times in Ofn's life where it would have been easier if he had simply laid down and died. So much struggling, and so much hate dominated his life. He stared at Banick for a long time, knowing that he should say something priestly at that moment. Even if he wasn't a real priest, this is what people came to the temple for: to be comforted. But no words came to mind. No inspiring story sprang to his lips. Instead he found himself asking a question.

"How do you deal with it?"

"I embrace them." Banick sniffed and rubbed at his wet eyes with the back of his hand. "I started talking to the ghosts of my past. They weren't going to leave me alone, so I figured we might as well start talking to each other."

He gave a shaky laugh before continuing.

"I think that's what ghosts really want. They just want to be remembered. We populate our world with all of these phantoms, these spectres that are out for vengeance and to visit pain and anger on the world. But I think they're just lost souls who are trying desperately not to be forgotten."

"What do they say?" Ofn asked, his voice filled with curiosity.

"Mostly they tell me what an ass I'm being," Banick gave another of those shaky laughs one has when trying not to weep. The sound was loud, and it burst against the quiet stillness of the temple. Banick gave a crooked smile in apology to Ofn, who waved it away.

"Other times," he continued, "they give me advice, or they talk with me about memories that we shared. Some of them can be quite funny, which is odd of me to say, because I'm fairly certain they are just my own thoughts taking on the disguise of the people who've died because of me. There was this one over-eager little shithead, Drewyn was his name. This little prick was always needing to be the center of attention. At every camp he would always be the first one to tell jokes, or sing songs, or whatever got the most people to look at him. He'd get so angry whenever someone outdid him or stole his thunder. It made him so easy to tease. He really got on my nerves." Banick took a shuddering breath and let it out as a sigh.

"But I realized later that it was just because he wanted so desperately to prove himself to the rest of us. He always volunteered for the most dangerous missions, and as rangers, we always had plenty of

those to choose from. One day I was really fed up with him, he'd been singing this new shanty that was catchy at first, but then it just got stuck in your head, ya know? Only he wouldn't shut up about it. Finally I told him to take his gear and two others and follow some tracks that we'd found. We were tracking a band of orc raiders, and a few of them had broken away from the main pack. So I sent him and his party to follow the smaller group. I figured that because they were going after the less threatening bunch that they'd be safe. I told them not to engage the enemy. But Drewyn wanted to prove he was just as good as the rest of us. When they found it was only four orcs that had split off, he had his group lay an ambush and attack them."

Here Banick paused, scrubbing at his face. Ofn waited patiently for him to continue.

"I think you can guess how that turned out. Drewyn was killed, and the other two barely made it back alive. I can't even remember if they killed the orcs or not. We didn't recover Drewyn's body in order to give it a proper burial, either. I tried to shrug it off, thinking it was his own fault that he'd been killed. But it was me who gave him the order to track the smaller group, all because I wanted some peace and quiet. So now…" he paused for a moment before continuing.

"Drewyn sits with me and reminds me of that story every time I feel like I'm reaching the end of my patience. Every time I find myself getting annoyed at some stupid little wet-behind-the-ears beardling that I have to teach, he's there. He always sings that damn shanty, too."

At this, Banick laughed ruefully; his eyes were still red, and his face had become haggard, but the laugh seemed genuine.

"He also usually pops up on his birthday, too, because that's the kind of self-centered ass he was when he was alive. Would not shut up about his 'special day' and wanted to make sure we made a big deal out of it, as if he were a child!" His words were harsh, but there was a real smile on his face, and the far away look in his eyes was replaced with a hopeful glow. He looked up into Ofn's eyes.

"That is how I deal with it. I have a host of victims in my head, just like any soldier in any war. Just like anyone who has ever made a wrong choice that has haunted them. I just have so many that they have to take turns, and I have to be careful not to play favorites with them." He gave another chuckle. "Although I do have a soft spot for that asinine Drewyn."

In that moment, Ofn tried to think of the faces of his own victims, those who had died as direct results of his actions. Only nothing came to mind. He couldn't remember any details from any of the faces of the people he'd killed. No, there was one, but she sat in a place where he found it difficult to look. His mind's eye reeled from the effort. He tried to force it, but the only thing that he could retain was a single name, and he said it aloud.

"Rhosyn." The name dripped with such guilt and regret that Banick had stopped and looked up at him quizzically.

"Did you say something?" he asked slowly.

"I was just trying to follow your advice. That's the first name I could think of among my ghosts."

"You mean Queen Rhosyn? From the book that you lent me? Why would you feel guilty for her death?"

"She was one of the few people that I have ever felt close enough to that their death impacted me in that way," he said, and he was surprised to realize that he meant it. All the other murders and deaths he had caused didn't haunt him, because at the end of the day, he hadn't cared about them. The weight of his actions bore down on his shoulders, but it was more generalized than what Banick had described. For Ofn, killing was part of survival. If he didn't kill, then someone would kill him, it was a simple fact of life. It was only now, when he'd come to Caeryn Golloch, when he'd lived among the Imperial Dwarfs for some time, that he'd come to realize that killing was not necessary to live. He had been shocked to realize that there were dwarfs in the city who had never killed anyone before. Such an idea was difficult for him to grasp.

"I get what you mean. I have several close friends whose death shook me to my core, and grief manifests itself in different ways." Banick shook his head and leaned back. "But surely that isn't the only death in your life that has affected you so. What about your parents? Or your grandparents?"

Ofn shook his head.

"My mother was a terrible person. She was from the north, closer to your people. She was rejected from her clan for reasons that I never really learned. I was just a babe when it happened. She wandered around in the wilderness for a while before landing in the bed of some dwarf who was a monster that kept her fed for his own appetites and used me as a beating post for his anger and frustrations. I left them as soon as I was able and began to study the worship of my goddess at an early age."

This was all mostly true. Ofn's mother had found her way to the Abyssal Dwarfs after she'd been ousted from her own clan for murdering her cousin over a dispute of some kind, Ofn had never bothered to learn the details. She'd found a lover there among the streets of Diew who had nearly killed Ofn, and when he'd come of age, he'd become a devout follower of Ariagful, the Wicked One of lava and the underground streams of fire. He had been a quick study, and his knowledge of the ways of torture was born from an intimate knowledge of the pain his life had brought him. It was this knowledge and talent that had placed him in a position to help convert Golloch to the ways of the Abyss. It was because of all of that he'd had the opportunity to come here.

It was because of the deaths that he'd caused that he'd been the one to prepare Rhosyn for her sacrifice, too. Rhosyn, the first person who had ever really shown him kindness – who had expected nothing from him in return for her friendship. Her ghost stood in his mind's eye and stared at him accusingly, her hands held out to him in a pleading manner, a single word on her dead lips.

Why?

Ofn was jolted back to the present. The memory of Rhosyn's spectre hovered over him like a cold mist, and he shivered. He turned to look back at the camp where he'd fled from Gruumen's sneering face. He realized now why the accusations that Gruumen had hurled at him hurt so much. Why they had caused him so much distress.

He didn't want Banick and Garrek to die.

He could barely stand the presence of Rhosyn's ghost in his mind. The thought of Banick and Garrek joining her made him break out in a cold sweat. He didn't understand these feelings at all! Banick and Garrek were his enemy! They stood in the way of Golloch's goals, and by extension, his own.

He was unfamiliar with the concept of caring for someone. Rhosyn had been his friend, and he'd offered her up to be killed by Golloch without any protest. Banick and Garrek had likewise only ever treated him with compassion and respect, and he'd betrayed them just as easily. But shouldn't they all have expected that? Wasn't their trust a weakness he'd exposed, just like he had done so many times before? Why was this time so different? Why did he struggle with the thought of their deaths?

You know why. Banick's voice seemed to say. Or was it Rhosyn's?

Ofn stared up into the night sky. He didn't understand these feelings at all, but he knew he didn't want to see Banick and Garrek dead. He also didn't know how he could stop it and still serve his purpose for being here.

He hated the feeling in his gut as ghosts of past and future sins circled in his mind.

5
An Inherited Legacy

Dwarfs are interesting creatures. To them, honor is everything, but they do not revere the individual so much as the society which raised them. In order for a dwarf to accomplish great deeds, they must have been raised in a community that harbored such bravery, or such skill. A dwarf is nothing without their family's legacy, and there is no telling the heights a dwarf can achieve if their family has established itself as honorable and just.

However, the opposite is also true. If one's ancestor has committed an egregious sin of pride, or worse, that of cowardice, then the sins of the fathers will be visited for generations upon the children, no matter what great feats those children achieve. Until the unforgivable acts have passed from remembrance, there can be no redemption. And dwarfs have extremely long memories.

–Kriet Torporus
Basilean Liaison to the Imperial Dwarfs

The morning sun peeked through the flap to his tent, lighting the air and the specks of dust motes that glittered like pieces of broken sunbeams. Garrek sighed and rubbed his eyes. The morning's arrival was the confirmation he needed that sleep would not be coming this night, and so he pushed himself up to sit on the edge of his cot. Outside, he could hear the early risers in the camp bustling about. There were some coughs and the clatter of pans being unloaded to prepare breakfast.

The long night had not been kind to Garrek. Sleep had been elusive, and instead, he had simply lain in his cot and stared up into the dark of the roof of his tent. His mind drifted back to the conversation that had spurred his restlessness. He had been sitting down to dinner with the other clan chieftains, as well as Rordin, to discuss the plan for the coming days.

They had already arrived at the location for the meeting of the clans, and their camp now only consisted of those chieftains who had also arrived, as well as their entourages. The larger camps of any accompanying armies had dutifully set up a day and a half's journey in whichever direction they had come, as was custom for such diplomatic meetings as this. Rordin had explained what Gruumen had told him about the meeting, that they would wait a few more weeks to allow as many clans as possible to make the journey to where they were so that they could all hear the talks and return to their homes to make their decision.

"I would be worried about what the Ashtels are planning," Garrek had spoken up. "They have us at a potential disadvantage here. They will be approaching from the east and have the majority of the empire at their backs. Most clans will have to cross their paths in order to get here, and they will have the opportunity to interrupt or block the arrival of any clans that they are worried about siding against them." This comment had caused some uneasy murmurs to circle around the table.

"I appreciate your concern, Garrek," Rordin had responded, nodding thoughtfully, "but we will just have to rely on trust at this time. We cannot afford to insult the Ashtels before it is decided which way the clans will vote on this issue."

"Trust the Ashtels?" Garrek snorted. "I trust them about as far as the reach of my hammer, and not an inch more. However, I don't suggest we outwardly accuse them, but perhaps it might be useful to send out some scouts to watch the perimeters and make sure that everyone is being given a fair chance to arrive, that's all."

"Oh, for Dianek's sake!" a voice from the other end of the table exclaimed, and Garrek turned to see Ddiangen Afalans thump his tankard down on the table. "We should not assume that the Ashtels are using subterfuge! They are not elves! We insult them just by having this conversation. And this is particularly rich as the source of these accusations is coming from you, Oathbreaker!"

Garrek's blood ran cold at the mention of his unfortunate title. His knuckles cracked as his fist tightened around his own mug. His vision took on a slightly red tinge as he stared at the Afalans chieftain.

"Yes, of course," he said, biting off the ends of each word as it left his mouth. "But please, tell me, what great deeds has the Afalans clan achieved in this, its present generation? I do not pay attention to these things much myself, being a lowly house with little honor and even less consideration in such things. But I have not heard of any great deeds or noteworthy things that have come from the Afalans since before your father, Lord Ddiangen."

By now, the table had grown completely silent. The other chieftains glanced about nervously between the two dwarfs, and several eyes bulged in disbelief at Garrek's words.

"I will not have my family's honor questioned by someone such as you, a chieftain for a clan of thieves!" Ddiangen rose to his feet. "My family has always been close to the throne, and their honor is beyond your snivelling reproach!"

Garrek also stood, his chair clattering to the ground behind him.

"It is your nearness to the throne that earns you my suspicion. I fear that you have taken to Golloch's treacherous ways. Tell me, would you defend his honor? Even though it was through his trickery that he took the throne and ousted your family from the succession?"

"You filthy gorachod*! You are beneath me! I will..."*

He was cut off as Rordin slammed his fist down on the table.

"You will do nothing, Ddiangen!" he shouted, and the sound carried out into the night. Garrek had been aware that there was silence all around them, but now it was as if the movements of the entire camp had stopped to listen to the chieftain's table.

"We are here for a meeting of diplomacy!" Rordin continued, his voice growing quiet but terrible. "Would you really be so dishonorable as to break the peace with your squabbles against someone whom you claim is beneath you? Where is your honor? Garrek has nothing to prove here, even though his outburst was unbecoming of him toward you, you have visited his slight back on him a hundred-fold over the years. It is you who pushes for conflict here, at a peaceful meeting of the clans. I wonder what our historians would say of your lowly brawl that you initiated at such a meeting? Especially if you were to lose against the dwarf whom you claim is without honor?"

"How dare you!" Ddiangen sputtered, his face turning a deep red as he spoke. "You are not our king! You are a drunken adventurer masquerading as a legitimate heir to the throne! You do not have the consent of the clans to rule, yet you hold yourself here as if you were our superior! You mediate in an argument that is not yours to meddle in!"

"I do nothing of the sort, Ddiangen. I am merely counseling you against your temper. I understand where it comes from. But I must remind you of the possible consequences of failing to reign in your passions, and your opinions, lest they should besmirch the legacy of your family by falling to common insults and petty fighting when there are much larger issues at hand. Think of what the histories will remember. Will your children be weighed down with unneeded shame because of your hasty actions done today? I am sure that Garrek could commiserate with them, having also needed to throw off the shackles of an unwanted inheritance."

Rordin's words caused several quiet gasps around the table, and Ddiangen's face had grown a deeper shade of crimson. The Afalans chieftain closed his eyes and turned toward the rest of the table.

"You must forgive me, my lords. It seems as though I have no appetite, there is something that does not agree with me and has pushed me to say things that are unbecoming of your company. As such, I think I will excuse myself." With that, Ddiangen turned and stormed off into the night, leaving the other chieftains sitting in an uncomfortable silence.

Garrek felt his own cheeks sting, and though he didn't want to, he turned to look at Rordin, who shot him a meaningful look.

"Garrek, this is no time for such petty squabbles. We must work together to protect the empire, and your words, however justified you may think they were, did not help us toward that unity. I expect more from you. I know your quality, and it is better than this." He turned to look at the other chieftains around the table. "Forgiveness is a difficult thing to ask, my lords. But we must take into account the strange and difficult times that we find ourselves in. We are facing a situation that has never occurred in our long history. We stand on the brink of war with our fellow dwarfs, and we must do everything in our power to avoid such a senseless conflict. Such a burden puts a strain on even the wisest and most honorable among us, and can push us past the breaking point. As such, I beg your indulgence to see past this matter and let us put it behind us."

Garrek had sat through the remainder of the meal without touching his food. Rordin's words weighed on him like a stone had been placed on his chest. His guts coiled at the thought of his own actions and the rather gentle rebuke that he'd received. He excused himself and retired to his tent where he had spent the rest of the night replaying the events of that conversation. He had wallowed in the burning irritation of his actions. Rordin was right, if they were to fight against Golloch and the Ashtels, they would need every ally they could find, and the Afalans were a powerful clan with deep pockets. Yet Garrek had insulted them because they had repeated the same insults they always did when they addressed him.

A small part of him wanted to rage against Rordin for not defending him outright, even though he knew that he had been right not to do so. Another part was embarrassed that he *wanted* Rordin to defend him. He felt the sting of Ddiangen's words and wanted to take that hurt and shove it down the Afalans's throat along with a list of all his accomplishments that he had to his name.

In the gray morning light that pierced through the walls of his tent, Garrek reached over to pick up his hammer – The Warp Hammer, as it was called. It was one of the twenty-seven God Boons that his ancestor had stolen from the High King's treasury all those centuries ago, long before the Free Clans had split from the Imperial throne. Stolen, and then lost, his great grandsire's greed turning to inevitable tragedy for the Heavyhand Clan. Gilgulli the Godless, as he was known in the records housed in Caeryn Golloch. Also known as Gilgulli the Thief, the Coward, the Faithless. His family had carried the weight of that one dwarf's sins for generations now. Their family had been branded as 'Oathbreakers,' and now they all carried that shame. Garrek's father had died a broken dwarf under that weight, buried under a thousand bottles.

Garrek had spent his whole life trying to fix the mistakes of this unfair past. He'd recovered or learned the fate of sixteen of the God Boons. But there was a problem in that there had been several that were destroyed in the intervening years between their loss and his discovery of them. This meant that there was no way to fully restore what had been lost. These artefacts had been ancient magical items given to the dwarfs from the Celestians, a race that had since been broken in half, and there was no way to replace these treasures. Garrek had wept many nights after the first of the destroyed Boons that he had discovered. He wept for their loss, and with it, his chance to absolve his family.

The Heavyhands would forever be known as 'Oathbreakers.'

Because of this, Garrek had eschewed the idea of marriage. He'd never sired an heir, not wanting to saddle any of his children with the weight that he'd borne. Instead, he had drawn the discarded of dwarf society to himself. Any who had fallen away from family and clan, for whatever reason, were welcome in the ranks of his clan, so long as they were willing to fight. Even though it was impossible to achieve, Garrek still sought to restore as many of the God Boons as he could, and his family of forsaken dwarfs followed him dutifully into every battle.

He turned the Warp Hammer in his hands. It was a masterwork tool. Garrek had often wondered at the purpose for its creation. Energy sparked around the heavy head, and when he swung it, the hammer crackled to life and increased the power of his blows tenfold. Garrek had split obsidian golems in half with a single blow of his hammer. But the angles of the weapon had him convinced that death was not its original purpose. The force of these blows on a similarly enchanted anvil could help shape the most stubborn of metals without tiring its wielder. The Warp Hammer was an object of creation, yet all Garrek had done with it was destroy. A part of him saddened at that thought, but it was lost among the myriad of other complicated emotions that swirled in his chest.

Sighing to shake off these morose feelings, Garrek rose to his feet and quickly dressed. Though he had no appetite, he still sought out the breakfast tents to find some of the bitter liquid that one of the famous dwarf traders, Billiam XXXVIII, had imported from the west. It had an alluring aroma, and the dark liquid invigorated him and put some warmth in his bones to help ward off the mountain chill that still hung in the morning air. He found a table and sat down with his beverage, his thoughts still warring with his emotions in his chest.

"Ho! Garrek!" Someone called his name, and Garrek looked up to see two dwarfs walking toward him. The first was an elderly, balding dwarf with a white beard that looked as though its ends had been burnt. A smell of smoke accompanied him as he drew closer. The other was short, even by dwarf standards, but her eyes were bright, and she smiled as they approached, pushing brown hair out of her face as it tried to cover her gaze.

"Mendeleev! Mimir!" Garrek couldn't help but grin as the two came and sat across from him at the table, plates of food in their hands. "I was not expecting to see you here! Your hold is so far off that I'm surprised that you could make it."

"Well, we got stuck in the capital after the mess that was the Claansvelt," Mimir said as she scooped up a steaming spoonful of mushrooms. "It was hard to secure transport with all the trouble after the assassination attempt. People were unwilling to let us travel with them for fear that we were part of the plot and trying to escape unnoticed. We were in the middle of waiting for that to die down when the announcement came of this new meeting of the clans, so we figured we'd come over and see what there was to see about all of this."

"Why were you at the Claansvelt? I didn't think you cared about all that political stuff?" Garrek looked pointedly at Mendeleev, and the old dwarf shrugged and shook his head ruefully.

"It wasn't my idea. This one here is convinced that we are going to need more Imperial sponsors to get us through this next winter." Mendeleev pointed at Mimir with his fork. "She says we're too isolated out where we are. I told her it was a fool's errand! Nobody wants to support a hold that mines pyrite! But she wouldn't listen, and was convinced that we could spread the word of what we're doing over there if we came to the great gathering. Unfortunately, it seems as though our presentation was grossly overshadowed by the other events of the evening."

Garrek's face darkened at these words. The Claansvelt had been where Ithel Ffionen had died, and where Banick had been set up for the assassination attempt on Golloch. Mimir must have seen the change come over him, because she cleared her throat.

"That's enough about those depressing matters, Mendeleev. Garrek has enough on his mind that he doesn't need us adding to his troubles."

"Ah, yes! We heard about your altercation with Ddiangen last night. I wish I could have been there to see the look on his pompous face!" the old dwarf grinned.

"Mendeleev!" Mimir hissed, but Garrek held up a hand.

"It's all right, I don't mind." He tried to smile, but he could tell the other two weren't buying it.

"What happened? If you don't mind our asking, that is." Mimir leaned in close, her previous apprehension completely vanishing.

"Oh, nothing more than is usual," Garrek sighed. "He insulted my family, called me a liar, and was ashamed that I had a seat at the table. The same old diatribe he throws at me every time our paths cross."

"Just got sick of hearing it, eh?" Mendeleev chuckled. "Well, good for you!"

"I don't know what came over me. Rordin is right, we can't afford to be alienating potential allies right now, no matter how onerous they are."

"Oh, I think I understand." Mimir smiled, and her eyes twinkled mischievously as she spoke. "They always tell you to have thick skin, that words shouldn't affect you, and on, and on. But after so many times of getting rubbed the wrong way, you tend to start getting sore spots. From the sound of things, Garrek, you did better than most others would have done in your position."

"Yeah well, I'm almost as old as this codger here," Garrek tapped Mendeleev playfully on the shoulder. "I should know better than to fall for those old traps. Besides, the Afalans can offer Rordin a legitimacy that my support can't. He needs the other clans more than he needs me, and I forced him into a bad situation last night. I should go and apologize."

"Well, you might be right in that regard, but I wouldn't sell yourself short, Garrek." The smaller dwarf shook her head. "You bring something that the Afalans are in desperate short supply of: integrity. The problem with all these big and major clans is that they are so caught up in their own honor that if anyone suggests that they may be wrong, they'll go to war before they ever admit it. You, on the other hand, are already thinking of how you can go about patching things up. Pride can be an excellent thing for a dwarf to have, but just like the greed for gold can be your downfall, pride can be just as dangerous. That's a lesson that I hope Ddiangen learns before it gets him killed, one day."

"I appreciate the compliment. But it was my pride that started the mess in the first place."

"Pah! Don't be ridiculous! He's the one that's constantly throwing dirt at you!"

"Doesn't matter. In the eyes of the clans, his opinion is valid, and mine is not." Garrek looked away as he said this last part, hoping to hide the hurt that welled up inside him.

"Do you remember what the nature of our expedition is? Why we've established a settlement clear out east?" Mimir asked slowly. Garrek heard her plate click as she set her utensil down.

"You mine pyrite," Garrek replied, turning back to face her.

"More commonly referred to as fool's gold," Mimir continued. She reached beneath the table and pulled out a small cloth bag and handed it to Garrek. He took it slowly and opened the drawstrings. He emptied the contents into his other hand. It was a single piece of pyrite that glittered deceptively in the early morning light.

"Do you know why we mine that stuff?" Mimir asked.

"I think you've tried to explain it to me once or twice, but I still have no idea."

"Well, it's all rather simple, really," Mendeleev began. "Mimir over here managed to separate pyrite into its components and discovered that pyrite is composed of iron and sulphur! She asked me what we can do with sulphur, and I explained that it reacts with saltpeter, that we can make with agricultural byproduct, and if we then start logging operations…" Mendeleev's rambling explanation was cut off by Mimir's raised hand.

"We use it to make a volatile liquid with similar properties to black powder. Golloch himself used to purchase it to supplement his own powder supply. Now we've working on a new formula for something that's similar but even more powerful than Dragon's Breath."

"That's incredible! Why haven't you brought this before the clans?!" Garrek exclaimed.

"What do you think we were doing at the Claansvelt?" Mimir smiled, but then waved her hand absently. "Mendeleev even brought all of the necessary components to show it off. But it didn't take. Our demonstration was flawed, and the process of making it is difficult. Not to mention that the results are too volatile and unpredictable. A small vial of the compound can either produce a bright flash and a lot of smoke, or it could split a cannon barrel in half with its force, as it has been known to do in our tests."

"The problem is that the process has to be absolutely precise," Mendeleev began talking excitedly, and even though Mimir tried to stop him a few times, he just continued talking over her. "One has to create vitriol from the pyrite before extracting oil of vitriol by heating it over a careful flame. Once that is completed, you must precisely mix it with saltpeter and collect the corrosive vapor. Finally, one must treat pig fat with a precise mixture of the vapor and oil of vitriol; being careful not to let it overheat, to make an unstable liquid. The less pure, the more unstable, and if any of these steps are missed or completed carelessly, then it can throw the whole process off. Not to mention that the final result is… less than stable and needs to be handled with extreme caution."

"Basically, the whole thing is too fiddly," Mimir translated with a shrug. "What we need is support from another clan. Someone willing to fund our research, as we've done all of this work ourselves, but it's getting more and more difficult to pay for everything."

"I'm sorry to hear that," Garrek said, placing the pyrite back in the bag and holding it out to Mimir. She pushed it back toward him, shaking her head.

"We didn't share all that with you so that you'd feel sorry for us. We did it so that we could make a point. Everyone thinks that we're insane for mining something like that. They've even given our settlement the nickname 'Fool's Hold' as a kind of joke. It was meant to be hurtful, but we've adopted it and now wear it as a badge of pride." She smiled, and Garrek was surprised at how genuine it was. She pointed at the bag with the pyrite in it.

"The point of all this is that people oftentimes misjudge the value of something because it doesn't fit a preconceived notion of what its value should be, just like with fool's gold. It has no monetary worth, but it has other properties which give it value. Fool's Hold is renowned for how little people value our research, but that doesn't mean that our endeavor isn't valuable. Some things are only worth what the opinions of others grant them, but the truly worthwhile things are intrinsically valuable." She reached across the table and clapped Garrek on the arm, her smile broadening. "We see your worth, Garrek, and you will always be welcome at Fool's Hold as an honorary Fool with the rest of us."

He sat there for a long moment. He knew that he had a crooked smile that was threatening to shatter on his face, but he also knew that it was the best that he could do in that moment. His throat was too tight, and he didn't trust himself to speak in any case. The other two dwarfs seemed to understand and didn't break the quiet moment between them.

"Thank you," Garrek said at last. Mendeleev and Mimir simply smiled and nodded before turning back to their food. He pushed back from the table, and they gave him questioning looks.

"If you'll excuse me, I have some bridges to mend after last night. I might be an old fool, but I won't be the reason that Rordin cannot convince the clans simply because of prideful arrogance."

"See what I told you, Garrek? Integrity and value." Mimir smiled, and Mendeleev raised his cup to him in salute as he turned and walked off to find Ddiangen and Rordin.

6
Troubling News

"To either die ignominiously, or to live with one's shame."

– An old dwarf saying used to indicate when someone is being faced with an impossible choice.

Rain was beginning to fall as Yorna sat under the eaves of the building where she waited for the storm to pass. It had blown in off the High Sea of Bari and caught them all unawares. She shivered against the damp air and thought how she would never understand dwarfs who would willingly live this close to the ocean and out under the open sky.

Yorna looked around at the building where she had fled from the rain. Construction tools and materials were strewn about where she rested. This was a common sight throughout the city. The Abyssal Dwarfs and their goblin allies had not been gentle while they had stayed here, and most buildings were not suitable to house anyone or anything without considerable repairs. Yorna had noticed quite a few buildings that were so structurally unsound that they would need to be demolished and rebuilt before they were serviceable.

Outside in the streets, dwarfs still hustled about with wagons and supplies moving up and down the stone pathways. Eastport was still recently recaptured and finding its feet after the long occupation by the enemy. But as it was the only port city the dwarfs had leading into the Halpi Mountains, it was already bursting at the seams with those anxious to return to their homes. Every day, the harbor was stacked with ships trying to find a place to dock so that they could unload the supplies and passengers they carried. The biggest problem came from the lack of food and supplies for return trips. These were sold at such a premium that many ships couldn't afford it and sat idly offshore with skeleton crews until the situation improved.

All of this made it difficult for her and the rest of the Ffionen Clan to secure transport back to Caeryn Golloch. Although, truth be told, she was not looking forward to reporting back to Ithel about the death of his son, Cerrig. Part of her was grateful for the delay, although her annoyance at it was beginning to overpower her gratitude. They'd been stuck there for weeks now, ever since they had accompanied Sveri and his ragged host when they had departed Cwl Gen and made for the port city to meet with their reinforcements. They'd left the majority of their army back at the northern hold to start on repairs to the keep. The title of *Hanner Brig,* or Broken Peak, had stuck with Cwl Gen since the battle with the Imperial traitors earlier that year after Yorna had blown away half of the mountaintop to stop one of their charges.

These thoughts inevitably led her to the strange set of circumstances that had brought her into contact with the elemental Craggoth. How he had begun speaking to her, or whatever weird way that elementals communicated with people. How she had begun to hear strange things in the stone. But most of all, it reminded her of Cerrig's death right before discovering these new abilities, and that caused her stomach to tighten and her head to pound. She leaned out and stared up into the sky to distract herself, letting the raindrops soak her mousey brown hair and run down her face as she did so. Thunder rumbled through the clouds, but it was distant and not the angry sound of a tempest. It was almost soothing in nature, and she began to think that maybe there was some sense to those crazy dwarfs who decided to live here.

She lowered her gaze, and her eyes caught a familiar figure hurrying through the rain. He was tall and thin for a dwarf, which made him a funny contrast to her shorter and more rotund stature, and his head was lowered against the storm. She called out to him.

"Wynn!"

The figure stopped, hearing his name, and turned in her direction. Recognition dawned on his features, and he hurried over to her. She started to smile at him, but then caught the look on his face and suddenly felt a chill that was not related to the weather.

"What's wrong?" she asked, hoping that she had misread the grim set of his eyes and his mouth. Wynn was her apprentice warsmith, learning the engineer's trade under her guidance. But their time together had made her a good judge of his moods.

"It's about Ithel and Banick," he replied, and Yorna took an involuntary step backward.

"No," was all she said. She didn't want to hear what came next, but Wynn pressed on anyway.

"They're both dead."

Yorna felt like she'd been punched in her stomach, and she let out a breath of air that sounded like a grunt.

"What?! How?!"

"Banick was accused of poisoning Ithel at the Claansvelt. Supposedly, Banick did it as a distraction for an assassination attempt on Golloch at the same time, but Golloch had sent his body double in his stead. The attempt failed only because of that. Banick was then taken and tried for the crime, to which he evidently admitted, and was publicly executed."

"That makes no sense! Why would Banick do that?"

"Golloch had been extremely negligent toward his promises of aid to the Free Dwarfs. In a way, it kind of makes sense that they would want to get him back."

"But to what end? What would that gain them? They still need help! Why would they waste time and resources on such a vain and empty gesture? Not only that but antagonize the Imperials so that they make an enemy on two fronts? They'll never be able to retake Halpi if that's the case!" Yorna stared down at the ground, her head was spinning.

"There's more," Wynn said hesitantly. She looked up at him. "The Ffionen Clan has been dissolved. Reports have reached the capital of us assisting Cwl Gen in an uprising against Imperial forces that had been dispatched by Golloch to assist Sveri as a sign of friendship."

"Again, this doesn't make any sense! They're the ones who sent us! Why would anyone believe this!" She took a few deep breaths to try and calm herself before motioning for him to continue. He rubbed his forehead before speaking.

"They mention how the Free Dwarfs defeated the Teirhammer Clan and the Imperial Garrison with the aid of the renegade Ffionen and extreme cowardice through subterfuge. In particular, your name is being mentioned a lot."

"What are they saying?"

"That you are a traitor to the throne, and that there is a reward for your capture."

"Well that's something," Yorna laughed weakly. "How much are they offering?"

"One hundred and fifty gold crowns." Wynn looked like he was going to say more but stopped himself.

"That's not a small amount!" She forced herself to smile. "What aren't you telling me, though?" Wynn hesitated, but Yorna reached out and hit him on the shoulder.

"The reward is offered if you are brought in dead or alive," Wynn winced as he spoke. The spinning sensation in Yorna's head worsened, and she felt bile creeping up the back of her throat.

"You thinking of turning me over?" She attempted a teasing tone, but it came out strained.

"Well, seeing as how I am listed as your apprentice, I think they'd just kill me, too." Wynn didn't even attempt at humor, his voice was flat. "All former members of the Ffionen Clan are also listed as fugitives, supposedly, and a bounty has been issued for each of them. Although it is for a significantly lower amount."

"How did you find out about all of this?" Yorna asked. Wynn produced a piece of paper that was well worn and torn at the edges. She took it. On the front was a drawn likeness of her, as well as the information that Wynn had just shared with her. She turned it over and on the back were listed the names of the Ffionen warriors who had gone with her and Cerrig to Cwl Gen.

"Piles of these were sent from Caeryn Golloch over to the Free Dwarf chieftains in Estacarr with orders to distribute them. They also came with a warning that they were to have no contact with Sveri or his clan if they wished to stay on Golloch's good side."

"What was the response to that?"

"It caused quite a stir. Several clans followed these orders, but most were enraged by them. Some even went so far as to return the papers back to the capital. One particular mad chieftain by the name of Gorvyn Treibmem lit a bonfire with them and forced the Imperial messengers to watch until all of the papers were consumed before releasing them. This paper was one that was brought across from Estacarr, and there were a few dwarfs distributing more down by the docks. They were spreading the word of Golloch preparing to declare war, it sounds like. When I asked about it, they also told me about Banick and Ithel."

"This is bad," Yorna whispered, taking a deep breath. She reached her hand out to steady herself but found nothing there. The dizzying feeling in her head grew more persistent, and so she knelt down to ward it off.

Ithel is dead, and I am a traitor.

The thought still struck her like a blow, and she reeled from it in her mind. She hadn't known Ithel very well. But she'd grown somewhat close to Cerrig, his son, during their march north to Cwl Gen. Cerrig had saved her life, though it had cost him his own in the process. Ithel had simply been the patron who had sponsored her in the first major appointment she'd had since graduating as a certified warsmith. He'd taken a chance on her when few others would have. The few interactions she'd had with him had given her a distinct impression of a warm, friendly smile and kind eyes.

It wasn't just Ithel's death that caused her anxiety, though, it was what it meant for her. How had things come to this? She was an outlaw, now. She could never go home. She could never see her family again: her parents and siblings, her cousins. All of these people were now separated from her as surely as the executioner's axe would separate her head from her shoulders should she try to go back there.

She stared out into the street, searching desperately for something she could focus on. Anything that would give her solid purchase in this swirling void of emotions. Fear, guilt, and anger all tumbled through her, each one stronger than the last. She began to see little details and desperately tried to latch onto them. She saw that the rain had stopped. She saw that people were beginning to gather together and pull away from the center of the road. She saw them whispering and pointing.

She followed these events, hoping that they might overcome the boiling mess inside her head. She looked to where the others were pointing. There she saw a group of dwarfs in heavy green cloaks walking purposefully down the road. She focused on the foremost dwarf and shook her head to clear it. She knew that face with his dark beard lined with gray…

"Herneas!" she cried, rising to her feet and hurrying toward him. Several of the other dwarfs gave her a scandalized look that she would approach the legendary ranger and use his name with such familiarity, but she barely noticed them. Herneas gave a start, then looked at her, and his eyes widened momentarily before nodding in her direction.

"Yorna," he said curtly and continued walking past her. She turned and hurried after him.

"Did you find anything?" she asked, trying hard to keep the desperation out of her voice.

"I thought you were leaving."

"I can't now. The Ffionen Clan has been dissolved and we've been branded as traitors. Herneas, Ithel is dead!" She found her voice was rising in volume as she spoke. The last part came out nearly as a scream, and she found that her eyes were stinging. Somehow hearing the words come from her own mouth made them hit harder, and she struggled to control her emotions. Herneas paused and turned to face her.

"I am sorry to hear this. What will you do?"

"If I go back, I'll be executed just like Banick was."

A wind howled through the drenched streets as Herneas's face drained of color. Suddenly he was inches from Yorna, a strange look in his eyes.

"What did you just say?"

"Banick was executed. They're saying that he was the one who killed Ithel, and that he tried to assassinate Golloch." Herneas stepped backward slowly, a stunned frown creasing his lips, his eyes open wide in disbelief.

"Who is saying that?" he asked.

"The Imperials. They sent this decree to the clans in Estacarr along with information regarding Banick's supposed betrayal." Yorna held out the paper with her picture on it and watched as her words registered with Herneas. His eyes grew hard, his frown deepened into something more closely resembling a snarl.

"The bastard will pay for this," he growled. His gaze fell on Yorna, and she found herself flinching away from it.

"What do you believe?" he asked.

"I… I don't…" she started, then shook her head and started again. "None of it makes sense. Why would Banick try and kill Golloch? If I hadn't witnessed the Imperial Garrison try and take Cwl Gen and kill all of us in the process, I'd assume that it was some tragic miscommunication. But now, my suspicions are far more sinister in nature." She was shocked at her own words. She hadn't realized that she felt this way, but as she said it, she believed it. Herneas continued to stare at her for a long moment before nodding.

"Good. I have to report to Sveri, but I will come by later, and we will talk more of this then." Herneas turned and continued walking. Yorna stared after him until he disappeared from view.

Above her, the rain again began to fall.

*****

"What are you saying?" Sveri asked, and he felt something unfamiliar welling up inside of him. "I think I know, but I want to hear it spoken aloud."

"Golloch has gone fully over to the Abyss." Herneas's voice was flat and emotionless. Sveri had known him long enough to recognize the tight control the ranger was being forced to employ in order to appear so calm.

They were in a private room in one of the few usable large buildings in the city. Sveri had been forced to get somewhat gruff with the local chieftain who ruled over Eastport in order to secure these quarters, but he needed a place such as this to conduct affairs of a more serious nature. It was spartan and bare, barely larger than a standard bedchamber, and the only furniture were a few simple chairs and a small table.

"By Dianek… By all the gods that have been or ever will be," Sveri breathed the curse into the quiet air. Outside, he could hear rain pattering against the windows as thunder rolled in the distance. The silence stretched between them. Then Sveri slammed his fist down on the table.

"*Uff'ran!*" he swore loudly. Red lines were beginning to form on the edges of his vision, and he had to take several long breaths to push them away.

"He seems to be building an army of golems," Herneas continued his report, and Sveri forced the rising bloodlust in him away. He focused on small details, such as the specific intonations of Herneas's speech, and the way the ranger stood as he spoke. Herneas seemed relaxed, but he was coiled like a spring, preparing to strike should Sveri turn violent.

"How is he doing that?" Sveri growled.

"I don't know, but Grodgni seems to think it has something to do with the Rift in the bowels of the keep. He thinks they are pulling energy or life force from it and imbuing the creatures with it. But they are unlike anything I have ever seen on the battlefield. The monsters rage and twist. They hammer at their restraints constantly. The best way that I can describe them is to compare them to an animal that has been infected with the frothing sickness that sends them into a murderous rage. Grodgni said that they were... *screaming* at him."

"What does that even mean?"

"It means that these are not your normal kind of golems. They are not subservient, nor controlled. They are feral. And there is something even more unnatural about these creatures than the average golem we encounter on a battlefield."

"May Dianek cast his soul into the deepest level of the Abyss." Sveri moved over to one of the chairs and sat down roughly. He put a hand to his forehead, willing away a headache that was forming there.

"Agreed," Herneas said. He walked over to the table and poured two glasses of rum, bringing both over to Sveri and handing him one. The sweet burn went all the way to his stomach as he drank the proffered alcohol, then he sat and flexed his fingers, feeling the ache of the old wounds and past broken bones there.

"There's more," Herneas said, placing his cup back on the table. "They are saying that Banick has been executed by the Imps."

Sveri felt his pulse quicken.

"What?" His voice came out in a whisper, but it seemed to fill the room.

"I just heard from Yorna that he was found guilty for attempting to assassinate Golloch."

"Those whoresons!" Sveri growled. He felt the Red Curse clawing at the back of his mind, begging to be released. He forced himself to push the anger down, knowing that if he were to let it off its leash here that Herneas would be the one to suffer.

"We know Banick would never have done something as rash as that," Herneas spoke slowly and calmly, and Sveri forced himself to focus on those details, "but the rest of the world, especially the Imps, they don't know that. This gives them the perfect excuse to declare war, it may even buy them sympathizers from the other races."

"May the Wicked Ones take them for this!"

"I agree, but we cannot afford to act hastily here. We have a more pressing matter." Herneas continued speaking in his soothing tone. Part of Sveri knew what he was doing and resented him for it, but he also knew that he needed to keep calm, and so he allowed the ranger his tricks. He was right. Golloch was in Crag Hudd and had control of the Rift. That was a more pressing matter than vengeance for their fallen friend. Sveri forced himself to take several deep breaths, and he finished his rum. The fiery sweetness of the drink dulled some of the anger, and he closed his eyes to relish it.

"What are we going to do about this, Sveri?" Herneas asked after a long silence. Sveri sighed and looked into the bottom of his glass wistfully, wishing for more.

"You know as well as I do that there's really only one thing that we can do. The problem is, how do we do it?"

"Even after recovering Eastport, so many of our forces still remain in Estacarr, and we don't have time to wait for them to get here."

"That's the kicker. Not only that, but we don't have the luxury of calling a meeting of the clans. We're so spread out that it would take weeks for us to gather and make a formal declaration of war as a united front. No, we have to march on Golloch now and take back Crag Hudd before he can unleash his golem force. How long would you say we have?"

"Based on the numbers that I saw, I'd say we have a month, maybe a little more. Then again, they didn't seem to have much control over the creatures. It might take longer if they need to figure out how to get them to do what they want."

"But we can't plan on that, though."

"No, we can't."

"Well, that settles it, then," Sveri groaned as he pushed himself to his feet and walked over to the table to refill his glass. "I will speak with those clans who are here in Eastport and Jarun's Bridge. I can only ask for volunteered help as one chieftain to another. We will raise whatever army we can and march out in a week's time. We can't delay any longer than that."

"What if no one agrees to help?" Herneas asked, walking over to fill his own glass a second time.

"We barely have what you would call an army. What we brought from Cwl Gen is small, but they are battle-tested and worthy. It was a fortuitous blessing that the Raven Clan and the Bowland Dwarfs arrived shortly after the battle with Gwrthod and agreed to hold the lands to the north of Cwl Gen against any fresh assaults from Tragar. The Daamuz Clan is still shoring up Llyngr Cadw and has been forced to repel a few sporadic ratkin assaults, which may be an indicator of things to come…" He paused a moment before continuing.

"I would take those who came with us against Golloch any day. I think that the majority of the chieftains here in Eastport would give us their aid if able. The problem that I foresee is if they are capable of responding and raising troops in sufficient time."

Herneas raised the bottle of rum toward Sveri, who sat for a moment considering it before shaking his head.

"No, I need to keep my head somewhat clear. I have letters to write. You should get some rest, too. I'll need you to deliver some of them and speak in my name tomorrow." Herneas nodded at this, set the bottle down, and walked from the room. Sveri scrubbed his face with his hands and began composing the missives in his mind. Weariness tugged at the edge of his awareness, but he shoved it down. It was going to be a long night.

*****

In the shadows of the evening, Yorna and Wynn made their way back to the shelter where the remnants of the Ffionen Clan had made camp. There they found the captain of the long rifles, Digaelion, beside a fire with a cup in his hand. Sitting across from him was the hulking form of Craggoth. Yorna staggered over and slumped down beside the giant elemental.

"Rough day, I take it?" Dig asked nonchalantly, and Yorna raised her head to stare blankly at him.

"That's a gross understatement," she replied while fishing out the paper from earlier and holding it up for him to see.

"Yes, I saw that unfortunate bit of business. We can't go home, it seems."

"I think this means that Golloch knew about the treachery. Part of me hoped that it was some tragic betrayal or misunderstanding. But at the very least, someone with some serious pull in the Imperial courts is in on it. That makes me more than slightly ill just thinking about it." Yorna sighed and closed her eyes, leaning her head back to rest against Craggoth's bulk. Images fluttered into her mind of a sunny, open field high in the mountains.

"I don't know what that means, Craggoth," she said, waving the image away with a hand.

"What's he saying?" Wynn asked.

"I have no idea, he just gave me an image of some sunny meadow somewhere. I don't get it."

Another image flashed in her mind, this time of Cwl Gen. It was followed closely with another image of her laughing and talking with the dwarfs who lived there.

"I don't know if that's how this will work, stone troll," she used her pet name for him as realization dawned on her. The other two dwarfs gave her a quizzical look.

"I think he's suggesting that we stay here with Sveri's clan and make that our home."

"Well, that might be our only option," Dig sighed with resignation, lifting a steaming cup of what Yorna assumed was cinnamon tea to his lips.

"What in the Abyss is happening?" Yorna groaned. "*How* did this happen? That's a better question, I think."

"Pride is what caused this," Dig said solemnly. "Somehow I feel that it has been a long time in coming, and it is worse than we could have predicted, but this storm has been brewing for some time."

"What will happen to us?" Wynn asked, and for a moment, his voice seemed so child-like that Yorna's heart ached for him.

"I don't know," she told him honestly. "For now, there's nothing that we can do. We can't go home. The Ffionen Clan is gone, dissolved away by order of the king, or one of his lackeys anyways. We've all been branded as traitors. Things look bad."

"What are you going to do?" Wynn stared at her, his eyes wide. She shook her head.

"Honestly, Wynn, I have no idea. I don't even know if I can call you my apprentice anymore as I've likely been disowned by the college that gave me the title of warsmith. I'm not sure that distancing yourself from me would do anything to help your position, but it likely wouldn't hurt your chances." She flinched slightly at the hurt look that came over Wynn's face.

"What about the clan?" Dig asked.

"What clan? The clan has been dissolved! Weren't you listening?"

"The Ffionen line is ended. However, the clan is still here."

"And what has that to do with me?" Yorna retorted sharply.

"Don't be insolent, it's unbecoming of you. You know why that matters. The clan is bereft of their leadership. We've suffered some major setbacks that they were never intended to undergo. They need someone who can lead them."

"Are you suggesting that I should be that person?" Yorna asked, incredulity coloring her voice.

"Who else?" Dig's face was solemn as he spoke, and Yorna could see Wynn was watching her closely throughout this exchange.

"I wasn't even a full member of the Ffionen Clan, though! Ithel hired me on after I graduated from the college, and while I liked his son, and those that I've fought alongside, I'm not one who was built into this position!"

"There are many who have risen to leadership under less auspicious circumstances than this."

"But I don't want this!" Yorna pleaded.

"Which makes you more qualified than most." Dig's eyes were harder than granite as they stared into her.

"Why me?" She tried defiance this time, but it rang hollow in her own ears.

"Because you are the one who has continuously made choices, and those choices have led to victories. You have carried us through the siege of Cwl Gen because of your plans and your actions. That battle would not have been won without you."

"I'm fairly certain that Sveri might not agree with you on that point."

"Sveri is stubborn, and also prideful in his own way, but he knows that you were a strong reason that Cwl Gen still remains in Free Dwarf hands. If he did not believe so, I don't think you would be free to walk around as you are. I think you would be rotting away in a cell at Cwl Gen if he did not think so."

"But I broke the mountain!"

"Yes, and that has become a rallying cry to the ragged Free Dwarfs, as well as an apt metaphor for the coming conflict with Golloch. Hail to the Broken Peak! Even now, the dwarfs from Cwl Gen have begun using that as a type of salute to each other."

"But I don't know what to do! I don't know what the right answer is!"

"That's okay," Dig said it simply, but it quieted something inside of Yorna, and she sat and thought for a few moments before speaking again.

"Then we will wait for the answer to come to us," she said at length. "We will continue to follow Sveri and Herneas. That has worked for us thus far, perhaps it will carry us the rest of the way."

Dig and Wynn both nodded, and Yorna felt a small twinge of irritation at the small smile on Dig's face as he did so.

"Yes sir," he said, and Yorna wanted to hit him.

7
A Call to Madness

> *There is so much of this wide world that we do not understand. How is it that when we speak to the earth that it answers to us? Why does something relatively inert and the opposite of living suddenly spring into movement when we call it into the form of an elemental spirit? How does something eternal such as rock and stone empathize with our emotions the way that they do?*
>
> *The only answer that I can come to is that Dianek truly is there, in the earth, and she knows our feelings because she, too, has felt what we feel. This tells us that emotions and feelings are powerful things, if even the gods are subject to them.*
>
> *But that begs the question, then, that if the gods have experienced the same emotions that we have, then what has caused them to quake with fear as we have been known to do?*
>
> –Athro *Qwarel Diacon*
> *First Priest of the Cennebrir Clan*

The giant creature swung its massive fist through the air, and it took everything in Argoll's willpower not to flinch as the obsidian block stopped inches from his face. Tendrils of arcane energy wrapped around the golem's wrists and led to two Iron-casters who stood to either side of the monster's limb with their faces twisted in concentration. Argoll nodded appreciatively at them both, the closest thing he would ever do to thanking them, and took a few minor steps backward.

The crazed golem bucked and twisted, trying to pull its arm free. When that failed, it lurched forward and slammed its other arm down, pulping the caster to Argoll's left in a gory spray of blood and bone.

"Restrain it!" Argoll bellowed, and two more Iron-casters ran forward, somewhat hesitantly, throwing their own magical bonds over the golem's still flailing arm. Together, the trio wrestled the construct backward in the direction of the Pens where it could be more safely contained.

Argoll sighed and looked around at the bloody mess surrounding him. That had been one of the more violent encounters at bringing a golem to life using the power of the Rift. Besides the one pulpy mass of bloody viscera that had been the unfortunate Iron-caster, there were several broken ratkin bodies littered about the room. He found himself grinding his teeth. His temples were throbbing, and he balled his hands into fists, feeling a heat rising up from inside.

A sudden clatter of metal on stone caused him to jump slightly, and he turned toward the sound. An unfortunate ratkin slave lay prone on the ground, staring up at him with wide eyes, a serving platter and a spilled goblet of wine lay before him where he'd dropped it. Argoll's fists let loose a stream of fire as a furious yell of pent up rage leaped from his mouth. The ratman burst forth with a series of terrified cries as the flames enveloped him. Each time the slave tried to take a breath, the scream grew higher and more urgent in its pitch, until it turned into a gurgling, choking sound and the mound of burning flesh grew still. But Argoll did not stop the fire until nothing was left but cinders.

Finally, he cut the blaze off. The room was filled with a terrible silence as the other ratkin cowered against the far wall and the other Iron-casters wisely kept quiet. The only sounds were the hissing sound of the cooling rock underneath the burnt ashes of Argoll's victim, and his own deep panting as he struggled to control his rage.

"Everyone out!" he bellowed, and they obeyed. The slaves scurried away as quickly as their feet would carry them, the other Abyssal Dwarfs walking at a more dignified yet still hurried pace.

When the giant chamber was empty, Argoll looked around the spacious cavern. The Rift swirled against the back wall, and the rough hewn stone flickered with strange and uneven shadows. The stone slab where the murderous golem had come to life lay empty except for some broken bits of bone and smears of blood from the throes of its angry birth. He raised a hand to his head, trying to soothe away the throbbing ache that pulsed behind his eyes. He wanted to scream again, he wanted to hurt something, to make *it* scream. He wanted to take whatever force that was responsible for his failure and make it hurt the way that it was obviously trying to do to him by turning fate against him again and again.

They had tried everything that he or any of the other casters had thought of. They had tried importing obsidian from the Abyss to make the construct's body more resilient. That had simply made it so that the golem's body burst into flames when it awoke, and that had been a nightmare to put down. They had tried linking the mind of a slave to a golem to see if that would make it easier to control. All the golem had done was target the slave that it was linked to as its first victim upon awakening. Someone had even suggested pushing a sacrifice through the Rift and then pulling the energy directly through afterward to see if that might appease whatever madness seemed to grip their creations.

Everything had failed.

If anything, the newer batches had become even more crazed and violent. It had been weeks since Golloch had given him this assignment, and they were no closer to understanding what was causing the golems to turn feral. The process was similar to what they normally did, granted there was more than one way to create a golem, but the method that they employed was one of the more reliable ones.

The main difference lay in the source of the spark for the golem. Instead of earth spirits, they drew upon the whispering souls on the other side of the Rift's shimmering face. Those voices that cackled and murmured just beneath conscious thought whenever one was in the presence of the infernal doorway. The effort was far less, as the owners of the voices flocked to whatever magical summons the Abyssal Dwarf casters sent through the vortex – they seemed almost eager. Yet when they were sealed into the construct body, they became violent and angry, and refused to follow the commands that they were given.

Argoll turned toward the Rift. He stared his hate into its depths with a single-minded determination.

"What do you want?!" he yelled at it. "What do we need to give you in order for you to do as you are told?!" He hurled a giant fireball through the air toward the maelstrom, and it disappeared into the void behind the swirling surface.

In the silence that ensued, Argoll could hear the whispers start. It was as if he were trying to listen in on a conversation happening in an adjacent room. Susurrations and muted gasps echoed all around him. Sibilant hissing slithered into his ears like a worm through fresh dirt. It left him feeling like his mind had been doused with dirty water, and he shuddered at the sensation. He wanted to claw the voices out of his head, cast them onto the ground and burn them to ash.

Then the voices suddenly stopped.

Silence pervaded the chamber, and Argoll looked around in surprise. The abrupt quiet left him feeling unnerved, as if some predator were sneaking up on him. But there was nothing near him. He was alone.

"Come here," a feminine voice whispered in his ear, and he stiffened in shock. He turned toward the voice. There was nothing there, but the room seemed to darken slightly. The purple light of the swirling Rift caused the shadows to grow even deeper.

"Come, forsaken child of Dianek. Come to me!" the voice came again, it was hushed and carried a sense of urgency.

"Where are you?" he growled, but his voice seemed far away to his ears. A rushing sound like that of falling water filled his hearing.

"I will take away your burdens," the voice spoke soothingly, like a mother calming a crying child. "I will give you the purpose you so desperately seek."

"I..." Argoll tried to speak, but his mouth would not respond. He found himself turning toward the Rift, and the great vortex filled his vision.

"Yes! I know that you are weary. Your anger weighs you down and makes existence so heavy! Come to me, and I will give you rest! Don't you want to rest?"

Argoll felt his eyelids drooping, and he was vaguely aware of his feet moving beneath him. The Rift swirled before him, its shimmering surface reflecting a non-existent light that danced across his vision. It was so beautiful! He wanted to touch that light. He wanted to join with it and be free of the worry and strife that dogged his waking hours. To no longer feel the pain of his old wounds. To forget the hurt of his memories, the betrayals, the death, and the rage. All of this relief lay just on the other side of the Rift.

All he had to do was reach out his hand and take it.

"Yesss!" the voice hissed, its quiet veneer breaking. "Your miserable existence is futile and brief! Give it away and trade it for something truly eternal! Come to me and rest! I will make something of you! Something that will shake the very stars in their firmament!"

Some desperate thing inside Argoll's chest was trying to claw its way free. He frowned, his hand was poised mere inches from the Rift's surface. When had he gotten this close? What was he actually doing? The thing in his chest finally broke through to his conscious mind, and it brought with it a single world which broke the voice's curse like a hammer through glass.

FLEE!

Argoll staggered back and away from the Rift, his knees trembling, and fell to the ground in a ragged heap. His chest was heaving while his heart hammered against his ribs. He had never felt such unadulterated dread in all his life as he sat there staring at the Rift. He couldn't move, his limbs were as useless as the stone beneath him. All he could do was stare at the purple ribbons of cackling energy as they pulsed hungrily before him.

For the briefest of moments, he thought he could see a face forming there. Its features were sharp and beautiful. Aquiline eyes stared out at him from the void, and he swore he heard laughter in the air as the voice ceased its whisperings and issued its threat.

"Next time, little dwarf!" The sound thundered around the chamber and reverberated back to him, causing him to tremble and fall back onto his elbows. He managed to sneer back at the face in the portal.

"Try it, *ci'ast*!" he cursed and forced his arm to rise. He blasted several tongues of fire at the Rift, and the face laughed before it disappeared. As suddenly as it had all appeared, the chamber was once again quiet. This time, even the ever-present whispers could not be heard.

Argoll felt clammy sweat across his forehead, and his limbs did not want to obey as he tried to rise. He managed to stagger back to the stone slab where the golem bodies were constructed and brought to life.

What in the seventh level of the Abyss was that? he thought to himself. At first he was inclined to simply label it a waking nightmare, but that didn't feel right. It had all seemed too real. Also, how had he ended up in front of the Rift if it were nothing but a dream? He had been poised to throw himself into the unknown depths of that spinning maelstrom, and to what fate that lay beyond?

Was he starting to go mad?

He took a few shuddering breaths to try and steady his still thudding heartbeat. It was during his third deep inhalation that the whispers started afresh.

He fled from the room, not caring who saw him or what it would look like if they did.

8
Peace Talks

We do not choose the clan into which we are born. Just like we cannot choose all the paths that our legacy must take in its formation. Some things will be required that are distasteful to us, some that are less than glamorous and will be left out of the stories told to our descendents. We cannot control these things from happening, they are a necessary part of our struggle.

What we can control, however, is how we rise to meet such obstacles. Will we wallow in self pity that our lot should have such misfortune in it? Or will we pull ourselves up, get the work done that needs doing, and fight on to greater deeds? That is the choice that faces all of us: do we shy away from uncomfortable tasks for the comfort of the familiar, or do we conquer such menial and base things as is our duty as dwarfs of the great clans?!

–King Golloch
At his address to the major clans after his coronation.

A crisp breeze caught the pennants and caused them to snap as they unfurled in the crisp morning air. Garrek looked up at the open palm emblazoned on his own flag. It was being held by one of the younger members of his clan, a rare honor for him that he would likely tell his children, if he ever had any. Those who found themselves unfortunate to be considered members of the Heavyhand Clan were likely outcasts or dishonored members of the rest of the Imperial community and thus not high on the prospects for marriage.

He pushed that dismal thought out of his mind and began making his way toward the center of camp, dressed in his full suit of armor. He held on his person three of the God Boons he had recovered in his journeys across Pannithor. At his hip, the Warp Hammer hung from a metal ring, its weight comfortable and familiar to him. On his back was slung the coffin-shaped Shield of Miph, and he could feel the waves of energy pulsing through his body from it. On his right hand was a small ring. The historians called it *Daeglwych.* For all the fancy embellishments on the other two Boons, the fact that this ring was a simple copper band still caused Garrek moments of wonder. He didn't exactly know what the ring did entirely, and he'd only learned that it was a Boon because he had shown it to the Imperial archivists who had confirmed its origins. All he knew was that when he wore it, it filled him with confidence; and on a day such as this, he would need all the confidence that he could muster.

As he approached the area where the rest of the clans were already gathered, he cast his eyes around. Canvas sun shades in the colors of all the clans in attendance littered the side of the mountain. The place where they were meeting was located inside a shallow depression at the top of one of the lesser peaks. The higher mountains that surrounded them blocked against the more violent winds, and the depression formed a natural amphitheater where a speaker could stand on a small, flattened boulder in the center and address all of the gathered chieftains and their counsellors.

In regards to the clans that had shown, less than half of what Rordin had hoped would arrive were present. Garrek waved to the dwarfs of Mynd Taranau, the sigil of their deep crimson dragon marching across an off-white field fluttering overhead. A heavily muscled and bare-chested Berwyn nodded in return, his fierce eyes likewise scanning the crowd. His younger brother Cefin also smiled at Garrek. These were the leaders of their clan and were sympathizers to the plight of the Free Dwarfs; they would likely side with Rordin in this debate.

Lord Thane of Anvil Mastery was also there. Proud and resplendent in his armor that was edged in gold, he didn't seem to notice Garrek as he walked past, but Garrek watched him closely. This leader was a bit more unknown as to where he might fall. While considered honorable, it was no secret that Anvil Mastery held Golloch in high regard, and Garrek wondered if today's events might change that.

Mendeleev and Mimir both waved in greeting as he walked past, and Garrek returned the gesture as he walked up to the spot that had been reserved for him. Mendeleev and Mimir were seated further back as they weren't even an official clan, as of yet, more of a guild, really. Technically so was Garrek, but that was more of a formality, as his family name was among the oldest in the empire, despite the dishonor that it carried. He sat down in the chair that was provided for him and looked out at the rest of the clans that were arriving.

The Bwaroc Clan, with their crossed arrows on a field of green, sat opposite to him. Rordin had mentioned them among those he hoped would be his supporters in the meeting today, but a lot could happen in the coming hours. Garrek also spied Quig Flintguard, which caught him a little off guard. Quig was the head of the Explorer's League, an organization that had been accused of looting Free Dwarf holds during the Halpi campaigns. There was another wild card that Garrek had not predicted.

There was the Draignos Clan in their midnight blue and golden mountain with a sapphire beneath its crest as their sigil. They would need to be watched closely, as they could influence several of the other clans if they put their weight behind one side or the other. Seated beside them were the Afalans, who were just as influential.

In all, there were close to two dozen clans present, and various other companies, guilds, and colleges also in attendance. It was nowhere near all of the potential parties needed at this meeting, but it was more than probably should have been able to arrive in such a short amount of time.

Garrek stiffened as his eyes fell on the black banner of the Ashtel Clan, with its hammer and fist emblazoned in white. He saw Gruumen, with his black beard and gray robes, sitting on the chair that had been prepared for him. He had to bite back a growl that he found stirring in the back of his throat. Here was the dwarf who had tried to kill his friend, Banick, and who was trying to start a war with the Free Dwarfs. If Banick was right, then he was an Abyssal Dwarf who was plotting for the destruction of the empire, and its unification with the lords of Tragaar to the north.

"His face is rather punchable looking, isn't it?" A familiar voice snapped Garrek's attention back to his surroundings. He stared in disbelief at the figure that stood before him. In the robes of the Dianek Priesthood, and with a nonchalant look on his face, Ofn gave him a lopsided smile.

"You!" Garrek hissed. "What are you doing here? Shouldn't you be with your master's company? Isn't your leash tight against your throat at this distance?"

Ofn looked shocked at these words, then a sad expression came over his face.

"I suppose it was too much to ask that you would greet me any other way."

"Why should I?! You tried to execute Banick!" This caused Ofn's brows to shoot up suddenly.

"You mean that you think we didn't? Does that mean that he is here?" Ofn looked around with a strangely hopeful look on his face. Garrek cursed under his breath.

"Why would he be here? Didn't you cut his head off?" he tried to recover, but Ofn dispelled that notion with a sad shake of his head.

"Let's not play those games, Garrek. We've known each other for far too long to try and trick each other with such paltry lies as these."

"I thought I knew you. But it seems that I am terrible at seeing through deceit."

"That hurts, Garrek," Ofn said, and Garrek was surprised at how sincere he seemed while saying it. "I never wanted to deceive you, I swear, but there are things in motion that not even friendship can impede. My dishonesty was a kindness, I assure you."

"What kind of twisted logic is that?"

"I mean it! You and Banick are…" Ofn paused here for a moment before continuing, "were my friends. I would have us still be friends if you would allow it."

Garrek stared at him for several long seconds, his mouth open in bewilderment. He forced his brows to lower and his eyes to harden before responding.

"I do not allow it. You are a snake! A viper that hunts in the dark and attacks its prey from behind."

Garrek glared balefully at the imposter before him, but Ofn nodded absentmindedly.

"Yes, that is understandable. You have no reason to trust me. In fact, you have every reason not to. But I swear to you that it is true. I wish us to be friends again. Our conversations at Caeryn Golloch… they were everything to me."

Garrek's eyes bulged. He didn't know how to respond. Instead, he sat back in his chair and brought a hand up to pinch the bridge of his nose.

"You are insane!" he almost whispered it, and Ofn leaned toward him.

"What was that?" he asked. Garrek sighed and shook his head.

"Is there a reason you are speaking to me?"

"I saw you from across the way as Gruumen was arriving and thought I would come and greet you as it has been months since we last were able to sit and talk."

"Why?"

"I already explained that."

"You are not my friend, Ofn! I don't know that you ever were! Get away from me!" These words seemed to strike the priest like a slap, and he flinched under the weight of each one.

"I am sorry that you feel this way, Garrek. I would like to talk to you some time, perhaps explain to you my side of the problem with Banick."

"Go away!" Garrek growled through gritted teeth. Ofn opened his mouth to say something more, but then just shook his head and turned away. He stopped briefly and looked back over his shoulder.

"Please don't spite my friendship, Garrek. It won't end well for you."

"You dare threaten me?!"

"No. I am warning you. Something is coming. It may even come today if our mistress commands it. A reckoning will come upon you as a fire from the depths. I don't wish this on you."

"I thought you were a servant of Dianek, and yet you threaten me with fire?" Garrek could feel the itch of violence in his hands, and a cold apprehension had tightened his spine. Ofn stared back at him for a moment, before turning to face him once more.

"I serve many masters, Garrek, and you know as well as I do that the stone may be where our race was born, but fire is what makes up its lifeblood." He leaned toward him, and Garrek felt a chill run down his spine. "It is fire that will be our doom when the time comes, and it is fast approaching."

A shadow covered his face as he looked at Garrek, who felt as if the rest of the world had grown silent as he stared at those eyes that glowed with a deep anger at him. He saw fire and death in that stare.

Then, in a moment, Ofn blinked and the heated look was gone, replaced with a pleasant smile. It was the same smile that Garrek had seen him wear every time he had visited the Temple of Dianek in Caeryn Golloch. Somehow, this filled him with a sadness that he could not explain.

"Goodbye, Garrek." Ofn gave a cheerful wave as he turned to walk away. "I hope things go well for you today, although not too well, or else I'll never hear the end of it!" He chuckled as he strode through the crowd. Garrek let out a breath he hadn't realized that he'd been holding.

"Kubrek!" he called to one of his attendants. A red-bearded dwarf came over and leaned toward him. Garrek grabbed him by the shoulder and pulled him closer.

"I have a bad feeling. Send some of our folks out to scout around the area. Send them in a wide net around the meeting place. Something doesn't sit right about this whole thing. They are to stop anyone that is trying to get into the meeting place, search them, and send them back the way they came from without giving them access, understood?"

"Won't this upset some of the lords here if their servants or members of their household are prevented from arriving?" Kubrek asked. Garrek snorted and shook his head.

"This is a top security kind of meeting, and I don't care who you piss off with these antics. You stop everyone and search them thoroughly. This comes straight from me. Rordin has nothing to do with this. If anyone gets uppity about it after the meeting, they can be angry at me. But there are too many of us here, and I don't trust all of the dogs who have summoned us to this place. I think some of them are feral."

Kubrek nodded and hurried away. Garrek watched him go, a deep unease filling his gut that wouldn't allow him to relax. He glared once more across the gathering at the black banners of the Ashtel Clan before motioning toward a server who was carrying a laden tray of tankards.

He needed a drink.

The rest of the clans were still filtering into the meeting place. In all, it took the better part of another hour before everyone was seated and the deep vibrations of an enormous drum further up the mountain signalled that the meeting was ready to begin. In all that time, Garrek could not get the fingers of anxiety to release their hold on his stomach, and he kept glancing about nervously.

A roll call was initiated, and each clan was allowed to speak a few words in regards to their expectations for the meeting. The other delegations, the colleges, guilds, and other powerful parties were not granted this honor, but it was the right of the chieftains to express their thoughts prior to the beginning of any formal discussion. This was to ensure that all involved parties were allowed to speak in the meeting. Many clans waived this right, as they were anxious to hear what both Rordin and Gruumen would say. A few spoke up and voiced their support for Golloch, or their concern for the events happening with the Free Dwarfs to the north.

By the time these formalities had concluded, the sun was already high overhead and the morning had been spent. Garrek wished that he could sit at ease and listen to the words of the clans, but his mind refused to focus on what was being said.

"Fellow chieftains and representatives from our illustrious society!" Garrek recognized the smoky voice of Gruumen Ashtel, and he forced himself to put aside his worries and listen.

"We stand before you in the wake of events that are unprecedented in the long history of our race!" the Ashtel chieftain's voice lifted into the mountain air, the other lords all sat forward intently, listening closely. "An attempt has been made on our king's life! Not by the assassins of the treacherous elves, nor the clumsy attempts of the feeble-minded humans! Not by the scheming Abyssals, or the warlords of Tragar! No! This betrayal came from those whom we called cousins! Those whom we took in from the storm of the Abyss and carried to a new home in our own lands! Those whom we helped to recapture part of their ancestral keeps!

"We bore them up in their time of despair and helped them to find hope in the lost days of their exile from Halpi! I speak, of course, of the supposed 'Free' Clans! We were kin to them, and they show their gratitude by sending murderers into our midst in the guise of emissaries!" Gruumen practically spit the term 'Free Clans' as if it were something that had spoiled on his tongue.

"I sat with the traitor who orchestrated the attack! I offered him aid! We sent troops to assist their ill-advised campaign on Cwl Gen, and they attacked our warriors who went willingly to help! What's more than that, I knew Ithel Ffionen! I saw him welcome the foul traitor Banick into his own home! I saw him dress that dwarf with his own threads and feed him from his own cellar! They drank in friendship, and I saw the reward that he received in full as he lay dying before many of you at the Claansvelt! His mouth bloody and his eyes weak! He thought he saw his son standing before him. Little did he know that his son Cerrig was already dead as well! Killed by Free Dwarf treachery! We have confirmed as much from our warriors who returned, broken, from Cwl Gen!

"Not only did this foul scheme take the Ffionen Clan from us, but it also claimed the life of Gwrthod Teirhammer! We gather here today to discuss the events of the empire and the worrying times that now sit at our door! I say unto you all that you are right to be troubled! Treachery the likes of which has never been known to our race since the great sundering of our people who took to the Abyss has spilled out upon the safe places of our keeps! Our hand has been bitten even as we have extended it in friendship!"

Here, Gruumen turned to look at Rordin.

"Now, I do not doubt the reasons that the heir-apparent has begun to question our king's wisdom! The world has been cast into doubt and uncertainty. War on a scale that we have never known in our lifetimes looms on the horizon, and it is understandable that one might sit and wonder at the choices and events that have led us to such a point as this! Such is the prerogative of a wise dwarf. A good king needs voices of dissent such as this around him! An advisor is worthless if he simply agrees with everything his lord says. But Rordin has perhaps taken this obligation too far! In a time when outside forces are building to tear us asunder, especially when those forces arise from such unexpected places as the violence and betrayal that we have experienced in the past year! It is to this challenge that we must bind ourselves more closely together, and yet Rordin hesitates! Why? Why would he do this and cause undue pressure to be placed upon an already troubled king's shoulders?!"

Garrek felt his teeth grinding, but then he heard several shouts of approval from various voices in the crowd. He looked around at the heads that were nodding, some with looks of approval, others with disgust. Not all – in fact, he couldn't even say if it was a majority or not, but it was more than he would have expected.

"Now is the time for us to be united! We waste valuable time sitting here debating the motives of the king when we should be rushing to his aid! The Free Dwarfs chafe under Golloch's rule, but it is obvious that they need his steady hand. Look at how he has guided our empire to prosperity! Then look again and see how the Free Dwarfs have fallen from their homes and now squabble in vain to regain some portion of their former glory! Golloch has a dream to unite us all under one banner! Dwarfs are superior craftsman, superior warriors, and superior thinkers than those other races which stand at our borders and look on in envy of our accomplishments! Think of what we might accomplish if the Free Clans were brought into our embrace! Imagine what might be if such were made a reality!

"This is Golloch's dream for us! And we now stand at the brink of its realization! If we can set aside our concerns. Our doubts. Our fears!"

Gruumen extended an open hand toward Rordin.

"You are a mighty hero to our people, Lord Rordin, and you stand now in a place that can help our people become the greatest version of themselves. What concerns do you have that would stop us from realizing the reality of a dream that has lived on in our hearts since the rift between Free and Imperial Dwarf first formed almost a millennium ago? Why would you wish to stop us from becoming whole once more? I extend my hand to you in friendship and ask you to lay aside those things that impede your willingness to respond to Golloch's call and join us in this great endeavor!"

Several of the chieftains and other delegates stood and cheered at this. Again, Garrek tried to gauge how many were clapping and calling out. But it was difficult to tell as some were arguing with their neighbors and adding to the noise and the chaos.

Garrek looked at Rordin, who lifted his hand, and after several long moments of continued cheers and yells, the noise fell to silence. He sat for a long time, looking over the other dwarfs in the amphitheater. Garrek felt his gaze linger on him as it passed by, and he nodded to the younger dwarf, not envying him his position. Finally, Rordin turned to look at Gruumen.

"Very eloquent, Lord Ashtel. I applaud your directness to the subject at hand. But I fear that you oversimplify things. There are many questions which you leave unanswered and would have us charge off to fight those whom, as you have stated, are our cousins. I feel that it is important that we be allowed to ask those questions before decisions of such magnitude are made." Rordin's words caused a ripple of murmurs to spread throughout the meeting, and several of the older and larger chieftains began rapping their knuckles on their chairs in support of his words. Garrek added his own fist to theirs.

Rordin produced a piece of paper and held it out toward Gruumen.

"Here is a list of concerns that I, and several other chieftains, have drawn up concerning the events of the past several months. If you would indulge us, Lord Ashtel, we would have answers to these and perhaps a small amount of time to consider your responses before we make any solid decisions. We do this in the sake of solidarity, so that if we do decide to follow Golloch into the north, that we may do so without reservation. I feel that such is best for us and our responsibilities as leaders of these people."

Garrek grinned. Rordin wasn't rising to Gruumen's bait. His level-headed response inspired more knuckles to knock on the armrests of their respective chairs. Rordin smiled and nodded to the assembly before turning to hand the paper to another dwarf who began reading the questions off to the gathered dwarfs.

"Excuse me, sir," Kubrek's voice at Garrek's elbow almost caused him to jump in alarm. He turned toward his scout.

"What is it?" he whispered with a scowl.

"There's something that I think you should see, something important." Kubrek motioned with his head meaningfully before turning to walk away. Garrek looked back toward the meeting before frowning and standing to follow.

Kubrek led him through the camp and back to the community tent for the Heavyhand representatives. There, he looked around anxiously before ducking inside. Garrek looked around himself, but the camp was deserted. Everyone was at the meeting. He pulled the tent flap to the side and walked in.

Inside he was met with a scene that caused his stomach to catch fire. A brown-haired dwarf dressed in black was tied to a chair, his face was pale and his eyes darted around at two other dwarfs who stood to either side of him, both Garrek's scouts he had sent out. Kubrek walked toward the ominous trio and nodded to the ones guarding the restrained dwarf.

"They caught this one on the outskirts of the camp. He almost made it."

"Wha... what is the meaning of this all?! Lord Heavyhand!" the captive dwarf pleaded, and Garrek met him with a cold stare that silenced his pleas.

"What was he doing?" Garrek asked, and Kubrek stepped forward, handing him a somewhat crumpled piece of paper.

"He was carrying this, said he needed to give it to Lord Ashtel."

Garrek sighed and closed his eyes. He had been afraid of this. He opened his eyes and took the paper. He saw that it was a letter, and that the seal had been broken on it already. He opened it and read the three sentences that he saw there.

We were delayed in the tunnels. We have arrived at Bor's Peak and will be marching to you as soon as we are able. Stall the meeting for as long as you can.

"You cannot read that! It is personal correspondence for Lord Ashtel's eyes only!" the captive shrieked, but one of the guards cuffed him to the side of the head, and he fell into a dazed silence.

Garrek looked up. Bor's Peak was a half day's march from here. He knew the underground highway that the Imperial Garrison used to move armies and supplies between keeps had a small way station there that opened to the surface. He also knew that the armies and attendants of all the clans, except for their personal guards, had agreed to stay a full day's march from where the encampment would take place in the spirit of the meeting's diplomatic nature. If this meant what he thought it did, they were all in serious trouble.

"Take this to Lord Rordin. Tell him to end the talks. We need to leave immediately." Garrek held the note out to Kubrek, who nodded and took the letter before hurrying away.

"As for you," Garrek said, focusing on the still dazed captive, "I need answers. How many dwarfs does Gruumen plan on bringing down on us? It can't be that many if he wanted it to be a surprise attack."

"I... will tell you nothing... Oathbreaker!" the bound dwarf tried to snarl, but the words that escaped his mouth were a contradiction of venom and fear. It only made Garrek smile.

"I am sure you feel that you are being brave by calling me that in your position, and I will give you credit, it did take guts. But you see," Garrek took a few steps closer and leaned in, "the problem with that insult is that I long ago embraced it, so it holds no power over me. And I can tell from the tremble in your voice that your bravery is already existing on borrowed bravado."

He straightened and took a step back, pulled the Warp Hammer from his belt, and placed it on a camp table that stood off to one side.

"Untie him," Garrek commanded, "but make sure that he doesn't try to run for it. He and I have things to talk about."

He did not turn to ensure that the other two dwarfs had followed his orders. Instead, he slowly and deliberately removed his helmet and his armor until he stood bare-chested, his white and gray hair spilling down over his muscles and scars. He kept the ring on his finger to help him remain calm. Then he turned to face the captive. He still sat in his chair, though his bonds had been cut.

"Stand up!" Garrek ordered him, but he only flinched backward. "I'm not going to kill you, beardling!" This insult seemed to spark some fire into the dwarf's eyes, and he glared at Garrek as he rose to his feet.

"I've found, in my years of experience," Garrek said, tilting his head from side to side, stretching out the muscles there, "that you can learn much more from the way a dwarf fights than you can from the words that leave his mouth." Garrek raised his fists and advanced on the messenger. "Try and hit me, whelp!"

Garrek threw out the challenge and followed it with a quick jab from his left hand. The other dwarf, not expecting the blow, took the punch straight on the nose, and Garrek felt the satisfying crunch of broken cartilage and bone as his hand connected. The Ashtel dwarf staggered back as blood blossomed on his face.

"You *ci'ast*!" he spat through pained tears.

"Put your hands up, beardling, lest you get another!" Garrek advanced again, and his opponent twisted away, running toward the tent flap. One of Garrek's scouts stepped in front of him to block his way, and he turned reluctantly back to face the old veteran warrior.

"There's no way out that way. The only way you get out is if you win our fight. If you knock me on my ass, my dwarfs will let you go. If you yield, then you tell me what you know, does that sound fair?"

"You're a barbarian!"

"So I've been told." Garrek grinned and threw another quick jab. This time, the other dwarf was able to dodge to the side of it, but Garrek had anticipated the movement and was already bringing around a strong undercut with his other hand. It caught the Ashtel messenger in the ribs, and he gave a choked cry before doubling over, gripping at his side. Garrek stepped back and allowed him to catch his breath.

"If you're going to go traipsing through potential battlefields delivering messages, you ought to learn how to fight, you know." Garrek rocked back and forth on his feet. Internally, he was screaming. They didn't have time for this! He needed answers and he needed them immediately. Who knew how close Gruumen's forces were to descending upon them?

As he was pondering this, the wounded messenger snarled and leaped at him. Garrek brought his arms up to defend as his opponent wailed on his proffered forearms. He felt the blows and could feel the bruises they would bring afterward, but he welcomed the pain. The other dwarf decided to try his luck at a similar move to what Garrek had done and went for his ribs. Garrek smiled and twisted so that the blow hit his core instead, tensing his muscles to accept the attack rather than taking it on his more tender ribs.

The dwarf over-extended himself, trying for a knockout strike. Garrek capitalized on his mistake by wrapping his arms around the messenger's head and bringing his knee up to slam it into the other dwarf's sternum. All the air went out of his foe at once, and he crumpled to the ground, desperately trying to suck in air that his lungs were currently unable to accept.

"There now!" Garrek said soothingly. "You've just had the wind knocked out of you, you'll be fine in a bit. Do you yield?"

The other dwarf gasped and stared hatefully up at him. Garrek reached down to grasp the front of his shirt, swatting away his feeble attempts to ward him off. Lifting him up, the old warrior raised a rock hard fist above his head.

"I'll ask you again, do you yield?"

"The Abyss take you!" came the gasped reply. Garrek shrugged and brought his arm down. It connected with the struggling dwarf's cheek, right below his eye, and the pressure of the blow caused a rupture. Blood immediately flowed from the wound, and the dwarf cried out in pain.

"Had enough yet? You can give up any time. All we need to know is how many troops Gruumen's surprise army has. You can answer that question, or I can let you get up and we can continue our dance."

"Enough! I'll talk!"

Garrek nodded and slowly stood up. He rubbed his stomach where the other dwarf had landed his blow. It was tender and already beginning to show the signs of a deep bruise.

"You got some good hits in there, beardling! You show some promise if you'd actually put some effort into it." Garrek smiled at the messenger, who scowled up at him with an eye that was already beginning to swell. Garrek motioned for one of the guards to help him up.

"Now," he continued, walking over to where his armor and hammer lay on the table, "how many soldiers is Gruumen bringing to this party?"

There was no response behind him. Instead there were a couple of sounds that happened more or less at the same time. There was a sound of metal rasping on metal, then a low surprised grunt, followed by the sound of something heavy hitting the floor. Garrek's instincts kicked in and he grabbed his hammer and turned, swinging it around as he did so.

The hammer hit the captive messenger who was charging toward him with an upraised, bloody dagger. The hammer glowed green as it connected with the attacker's chest. For a moment that seemed to hover in the impossible eternity of when fighting becomes bloodshed, Garrek met the surprised look on the Ashtel dwarf's face with a stoic one of his own. Then time caught up and the dwarf went sailing across the tent to slam into a table and some chairs which splintered apart on contact. Garrek didn't need to check him to know that he was dead; instead, he rushed over to the prone form of the guard he'd told to help the treacherous captive. It was too late, and Garrek knew it as he saw the blood pooling underneath the body. The Ashtel messenger must have pulled the knife at his guard's belt and stabbed him in the chest before charging Garrek from behind.

He cursed quietly and reached out to close his warrior's glazed eyes as they stared into the roof of the tent. As he did so, he noticed sounds coming from outside the tent. He strained to listen, and then the anxiety that had been gripping his stomach that whole day suddenly tightened its grasp.

It was the sounds of battle.

9
The Start of the Avalanche

I looked and there beheld a mighty panther
Who prowl'd before the gates of Death and Dismay
Her eyes were red, like crimson fire, and to me
She did come with mouth agape and her
Words upon the wind. She spoke to me and said:

"Man! Be warned! For when the sons of Dianek
Do bathe in brothers' blood, and icy Chill is
Broken upon the edge of Nightmare's mad cry.
This will be your land's lament: That doom is nigh
When gods shall weep, and Death shall creep into the

Sacred home. Beware the fires that then will come,
From Frost, to Stone, to Fire. And then a new child
Comes to slaughter those who were not there to watch
The ways across the Eastern Sea where dwarf clans
Still wait on. There is where Death awaits you all."

–From the Song of Sagacious the Mad Prophet
Canto III, Lines 15-30

Ofn was starting to nod off when things began to unravel. It started when some kind of messenger or servant approached Rordin with a piece of paper while whispering in his ear. Rordin's face grew grave, and it became more so as he read what was on the paper. Gruumen was in the middle of answering one of the several questions that the assembly had asked as to the events of the Claansvelt and the events that were connected with the Free Clans when Rordin interrupted him.

"Gruumen Ashtel!" his voice cut across the amphitheater like a volcano's eruption to break the silence of a formerly calm day. "Why do I have reports of a messenger trying to make contact with you detailing the arrival of a possible army that is marching on this peaceful meeting?"

The world seemed to freeze. In that instant, Ofn swore he could hear the veins in Gruumen's forehead popping as he restrained himself from screaming with rage.

"I have no idea what you are talking about," he denied. Ofn could feel the tension in the meeting rising.

"You would lie while under oath? Here? At a meeting that *you* have orchestrated to talk about unity within the empire?" Rordin pushed himself to his feet and held the letter out in front of him. "Then how do you explain this?"

"I don't even know what that is!"

"It was meant for you."

"So why, then, did it not come to me? Why do you have it?" Gruumen sneered the question, but Ofn was impressed. He'd laid a good trap for Rordin. Why, indeed, did he have a message that was supposed to have reached Gruumen? On what authority did he feel that he should intercept messages that were intended for another? Ofn waited to see how he would respond.

"It is because I don't trust you." There was a collective sharp intake of breath from the other chieftains present. Ofn had to restrain a feral smile from forming on his lips. *The boldness of this would-be king!* He thought to himself. But the exchange wasn't over, yet. Many clans would see this as an affront and be upset at Rordin for his lack of decorum.

"What have I done to make you distrust me so?" Gruumen sneered.

"Many things, many of which you would deny were I to accuse you of them presently. But I know of your worth, and this letter confirms it. The source of my information comes from sources that I trust, and I see you for the sickness that you are. You are a blight upon the empire, and now you would use treachery to secure your ill-gotten power over this proud people."

"You speak as if you have proof! Yet I see nothing here but a letter which I have no idea what it says and vile accusations that are baseless and untrue!"

"You say that you sat with Banick Kholearm in Caeryn Golloch? That you promised him aid and sent it to Cwl Gen at his behest?"

"What does this…" Gruumen began to say.

"Answer the question!" Rordin's voice was thunder, and it quelled the quiet whispers of the audience and the sneering protests of the Ashtel chieftain.

"Yes! I already said that I did so, and he returned our generosity with treachery!"

"You also say that you know that he was sentenced to death and that you witnessed it?"

"I was the one who sentenced him, but I was not present at his execution."

"But you swear that it was?" Rordin pressed the question, and Ofn knew what was coming. He was certain that Gruumen had also guessed at Rordin's tactic.

"I can only say that he was sentenced to death and that I was told that his sentence was carried out."

"Why do you argue semantics such as these? Are you a human politician? A would-be courtster who plays for titles? Or are you a dwarf?! Give me a straight answer!" Rordin raised an accusing finger at Gruumen. Ofn again marvelled at his boldness. Around the assembly, several of the chieftains and representatives rapped their knuckles on their chairs.

"I was told that he was dead," Gruumen persisted, but it sounded hollow to Ofn's ears.

"Then why did a dwarf proclaiming himself to be that very same Banick Kholearm show up at my camp a couple months ago to warn me of a danger growing in the capital? This dwarf's identity was confirmed by other dwarfs whom I trust and who knew Banick on a personal basis. Why, then, would you publish his death if it had not happened?"

"You would harbor a fugitive of the law? Where is this individual who claims to be the now infamous Kholearm?"

"Banick's guilt is a topic for a different day, it is not what we are discussing here," Rordin brushed Gruumen's diversion away and took a step closer. "What is up for discussion is the reason that the Imperial court would issue a declaration saying that he is dead if that were not a verified fact. The only conclusion that I can come to is that someone wished to antagonize the Free Clans. Somebody wants us to go to war with them. And the leader of that charge, the dwarf who has argued for that course of action more than any other is none other than yourself, Gruumen! This explains why I distrust you, at least in some small way. There are many other reasons, but we do not have time to discuss them at present."

Rordin turned to the rest of the chieftains and raised the letter to them.

"Unfortunately, I fear that this meeting of the clans has been a trap for us all, my friends. The evidence I hold in my hand declares that there is someone who is coming, and they do so in a cryptic and secretive way. I have reason to believe, and it is a strong reason, that this is a force acting under the Ashtel Clan's orders, and they are coming to either capture or kill those whom they cannot convince this day to join them."

"You slander my name without any real evidence!" Gruumen practically screamed it at him. "You accuse me of heinous and unspeakable acts, and you would have me stay silent?"

"I am not concerned with appeasing your honor. It has already been sullied in my eyes and is not worthy of respect." Rordin's eyes were hard, and Ofn was surprised to see the Ashtel chieftain take a step back from where the younger dwarf now stood with the upraised paper.

"I am leaving!" Rordin declared. "I would urge you all to do the same, lest something terrible befall you by staying."

"You would threaten us?" Gruumen tried to reverse the accusation, but Ofn could see that it was weak and desperate. "You wish to be king, yet your first orders are veiled in threats?"

Rordin shook his head.

"I never said I wish to be king. Far from it, in fact. I don't know why Golloch named me as his heir. Perhaps because I was an adventurer, and a drunkard, and he thought that I would be easy to control. Maybe he thought I wouldn't live to inherit the throne. But all of my travels, all of my adventures, they all drove home for me the importance of having a home, someplace that you call your own. That is why I ask these questions, and that is why I will not sit here and listen to your poisoned words any longer."

Rordin raised his head and spoke once more to the assembly.

"Our empire is sick, my brothers and sisters. Behold, here is a symptom of that sickness. Golloch is the source, and he has much to answer for. Ever since we allowed him to have power over us. Ever since we allowed him to take his authority which he bought and bullied his way into, he has been leading us to this point. I wish we had not let it come to this, but we all expected him to act as a dwarf should. Honest and direct. But he is not what we should aspire to be. He is the definition of authority derived from taking, not leadership through merit. I weep for our empire and the months that are to come, for there are many hard decisions ahead of us, and many sacrifices to be made."

"He speaks treason!" Gruumen yelled, a wild look in his eye. There were a few shouted responses, but overall there was a stunned silence that hung like a weight around the shoulders of all who were present. Gruumen snarled and pulled his axe from where it hung at his belt. "I will not allow it!"

There was a series of staggered cries as others of Gruumen's supporters stood up and drew their weapons in support of the Ashtel chieftain, but the majority of the assembly still sat without moving. Rordin glared daggers at Gruumen.

"Is this wise to show your forked tongue here where all can see it?" the younger dwarf growled through gritted teeth, somehow making the sound carry to the other dwarfs in the amphitheater. "You would break the peace of this meeting? Wouldn't that make you the one in bad faith? I spoke my honest thoughts, and it is either a foolish king that cannot abide criticism or an evil one."

"That is twice that you have spoken ill of our king and accused him of wickedness. You will pay for your idle threats and your unfaithful words!" Gruumen turned to the rest of the dwarfs and addressed them while pointing at Rordin. "We must seize him and bring him to the capital where he can be tried for his offenses! He is a friend of the Free Clans!

He has admitted as such! Seize him!"

"He speaks truth, though!" A voice yelled from one of the other clans. Ofn couldn't identify which of them it was, but it was soon joined by another.

"We've all wondered about Golloch's intentions! He's only voiced what we've all thought ourselves. Why should he be punished for it?!" This time Ofn recognized the Bwaroc Clan as the speaker.

"He's right! Golloch has been dodgy since before he ascended the throne! Now things are worse than ever!" The Afalans cried out. Ofn felt his blood beginning to rise as the sense of impending violence built in the air around him. He found himself gripping the axe at his side.

"You fools!" Gruumen practically screamed, his normal composure was shattered, and Ofn gaped at the open display of hostile emotions that played across his face. "You utter fools! You have no idea of the wonders that Golloch has planned for us! We will become the rulers of Pannithor! Why would you fight against that?!" There were several shouted replies, but Rordin stepped forward, and everyone immediately fell silent, all eyes on him.

"It is not meet that one should rule at the cost of all of our souls," Rordin spoke slowly, and it was as if every word were a blow to Gruumen, who flinched with each syllable. "Golloch would have us as shells of our former selves. He would trade us as livestock or jewels to be used as currency for his own pride! If we were to accept this, then we would be no better than that. Valuable, useful, and lacking in our own purpose."

Rordin stared Gruumen down, and the air crackled between them. It was Gruumen who eventually broke and turned his gaze away. Rordin nodded and turned to walk away. Even as he did so, the Ashtel chieftain snarled and threw his axe at Rordin's retreating form. The world slowed as the axe spun through the air toward the younger dwarf.

Ofn watched the flight of the weapon and held his breath, unsure as to what he hoped would happen next. He didn't notice one of Rordin's guards move to intercept the blow until the axe bit deep into the raised forearm. The force of the throw was so great that it nearly cleaved the dwarf's arm from his elbow, and he fell back screaming. Rordin whirled back and took the scene in with sharp eyes. Ofn smiled in spite of himself as he saw the anger wash over Rordin's face.

Then, chaos ensued.

Gruumen's allies were the first to act. They drew their weapons and ran toward the dais where Rordin stood glaring down at the Ashtel chieftain, his wounded warrior screaming in pain at his feet. The other clans were slower, but Rordin didn't wait for any to rush to his aid. He pulled his hammer from his belt and held it up in challenge to Gruumen, who snarled in response. The two dwarfs glared for a moment, and

Rordin advanced. Ofn watched in rapt fascination as the heir apparent to Golloch's throne threw himself at Golloch's most trusted advisor.

Rordin let loose a mighty war cry and slammed his hammer down where Gruumen stood, but the other dwarf dodged to the side and pulled a small knife from its sheath. The Ashtel lord leaped forward, thrusting the point of his blade toward Rordin's face. The younger dwarf flinched backward, and the knife passed within a breath of the bridge of his nose. He then brought his hammer up for another swing, but it was so heavy that Gruumen was able to get in a few more thrusts, causing Rordin to become unbalanced as he tried to dodge the knife.

Then several of Gruumen's allies arrived. Liethbred of the Slatebeard Clan rushed forward to hack downward at Rordin's exposed side. The dwarf lord allowed the building momentum of his hammer to pull him into the blow so that his helm took the brunt of the strike and glanced it aside. Rordin followed up quickly and swung his mighty hammer into the chest of his assailant, sending him flying through the air to crumple into the dirt. Blood poured out of Liethbred's mouth, and he squirmed as if fighting for breath before laying still. Gruumen took advantage of Rordin being distracted to fade into the back of his allies.

Battle lines began to form as chieftains and their guards picked sides. Ofn noticed with some disdain that there were several clans who remained seated, as if waiting to see which side would win before choosing. Among them were the Afalans, who had been so vocal in their support for Rordin only moments before. Perhaps they weren't as convinced as they had made it seem. Not that it mattered. Most of those who had jumped into the fray were running to support Rordin. This made sense. Gruumen had been hoping to wipe out support for the would-be king and had therefore invited most of the clans he felt would rally to him to this meeting in the hope of dispatching them in one fell swoop.

Now, though, that tactic had turned against them – Gruumen and his allies were heavily outnumbered. Weapons clanged against shields as Imperial fought Imperial, and the sounds reverberated throughout the natural arena, causing the very ground to vibrate. Ofn watched as a younger dwarf's skull was pulped not far from where he stood. Blood sprayed across the stone of the peak and coursed in bright red rivulets into the cracks, draining down into the bones of the mountain.

Ofn stared at it in bewilderment. The blood was scarlet, like rubies that ran like water, or coursed like lava streaming from the ruptured volcano of the dwarf's head that lay nearby. Soon more blood mixed with his, and then there were puddles of hot crimson that splattered the air whenever a foot stomped down into the depths. Ofn wondered absently if the red would be enough to turn the sky to blood. Perhaps if sufficient dwarfs were sacrificed then…

"Ofn!" Gruumen shouted, and the false priest shifted to stare at the Ashtel lord. "Get in the fight! They're killing us here!"

Ofn shrugged carelessly and lifted his hand. A ball of fire formed at the ends of his fingertips, and the heat threatened to blister his face. The flame pulsed for a moment before he thrust his arm forward, sending the magical blast forward to explode at the feet of a group of nearby dwarfs. Bodies went flying from the ensuing explosion. Ofn didn't really bother to check and see if they were friends or foes before sending another ball of fire into the massed ranks of dwarfs before him.

He heard screams. He smelled the scent of cooking meat, the stench of burned hair. He smiled, and laughter bubbled up as he released another orb of heat. The sounds of death surrounded him. Oh, it had been so long since he had relished in this delightful symphony of pain!

A hand clamped onto his shoulder, and he looked down at it in disgust. He followed the length of the arm attached to it in order to discover the owner's face. Gruumen stared at him with a scowl on his face.

"That's enough!" he bellowed. "We need to leave!"

Ofn squinted, trying to comprehend what he was being told. They were retreating? But why? There were still so many screams to wrench from their charred corpses!

"Let's go! Damn you! Or stay here and be slaughtered! We don't have enough warriors to win this fight! I am ordering you to pull back! But if you won't listen, then good riddance!"

With that, Gruumen turned and took off running in a direction that took him away from the fight. Ofn sneered, but when he looked back to the fight, he saw that Gruumen was right. More of the bystander clans had made their decision and were running to Rordin's side. Soon they would overwhelm those warriors that had fought beside Gruumen. Ofn grunted in disappointment, threw a few last fireballs into the fray, and then turned to follow the retreating forms of the Ashtel warriors and their allies.

*****

Garrek wiped the blood and viscera from the surface of the Warp Hammer, tossing the soiled rag aside after he finished. He looked around at the splayed bodies that lay about the amphitheater and sighed inwardly. It was hard to tell which dwarfs fought on which side. Rordin had won this small skirmish, but that didn't change the fact that all the dead bodies were those of Imperial Dwarfs. What made it worse was that this was only the opening scene on a much more troubling act in the drama that was unfolding.

He had arrived just as the bloodshed was reaching its fevered pitch. He was still bare-chested, having rushed here as soon as he'd heard the sounds of fighting, and there were several small cuts that wept bitter red tears across his skin.

"This is terrible!" a familiar voice rumbled, and Garrek turned to see Ddiangen standing in front of Rordin with his hands outstretched toward the carnage around them.

"You have a talent for describing the obvious and not doing it credit," Rordin stated dryly. His face was covered in blood splatters, and his clothes were likewise spotted with bits of brain and drying gore.

"I thought you guaranteed our safety for this meeting!" Ddiangen continued, seeming to ignore Rordin's snide remark.

"I thought I could trust on the basics of dwarfen courtesy from the Ashtels. It seems I misjudged them, and badly at that."

"What was the meaning of all this?"

"That seems obvious enough, doesn't it?" Garrek spoke up and walked over toward them. Ddiangen and Rordin turned to face him, the Afalans chieftain had a sour look on his face.

"What insight can *you* offer?"

"It was a simple ploy. Gather all of Rordin's potential allies in one spot, and then kill them or take them all hostage so their clans would not fight when a new succession was announced."

"Gruumen didn't like being called on his lies. I feel as though he has grown used to people believing them far too readily in the capital." Rordin tried to wipe some of the drying blood from his face with his sleeve and only succeeded in smearing the substance further along his cheek.

"You sound so sure that this was, indeed, a trap laid by the Ashtels. Do you really believe that?" Ddiangen retorted, and Garrek had to bite back a snide response.

"I said that, didn't I?" Rordin said bluntly.

The Afalans leader frowned and opened his mouth, but before he could speak, Rordin cut him off.

"Listen Ddiangen, I have already stated my piece and given you my evidence. There is nothing more that I can say to convince you, and I think you know that. All that is left is to decide where you stand, and then follow through."

This statement hung in the air for a long pause. Garrek became very aware of the eyes of all the other clans watching this exchange, and he realized that most of them must have the same questions that Ddiangen had been asking. Rordin's statement must have been addressed to them as much as it was to the chieftain of the Afalans, and now they were all waiting to see how he would respond. Garrek forced himself to let out a breath that he hadn't realized he was holding.

"Do you think the rumors are true, then? Has Golloch gone over to the Abyss?" Ddiangen asked, but the bluster in his voice was gone, and Garrek felt the temperature drop as the unwanted question was finally spoken. Rordin must have realized the weight of his next words, because there was another long pause before he spoke.

"I have strong reason to believe that this is true, but I will not condemn a dwarf who is not here to defend himself. All that I can judge for certain is that Golloch has started a war with the Free Clans at a time when there are enemies at our very doorstep. He has used trickery and politics to try and bring our cousins from Halpi into the empire rather than open invitations which would likely have been met with better success. He has divided all of the clans with his actions, as evidenced by the events of today, and for that, he must be brought for judgment."

Rordin stopped and took a long breath before continuing. Now he turned openly and addressed the rest of the assembled clans.

"Golloch has poisoned our society for too long. He must be stopped before his vanity and greed destroy all of us, both Free and Imperial alike. That is my purpose from here until either I die, or Golloch is defeated."

His words rang out through the amphitheater, and Garrek noticed nods of approval from several chieftains. Ddiangen himself still wore a frown, and Garrek felt himself groan inwardly as he stepped forward.

"And then what?" the Afalans chieftain asked, lifting his chin accusingly at Rordin, who gave a tired sigh and looked down at him.

"I assume you mean what my intentions are toward the throne, am I right?"

"Of course! Why should we replace one tyrant with another?"

"I do not want anything from Golloch, nor would I accept the throne from him, even were he to offer it to me. Golloch rose to power through trickery and politics. He blackmailed and cajoled his way there, and I will have no part of that. When we have defeated Golloch, there will be a need for a new ruler, that is certain. But it will be a king who reigns by the consent of the clans! I do not want, nor do I wish, to pursue the throne. The new king will be someone who all of the clans will gather and cast their votes as to who should rule, and that king will be charged with an extremely unenviable task of restoring order to our sorely wounded empire. I put forward to you my word and my oath that this is not a power grab. I do not wish to even be considered for the title, and I will gladly support anyone the clans choose. But that is something that must wait until its proper time. For now, we have to win the war before we can begin to consider who will rule. We must cut out the rot from within before we can begin to heal! We cannot splinter further into camps vying for the throne when there is still the threat of Golloch over our heads, or else we will be arguing over an empire of ashes over which Golloch will still hold his fetid fist!"

The mood of their gathering was too somber to warrant a cheer, and Rordin's words were not triumphant, but Garrek could feel the sensation of anxious energy welling up inside him. Rordin stood before them with the blood of his fellow dwarfs covering his face and hands while the thin air of the mountains blowing gently managed to stir his cloak so that it billowed around him. He stared around the assembly with eyes that could chip the very stone beneath their feet, and there was none that could look away from him. The moment held for the space of several heartbeats, but Garrek felt the weight of generations behind it.

"Fine, I'll accept that," Ddiangen spoke and shattered the spell of silence.

"As will I!" Lord Bretsnag of the Draignos Clan added his voice. Several other chieftains voiced their support, and nearly everyone was nodding in agreement.

"I welcome your aid in this." Rordin's face looked relieved, and he nodded his gratitude toward them all. "I will take my forces back to Dolgarth, where I will welcome any clans that wish to join me! We will muster our hosts and march them on Caeryn Golloch to reclaim our homeland, and then we will set things right there."

"I will rally those clans to the southeast to join you, we will gather at Gaer Carric and march inland from there," Bretsnag spoke again. "We will meet you at Caeryn Golloch where we will continue the conversation that you began here today, Lord Rordin."

Then, Lord Bretsnag did something that caused a ripple of whispers to move through the other dwarfs. He bowed before Rordin before turning to walk away.

"I urge the rest of you to return to your holds and gather your warriors, they will be needed in the days ahead." Rordin frowned at a thought before continuing. "Gruumen's forces are larger than we can resist at our present strength, but he only has enough to chase one of us, and for some reason, I feel as though he will be targeting me. So I shall lead him away from you so that you can have a better chance of reaching your homes."

"I will go with you!" Garrek called out. Then, before Rordin could protest, he said, "You know that my clan has nowhere to go in any case, we might as well start heading to Dolgarth, as that is the meeting point for us anyways. You can't really stop us from doing that."

Rordin shot him a sour look, but it didn't hold, and he ended up smiling a sad smile before shaking his head.

"I will also accompany you," Ddiangen said, stepping forward. "I have brought a quarter of my troops that we can muster, and I am angry at Gruumen for making a fool of us here today."

"No, that is unnecessary. You need to return to your hold and gather the rest of your forces," Rordin said, but his voice was less sure than it had been while addressing the entirety of the dwarf clans.

"I will send a messenger and have my eldest son prepare the troops. I will not pass on the opportunity of having the Afalans Clan take part in the opening battles of this war, and you will not deny us the honor that is to be won from that. Besides," Ddiangen grimaced in Garrek's direction, "we can't have an Oathbreaker showing us up!"

Rordin let out a tired sigh, but he made no further argument and instead turned to walk away. The rest of the chieftains were already moving about and talking with their servants. It was obvious the gathering was concluded. Garrek hurried after Rordin.

"That was rather well done, m'lord," he said out of the corner of his mouth. Rordin shot him a nasty look.

"I wasn't trying to do anything. I just want everyone to work together for the first time in what feels like centuries. How we have let things go this far is beyond me!"

"You are a good leader. You gave the rest of the chieftains a clear goal, and you were straightforward and honest with them about our chances and what was needed. That is refreshing and is something that we haven't seen since before Golloch took the throne. If you aren't careful, the Draignos aren't the only ones who will be bowing to you."

Rordin stopped walking and Garrek took a few more steps before turning back to face him. The younger dwarf had a fierce look on his face.

"I will not stand for that, Garrek. You speak of me being honest in one breath and then accuse me of politicking and currying favor in the next. I do not want to be king. I am not meant for that crown, nor do I wish for it. I will not campaign for it, and I will not stand for that indirect comparison between myself and Golloch, I will *not* be like him!"

Garrek found himself looking away from that piercing gaze.

"My apologies, I meant no offense," he said after a moment. "However, it's funny how fate works. Many times the things that we want and the things that happen are not always the same thing. In fact, in my experience, the more you want something then the less likely it is to happen that way, and even when you do get what you want, it isn't usually the way that you want it." He glanced back at Rordin who was giving him a quizzical look. Garrek laughed. "I'm sorry, it is the prerogative of your elders to speak in circles like that. But all that aside, what is your plan?"

"Exactly what I said." Rordin shook his head and turned to begin walking again. Garrek fell into step beside him. "However, even with you and the Afalans joining with my own forces, the Ashtels and their allies still outnumber us by a significant margin, even without accounting for this unknown force that was attempting to ambush us. We can't stand and fight. Our best bet is to try and retreat to Dolgarth where we can put some walls between us and rally the rest of my forces while the other clans gather their strength. I don't think Gruumen will pursue us all the way there, anyways. That would leave him too exposed."

Garrek nodded. Dolgarth made sense. It was outside of the Abkhazla mountain range, and there was a fair amount of open plains and a few major rivers between them that would leave a large army vulnerable as they tried to march across it. Also, it was right on the border with the Basilean Hegemony, and the Hegemon was always spoiling for a fight with Golloch. The last thing that Gruumen would want right now is to antagonize the Basileans and give them a reason to attack.

"Do you think that we can do this?" Rordin's voice was low so only Garrek would be able to hear. "Can we actually win against Golloch?" The mountain breeze suddenly became colder and bit into Garrek's bones. He became painfully aware of his bare skin and shuddered as snow began to fall like ash from the skies. He was slightly shocked; the day had been mostly clear and warm up until just a few moments ago.

"Whether we can win or not matters little at this point. When you've already jumped from the precipice, it's too late to consider whether or not leaping was the right choice." Garrek's teeth began to chatter from the sudden cold, and he cursed the uncharacteristic spring weather.

"That's not very comforting."

"That's the thing with choices. The more important they are, the less comfortable it is to make them." Garrek clamped a hand on Rordin's shoulder. "But I will say this, something needed to be done about Golloch. Whether or not we win isn't as important as *how* we do either. Golloch needs to be reminded what it means to be a dwarf, and I think that we are as good as any generation for doing just that."

A strong gust of cold wind blew around them as Garrek gave Rordin the most convincing smile he could muster.

10
On the Move

I actually envy the Free Clans and their sense of identity that they have created. Where Imperials have crafted a unifying code of culture and ethics that is practiced regardless of what clan you belong to, the Free Clans are different. Each clan is unique in how it approaches problems, and is free to choose which clans they wish to ally with and which ones they do not.

That is not to say that the Free Clan way is superior to the Imperial one. In fact, it seems as though there are some serious hindrances in the way they deal with things. But the sense of individual pride each clan possesses far outstrips anything I have seen in Golloch's empire. The term Free Dwarf is not just a moniker, it is an apt description of their way of life in many ways. It may be the cause of their downfall one day, should infighting and pride ever prevent them from helping one another, but I will say this: I highly doubt that Golloch would have risen to the heights of power that he has if he had been born into the Free Clans instead of the Empire.

–Garrek Heavyhand, when asked why he regularly fought alongside the Free Clans.

Yorna's feet hurt. In her relatively short career as a soldier on campaign, she had come to one definitive realization: marching was awful. She sighed wearily and glanced over at Dig walking beside her. The veteran soldier carried his rifle across his shoulders like it weighed nothing, and his steps seemed light and almost youthful. Craggoth clumped alongside her, and his boulder-sized fists acted like another set of legs, turning him into some giant rock beast that ambled along and towered over his companions. Wynn walked behind them with a faraway look on his face, his eyes clouded with the same discomfort that she felt. She shook her head.

"Does it ever get easier?" she asked.

"Does what ever get easier?" Dig asked, shooting her a wry glance. She waved her hand around motioning to their surroundings.

"Oh! The marching? I suppose it does, at least physically."

"You have time and mental faculties available to focus on things other than how badly your feet hurt?" she asked incredulously. He laughed in response.

"Ah, I went numb from the knees down several miles ago. Not sure if that's a good thing or not, but it leaves me the ability to think about what's waiting for us at the end of the march."

"Ah, yes... that." Yorna scowled. "At this point, I'm not sure if I mind the hopeless battle that's ahead if it means I can stop the blisters on my heel from growing."

"Come now!" Dig laughed. "You can't think it's that hopeless if you volunteered us to go."

"We weren't exactly spoiled for choices. We either joined Sveri, or we got kicked out of Freeport as the treacherous Imps that we are. I suppose there's also the option of going home and facing our charges of treason, for which I'm sure we'll receive a fair trial."

"Don't be so despondent!" he chided her, and she rolled her eyes.

"Look, I'm tired, my feet are killing me, and I am still dealing with the fact that we don't have a home. Forgive me if I am a bit cranky."

"Oh, we have a home. We're still a clan, even if it's just a clan of misfits and outcasts. We wouldn't be the first clan of such."

"Who are the others? And how did that turn out for them?"

"Surely you've heard of Garrek Heavyhand and his followers?"

"Of course," Yorna groaned and shot him a venomous look. "At least they are welcome in the empire, though!"

"'Welcome' might be stretching the word a bit far. They are tolerated at best, for the most part. Although Ithel was always on friendly terms with him." There was an awkward pause at the mention of their former chieftain's name. Yorna coughed and tried to keep the conversation going.

"Why was that?"

"He was always more focused on what a dwarf did in living memory rather than what his parents or grandparents did. He always used to say that if Garrek had been born into a worthy family that he could have been the one who challenged Golloch and took the throne. He said that the Heavyhand Clan had done more to ensure the safety of all dwarfs than practically any other clan. He'd even suggested a few times that it might be worthwhile to revisit the need for Garrek's ostracization. He was shouted down by his peers each time, though."

"You knew Ithel best, what do you think he would say to a clan in our situation? I mean if he were alive and we had belonged to a different clan, that is." Yorna kept her gaze straight ahead, hoping not to betray anything she felt on her face; but when Dig took several moments to respond, she turned her head to look at him. He looked over at her with a sad look on his face.

"I can only imagine. But I think he would have fought for us. He would have been one of the nobles we might reach out to in order to secure our defense for a trial… But with him gone, and the manner of his death, I think we aren't so lucky as that. I don't know that there's anyone in the empire that would listen to us."

The conversation seemed to die after that, and they trudged along in silence for some time before the quiet was broken by Wynn, who coughed politely.

"I don't think it's all that hopeless. Ithel was well-liked by the clans, as evidenced by his appeal to the Claansvelt. Maybe there's still someone out there who will believe us and will help us to come home."

Yorna looked over her shoulder and smiled at him. He grinned sheepishly back at her and shrugged.

"It's better to hope in something like that than to just give up and accept our exile," he said.

"I suppose you're right," Yorna sighed and shook her head ruefully. "Really, for me, I have my parents and siblings back home, but my father was never really keen on me joining the warsmith college. He was always hopeful that I would come back to them with my tail tucked at the sight of my failure. He had always hoped for a demure daughter he could marry off to gain power to hand off to one of my brothers. My mother is the one that I miss. She always believed in me and encouraged me to follow my goals. She sent me money when my pa refused to do so. She's the one I'm going to miss the most, I think." She smiled as the melancholy threatened to overtake her.

"I have two daughters back home, but they're married with families of their own," Dig said. "My oldest was more traditional and married a chieftain's third son. They now have three little ones all their own, and they have me wrapped around their little fingers. My other daughter married a stone priestess, and that caused quite a stir! They don't have any sons or daughters of their own, but her wife helps organize one of the largest orphanages in Caeryn Golloch, so she always says she has a couple hundred children to take care of!" He chuckled.

"What about your wife?" Yorna asked. Dig grew a little quieter before responding.

"My wife died about fifteen years back, caught a blood infection that took her shortly after we discovered it," he said slowly.

"I'm so sorry!" Yorna gasped, but the sharpshooter held up a hand to stop her.

"It's alright! She had a good life, and I don't regret anything we did. It was quick and relatively painless, which is more than most mercies some people get."

"What orphanage does your daughter help run?" Wynn asked. Dig turned and gave him an appraising look.

"The one that's about two streets down from the Temple of Dianek. Like I said, I think it's probably the biggest one in the capital. Why do you ask?"

"Because that's where I grew up! I'm an orphan, so I grew up a ward of the empire. What's her name?"

"My daughter's name is Jesa, my daughter-in-law's name is Qaiwyn. My daughter took her last name, so you'd probably know her as…"

"*Athro* Lief! I know them!" Wynn called out excitedly. A grin split Dig's face.

"That's her! You one of hers, then?"

"Kind of. I was less than a decade away from reaching adulthood when she took over. She was really young to be put in that position, and I think she struggled a lot while I was there. But I do remember that she was always smiling, even when she was chewing out one of the others."

"You saying that she never yelled at you?" Yorna asked, her face hurt from smiling at the thought of a younger Wynn being redressed by an *Athro*.

"No, like I said, I was already pretty old for the most part, beyond the age where they assume that you might be adopted by anyone, and I'd pretty much figured out how everything worked there. I wasn't much trouble for her; in fact, I'll bet she doesn't even remember me."

"I doubt that," Dig said. "She remembers everyone at her orphanage. Qaiwyn has a memory for names and faces that would put any imperial archivist to shame. She loves you kids. So does my Jesa."

Yorna looked back and saw Wynn blush and smile while looking down at the ground in front of him while he walked.

"That kind of makes you his honorary grandson, doesn't it?" she asked mischievously.

"You know, I think it does!" Dig gave her a sly wink and fell back to throw his arm around the young apprentice, whose blush deepened as he tried to shrink down further into himself.

"Thought you could hide from your granddad, did ya? For shame!" Dig chuckled as he crushed the other dwarf's shoulder in a one-armed hug.

"So, uh… Yorna… What about Craggoth? Isn't it a good thing you're staying around for him?" Wynn sputtered, desperate to change the subject. Yorna gave a laugh that she felt in the depths of her belly. It felt good, and she was almost sad at its brevity. She turned her smile toward Wynn and decided to take pity on him.

"I suppose it is at that. Although, I don't know why he's been following me around so much. Don't know what I did to get his attention."

"It's odd that he's an elemental that doesn't fade away like all of the others," Dig said, but his tone was curious, not cruel. "I wonder what keeps him here."

"I've been studying him now for a bit," Wynn said, perking up. He pointed to the metal furnace that was attached to his back. "That's what sustains him. Just like we eat food for our sustenance, he consumes the fires of that furnace for his victuals."

"Seems odd that a rock would need fire to live," Yorna cocked an eyebrow at the puzzle that the earth elemental represented.

"I think it makes perfect sense," Wynn replied. Both her and Dig shot him quizzical looks at this, and he shrugged awkwardly under Dig's arm.

"Think of our society. We live in the heart of stone, and we use fire to purify ore and shape our homes out of rock. We have two religions, which are really just mirrors of our culture. We worship our mother Dianek, but also the Shining aspect of Fulgria, the goddess of fire. It was Fulgria who brought us the gifts of the forge in ways that Dianek could not provide us. It is because of both stone and fire that we are the people that we are today. Craggoth is a living embodiment of our people, or at least of what our people could be if we'd stop arguing and fighting. Maybe that's what he's here for: to remind us of that potential."

Silence prevailed except for the sounds of the army's marching. Yorna stared at him for a long moment while they walked, and Wynn couldn't meet her gaze.

"It's just a theory," he mumbled.

"I'm not saying anything!" Yorna replied. "I'm just wondering if you missed your calling to the priesthood rather than joining the college! I had no idea that you had the soul of a poet in there, Wynn!"

Dig let out a loud laugh at that, and Yorna joined him. Together they drew several gloomy and disapproving looks from the other dwarfs around them, but they didn't seem to care. Eventually even Wynn joined in with some nervous chuckling.

"Oh, I needed that," Yorna said while wiping her eyes as their mirth died down. Then her face took on a more somber expression. "Although that does make me worried about one thing."

"What's that?" Dig asked.

"Herneas reported that the golems at Crag Hudd were insane, and he thought it might be because they were trapped in their bodies, like they couldn't return to their natural state. What if..." she paused here, looking up worriedly at Craggoth. "What if the same thing will happen to him?"

"I don't think it will," Wynn said, shaking his head.

"Why's that?"

"Well, for one thing, Craggoth has already been around for years and hasn't gone insane yet. The golems at Crag Hudd seem to be born into their madness. That means that there is something inherently different between them."

"Like what?"

"I don't know. Maybe it's the nature of their creation? The Abyssal Dwarfs use infernal sorceries to bind them, so that could have something to do with it? Also, didn't Herneas say that they were using the Rift somehow to create them?"

"That's what Grodgni thought, yes."

"Then maybe the spirits being bound to the golems aren't even elemental spirits? Maybe they are something else? Something that thinks our world is filled with madness?"

A shiver ran down Yorna's spine.

"What other kind of spirits are there besides elemental ones?" she asked.

"I don't know," Wynn replied.

"And that's the problem with this situation," Dig said, his voice was cold and he looked away from them both.

"What's that?"

"There are more things in our existence that we do not understand than those things that we do, and whenever we encounter the unknown, it should be done cautiously and respectfully. The things we do know are terrifying enough to warrant that. What Golloch is doing at Crag Hudd screams that it is a sin against the natural order of things. Is it any wonder that the results of his haphazard dash into the unknowable realms of another plane of existence yields anything more than madness?"

With that, he released Wynn and continued walking in silence. Yorna again felt the familiar twisting sensation in her gut as she followed his lead.

*****

The drumming sound of a thousand boots pounding against the dirt resonated through the valley. Herneas grit his teeth and swore that everyone within a hundred miles could hear the noise of their passing. Even though only three clans had responded to the Sveri's call for help, they had managed to gather something resembling an army, and Herneas surveyed them from his vantage point on a low hill that the army was slowly marching past.

Ari Shatterpeak and the Shatterfist Clan marched in their olive drab banners striped with bars of gold across them. Alongside them marched the symbol of the Rivermark Clan with their runic book on a field of blue with gold crenellations above that, their chieftain Arktos Rivermark bellowing orders to his troops at their head. There was a contingency from the Green Valley Confederacy, a strange alliance from a fringe clan and a group of halflings that had been expelled from the League of Rhordia on the western edge of the Halpi Mountains. They had come to Freeport after the war for Halpi's Rift to help with reconstruction and had eagerly answered Sveri's request for help. Their banner was a black hammer crossing a gray butcher's cleaver on a field of deep green slashed with a ruddy orange. Their leader, Baldr Balhertogi, bore their standard himself as they marched.

There were a few other oddities and smaller bands that had been sent by other chieftains, but these were token squads meant to express their support. The problem was that too many clans were hard-pressed trying to get into Freeport, or to reestablish their own lands, that they couldn't afford to send many troops. There were some mercenaries whom Sveri had been able to enlist. Daladamir Platebreaker in his battered plate was easy to spot, even at this distance, with red runes engraved across his armor. Kyah of Carric Gulf had been another oddity that had joined them. They were a dwarf raised by the druids of Galahir, but had returned to Halpi to help reclaim their ancestral homeland. A few other small bands dotted the landscape of the other, bigger clans.

There *was* a fourth clan that marched to the back, but Herneas didn't know how to place them. They were the smallest of the contingents that had responded, but only because they were all that was left. Yorna had approached him about staying on with Sveri after the news of Banick's execution and their branding as traitors to the Imperial throne. Herneas had agreed, but he knew that the presence of Imperials marching alongside the other clans had made the chieftains nervous. It didn't matter that Herneas had vouched for them. They were still outsiders – and worse, they had been subjects of Golloch, who was an obvious oathbreaker; by extension, these individuals must be as well. Herneas sighed, that was an issue that he would have to deal with at a later date.

"Are we sure we can pull off this stealthy thing?" Grodgni asked, standing beside Herneas and surveying the small valley.

"It's the only plan we have, and at this point, we don't have any other choice, really," Herneas replied. Grodgni was referring to the strategy that Sveri and Herneas had concocted. With all the combined might of the clans and mercenaries that had responded to their summons and the forces Sveri had been able to bring from Cwl Gen, they had mustered a force of nearly four thousand troops. It wouldn't be enough if Golloch saw them coming, but if they could surprise him and strike hard and fast, there was a chance that they could penetrate their outer defenses and possibly steal back the Rift before the Imps could react. What that attack might look like was still a work in progress, and the uncertain aspects of what lay ahead made Herneas's stomach twist uncomfortably.

"How did you convince Sveri of this plan?"

"He didn't like it, that's for certain," Herneas responded, wincing as he spoke. "I impressed on him the need for urgent action if he didn't want to see a tide of insane golems descending on Freeport or Cwl Gen in the near future."

Grodgni gave a dry laugh at that.

"Can't imagine that was an easy conversation. I know how much Sveri hates subterfuge. I remember how hard it was to convince him to follow the strategy to retake Cwl Gen, what with the distraction and the misdirection that required. As I recall, the only reason he agreed to it was because we were fighting goblins, and they didn't count as honorable opponents in any case."

"I used a similar strategy here," Herneas replied, nodding. "I argued that Golloch was not held back with Sveri's principles of honor, and that if we didn't act soon, then he would be able to take even more of our home away from us with his treacherous schemes. He didn't like it, but he's not a fool. He understands how important it is for us to take back Crag Hudd. He knows that if we don't, then Golloch will take back all of our homeland that we have struggled to reclaim, and that we may never be able to come back from that loss."

"Essentially, if we don't take the Rift back from Golloch, then he'll win and we'll be subjugated to the Imperials."

"And by extension to the Abyssals."

Grodgni gave a low whistle. Herneas gave another scan of the columns of warriors moving through the valley.

"Even with all that, I imagine he wasn't too happy about it."

"When is he ever happy about anything these days?" Grodgni grunted.

"When are any of us?" Herneas replied, his eyes narrowed as he caught sight of Brethod running toward them. The sandy-haired youth was red in the face from running, and his beard swayed erratically as he approached. When he finally drew close enough to speak, his voice came in between sharp gasps of breath.

"You need… to come with me… There's trouble…" he wheezed.

Herneas raised an eyebrow.

"What kind of trouble?"

"The kind that you need to see," Brethod took a deep gulp of breath and swallowed. "Something is coming, and it doesn't look good."

"*Uff'ran!*" Herneas cursed. "What is it?"

"We can't tell exactly. From a distance, it looks like dwarves. They wear dwarf armor and I see a few examples of regalia, but their columns are disorganized and their banners are strange."

"Are they Golloch's dwarfs?"

"Couldn't say. We sent out scouts to investigate. Whoever they are, they're marching through the mountains, and they don't seem to care if they are seen. I'd say they won't reach our forces for another few days, but they are coming."

"We need to take this information to Sveri, then. How long ago did you send the other scouts?"

"I left them this morning and ran straight here, so I imagine that they will likely be back by tonight with a report."

"We can't afford to wait that long. I'll have to tell Sveri with the information that we have so we can begin making preparations."

"There's more." Brethod placed his hand on Herneas's arm, who turned back with a questioning look on his face.

"What is it?"

"There is an elf..." his voice trailed off.

"An elf?" Herneas's brows furrowed.

"She snuck up on us. We didn't see her until she was practically on top of us..."

"What is it, dwarf?" Herneas growled, the edge of his voice betraying his impatience.

"She's demanding to see Sveri, or rather, whoever is in command of the army. Says she has information about what's coming, and about Crag Hudd as well."

"What in the Abyss is an elf doing here?" Grodgni muttered. Herneas frowned, it was a good question.

"Take me to her," he ordered.

11
Allies of Inconvenience

The Battle of Black Pass is considered the ultimate example of the treachery of the elfs. It was here that they showed their true colors as they cut down the Ironhelm Clan. Every dwarf learns this history lesson as they grow into adulthood, and with that story, there is always this outspoken moral given:

'The only thing reliable about an elf is their deceit.'

–Breva Corriger
Imperial Dwarf Archivist

The evening sun slid hesitantly behind the peaks, covering the ground with a cold blanket of shadow. A strong wind blew through the mountains towering above, and the ratkin general fancied that it brought with it the smell of the dwarfs that were so very close. Krut Stonepaw lifted his nose and took in the scents, the whiskers on his snout shifting as he snuffled and fidgeted to try and get a better sense of how far they were from their prey. The ill-fitting armor that he wore rattled with his movements. In particular, the dwarf helm shifted uncomfortably on his head.

The ratman surveyed the tide of furry bodies that marched all around him and allowed himself a sly smile. His scouts had brought him news that the stonebeards had not changed their course. This meant that they were either unaware of his army marching on them, or they thought that they could defeat the might of his endless hordes. Either way, they were doomed.

Krut turned and pointed the heavy pickaxe which he used as his chosen weapon at a group of Scurriers, who shrank back under his attention. Krut grinned at their discomfort, he liked the taste of fear that escaped from his followers when he gave orders. The Abyssal Dwarfs, their former masters, had been right in this aspect. His army worked so well because of the terror they felt if they displeased their new master, and his whips were far crueler than the Fire Lords' had ever been.

He chittered his orders at the Scurriers; light and fast, they would serve as his vanguard in the coming fight. They sniveled and pleaded for him to change his mind, but all it took was a single crack of his pick against the stone at their feet and the flash of sparks from the blow to silence their complaints. Their clicking and squeaky tongue was not as harsh as the words their former overlords had used on them, but violence worked in whatever language, and the lightly armored rats made like their namesake and scurried away to follow his orders.

Behind them stood Pratter, Krut's commander of the more elite and better-equipped shock troops. Pratter was almost as big as Krut, so much so that the dwarf armor that was strapped awkwardly to his shoulders and chest nearly seemed to fit him if he stood still.

"The stonebeards come, it seems," Pratter said, moving forward to stand beside Krut.

"Yes. They think they are to beat us with little trying," Krut sneered.

"Maybe they think we will run from them?"

"Or that we do not exist in numbers that will be able to kill them." Krut shifted the helmet on his head so that he could see more clearly. "They do not know the might of the Stonepaw! We took their mines from them, and we did it too well! None of the stonebeards survived to tell the tale of our murderings. They do not fear what they do not know!"

"They will know when they see our banners with their packmates' skulls on our spears." Pratter smiled a wicked grin. "When they see their armor on our backs, and we take their axes in our claws and kill them with their own weapons. This is when they will know to fear us, but then it will be too late!"

"This time we will be smart. We will not kill them all. This time we take captives so that they tell others of our might. We cut off their hands, they do not need these to tell stories, and stonebeards without hands cannot return to fight us again. They will know to fear these mountains. They will know that this is now our home, not theirs as it once was!" Krut sniggered at the image of wailing dwarfs waving around bloody stumps where their hands had been, and the fear that it would inspire in those that saw this and heard of his name that caused it.

"They will know fear," Krut growled as his mirth died away. "They will learn to hate the homes they once held, and our pack will grow stronger and will fight back at the Fire Lords in their cities by the Abyss. We will make all of the bearded ones pay for the pain that they have given us. They will know to fear the rats they used as slaves before. We will show them this fear. We started with the mines. We will continue by slaughtering these stonebeards, and we will not stop until all of them feel terror at the sounds of our paws within their walls and beneath their feets!"

*****

"His name is Krut Stonepaw, or at least that's what he calls himself," the elf stood with her chin tilted back and her face as cold as a winter's morning. Sveri found himself grinding his teeth as he looked at her; and several times he had to avert his gaze in order to calm his already frayed nerves. They were in a hastily-pitched tent with the other clans' leaders. Herneas had even brought Yorna as a representative of their ragtag band of Imperial outlaws.

"How do you know this?" he asked, forcing his jaw to unclench and his head to turn back to the pale elf before him.

"My troops have had several run-ins with him since we escaped Crag Hudd. Some of them were taken hostage, unfortunately, and those that he didn't kill were returned to us maimed and with horrifying tales of what he did to those who weren't so lucky."

"What was your name, once more, elf?" Sveri saw her lips tighten at his question and felt a small surge of satisfaction at her irritation.

"I am called Inei Sertsuey, Icekin hunter from the north and emissary to..."

"Yes, yes, I remember the rest." Sveri waved a hand dismissively. "Why does this ratkin horde seek a fight with us? Are they truly that strong that we should be worried?"

"Stonepaw was the one who killed the dwarfs stationed at Creidd Aram, one of your mines to the east of here. He hates all dwarfs, and he seeks to kill as many of you as he can. He styles himself as your equals. He even wears your armor and refers to himself as a lord in order to press home this point. His army could very well be a match for the force that you've gathered here. He certainly has the numbers to challenge you."

"This poses a significant problem for us, as I am sure you are aware," Herneas spoke up, and Sveri shifted his gaze to the ranger impatiently. "We are already short on soldiers that we will need in the battle for Crag Hudd, we cannot afford a costly engagement such as this."

"Yet it is unavoidable," Inei quipped, "so you must either find a way to deal with it or retreat, and I would caution you against retreating."

"I don't recall asking your advice, ice elf," Sveri growled.

"But I give it nonetheless," she replied with a tone that made Sveri wonder if it might start to snow, and he had to suppress a shudder. "You know that treachery has taken the hold, but you were not there when he did it. You did not see how your king..."

"He is ***not*** our king," Sveri interrupted her, growling. She fixed him with her sharp stare, and he met it full on, his hot rage melting her cold insolence. Finally, it was she who looked away, even as she continued speaking.

"You were not there to see him plunge his knife into the backs of your allies. You did not see what he did to your brothers and sisters. He entered the keep as an honored guest, and within an hour of doing so, he had butchered almost everyone there. He is cunning and ruthless, and if you allow his plans to come to fruition, then the whole world will suffer for it."

"In all your wisdom, you couldn't have seen that coming, huh?" Sveri glowered at her, but his anger had lost its edge.

"It was only because of my suspicions that I was able to escape and keep as many as I did alive." At this, Inei lowered her gaze to the floor, and Sveri found that he couldn't bring himself to break her reverie as she stood there for several seconds. He knew the look that was on her face. He'd worn it himself many times on long nights when ghosts howled up from the darkness and refused to be silenced. When the quiet was broken, it was done so hesitantly, by Herneas, who spoke low and soft.

"So what are we to do? Even if we prevail against the rats, they will potentially cause enough damage to prevent us from being able to take the fight to Golloch."

"Do we have any other choice? They already know we are here. I don't think that we can avoid them." Sveri pursed his lips in thought. There were no good options here. They could attempt to take this new threat on in open battle, but there was no guarantee that they could even win that fight. Victory would be hollow; even if it was possible for them to win without taking large amounts of casualties, they would still be depleted. Further, the battle might make Golloch aware of their presence. They would lose the one advantage they might have had in the coming fight against the fallen king.

"I have a suggestion," Inei spoke quietly as if she was waking up from a deep sleep.

"What wisdom would you deign to give us, frost-skin?" Sveri's teeth ground against themselves as he forced his eyes to turn to her, his former reticence to address her fleeing in a sudden flickering fire of irritation boiling up inside him.

"The head of a ravine is within two day's march of here, it is at the head of a very narrow pass with steep walls to either side. If we do a forced march, we can stay ahead of the ratkin and arrive with enough time to prepare to meet them at the entrance with a small force that will fall back into the pass where we will be waiting with our ranged weapons to..."

"No." Sveri's voice cut through hers, and the quiet that followed was absolute.

"Sveri," Herneas began, but Sveri silenced him with a look.

"You would have us commit another Battle of Black Pass?" Sveri turned his quiet rage back on the elf. He clenched his fists so hard that he felt the knuckles crack under the pressure.

"I..." she started to reply, but some desperate instinct for self-preservation must have clawed its way forward, and she stopped.

"You come here, with your sneering disdain for our kind. You bring us heart-breaking news that we already suspected, and then you have the audacity to flaunt your conniving race's backstabbing tactics as a solution to our problems, which you see as 'self-inflicted' because those problems were caused by another dwarf. As if your people haven't produced enough shameful individuals that have nearly brought the world to its knees! Perhaps this is your way of getting back at the rest of the world for your damnable Calisor Fenulian? What has your race done to atone for that sharp-eared bastard's sins? Wasn't he considered the greatest among you? Granted, that's an easy target, but there have been other examples. Shall we compare ancestors, elf? See whose lineage has more black spots? I don't think that you will enjoy that contest."

The elf refused to meet his gaze. Her brow was furrowed, and she seemed to be looking at the space just above his head.

"I never said anything about your ancestors," Inei's voice was barely a whisper. "I came here as a courtesy to try and warn you of what is coming. If you meet Stonepaw in an open fight, then you may win that battle, but will you then be in any shape to march on Halpi's Rift?"

Now, her flint-like gaze flickered down and held his own hot stare.

"Do not assume that I bear any grudge against your people, Berserker Lord. I know your name and I know your accomplishments. They are many. If you and I were to come to blows, I have no doubt that you would emerge the victor. But I..." her voice seemed to catch in her throat and she coughed. When her eyes once again met his own, Sveri was shocked to see the wetness of tears there, and a fierce fire had ignited behind her steel-blue irises. "I had to watch as Golloch's forces cut down your warriors that were stationed at Crag Hudd. Many of them I considered friends. I know the rage that you feel toward him. Maybe not as deeply, and I know that I do not understand everything that you feel toward him. But I do know that I want to see him pay. I want to drive my blade through his chest and watch as the life slips from his eyes. You had good people who had sworn to protect the Rift there, and they deserved better than the knife they received in their ribs. Camwedd deserved better than that..."

At this, Inei blinked and looked away again.

"These ratkin that threaten you now," she continued without looking back at Sveri, but her voice still continued to sound strained, "you want to treat them as though they are equals. You treat them as if they deserve your respect, like they deserve a fair fight. Do you know how many dwarfs they slaughtered in ambushes? How many children were stationed with their parents at Creidd Aram when Krut Stonepaw's monstrosities fell upon them?"

"Do not cite their crimes against us, elf," Sveri growled, but he could feel the anger ebbing out of him. "We know what they have done. Their crimes against us are many, and we will make them pay for each one."

"Then why do you treat them like they deserve a fair chance? Why do you not slaughter them as you would a pack of wolves that have gotten in amongst your livestock? Would you stand your ground against a bear that is bearing down on you? Or would you set up traps and pits to catch the creature so that you could put it down safely, without risking your life?"

"It isn't the same thing."

"Isn't it? Then explain it to me. How is it different? Why should we give these beasts a better chance at killing us?"

"If we stoop to the same levels as our enemies, how can we claim to be better than they are? How can we claim to be good and just if we only justify our treachery because it is more convenient?"

"You speak about these rats as if they held the same morals as you! They don't care about your honor! They were raised in darkness! They do not understand what you are trying to teach them with your honorable tactics in war. They will exploit your honor as the weakness that it is!"

"It isn't for them that we hold to our honor!" Sveri's voice rumbled now, and he saw the faces of the other dwarfs flinch and step back. To Inei's credit, she stood firm and only winced under the force of his words. "If we retake our homeland through deceitful tactics, it will undermine our entire way of life! Honor is the only thing that binds the Free Clans together! We do not force our fellow clans to come to our aid! We do not coerce allegiances! We do not fight in ways that would have our foes question our integrity! For if we did that, how are we better than Golloch and the deceit that he has sold the Imperials?! If we take the easy path now, what is to stop us from doing the same thing later, when a problem arises that could be solved with a knife in the dark?"

"Those are not the same thing!" Inei cried, but Sveri shook his head.

"Isn't it?" he threw her former words back at her. "Then explain it to me. How is it different?"

"You are talking about killing a pack of animals like the ratkin and equating it with sending assassins to kill a political rival! One is against your enemy, the other would be used against another of your own kind!"

"You argue that the recipient of the action is the difference. For me, it is the intent of the action that matters. Both of those are easy responses to difficult situations." Sveri waved a hand in dismissal. "I will not waste further time discussing this, we have a battle to plan, and we must draw up viable solutions to the problem that is before us."

"You will allow ruin to come to your attempts to retake Crag Hudd before you even reach its walls?" Inei stared at him, a look of disbelief in her eyes. Before he could respond, Herneas strode out and interrupted them.

"Before any plans can be made, we need to prepare the troops. Whatever decision we make, our warriors will need to know that a fight is brewing and to prepare for it. Send word through the lines to disembark weapons and armor from the luggage train and get everyone situated for the fight. Have all units form up for marching orders, and once those orders have been relayed, we will convene once more to discuss strategy. Inei, we would appreciate it if you stayed to help us. Since you already scouted the surrounding area, we could use your counsel on potential battle sites."

"She will not..." Sveri started to speak, but Herneas turned toward him and glared.

"*All* of the clan chieftains will gather to discuss strategy before any decisions are made. We are not beholden to a single chieftain or king as the Imperials are, right, Sveri?"

Sveri stopped short as a confusing range of emotions ran through his mind. He felt the violence growing inside him. He wanted to reach out and slam his fist into the side of Herneas's glaring face. He wanted to holler and yell at the other dwarfs around him. He wanted to kill the damn elf behind Herneas, with her icy eyes and sneering face! He bit the side of his cheek until he tasted blood and forced the raw emotion to ebb and flow away. He didn't respond to Herneas, but instead simply turned and walked over to a small table where a pitcher of ale had been deposited. He poured a cup and forced himself to take small, careful swallows of the chilled beverage and focused on the taste to distract himself from the rage he felt burning inside of him.

*****

Yorna stared at Herneas's back for a long set of moments after Sveri had turned and walked away. She was certain that she had been about to watch Sveri cut her friend down in front of her in a fit of rage. But several seconds had passed, and as the seconds continued to stretch even more, nothing happened and the rest of the tense crowd of chieftains or their representatives turned and began to shuffle out of the tent. Yorna shook her head and caught sight of the ice elf ducking through the tent flap. She cursed and took off after her.

"Hey!" she called out, but the elf didn't turn. Yorna forced her short legs to pump quickly, and she sprinted to catch up, finally touching the edge of her tunic, causing her to stop and turn. Yorna took a few deep breaths to try and steady herself before talking. The elf raised an eyebrow in question.

"What is it?" she asked, and Yorna shivered in spite of herself.

"I just wanted to say that I respect what you said back there," Yorna said in between small gasps that she made to try and catch her breath. "As an outsider here, I get how hard it can be to speak your mind with this bunch."

"You are an outsider?"

"Yeah, I'm an Imp."

"An 'Imp'?"

"It's a slur for Imperial Dwarf," Yorna explained, feeling her cheeks grow warm as she spoke.

"You're an Imperial?!" Inei's eyes widened almost imperceptibly, and her hand slid to the knife at her belt. Yorna held her hands up submissively.

"Oh! Sveri already knows! In fact, he's always known. We fought with him and Herneas at Cwl Gen… I'm kind of the reason that the mountain was blown up…" Yorna looked up sheepishly and saw something that might have been incredulity on Inei's face, also more than a little bit of alarm and suspicion.

"I had heard stories of Cwl Gen's defense, such as it was. But I always thought they were a bit exaggerated, most rumors generally are. Besides, the majority of the news we'd gotten has been pretty scarce, as we'd only heard snippets here and there since Crag Hudd fell."

"Well… I mean, I haven't heard all of them, but the ones I've heard have mostly been true… some of them have even been toned down from what actually happened…the biggest inconsistency that they've had is to who ordered what, and of course they always struggle with my gender!" Yorna felt her brows furrowing at the last bit. It was true, half the time the stories painted her as a male warsmith, while the other half that got her gender right confused her as a secondary character in the story.

"You are the warsmith?" Inei asked, somewhat hesitantly.

"Yes! I am!" Yorna half snapped, half beamed at this, and Inei took another step back.

"Anyways," Yorna continued, tripping over her words. "I also wanted to say that I agree with your tactical advice. I think an ambush like what they did at Black Pass would be perfect for our situation, or at least as perfect as we could hope for. I'm sorry that Sveri didn't agree…"

"He's a fool," Inei spat, looking back in the direction of the tent.

"No, he's not!" Yorna protested, and the elf looked back at her with surprise. "I think he's wrong here, but that doesn't make him a fool. I understand his reasoning, even if I don't agree with it."

"He's going to get your whole army killed," Inei said, but Yorna shook her head.

"No, I think his decision is wrong, and that it will likely end up with more casualties than we could have had if we followed your plan, but he doesn't throw lives away without purpose. He has a heavy burden to bear. There isn't anything like a king of the Free Clans, but many of the other chieftains do look to him as a type of leader, or at least as a first among equals. There are a lot of expectations that come with that kind of responsibility. Sveri is a hero because of his morals, and if those are taken away, then what is left for him?"

"I hope his morals help him sleep at night. It's hard to rebuke ghosts with morals."

"See, that's where I disagree with you. I think his morals are the only thing that keeps him going, they are his guide. He has so much anger and rage inside him, yet he can be exceptionally kind and wise, too. He is a host of contradictions, just like we all are, I guess. But his honor and his morals are those things that he clings to when he doesn't know which way to turn. If he didn't have them, he would probably just go with whatever thing pulled at him the hardest, and that would likely end in violence. Just because his morals have led him to a choice that you or I consider to be wrong, that doesn't mean that he himself is wrong. I don't know…" Yorna shook her head and shrugged. "I feel like I'm not making any sense."

She looked up at Inei and was surprised to see a small smile on her face. The elf sighed and nodded.

"No, I think you make plenty of sense. It's very… umm… logical."

"What does *that* mean?" Yorna said, raising an eyebrow. Then her eyes widened in surprise and she again felt her cheeks blushing. "I mean… um… that is…" she stammered. Inei chuckled and the burning in her cheeks deepened.

"I'm just saying," Yorna continued, trying to brush off her embarrassment, "that I hope you will not abandon us, yet. Especially if it's just because you don't agree with a leader's decision. How many times have we received orders from a leader that we didn't fully understand or agree with, and had to follow through with them anyways?"

"I see your point, Master Warsmith," Inei smiled, and Yorna quietly wondered how even her smiles seemed to be carved from ice.

"Please, my name is Yorna, just call me that."

"Very good, Master Yorna. I will stay and see how I can help your forces as much as I can."

"This is good to hear." Herneas's voice cut into their conversation, and Yorna whirled to face him in surprise.

"Herneas! What are…?" she sputtered.

"I had to wait for everyone to clear out of the tent to speak with Sveri in private, but I wanted to speak to you first and was afraid I wouldn't be able to catch you. I was pleasantly surprised to see you chatting with our resident Imperial commander when I emerged." Herneas placed a hand on Yorna's shoulder as he spoke. She felt her blush deepen and wondered if her face was about to burst into flame.

"Sveri is going to get a lot of you killed. Master Yorna has said some rather wise words to me and has helped me to understand him better. But I still stand by what I said in the tent."

"Sveri is a good dwarf and an even better chieftain. But in this situation, I can see the merit in the plan that you are suggesting. I wish that you had come to me with it first, but there was no way you could have known that."

"You… *agree* with me? Over your commander?" Inei squinted in disbelief, and Yorna wondered if that was the equivalent of being slack-jawed for an elf.

"Don't be so surprised. Dwarfs are nothing if we are not logical. Sometimes that logic is different from the other races, but I know a good plan when I see one, and yours holds merit. But surely you understand how an elf suggesting that we follow the strategy that your kind used against us in the Battle of Black Pass was a bad idea?"

"If it is a good plan, does it matter what the source is?" Inei lifted her chin.

"Of course it does! You placed Sveri in a terrible situation! Stories will be told about what happened in there. If he were to side with an elf suggesting the same strategy that is *still* taught to our youth about the follies of treachery, think of how that would have looked! While not all of our clans are bound by the same xenophobia that has plagued previous generations, there is still a deep sense of tradition within our culture, and old prejudices die hard."

"You are saying that the reason he disagreed with me is because of appearances?"

"I need to speak with him at greater length and see how he wants to proceed, but in future situations, if you have suggestions, then please pass them by me first and I can help advise you on how to bring it up."

"Are you sure you weren't born to statecraft, ranger?" Yorna blurted out, interrupting their conversation. They both fixed her with placid stares, and she smiled sheepishly and took a step back.

"If I am able to convince him to follow your plan, you said that this ravine is about two days' march from here? Won't the ratkin overtake us before we can reach it?"

"Not if we leave by tomorrow morning. Stonepaw is still over a day away, and the ravine is moving away from him. It will be a tight fit, but if your soldiers can keep up a forced march, we should still be able to make it."

"I see." Herneas nodded and brought a hand up to scratch at his beard. "We will need a body of soldiers to act as the decoy. They will be the ones in the most danger, and with the nature of this plan, there may be some hesitation to volunteer for such a difficult assignment."

"We can do it!"

The words tumbled out of Yorna's mouth before she'd even realized she had been considering them. Herneas turned a quizzical look in her direction.

"Your group is already rather depleted. Plus you are a warsmith. Wouldn't you be more comfortable and useful manning artillery within the pass?"

"More comfortable? Yes! Absolutely! But..." Yorna hesitated, taking a deep breath before continuing. "The other clans don't trust us very much. They see us as outsiders, and this could be a good chance to prove ourselves."

"You don't need to prove anything, Yorna. We still have Cwl Gen because of you," Herneas said.

"I know that *you* trust us. But the other clans still see us as Imperials. If we are going to have a future among the Free Clans, then we need to shrug off that label. We need to show the clans that they can trust us. Otherwise, we'll spend our whole lives as outcasts, and I can't subject what's left of our clan to that kind of life."

Herneas stared at her for a long time, then nodded.

"Talk with the rest of your clan and make sure that they are okay with it. I will keep it in consideration if we decide to go in that direction."

"That's it?! That's all you're going to do to try and talk us out of it?" Yorna felt a conflicting mass of emotions wrapping through her chest.

"You make a sound argument. I still need to talk to Sveri about all of this anyways, so nothing is set in stone, yet. Talk with your clan and make sure that they are on board with this, and if it becomes necessary, we can revisit your decision then. But I will keep you as our first consideration unless I hear otherwise." He then faced Inei and nodded. "I am glad that you will be staying with us. We will speak again, I'm sure of it."

The ranger then turned and walked back in the direction of the tent while Yorna and Inei stared after him in silence.

*****

Herneas took a deep breath before ducking back into the tent. Sveri was still standing in front of the small table, taking small sips of ale from a cup made of horn in his hand. From his outward appearance, the berserker lord looked calm and collected, but Herneas knew him well enough to know that the rage was merely being concealed by a thin layer of icy indifference. He would have to tread carefully in the coming conversation, he knew, lest he fall through that thin ice.

"Sveri," he said, breaking the stillness. Sveri did not even acknowledge him. "We need to talk about what we are going to do."

"I should think that would be obvious," Sveri replied without turning.

"I think we both know it's not that simple."

"And what would you have me do?" Sveri finally turned and fixed a dangerous glare on Herneas.

"I would have you listen, and keep an open mind."

Silence prevailed here, and it stretched out anxiously in Herneas's mind. Sveri's expression did not change.

"Well?" Sveri finally said impatiently. "What is it that you want to say?"

"I think we should listen to the elf's idea. It makes the most sense in our present situation." Herneas took a breath to say more, but there came a resounding crack from Sveri's hand where he had crushed his horn cup, spilling ale across the ground. Herneas shifted his stance, preparing for the potential of violence should rage overcome his friend.

"You want to follow the elf's suggestion? You would follow that frozen *fythcyn* over me?" Sveri's voice was low and menacing.

"Don't put it like that, Sveri. You know what I am saying. We have more at stake here than just the simple breakdown that you presented her just now."

"You can't be serious?!" The quiet menace was now gone, Sveri was yelling now. "You want us to use elf trickery to win this battle? What will the other nobles say when this is done? We need the clans to be united in order to win the fight against Golloch! If we give legitimacy to the very elf treachery that has festered like a sour wound between our races for untold generations, then what will those other clans back at Freeport say? There are already many who think we should just roll over and accept Golloch as our king! You would paint us as cowards and tricksters before them? That is besides the fact that they would be right to call us such!"

"I would answer that any dwarf lords who are not here have no right to criticize what choices we were forced to make," Herneas's voice was icy cold to counter the heat of Sveri's rage. "Beyond that, if we are unable to succeed here, then will there be any hope of us reclaiming our homelands? Won't the Free Clans be forced to accept Imperial rule if we cannot remove Golloch from Crag Hudd? Even if we manage to convince the other Imperial clans that their king has gone over to the Abyss, Golloch will have the Rift and an unending supply of crazed golems that he can unleash upon his enemies. Do you think that we will ever be able to retake the Halpi Mountains with that there? What good does it do us if we are forced to retreat because of the misfortune that we've stumbled upon? We have been fighting on our back foot since we lost our homes in the first place, and every victory has been more hollow than the previous. If we finally have an advantage, why don't we use it?"

"Because what are we if we don't have honor? That is everything! What is the point of winning if it tarnishes our legacy and leaves us alone to face the storm that is approaching?!" Sveri yelled, and Herneas felt anger beginning to seep into his own words. Some part of him screamed a warning at the back of his mind, that this was not a safe way to confront Sveri, but his own frustration and weariness drowned it out.

"If this is all it takes to push them away, then were they ever our friends to begin with? Because we used a morally questionable tactic to survive?! I wouldn't even call it a morally questionable tactic, but rather a social misstep!"

"They are the same thing to a dwarf!"

"Then maybe it is time that we changed that!" Herneas shouted. Sveri's eyes widened, and Herneas found that he was just as shocked by his own words.

"What?" Sveri asked.

"Haven't you seen enough to understand what I am saying? Look at Banick! He was a dwarf who was ostracized because of his failures. Yet when the society that rejected him needed him, he rose up to the challenge! He was someone who had lost his honor because of his choices, and yet you trusted him enough to send him as your own personal envoy! He was a hero of our people!"

"For all the good that it did him! He's dead now because of my choice, and he's being held up as an assassin and guilty of more underhanded deeds. The fact that I am associated with him has actually made it harder for me to approach the other clans! If I cave and start using elf trickery, that will only confirm more of the lies and rumors being spread about both Banick and myself!"

"But that is just more evidence of the need for change, though! I am the worst person to speak of these things because I have always been resistant to change. When I was younger, I boldly held to the ideal that I should only give to my community, that I should never take. I felt that if I asked for help, then I was showing weakness. This led me to try and attack an enemy encampment on my own, and it was only because of my comrades going against those expectations that I believed were my duty that I was saved from certain death. Because they disobeyed my orders and my sense of honor, together we were able to win the day. But the thing is, had I died on my own, I would have been hailed as a hero even though my hold and my community would have perished because of my pride! Tell me, is your honor worth the survival of your people?"

Sveri was silent in response. He stared at Herneas for a long pause, then looked away. Herneas could still sense the anger and resentment in that look, but it no longer seemed to be directed at him.

"Sveri, we all know that life is not as simple as we would wish it. Sometimes we have different ideals that come into conflict with each other, and when that happens, we have to decide which of those ideals is more important. You want to see your clan restored to its homeland and your family and friends established for future generations. You also want to win all of your fights honorably so that songs may be sung of your achievements and you will be remembered as an unblemished hero of our people. When the time comes that you must choose between these two strong desires, which of them will win out?"

More silence met Herneas's question. Sveri refused to look at him and eventually turned and walked back over to the small table where he picked up a new cup and filled it with ale. He took a long draught of the drink before placing the cup carefully back on the table.

"I will not change my mind on this matter. I feel that this is an underhanded tactic and that we are better than resorting to trickery in our battles. But I also understand that I am not the only commander here. If I am outvoted in this matter, then I will follow the rest of the army. But I will refuse to participate in the ruse. If it comes to open battle, then I will lend my forces to the fight, but I will not partake in foul trickery in order to win an easy battle."

"I suppose that is the best that I could hope for. Thank you for not forcing the matter unnecessarily." Herneas sighed and moved to the edge of the tent.

"I cannot condone this plan, Herneas," Sveri said as Herneas lifted the flap to exit. The ranger paused and looked back at his friend who was still facing away from him. "And I am disappointed that you are in favor of it."

"I know that you have suffered as much as I have in the course of our lives, Sveri. But when it comes to survival, I'm not sure that there is anything too underhanded, save the threatening of innocent lives perhaps."

"May our ancestors forgive us for that, I hope." Sveri took another drink from his cup. Herneas opened his mouth to say more, but he knew when he was being dismissed. He shook his head and stepped out of the tent without another word.

12
A Feeling of Home

All dwarfs have an innate resonance with the idea of home. The dwarf term for home is guirtref, *and the word has more meanings than its mundane interpretation in the common tongue.* Guirtref *is most literally translated as 'the place my soul resides in sleep.' This is a haunting concept; the dwarfs view their homes as sacred, even to the point that it is their home that is the final resting place of their very spirits once they die. This is further enforced by the referring to their 'ancestral halls' in their burial hymns and funeral prayers. Home, to the dwarfs, is something holy. To see the home desecrated by an outside force is the ultimate insult, and to be invited into a dwarf's home is considered one of the highest forms of respect.*

–Brienne Cothsefult
Professor of Linguistics at the College of Eowulf

The sound of Golloch's fist slamming into the stone table made a thunderous boom and caused a portion of the smooth rock to crumble and break away. Argoll flinched unconsciously and forced himself to not take a step back. Golloch's face was a mask of rage.

"You mean to tell me that you still haven't made any progress?" Flecks of spittle leaped from Golloch's lips. Argoll tried not to stare, but it was obvious that the dwarf king before him had been experimenting with the dark powers of a fleshcaster. His limbs had grown thicker, his eyes had developed an unnatural glow, and his jaw had widened noticeably within their time at Crag Hudd – plus the fact that he had shattered a piece of stone from the table which had been carved from the mountain and had survived goblins, ratkin, and Abyssal Dwarf occupants without so much as a scratch until now. All of these things made it difficult not to stare at his enhancements, and these all made him all the more intimidating. Even so, Argoll was determined not to let his trepidation show on his face.

"My lord, this is a unique puzzle that you have set before us. Never before have we utilized the powers of the Void to imbue our golems with life! It is only natural that we would encounter some impediments. We are getting closer, I can feel it, but the golems that we create remain feral and unyielding to our commands, as of yet."

"Natural?! The very essence of your power is the most unnatural resource in the universe! You mold flesh and stone together with infernal devices! Do not talk to me about the 'natural' impediments that you have come across! I need an army of immortal golems at my side to accomplish what I must do! Do you understand that, Argoll? Do you?!"

"I understand, my lord." Argoll struggled to keep his voice from wavering.

"I'm not sure that you do, because I still do not have what I need, and I am growing short of patience! Perhaps I should cast you into the Rift and see what you can find?!"

Argoll recoiled at this, his stomach coiling in a queasy knot at the idea. He held his hands up defensively.

"That will not be necessary, my lord, I swear. We do have an army prepared for you, but it is one that may require some... unique applications."

"That's one way to put it. You have hordes of wild animals down there and would call that an army? How am I supposed to use golems that won't take commands?"

"We have enough, and they are expendable that we could simply deposit them on the edge of our enemy's location and allow things to take their natural course."

"You are desperate, aren't you?" Golloch sneered and rubbed his face with a large hand. "Even if that went exactly as we hoped, how would we take the land from our foes? All we would be doing is infesting it with feral golems that we would then have to go in and eradicate on our own! We'd be replacing an enemy whose tactics we know with one who is wild and unpredictable!"

"My lord, please, we are close. We've been able to make some progress. Limited communication has been possible from some of the golems. We have learned through some very crude methods that the spirits that we have housed in these bodies are angry, and scared. They don't know what is going on, and so they react violently. Our whips and our magics do nothing to move them toward obedience because they do not comprehend pain the same way that we do. It's almost as if the spirits that we have torn from the Void are used to a different way of viewing the world, and when they are encased in obsidian, they lose what little sanity they had before. We just need to learn how to reach them in a way that they can understand. These aren't the simple creatures like earth elementals that we have dealt with before."

"All of that is fascinating, Argoll, and if I cared I'm sure I would be appeased by that bit of information. But I'm not, because I need an army, not a scientific study of the nature of the Void and its inhabitants."

Golloch fixed him with a scowl. "This is your final warning. You have a fortnight to figure this issue out. If you do not, then I am removing you from your duties and sending you back to Diew in chains. I'll let your successor decide in what state you'll be transported, too. If that isn't enough motivation, well, then I can't help you."

Argoll bowed, trying to hide the shaking in his hands, and then retreated from the room. He hurried down to the chambers where the Rift was housed and took his frustrations out on several ratkin slaves; and once that was accomplished, he set himself to work.

Hours passed, and Argoll pushed himself harder and harder to produce results. Between himself and another Iron-caster, they managed to animate three more golems, each with a different method applied. On the first, they carved runes of pain into its back; the creature didn't act any differently than its predecessors. On the next, they tried animating it without limbs to see if they could try to reason with it through their simplistic form of communication, which left Argoll sick as it reminded him of the methods employed by the Stone Priests of his former home. This limbless abomination simply screamed into their minds about incomprehensible images of cosmic horrors so foul that it had set Argoll's assistant to vomiting.

Finally, on their third try, something different had happened. Argoll had crafted a set of rudimentary eyes made from cheap gems and had affixed those to the head of the golem's body. He had woven strands of magic connecting those eyes to every part of the inanimate form before them. Then, when they had summoned a spirit from the Void and had infused it into the prepared body for it, something had changed. The creature had sat up and appeared to look around. But when it appeared to notice its own body, the same screaming that had accompanied the previous attempt filled their minds, and the golem had proceeded to rip itself apart violently.

Now Argoll stood in an empty chamber, the purple light of the Rift casting the walls of the cavern in the dark hues of bruised flesh. The other Iron-casters and slaves had all been sent away, and he was left alone. He cast his eyes about at the ruin of his latest failure as it lay strewn about the floor. Despite this golem's destruction, he had managed to create a small army for Golloch, if one didn't count the fact that the army was feral and refused to follow commands. He sighed and placed his hands against his temples, sinking down to sit on a stool as he did so.

"What am I going to do?" he whispered aloud, and the sound was swallowed by the emptiness around him. The heat of rage was absent in his voice; he was past such emotions, he was empty. The whisper of despair echoed deep into his chest, and he didn't bother fighting to contain it. Exhaustion, anxiety, and fear warred inside him like a tavern brawl that had gone on for far too long, each participant struggling to keep itself upright while the space they occupied was destroyed by their contest. He let the weariness take him, he had no strength left to resist it.

A familiar scent seemed to brush at his nostrils, and he took a deep breath. It was the loamy scent of grass after the first winds of spring had begun to melt the snow. Argoll filled his lungs with the scent and leaned back while closing his eyes. He was transported back in his memory to a far distant time when he had far fewer scars and his fury hadn't yet overcome him as it now did.

He remembered sitting on the side of a hill, the great granite mountains of Halpi soaring high above him as the sun set in the distance. He stared off into the glowing embers of the dying day and felt the cool breeze send a slight chill down his back, but he welcomed the cold. He shivered and pulled his cloak tighter around him. It felt like a dream, or a strange vision. Was it a memory? It had been so long ago, even before the Abyss had expanded and the Free Dwarfs had lost their home in the Halpis.

"Come now, my boy, help me with this fire," Cwythn grumbled from behind him. Argoll turned to stare down at the former stone priest.

"Why are you here, Father?" Argoll spoke, and the memory flickered into place as if it had always been right. Argoll felt the sense of something being off sputter and fade, and he blinked slowly.

"You know why, Anobreth. I'll not leave you to wander in the wilderness on your own."

Anobreth? Argoll thought. *Yes, that was my name, so long ago. Dead names belong in the past. I haven't been Anobreth for some time now, I thought I had killed him when I came to Tragar.* Out loud, he simply said:

"Yes, but I am no longer your son. I have no clan. I have no kin. I am exiled for my sins. You haven't committed any sin. You are not forced to wander."

"You know that's not true. I know why you did what you did, and I know that the chieftain's ruling was wrong. You are a good dwarf, Anobreth. You made a mistake, but you are not evil."

"It wasn't just the chieftain. The stone priests seemed to sense something wrong with me. One spoke of a darkness within me. How else could I be responsible for all those deaths and not feel remorse?"

Cwythn stood up from the small fire he was nursing and looked at Argoll, who couldn't meet his gaze.

"That's a load of *griek* and you know it," the older dwarf said after a long pause.

"Seemed plausible enough to have me banished," Argoll replied, still staring off into the distance.

"You were thinking of your squad! They ordered you into a suicide mission without telling you why, and that makes *you* the one with evil intent? Just because you refused to risk the lives of you and your regiment?"

"Because we let those orcs go, the farming settlement was slaughtered and the flank of our marching column was exposed to their ambushes. Over ten times the number of dwarfs died because of my pride! Because I wouldn't follow orders!"

"If you had, then you would be dead now."

"Dead with honor is better than alive and disgraced!"

"Why? Why is that the case? I don't see it that way!" Cwythn's voice was soft, but there was an edge to it. "Why is it better to be dead than it is to live? You can't enjoy your honor if you are dead!"

"A priest telling me there is no afterlife is hardly what I would call a compelling argument." Argoll found himself suppressing a sneer.

"I am no longer part of the priesthood. I will not deceive you with their comforting lies."

"You call your life's work a lie?" Argoll's eyes narrowed.

"My life's work was you and your mother, the priesthood be damned. The clan can be damned, too."

"My mother is dead, and your son is exiled. I would call your life's work a failure, then."

"Not so long as you are alive, my son. You are my salvation. You always have been."

"Don't you dare put that on me!" Argoll growled, and a strange weight seemed to settle in his chest. "I will not be the reason that your life has meaning! I can't even find meaning in my own existence, much less give it to yours! I am a failure! My best hope is to find some mountain troll or band of goblins and find a glorious and violent death that will suit the sins I've committed to bring me to this point! I will not be your 'salvation,' old dwarf! I cannot save you! I can't even save myself!"

Cwythn took a few steps toward him, his eyes were pained and his hand outstretched.

"Every day you are alive is a victory for me, my boy. Knowing that you still draw breath is enough salvation for this old dwarf."

"A fine sentiment," Argoll felt his throat constricting. He wanted to shut his eyes, he wanted the memory to end, but it refused to be silenced. The next words left his mouth as if torn from his throat. "But we are lost. *I* don't want to live anymore! It is my life's mission right now to ensure that your 'victory' is taken from you! There is nothing left for me! You have your mission to protect me, but I will be your greatest enemy in that regard! I will look for every way to damn you, Father! Do not make me your hope, for I will turn that hope into damnation! My greatest ambition is to meet a violent end. I will not enter into the stone halls of the Earth Mother's embrace. I mean to burn bright, hot, and violent, and I will consume all that are near me. I swear to you, leave me and let my despair take me! It will be better for you and all the rest of this world if that is to be my end. Do not force your salvation on me at the expense of everyone else, for in saving me, you would also condemn me to even more suffering. Let me go!"

Something seemed to shift in the memory of his father's face, some kind of shadow that darkened the light in his eyes. Cwythn stepped forward and extended his hand toward Argoll, who unconsciously flinched back and away from him.

"My dear sweet boy," Cwythn's voice was strained, and a smile stole over his face that seemed slightly too wide for his face. "I already tried to let you go, but then you couldn't leave me alone. You dragged me down into damnation with you, and now my body is cold and empty beneath the stone of Cwl Gen!"

Now the toothy grin spread wide, and Argoll saw that his father's teeth were sharp and pointed, like the jagged spikes of a dragon's mouth. He forced himself not to react, but he slowly began to reach out with his other senses. He knew he couldn't trust his eyes, and his sense of smell was somehow not trustworthy, either. He closed his eyes and pushed out with his magic. He could sense the presence in front of him, it felt like a frozen void of nothingness that spread its mouth wide. Argoll bit his lip to stop from crying out in alarm. Instead, he opened his eye and stared up at the face of his father staring down at him with empty eyes and a mouth that wrapped across where his jawbones should have been. It looked like something that knew what a smile was in a purely theoretical sense and had tried to make it work in a painting or some abstract art.

"Who are you?" he asked, the words coming out slowly and deliberately.

"It's me, dear child, your father!" came the response, though the voice no longer sounded like Argoll's memory of Cwythn; now it sounded like a thousand sibilant whispers chanting the words in unison.

"If you knew anything about me, then you'd know that this is not the means to tempt or trick me. My father and I were not on the most amicable terms last we spoke."

"And yet I can tell that there is sorrow there, maybe even a hint of regret?" The face's grin grew wider somehow, stretching the skin at the corners of its eyes.

"I suppose, what is your point? You still haven't answered my question."

"Why should I? How will that serve my needs?"

"If I knew what those were, then maybe I could be more accommodating."

"Or maybe you would struggle against us. Other things of this world all seem to do so whenever they know of our madness."

"Let me rephrase, then. How can I assist you, or make you go away? Either outcome is fine with me, so long as you leave me in peace at the end."

"You are a strange creature, little dwarf. But I mean you no harm. That is, I wish you no more harm than I do to the stone at your feet, or the sky over your head."

"Forgive me if that is not the most reassuring comfort for me that you may have intended it to be."

"Not at all! You are wise to be wary of me. I am something frightening and new. Most of your world that would call themselves wise would caution you to do the same!"

"You flatter as though you were part of this world. Now, what do you want?"

"We want a conduit. We need a way to pass through the door and return to that which we once knew! We need to return the old glory to its former beauty!"

"You speak in riddles. I don't understand what that means!"

"Come to me and I will tell you in person. It is so much more difficult in this form, I am nearly not real in a dream. It is easier for me to speak in a straightforward way when we come face-to-face."

"How do I do that?"

"Simply take another step, little dwarf." The being that was wearing Cwythn's face took a step back, and Argoll found himself rising to his feet.

"What?" He took a step forward and felt something cold touch his feet. The sensation shocked him, but he could not arrest his forward momentum. Suddenly he saw that he was standing on the edge of a cliff. His step had taken him over the lip and about to careen into the depths far below. He opened his mouth to scream, but nothing escaped his lips as he fell forward slowly.

A hand clamped down on Argoll's shoulder, and he blinked. His eyes focused, and he saw that his face was inches from what looked like a swirling pool of purple water that shifted and rippled in front of him. The hand on his shoulder pulled him backward, and he recognized the Rift's pulsing surface in front of him. A Blacksoul guard stood behind him, keeping him from falling into the portal, a frown permanently frozen on his empty features.

"Wha..." Argoll stammered, and then the horrid realization dawned on him. He threw off the Blacksoul's hand and stalked away from the Rift. He spied several other Iron-casters in the cavern, and they were all staring at him.

"What are you all looking at?!" he bellowed, and they all shrank back from him, knowing the edges of his anger could cut them as surely as a knife could. "Why are you here? Didn't I send you away for the evening?"

"But, my lord, it is morning! We thought you would want to resume testing the Rift with more experiments?"

This caused Argoll to pause. It was morning already?! But it had been the dead of night what felt like only minutes ago! He glanced back at the swirling energies of the Rift. It pulsed steadily, unchanging in its constant motion.

He swore he could hear a woman's laughter on the air.

"Of course!" he growled and turned to begin issuing orders in an effort to suppress the shiver that ran down his spine.

13
The Firing of the Crucible

A crucible is used to melt and purify metals. It involves the process of placing ore in a container and super-heating it so that the metals separate from their impurities in a process known as smelting.

In the dwarf culture, the process of forging and metalwork is an integral part of their society, and as such, they have many sayings that permeate their language which reflect that. One such saying is:

'Crae tân y chrwsibl yn et etwyllthysio.'

This translates, roughly, to: 'The crucible wills it so.' It is meant to be a comfort or explanation for why hard times befall an individual, as it means that fate is working to purify one's life, much the same as how a crucible purifies its metals, through the fires of tribulation.

–Phet Ilysio
Author of 'The Lexicon of the Dwarfs: A study of dwarf linguistics'

The shouting had become a sea of noise, one in which Garrek felt that he was drowning. The fact that the shouting was being done in the open air and *still* threatened to overwhelm him only added to the aggravation that he felt. Ddiangen Afalans's voice was the loudest of all, and this was probably the reason that Garrek's teeth were grinding together and causing the ache to rise from the back of his skull.

"We can't keep this up any longer!" Ddiangen shouted, slamming his fist down on the camp table in the center of the other commanders that had accompanied Rordin in his retreat from the failed peace talks. Banick had been allowed out of his prison tent at long last and revealed to the other dwarfs there. He now stood beside Garrek. A few other dwarf nobles that had followed Rordin from the meeting stood in a huddle a few paces away.

"We have managed to outpace Gruumen thus far," Rordin's voice was loud, but calm. Although Garrek felt he could hear the strain in his words. "I think we have a good chance of escaping him altogether if we shorten our rests and put on a final burst of speed to give us a bit more time to cross the river."

Rordin was referring to the fact that they were about to leave the last of the Abkhazla Mountains and enter the Plains of Difetth. They were roughly about a half day's march ahead of Gruumen and his allies, but there was a problem coming up. A river called the Wyrmtung spread from the Low Sea of Suan almost all the way down to the Infant Sea. It acted as the official division between the mountains and the plains. It was roughly a quarter mile in width, and it ranged in depth from the ability to swallow a fully formed greater earth elemental to only a few feet, but its current was so strong that fording it became nearly impossible in most places.

"We're coming up on Tyr's Crossing, but it will take us most of an entire day to get all of our warriors across the Wyrmtung. Do you think Gruumen will just sit back and wait for us while we file over the bridge?" the Afalans chieftain sneered, and Garrek felt himself bristle at his words, but Ddiangen wasn't finished. "Besides that, we'll be on the early parts of the plains, and Gruumen has artillery. Unlike us who don't have enough blasting powder to light off a spark. He'll be free to rain down fire on us at his leisure while we sit huddled around just waiting for him to pick us off."

"You act as though we haven't already considered this," Rordin replied in a voice that was far calmer than Garrek felt was warranted.

"From everything you've shared, it sure seems as though you haven't!"

"Well, if you would calm yourself enough to listen, Lord Afalans, then it will all be explained." Rordin's eyes could have split a granite boulder as he stared down the loud chieftain before him. Ddiangen seemed to wither under his gaze and stepped back with a sullen glower. Rordin seemed to fight a smile as he turned toward Garrek and nodded at him.

"Master Heavyhand, if you wouldn't mind explaining the plan that you have suggested?" Rordin raised a hand to him while shooting another glare at Ddiangen, which stifled the chieftain's spluttering protests long enough for Garrek to step forward. Garrek couldn't help but smile as he spoke, but his words quickly brought his mood back to the present.

"As you have already pointed out, we are reaching the edge of the Abkhazla Range. In fact, we should be entering the foothills by midday tomorrow at our current pace. That would put us at Tyr's Crossing the following day. But there is almost a day's worth of marching across the flatlands of the plains. Gruumen has artillery, and far more firepower than we do. Most of our troops are Ironclads except for the few rangers that Rordin and I each brought with us. We have no war engines to combat against Gruumen. Plus he has an advantage also in numbers, so facing him in an open fight on the plains would be a massacre. So we shouldn't do that."

"I already said all of that," Ddiangen growled. "What else can you offer besides restating the obvious?"

"Patience, Lord Afalans," Garrek said slowly while trying to prevent his teeth from grinding as he spoke. "The fact of the matter is that we will be unable to beat Gruumen in a straight on fight. But we are reaching the edge of the mountains, and the tunnels that he used to ambush us at the peace talks don't extend out this far, at least according to the maps that I have studied, and Rordin has agreed with my assessment. So he won't be able to use them to get around us."

"But he doesn't need to, does he? All he has to do is keep punching us until we're dead."

"I'm getting there…" Garrek forced himself to break off his words before they turned acidic. "If you'll notice, we currently find ourselves in a valley. There are steep cliff walls to either side of us that extend up to nearly the caps of the smaller peaks around us. This valley follows around the mountain before us before opening out onto the plains. It is there, at the bend in the pass, that we will make our stand against Gruumen. It is our best chance. The valley is narrow enough that we can mitigate his advantage in numbers, and he won't be able to make effective use of his war machines because they won't have room to deploy with any real vantage point."

Ddiangen paused for a moment and looked up from the table with the map. He frowned as he stared down the pass to the spot that Garrek had indicated, then slowly he nodded.

"Alright, I see what you mean. That may be our best chance to defeat the bastard," the older chieftain said at length.

"I don't know that we can fully defeat him here. We cannot press against any retreat that they may make for risk of exposing ourselves to the longer corridor and their artillery." Garrek shook his head as he spoke, shocked that the other dwarf had agreed so quickly to the plan.

"That remains to be seen, doesn't it?" Afalans said.

"That isn't our objective at this time." Rordin leaned forward, his eyes fixed on Ddiangen.

"But if the opportunity presents itself…"

"No! We will not overextend ourselves. This battle is about survival, not glory," Rordin cut him off, and the older dwarf shook his head.

"We shall see. Remember, you are not our king, and you have said that you will not be so, or did I misunderstand you?"

"No, you did not, at least in that regard."

"Then do not presume to give me orders. I have been fighting in battles since before you were born. I know when to play my hand and when to hold back."

"Actually, it will be Garrek that you must take your orders from. He has the largest force here, and so his troops will form the center of our defensive line. He will be in the best position to issue commands for the upcoming battle, and last I checked, he had a much higher amount of victories to his name than you do, Lord Afalans." Rordin glanced over at Garrek and gave him a small smile. Garrek, in turn, felt the heat rising on the back of his neck. What was Rordin doing? They couldn't afford to antagonize Ddiangen at this point!

"The Oathbreaker?! No! I will not take orders from him."

"I..." Garrek began, but he was surprised to see Banick jump in before he could get his words out.

"That is not your choice, though! Gruumen is ruthless, he will take every inch that you give him, and he will strangle you with what's left." Banick's voice held an edge of panic.

"I would expect a freeloading dwarf such as yourself to side with the Oathbreaker, but I will not listen to either of you."

"You arrogant..." The insult was in the middle of leaving Garrek's mouth when the whole meeting was silenced by Rordin's voice.

"Enough!" he bellowed, and all eyes turned to see him. "We are all equals here, are we not?"

"*Some* of us are equals," Ddiangen growled.

"Well, even if you only accept me as a fellow commander, and Garrek as a secondary one, it is still mine and Garrek's votes against your singular one. In order for us to prevail, Lord Afalans, we must be willing to see past our old prejudices. The days ahead are already going to be difficult with few allies we can trust. Let us not dismiss a capable friend simply because tradition wills it so."

"You speak like a human, or worse, like an elf."

"I speak sensibly. Logic is what we prize as dwarfs, do we not?"

"Rightly so."

"Then logic dictates that soldiers are more willing to follow a commander whom they know and respect. Most of our warriors are from Garrek's camp. I don't know about you, but I think that most of his troops would not act favorably to your commands, since you have expressed so vocally your disdain for the Heavyhand Clan. They might even refuse your orders as they think you may be throwing their lives away, as it is obvious that you do not value them. Is my logic sound to your ears?" Rordin's tone was short and clipped, but he paused to glare at Ddiangen meaningfully.

"The curs would dare to disobey an order from their commander? That only confirms that my judgments on their character are correct."

Garrek bristled, but he forced himself to remain calm. He trusted Rordin, and whatever he was doing now wouldn't be helped by him blowing up at the Afalans's chieftain.

"That only further proves my point. If your judgment is sound, then they will not follow you. I have only a small force of my retainers, so I do not know them either. Ergo, Garrek must be the one to command the coming battle."

"And why should my soldiers follow his orders, then? If they would not follow mine?"

"Because," Rordin said, and his voice dropped into a gravelly tone as he stared across at the Afalans's chieftain, "they want to live as much as the rest of us." Garrek shivered at the sounds of violence hiding in Rordin's words.

"Is that a threat?" Ddiangen tried to puff his chest out, but he could not hide the hitch in his voice.

"No, it isn't." Rordin looked like some kind of predatory animal preparing to lunge on its prey. "If we are not united in the coming battle, it will not end well for any of us, and many of our clansdwarfs will die. A threat sounds more like this, Lord Afalans: Banick is my guest, and if you insult him again, then I will personally make sure that it will be the last time."

This time, the older dwarf was not prepared with some kind of retort, and instead turned and walked away while the rest of the crowd dispersed shortly thereafter. Eventually it was just Banick, Rordin, and Garrek left standing at the table, and Rordin let out a long sigh.

"That was… impressive," Garrek said at length, and Rordin shot him a broken smile.

"I really shouldn't be antagonizing our ally when we are still so early on in this conflict." Rordin grimaced and then brought his hands up to scrub at his face. "We're only just beginning to fight against Golloch, and already we're walking on a razor's edge. If we can't push Gruumen back here and escape, I don't know if the southern clans will have the spirit to unite against Golloch. It is imperative that we win this fight, Garrek. This all rests with you."

"What is his problem, anyways?" Banick asked. "Sure, Garrek's family has its history, but hasn't Garrek's victories won him some reprieve from that reputation?"

"That will never happen," Garrek said slowly. "He hates us for what we represent. A clan that manages to continue existing even though it has no right to do so. What my grandsire did was unforgivable, and it should have resulted in the dissolution of my clan, yet it didn't. My father's lackluster leadership only cemented that legacy."

"But that shouldn't give him the right to treat you like that."

"Propriety and respect are an inheritance amongst us Imperials," Garrek shrugged. "My only birthright was scorn and disillusionment. My grandsire took on an impossible debt, and that is the only thing that has passed to the generations since. I have worked hard to repay it, but the scales will never balance in my favor. Perhaps if I'd had children, they would have eventually broken through the issue, but that wasn't a problem that I was willing to pass on, so I never had any."

"Banick's right, though," Rordin cut in, "you don't deserve this treatment anymore. I have long suspected that many of the clans hold it over you because they are simply afraid and intimidated by you, and this is the only way that they will be able to hold you down. You've done more than enough to make amends, and the clan that you've built! Garrek, you've taken the discarded and disillusioned members of our society and you've given them hope and a purpose! Your clan now consists of the supposed dregs of Imperial society, and with them you have created one of the most impressive forces we have had in the empire!"

"I appreciate the kind words, but they don't change the reality of our present situation. Ddiangen is a traditional dwarf, and tradition among the dwarfs is that I and my clan are outcasts. We will never have the respect of the others, and that will likely cause you only grief, Rordin."

"I'll be damned to the Abyss for this, Garrek, but I will find a way to fix that if it's within my power somehow. I don't know how, but you are worth more than a dozen Ddiangens." Rordin's voice was hard as he spoke, and Garrek smiled sadly at him.

"You shouldn't say such things, Rordin, they'll accuse you of favoring a clan that is devoid of honor."

"And why should I care what they say of me? I'm not going to be king, I have no desire for their approval. I see a wrong before me and I mean to see it fixed."

"Besides, Garrek," Banick added, "you're talking to two fellow outcasts. I chose exile and fell from grace, and Rordin has avoided decent society for so long that many players in the political world have forgotten him as he tries to dodge his uncle's shadow. We know that real value is not always reflected in one's reputation, especially when that reputation is second-hand."

"I am glad that I have such friends as you," Garrek responded and clapped both of the other dwarfs on their shoulders. "However, you are the exception that proves the rule. The majority of the clans have functioned on the basis of familial reputation for thousands of years at this point, and I don't see that changing any time soon. Now, if you'll excuse me, I need to start making preparations for the coming battle that will hopefully see us to safety."

He didn't wait for their replies and instead walked past them quickly, plastering what he hoped was a convincing smile on his face as he did so.

14
A Matter of Pride

> *Garrek Heavyhand is known throughout the world. He is one of the most feared and respected dwarfs in living memory. None other, Golloch included, have the variety of names and curses used to refer to him among the other races of Pannithor than he does. What does that say about us that we hold him in such low regard amongst our own clans? That the only title we have bestown upon him is that of Oathbreaker?*
>
> *–Rordin the Dwarf*

"By the Earth Mother, this is tedious work, isn't it?" Banick grumbled as he stifled a yawn.

"The best battles to fight are those that are boring. Exciting battles make for good stories but terrible memories." Garrek shifted uncomfortably from one foot to the other, trying to find a stance that was most comfortable.

They stood about fifty yards from the bend in the valley. A cold morning wind whistled amongst the stone peaks high above them as the shadows crept slowly back into the nooks and crannies of the rock walls around them. The sun wouldn't penetrate the gloom fully until almost midday, and as such, the air was cold and felt heavy, like someone had covered them with a damp blanket.

"Rordin could be halfway to the river by now. Why hasn't he left?" Banick rubbed his hands together and looked back to the rear of their forces. Their relatively small army spread out behind them for a good ways, to the point where Banick wasn't sure where Rordin would actually be.

"Doesn't want the troops to think that he's abandoned them," Garrek replied.

"But surely they know what's at stake here, don't they? They should understand why he can't stay."

"Knowing something and feeling it are two different things, though, aren't they? Having him here makes them think that he has faith in them to win the day. Leaving would be a sign of no-confidence, even if it makes more sense. They'll fight harder because he stays."

"We are a contradictory bunch, aren't we?" Banick sighed, and Garrek shot him a raised eyebrow.

"What do you mean?"

"Well, we talk about our actions and how we do what we say, and honor and logic and reason and all of that, but at the core of everything we do, we are just as emotional as any elven maid in Elvenholme."

"Don't let Ddiangen hear you say that. I'm offended by it, and I like you. Imagine how he'd take it."

"I imagine his head might explode as all the blood would rush to his forehead." Banick chuckled, and Garrek couldn't help join him as the macabre image formed in his own head.

"I think that emotion and reason are two parts of the same thing. You can't make a decision without consulting both," Garrek said after a few moments of silence.

"I don't disagree, but our society as a whole might. Emotion is seen as a negative thing, unless it's anger over some perceived slight or pride in one's ancestry or accomplishments. Fear, doubt, sadness, dissatisfaction, all of these things are looked down on, yet those are the emotions that inform our decisions more than anything else."

"Are they?" Garrek shot Banick a look of confusion that was only slightly disturbed by the nervous smile he wore with it.

"Well, among others..." Banick shrugged and gave a small laugh.

"I think you gave up more information about yourself than you really meant to there, my friend. Has fear guided your actions more than hope? More than love, or a desire to see your home again?"

"I see your point. It's possible that our current circumstances might have colored my own perceptions." Banick shook his head.

"You can be downright melancholic at times, you know that?"

"I would say our circumstances warrant a little melancholy, wouldn't you?"

"As long as you leave some for the rest of us, you sad, little, *griek*." They both chuckled at that, but then an uncomfortable silence once again settled over them. The wind whistled through the cold air as if trying to fill the emptiness with sound. It only came across as a pitiful cry.

"Always the worst part, the waiting," Banick grumbled. Garrek only nodded.

"Why are you up here, though?" Garrek asked without looking up. "Not that I mind having you here, but you could be back with Rordin in relative safety."

"Didn't feel right. I'm not important enough for that spot."

"You can't be serious!" Garrek harrumphed. "You're the one that brought Golloch's treachery to Rordin's attention. You're the one who basically started all of this. If that doesn't make you worthy of standing beside him, then I don't know what will."

"That's not what I meant. I'm not an Imperial like you. I'm an outsider, and one that has caused a lot of problems, too. Besides, my usefulness to Rordin has been spent at this point. I thought that my time would be better spent up here on the front, with you."

"With your fellow pariah, huh?"

"Well... yeah, actually." Banick smiled, and Garrek couldn't help but return the gesture.

"I'm glad to have you with me, then." Garrek's smile became pensive, and his eyes turned back to the bend in the valley, but they refused to focus on anything in particular. "I don't think I've told you how much your friendship really means to me. You're one of the few who has freely given it to me. Probably one of the only ones who hasn't required me to earn that friendship in one way or another. It's not something that I am used to. But I really do appreciate it." Banick didn't respond for a few moments, and the silence filled Garrek with trepidation.

"Now who's the one being melancholic?" Banick said. Garrek laughed and was surprised at the ferocity of the sound. He wanted to say something else, but before the words could form, there came the blast of a warhorn in the distance.

"They're here," he said instead.

*****

The noise was different than most battles that Garrek was accustomed to. The lack of artillery and the concussive sounds of black powder igniting left him with a sense of being exposed, like there was something wrong, but he couldn't place it. The sensation left him feeling unnerved, but he forced himself to think of it as a good sign. It meant that the enemy was unable to use their biggest advantage in the fight, and this was the biggest sign that their strategy was working.

This is not to say that the battle was a quiet affair, either. The sounds of metal clashing against metal, the screams of the dying and the warcries of the living, mixed with the stomping of thousands of boots all combined to create a grand cacophony of sound that threatened to overwhelm him.

He looked out over the mass of struggling bodies that writhed all around him. Because the battle took place where they had designed it, there was no missile fire from either side, and the entire affair was one large mass of violent brawls. It was easily one of the most violent scenes that Garrek had ever witnessed, and as he looked out over the shoulders of his troops, he couldn't help but feel sorrow for what he beheld. He stood on a small boulder that lifted him just a few feet above his fellow warriors, and it gave him the feeling that he was standing on a small island surrounded by rivers of dwarf blood.

Melancholy aside, however, the battle seemed to be progressing well for Rordin and his allies. Gruumen had been unable to make any headway in the hour since the battle had begun. Thus far, the Afalans to the left had held their ground for the most part, but Garrek had needed to send messengers regularly reminding them to pull back as they continued to inch forward from their initial position. Rordin's troops to Garrek's right held firm against the constant onslaught in a true stoicism worthy of their race. But fatigue was beginning to take its toll on both sides of the fight.

"Brekka!" he bellowed, and a rough-faced dwarf looked up at him. "Start initiating regimental swaps down the line! Have each unit currently fighting on the front step back, one at a time, and push in a fresh group to rotate through. I won't have our dwarfs dying from exhaustion!"

"Aye, sir!" the rough dwarf grinned up at him and began yelling colorful insults accompanied with commands that were equally as colorful. Garrek watched him walk away and nodded to himself.

"Things look much better from up here!" Banick grunted breathlessly as he practically threw himself on the boulder, beside where Garrek was standing.

"I think it's going about as well as we could hope for," Garrek replied without looking down at him.

"Yeah well, it isn't easy to understand that when your only view is the enemy dwarf right in front of you."

"Agreed, that's why we're swapping regiments out. The front fighters need some reprieve. The tunnel vision of bloodlust is a damnable thing and will get you killed as surely as an axe to your chest."

"Such poetry you speak." Banick wiped the grime and viscera off of his face.

"This is a working day," Garrek spat out of the corner of his mouth, "this is no time for poetry. *Uff'ran!* Gilwyd! Send a runner over to that damnable Ddiangen and tell him to pull his troops back! He's almost pushed the Ashtels to the edge of the bend! If he keeps going, they'll be able to pummel them to death with their cannons and artillery!"

*****

Ofn smiled to himself as he surveyed the battlefield, even though his side was losing. Part of him was proud to see Garrek's banner in the center of the opposing army. Garrek, who was the outcast of the people he was constantly striving to help, had finally risen to the top – for at least this battle. He felt no small amount of regret at having to be the one to tear his friend's victory away from him.

He cast his mind back to the tirade that Gruumen had given that morning to the chieftains that had followed him. His words had echoed across the crisp morning air as the Ashtel lord had half berated the other commanders with a speech that Ofn had assumed was meant to inspire them.

"Today," Gruumen had declared, "we have the opportunity to end this civil war before it even begins! If we can defeat Rordin here and now, then we can stop the sundering of the empire even as it stands on the precipice of greatness! Golloch cannot stand to wait for an usurper to be put down now, not at the most crucial moment of the plan for which we have all worked so hard to achieve! Slaughter these traitors and grind their corpses into the mud beneath your boots! They will not stand in the way of the destiny which Golloch has prepared for them! Absolute unity lies on the other side of this conflict! They have nowhere to flee! The river ahead cuts them off from escape, and there is no way for them to make the crossing without leaving themselves vulnerable. If we cannot carry this victory, then perhaps we are unworthy of that glory! Go now, and do not disappoint me in your efforts. Glory awaits!"

Ofn shook his head at the memory. The speech had been met with confused cheers, and anxiety had been high as the battle had commenced. No doubt Gruumen was frothing at the mouth due to the lack of progress the army had made over the course of the day. But Rordin had been clever to pick this particular battlefield. A good portion of Gruumen's firepower was wasted on this fight, unable to set up in any way that would be useful. Even though they had the superior numbers, the narrow confines of the valley evened the fight considerably.

But Ofn knew something of the pride of the dwarfs.

He looked out across the way at the Afalans Clan across from where he stood, and he gripped the weapon in his hands. Behind him stood a dwarf holding the personal sigil of Gruumen Ashtel, an anvil in the likeness of a fist. He'd borrowed it from Gruumen's personal tent without permission. The fabric waved softly in a light breeze. It was the perfect bait for the trap that Ofn had in mind.

"Stick close to me and make sure that banner stays upright and high above the press, you understand?" he muttered to the standard bearer, who nodded grimly behind him.

Ofn placed his helm on his head, its crest adorned with the Ashtel clan colors of black and white, and hefted a shield which bore the same sigil as that of the flag behind him. He then began shouldering his way through the press of dwarf warriors, making his way slowly toward the sound of combat.

Before he knew it, he found himself directly across from the silver and blue tabards of the Afalans. He hefted the heavy hammer in his hand and brought it down on the helm before him. The metal collapsed under the weight of the mallet, and blood gushed out from under the visor's edge before the dwarf toppled to the ground. Ofn didn't slow and quickly brought down another warrior who turned to face him. The hammer rose and fell in practiced motions, much like a miner hewing at stone.

Ofn had always preferred the terror that a warhammer caused in his victims. There was something so visceral about the snapping of bones caused by the weight of a weapon. Blunt force trauma was far more shocking than the cleaving edges of blades. The sight of a head being cut from one's shoulders had a certain shock value, but the screams that came from the hammer slamming down to crush the small bones of an exposed ankle or the gurgling cries of a crushed sternum were far more terrifying to hear.

Ofn's ferocious attack quickly had the desired effect. The enemy warriors before him pressed back, each one glancing nervously at the mostly dead dwarfs around him. Ofn tried to avoid outright killing when possible. The suffering of the fallen was the perfect weapon for both either a torture chamber or a battlefield.

Beneath his helm, Ofn grinned and raised his hammer once more to strike.

*****

Garrek saw the banner and something twisted in his gut.

"Why is Gruumen in the middle of the fighting?" he wondered aloud. Banick followed his gaze and looked out over the battle.

"Could it be a champion or something of that sort?"

"I don't know, but those are his personal colors. It would suggest that he is the one in that armor. From what I've heard, he's actually a rather formidable fighter. Maybe he's come to bolster that side of the fight? The Afalans have been giving them quite the beating today."

"I don't know," Banick shrugged, "but maybe it provides an opportunity? What if Ddiangen is able to capture him? Even if it's just a champion, wouldn't that be a blow to the enemy's morale?"

"Maybe," Garrek grunted, "but something doesn't feel right about it at all. Why would Gruumen risk himself in such a way? They outnumber us and haven't seen a sufficient loss of troops to make them as desperate as that."

"It seems to be working, though, look!" Banick pointed, and Garrek nodded. The Ashtels were pushing the Afalans back. The line was moving slowly, but it was a perceptible shift. Garrek bit his lip anxiously.

"Ddiangen better not do anything foolish," he muttered under his breath. But even as he spoke, he looked over and saw the Afalans chieftain making his way toward the thick of the fighting, his own standard bearer following him to mark his progress.

"No! The bloody fool!" Garrek hissed.

"What?! What's happening?!" Banick asked.

"Ddiangen is moving to challenge Gruumen!"

"Can he beat him?"

"I don't know, Ddiangen is a good warrior, but it's a risky bet any way you look at it. What if he falls?" Garrek turned and bellowed for a messenger. "Tell Ddiangen to pull back! We can't have him taking such big risks! Get over there and tell him to stand down!"

Even as he sent the messenger off, though, he knew that he wouldn't make it in time. The twisting in his gut grew worse.

*****

Ofn smiled as he saw the Afalans chieftain moving through the press toward him. He took a few steps back and allowed the soldiers around him to close the gap before him. Then he turned and spoke to the standard bearer.

"Sound the retreat! Ordered withdrawal!"

The dwarf nodded and raised a horn to his lips, giving three prolonged blasts that echoed throughout the valley. Three other horn blasts from across the battlefront replied, and Ofn nodded to himself in satisfaction. Then he took the horn from the banner dwarf and tucked it in his own belt. He snatched the standard out of the dwarf's hands, too.

"Go and make sure the artillery is in position for when we pull around the bend. I want them to open fire on signal, and not a moment sooner, you understand?" He didn't wait to see the other dwarf's response and instead turned back to the fighting. The warriors around him were making a fighting retreat, slowly and steadily, one step back for each stroke they made with their axes and hammers.

He hovered at the edge of the fighting. Staying just outside of the combat, but within sight of the Afalans banner as it drew closer to him. Just like a fly to a honey trap. Ofn took note of their location as they continued to fall back. They were now level with the bend in the valley, just a little bit further. The enemy banner seemed to have slowed its advance. Ofn growled and grabbed a nearby warrior, thrusting the banner into his hands.

"Stay right behind me, do not let us get separated, no matter what happens, you understand?" he snarled, the other dwarf's helmet bobbed in acknowledgement, and Ofn stepped back into the fighting, swinging his hammer around to crush in the chest of an unfortunate blue-clad warrior before him.

The hammer rose and fell, and soon Ofn's hands were numb from the constant collisions of his weapon with metal and bone. He felt the breath burning in his lungs and the sweat that dripped from his brows under the oppressive heat of the helm which he wore.

The Afalans chieftain stood before him, shield in one hand bearing the blue bar slashed diagonally across a white field, the other hand holding a simple bearded axe. The chieftain extended his axe out toward Ofn and called out to him.

"Fight me, you filthy traitor!"

Ofn did not bother to respond, he simply launched himself forward, swinging his hammer down in an overhead attack that would have crushed most anything that got in its way. Ofn was somewhat surprised when his blow was arrested mid-swing by the other dwarf's shield. The weight of his hammer bounced off the metal rim of the diamond-shaped armor and sent a shockwave of force up the shaft that Ofn felt in his shoulders. He staggered back in surprise, and his opponent capitalized on his backward momentum by taking a few quick swipes with his axe at him. Ofn threw himself backward even further in a desperate attempt to avoid the edge of the axe blade.

Ofn jabbed the head of his hammer forward like one would thrust a spear and punched his opponent in the chest hard enough to throw him backward a step. He then followed up with a quick swing aimed at the chieftain's knee. This was blocked by the shield again, and Ofn was quickly forced to step back to avoid another series of attacks from the enemy's axe.

One of the chieftain's strikes caught him across the shin and sent him sprawling onto his side, and he rolled onto his back just in time to block his opponent's axe with the haft of his hammer as it came hurtling toward his face. He twisted his hammer and the blade went wide, and he slammed the butt of his hammer's handle into the chieftain's stomach. He pushed up hard and flipped the older dwarf over to land on his back. Ofn sprang quickly to his feet and glanced up at the bend in the valley. They were losing ground quickly now.

He looked once more to the fight and had to dodge back as the axe again came within inches of his face. He could see that his opponent was tiring. But it wasn't time just yet.

Ofn backed up warily, leaning on his hammer and breathing hard. The Afalans chieftain roared another challenge and charged forward, Ofn responded by backing up desperately. Several times he almost fell over fallen corpses beneath them. The blood turned the dirt into a gory mud that threatened to slip out from under him at every step. He dodged blow after blow, but he didn't strike back except for a few tired swings when his opponent seemed to slow to catch his breath.

Finally, Ofn looked behind him and saw the valley open up. The time had come.

In one swift motion, he ducked under the Afalans's blow, spinning as he did so, and used the momentum of his body to bring the hammer down on the chieftain's exposed knee. There was a sickening crunching noise, and the older dwarf fell forward onto the ground with a sharp cry. Ofn stood and quickly brought his hammer around for another blow, this one fell on the hand that gripped the chieftain's axe, pulping it into a gory mess and bringing another howl of pain from the downed dwarf.

Ofn reached a hand down and pushed the Afalans chieftain onto his back so that he could look into his face. The older dwarf glared up at him with a strange mixture of fear and anger. Ofn removed his helm and stared back for a short moment. Then he extended a hand and launched a ball of fire into the air. It arced over the heads of the pursuing Afalans who had crossed the protective boundary of the valley and erupted into a wall of heat that cut them off from retreating. He then blasted the ground a few feet in front of him, and a similar inferno extended across the battlefield, closing the trap around the Afalans.

The Ashtel troops fell back another fifty yards or so before forming up and halting their retreat. Seconds later, the resounding concussive reports of artillery fire were heard. Explosions soon followed among the lines of the confined Afalans that had followed their leader's reckless advance.

Ofn looked down into the pained expression on the chieftain's face. He relished the fear and despair that he saw there. Then he raised his hammer high above his head and brought it down with a sickening crunch that smashed that look into a thousand, bloody pieces.

*****

"*Uff'ran!"* Garrek cursed. "Order the retreat!"

"What just happened?" Banick asked.

"We just lost our entire left flank and almost the entirety of the Afalans Clan in one fell swoop!" Garrek growled.

"But we're doing well with the rest of the battle, can't we still hold them?"

"The enemy can now sweep around and hit us from two fronts. They have the advantage of numbers, and if they can get a decent enough foothold, they can bring their artillery around to begin bombarding our rear troops. What do you fancy our chances are if they manage that feat?"

"But what are we going to do instead, then?"

"If we retreat now, we get to the bridge, get Rordin across, and then hold them off for as long as we can so that Rordin can make it to Dolgarth and has a chance of holding out until more help arrives."

"That's a terrible plan."

"True, but it's better than staying here and simply dying while being overwhelmed. If we retreat now, it gives us some time before they can get their artillery around and begin attacking us with it."

Banick didn't reply to this, and Garrek didn't pursue the argument. Instead he looked out over the battlefield as the horn blasts signalling the retreat rang out. He felt a creeping despair that clutched at his chest and he stared sadly at the collapsing lines before forcing himself to turn away and begin his plans for what he was going to say to Rordin.

He also began to mentally tally the dead and add their names to his list of penances.

15
Inherent Value

> *Ah yes, the dwarfs are fantastic creators! Among the finest crafters of any who live among all the breadth of Pannithor. But they have the single greatest disadvantage that an inventor could ever be cursed with: a reverence for tradition!*
>
> *They wouldn't recognize a good idea unless it comes furnished with a full pedigree chart and two letters of recommendation. Tradition is the death of innovation.*
>
> *–Lopen Weedrop*
> *Halfling Tinkerer and*
> *World-renowned Showman*

The moon shined silver across the rippling currents of the Wyrmtung as it strained against its banks, hurrying south and away to the Infant Sea beyond. The sound of muted marching acted like distant thunder beaten into a regimented drumming of a thousand boots in lockstep.

Garrek looked on in forlorn melancholy as the moon continued its steady climb into the night sky. His neck and shoulders felt tight, and a wide strip of aching weariness wrapped itself around his head. He glanced behind him toward the foothills where Gruumen's army had stopped their pursuit, at least that was what his scouts had reported. It was likely that Gruumen's forces were as exhausted as Rordin's. Rather than pursuing them out onto the foothills, they knew that the river was a natural chokepoint; that they would be able to catch their prey tomorrow before they had all gotten across the bridge.

He shifted over to look at Tyr's Crossing. The bridge itself was made of sturdy timbers, with stone pillars extending down into the swirling depths of the river beneath it. It was a sturdy bridge built by dwarfs. It was wide enough that five soldiers could make the crossing side by side without touching shoulders. A large wooden awning was built over the top that was reinforced with iron bands that could provide cover from a storm to any travelers that might be passing by. Heavy embankments were carved out of both sides of the river and were fortified with additional supports.

Garrek moved closer to where the bridge met the bank, stepping beneath the bridge itself. Above his head, the wooden cross beams shuddered under the footfalls of soldiers passing by. Something glittered in the reflected light of the river. At first, Garrek had thought it was merely the moonlight playing off the ripples in the water, but as he drew near, he saw something metallic bouncing the light of the reflections off the embankment in a tantalizing yellow hue tinged with rainbow edges.

Was it gold? Garrek leaned further toward the embankment, reaching up a hand to brush against the wall. Dirt came away to further reveal the material, and Garrek found himself grinning despite his current melancholy.

Pyrite. It was fool's gold. Veins of the stuff split the rest of the stone that made up the embankment like a spider's web.

He reached into his satchel and pulled out the small pouch that Mendeleev and Mimir had gifted him, remembering their words about his worth.

"Think that we'll make it before morning?" Rordin asked, coming up to stand beside Garrek, shocking him out of his reverie.

"You should already be across and making your way to Dolgarth with an entourage," Garrek grunted in response. He reached up a hand and rubbed his forehead in an attempt to ward off the fatigue that made him want to lie down right where he was and just fall asleep.

"What good would that do? It would just dishearten our troops, and without them, even if I make it to Dolgarth, I won't be able to do anything but surrender once Gruumen arrives with his army."

"Then don't stop at Dolgarth. Head north to the Golden Horn. Seek refuge with the Basileans. Even Golloch couldn't touch that city."

"That would be tantamount to admitting defeat, though. The end result would be the same as surrender. Worse, because it would make me look like a coward."

"But you would be alive. Maybe the humans would be willing to help you fight back, even. After all, if Golloch really has gone over to the Abyss, then they will likely be his first target once he has subjugated all of us. The combined might of three nations, and with infernal aid, might be more than even the Hegemon could handle."

"And I would be trading one tyrant for another. Golloch would simply be replaced with the Hegemon, for we would be indebted to him as surely as we would be enslaved by Golloch. The chains might be more comfortable under Basilea, but that wouldn't erase their presence." Rordin sighed heavily and squatted down on his heels. He reached down, began pulling stones from the riverbank, and tossed them out to have them splash into the water.

"So what will you do?" Garrek asked.

"I don't know, Garrek." Rordin paused. When he spoke again, his voice was tinged with sadness. "I think I'll do the only thing I can.

I'll go down fighting. We'll send out messengers telling of our defeat and the underhanded tactics that Gruumen used. Perhaps our sacrifice will inspire others to rise up and fight. We'll warn them of Golloch's treachery and let them know that he has allied himself with our enemy."

"There has to be something else," Garrek began, but he couldn't think of what else to say.

"What else could there be? Even if we were able to make the crossing, the bridge is still here for Gruumen to use. He'll catch us on the flatlands and blast us into oblivion. The only source of any meaningful method would be to have Banick light the bridge on fire with his magic. But we wouldn't be able to get everyone across before Gruumen and his troops reach us, and even if we cross the river completely and light it on fire, they'll just put it out before the bridge is destroyed. At least if I face him on my terms then I can make him pay, and we can send off messengers that will tell our side of the story. Remember that there are other nobles who saw what he did at the peace talks. There will still be a chance that the other clans will fight back."

"But Gruumen already has so many cautionary tales," Garrek spoke, and he felt his chest constrict at the harshness that he found in his voice. "Between you, and the Ffionen Clan, now the Afalans as well, he has successfully crushed three popular leaders who have tried to oppose him. Even if Ddiangen's sons rise up to avenge him, will they be able to gain support from the other clans when they see the fate that has befallen all else who attempted to fight? Why would they? So that they can end up like Ithel? And for all we know, Cerrig is dead, too. The whole Ffionen line ended for daring to simply be in the way of Golloch's ambition."

"What do you want from me, Garrek?" Rordin's reply was not heated, there was no anger in his voice, only weariness. "I am not the leader that our people need. My parents were not beloved. The only reason people look at me is that Golloch once named me his heir because he didn't have any children of his own. I am laughed at because of my raucous lifestyle as an adventurer, which is justly earned. I marched right into Gruumen's trap because I felt the need to defeat Golloch on the terms and traditions of our people. It seems fitting that my fate has been brought about by my hubris. I can't think of a death more fitting for a dwarf." He gave a humorless laugh and threw another rock into the stream.

Garrek stared down at him. His mouth opened several times to protest against what Rordin was saying, but nothing came out. Everything he thought to say felt trivial and patronizing. He clenched his fists, and again he felt the small pouch of pyrite in his hand. He lifted it up and poured the contents into his palm. The small chunk of rock glittered deceptively in the dark.

"Here, look at this," he said and held the fool's gold out to Rordin. The other dwarf took it and gave him a wry smile.

"That's an apt metaphor for our conversation. I feel a certain kinship with this rock. It looks valuable, when in reality, it is worthless. Just like me."

"Oh, for Fulgria's sake!" Garrek cursed and Rordin raised an eyebrow, opening his mouth to say something, but Garrek cut him off. "Just listen! You are acting as if you're like this lump of pyrite here. That you have no inherent value, that you're worthless, that you haven't accomplished anything. I say you need to get off your ass and quit complaining so much!"

Rordin's eyebrows raised even further in response to this, but Garrek barrelled on.

"You have reclaimed Dolgarth, our empire's ancient capital. You have saved lives through your adventures, and I have witnessed how you have risen to command these past few days. The clans respond to you. They respect you. More than anything else, they are looking to you to see how they should respond to these unprecedented events because you are different from the rest of dwarf society! If you haven't noticed, we as a race are not good at adapting to change, especially when that change is within our own ranks. Yet you are the one who is navigating this business. You are the one who has taken charge. You have claimed responsibility for our people, and the reason that they listen is because you *aren't* the same as others. Your value is different to the other clans and their leaders. This causes some resentment, but it also makes you ideal to lead us through this crisis."

Here, Garrek paused and Rordin gave him a sad smile.

"I appreciate your kind words," he said at length, "but I do not want to be that leader. I doubt others would want me to have it either. Besides, it is a moot point, because we are likely to die soon, and then we will be beyond the cares of what our society thinks anyways."

"But that's just it," Garrek was surprised by the heat in his voice. "You aren't what tradition dictates is the most honorable. Tradition is well and good, even necessary at times, but it is also the reason that we are in this predicament. Golloch weaponized our legacies and expectations. He used them to hide his intentions under a veneer of 'honor' when all he was doing was using the privilege of his station to set himself up to dominate and enslave us. Yet you, in all of your adventures, you have only ever sought glory, never power. Most nobles of the major clans have gotten by these days by following Golloch's lead and calling great feats of violence as 'honorable,' yet you do not value the same things. That makes you better suited to lead us in this because you are able to see things that others overlook. You are an ally to those who are often times forgotten by our people. Like me."

Garrek paused again, feeling his throat tighten at this admission. He coughed and forced himself to continue.

"You have been a friend to me when most others see an outcast. Because of that, I would gladly give my life for you if you asked it of me. These are not traits that our society generally holds as worthy of praise…" Garrek broke off here and glanced down sadly at the Warp Hammer that hung at his side. He felt the pressure there, the burden. It was a powerful artefact and the ultimate reminder of his family's shame. He touched it with the tips of his fingers, and he could feel Rordin's eyes watching him closely. "...but perhaps it's time that some of those traditions were changed."

His voice was a choked whisper by the end, and he felt a tear escape down the side of his face despite his best efforts to force it back. A weariness stole over him that had nothing to do with the fatigue from the battle. He was exhausted as the decades and even centuries of his existence seemed to settle on his shoulders like a mountain.

The weight of that mountain was grinding his bones into ash.

He felt Rordin's hand on his shoulder, but he couldn't bring himself to look the other dwarf in the eye. He took a deep, shuddering breath and willed the concussive forces in his chest to stillness.

"Garrek, you have done…" Rordin began, but Garrek cut him off with a sudden glare, a sheet of hot anger flashing through the heavy grief.

"Don't!" he growled. "That only makes it worse. If I hear one more friend tell me how much I have accomplished with my life, how much good I have done… It may very well kill me. Because despite all of my efforts, I am still an outcast! I am still a name that is said with an accompanying bout of phlegm that is spat on the ground. I…" he forced himself to stop and took another deep breath. He steeled himself and looked directly at Rordin's face. There was hurt there, but no anger. No blame.

"I'm sorry about that, Rordin. I do not blame you for any of this. I do not blame anyone, or at least I try not to. I'm sorry that you had to see that."

They stood in silence for a long stretch of time. Finally, Garrek straightened his shoulders and stretched his neck.

"For now we have the problem of getting across the river, and stopping Gruumen once we do so." He forced a smile onto his face and shrugged. "Sometimes it helps to focus on the problems in front of you rather than the bigger ones that hang around like an unwanted relative."

Rordin stared at him for a few moments longer, then he lifted his gaze to look at the bridge overhead.

"If we could somehow destroy the bridge behind us, then Gruumen would have to march twenty miles upstream where the river levels off and it's possible to ford across. It would give us a couple days' lead on him, and we could easily reach Dolgarth ahead of him." Rordin's voice was strained. "Unfortunately, I don't think there is a single keg of black powder in the entirety of the camp. We have no artillery, and if you take all the powder possessed by every one of our rifles, you still wouldn't have enough to make a dent in this bridge. We could take our axes to it, but it would take us several days to tear it down."

Something niggled at the back of Garrek's mind, and he glanced down at the small pouch that had held the pyrite. Then he looked up at the deceptive glitter emanating from the bridge's embankment. He stared for several long moments, then his eyes widened and he turned back to Rordin.

"I may have a solution to that problem!" he said and stepped past the younger dwarf; he spoke over his shoulder as he moved. "Wait here! I'll be back shortly!"

*****

"What's this about, Garrek?" Mendeleev muttered while rubbing the sleep from his eyes. Mimir stood beside him yawning. Garrek had found them sleeping beside their cart, waiting for their turn to cross the bridge. Soldiers were laid out all around them trying to catch a few desperate moments of rest before the coming dawn and their potential doom.

"You said you had a way of transmuting fool's gold into blasting liquid, right?" Garrek couldn't keep the anxiety out of his voice, but he needed this to work.

"What? No!" Mendeleev declared, shaking his head as if he were scandalized. "Pyrite is just a component of the process in order to create the explosive substance which we use. I thought we explained this to you."

"I don't have time for another lesson on alchemy, Mendeleev. Can you do it?"

"He already answered that question, Garrek," Mimir said through another yawn. "Pyrite is just one part of the recipe. But even if that was it, the end result is too volatile to use in any really predictable way. It could just as easily blow up and kill the person using it as fire a gun or a cannon."

"So you can't do it." Garrek felt his stomach twist and fall, the despair he kept trying to ward off was clawing at his insides once more.

"Not just from pyrite, no. But what is this about, Garrek?" Mimir asked, a look of concern passing over her face as she looked up at him.

"We need to take out that bridge once we get across it so that Gruumen can't follow us." Garrek sighed and shook his head. "But we don't have any black powder in our camp, and I was hoping that you could compensate for that. But if it's not possible, then..." He cut off as Mendeleev broke in.

"Is that all you need?" the eccentric old dwarf exclaimed loudly. Several voices around them hissed for them to be quiet. Some even threatened violence.

"Is that all?" Garrek echoed, lowering his voice. "Yes, that's all, but the only thing I can offer is the pyrite that's part of the bridge's base. I thought you might be able to use it to craft some powder for us."

"Oh, never mind the pyrite, I have plenty of that with us already!" Mendeleev's voice continued at almost a shouting volume, and the grumbles of the soldiers around them were also getting louder. The old dwarf walked over and opened what looked like a cupboard on the side of their cart. Inside were a series of drawers. Mendeleev pulled open several of them and selected a handful of small vials before turning back to Garrek with a triumphant smile.

"I assume that you will need about twenty to thirty pounds of our blasting compound. It may take me a few hours, but I think I can manage to make that much before mid morning if I start right away!"

"What?!" Garrek asked, his brow furrowing. "You mean you have everything that you need to make the stuff already? Why?"

"Did you forget what we came to Caeryn Golloch for in the first place, Garrek?" Mimir gave him a huge grin. Garrek looked down at her. "We came to show how useful our compound was that we discovered and what its potential uses might be for. We were looking for some sponsors to help fund our expedition. What is a demonstration if there is nothing to show? Of course Mendeleev brought all of the ingredients necessary."

Mimir laughed as she watched Mendeleev setting to work. The grumbling soldiers were starting to stand up and walk away. Some of them threw curses back toward the noisy trio, but Garrek barely heard them.

"This is excellent news!" he declared just as loud as Mendeleev's exclamations. "You say it will be ready by midday? How long will it take you to rig the bridge with it?"

"That will be a somewhat tedious process, as we must be very careful with the transport and application of the completed compound. It is very combustible and unpredictable. I will produce a double batch just to make sure that we have sufficient force to destroy the bridge. This will be an excellent experiment to determine how well the components handle a damp environment! This is perfect!" Mendeleev began humming softly to himself as he mixed several vials together and lit a small candle.

"Um... should he really have an open flame that close to the cart?" Garrek asked, taking a step backward. Mimir chuckled.

"Oh, you've got him started now. The old boy will be going without stopping until he's finished. As for the candle, don't worry, the components aren't explosive until near the end of the process, but he needs the heat to cook certain portions and extract other substances." Garrek gave her a confused look, and her grin only widened. "Don't worry, you get used to it. He knows what he is doing, and he'll have it all ready when he says he will."

"Of course, I will need to be the one to detonate the compound," Mendeleev said over his shoulder. "Wouldn't trust anyone else to do it right. Plus I need to observe the results for my own notes. There is a lot of valuable data to be had with this experiment!"

"I don't know that I would trust anyone else to do it, either," Garrek replied and gave a shrug to Mimir as well.

"I'll need to stay back with him, too, of course." Mimir watched her partner with a glint in her eye. "He doesn't trust others to handle his compound, and I don't trust other people to handle him."

"That's fair," Garrek said before turning to walk off. "I'll let Rordin know that we have a plan and to get things ready!"

For the first time since the failed peace talks, Garrek actually felt some hope that things just might work out for them. A grin began to split his face.

16
The Price of Worthiness

"I long to return to my Mother Earth's embrace. If it were not for my debt to my friends and my family, those who have already paid for their place among my hallowed ancestors, I would have guided myself there long ago. But I know that in the eyes of those who watch me, I am still in want of deeds that would secure my value amongst my clan. The heaviness of that value is too much for me to lift alone, yet I dare not ask another to bear such a burden with me and shame them with my fellowship.

Therefore, I stay my journey here, neither advancing nor retiring. For retreat is worse than death, and to press forward is more than my strength will allow. The weight of my unproved value shackles me here as I wait for the earth to take me at its leisure.

Perhaps then I will finally be allowed to rest."

–Excerpt from 'The Mother of My Burden: A Dwarfen Tragedy in Three Acts' Act III, Scene IV

The morning sun was just beginning to peek over the horizon. Its first blushing rays touched Sveri's cheek where he sat on the ridge overlooking the valley floor far below him. From this distance, the remnants of the Ffionen Clan were almost specks sitting at the bottom of the steep incline that began just inches from where he stood. Thankfully, Herneas had talked the Warsmith Twilip to abandon the fool task of joining her troops at the front of the lines. She was no warrior to be caught in the thick of the battle and was better suited commanding the artillery toward the back of the trap that had been set for the fiendish ratkin that were even now bearing down on their position.

He hated that they were here. He hated the purpose of their deception. He hated that they were putting themselves in danger for such a cowardly tactic. Mostly, he hated that he had agreed to put them in danger like this.

"My lord," a voice at his elbow said, and Sveri turned slowly to look at the speaker. A grungy, wind-swept dwarf stared back at him through misty tendrils of gray hair. Myrgwyddn, he was the captain of the rookery and the leader of the stoneclaw riders, massive ravens that were able to carry a dwarf high above the ground where they could rain down mayhem with their explosive ammunition. Outside of battle, they served as excellent outriders and scouts.

"What is it?" Sveri growled. "Have you spotted them?"

"The vermin are approaching quickly, my lord, they should be here within the hour. But there's something odd that we can't quite place."

"What's that?"

"Seems like there's less of them than we first counted. Makes me uncomfortable that our earlier reports don't match up."

"You think some of them ran away?"

"I don't know that we're that lucky, my lord. I think they're preparing some kind of devilish trickery."

"It would serve us right," Sveri grumbled and turned back to looking down the slope. "Keep a lookout and do not engage with the enemy. If you find our missing rats, report back to me immediately."

"My lord." Myrgwyddn bowed and turned to walk away.

Something uncomfortable nestled itself between Sveri's shoulder blades, almost like an itch but deeper and more insistent. He rolled his arms in their sockets to try and alleviate the feeling, but he knew it was a futile gesture. The itching sensation wasn't a physical problem. Sveri felt his gut tightening and the nervous energy began to rise up through his fingertips. The edges of his vision began to show flecks of light, a precursor to the onset of a bout of rage. He took a deep breath and gritted his teeth, forcing the emotion back, trying to prolong the time before the Red Curse took him.

He knew what the cause was. Everyone always assumed that he was constantly angry, that his fury was always simmering just below the surface. In a way that was right, but he knew that this was only half of the truth.

He reflected on his latest conversation with Herneas, which may have been a mistake, as the berserker lord had to force his teeth to stop grinding against themselves as the memory replayed in his mind.

"When it comes to survival, I'm not sure that there is anything too underhanded, save the threatening of innocent lives perhaps."

The ranger's words echoed in his head, and it sent a shiver down into the depths of his guts. He felt the cold sensation spread out from there until he was forced to clench his jaw to keep it from chattering. Again the edge of his vision stuttered and threatened to turn pink. The cold always came before the fury.

That was the other half of the truth. The anger was not the constant companion that everyone associated with Lord Sveri, Master of Cwl Gen. They assumed he was filled with rage and bloodlust, and that was true. The Red Curse ensured it was so, but what people didn't know about was the frigid sensation of dread that always preceded the onset of the rage.

That was the nature of the Red Curse, at least it was how it affected Sveri. It stole over him and fed on his fear, using it as fuel to stoke the fires of vengeance hidden deep within the blood. It was terrifying, and Sveri would rather face a thousand battles than have to deal with that fear.

He thought back to his youth before the Curse had descended upon him. His mother had been hopeful that it would pass him by, as it was known to do from generation to generation. Not all members of his line were claimed by its violent claws, but it was rare that an individual was not possessed by it.

Then the nightmares had started.

He'd dreamed that he was lost among the corridors of Cwl Gen, where he had grown up. He walked among the dark halls, the only movement was that of the flickering fires in the torches that barely managed to illuminate the way before him but sent shadows scattering across the stone walls. All of the shadows were only made deeper by the scant light.

He became aware of a scent in the air. It was warm, and it smelled delicious. His stomach rumbled with hunger and he followed the smell deeper and deeper into the bowels of the mountain hold. Finally, he came to the source, it was hidden behind a large wooden door. It was locked, so he raised a fist and struck the thick panels. The sound of his hand hitting the wood boomed and resonated through the darkness, making his blow seem much larger than he could possibly have made it. He looked behind him as the sound echoed away into the hall, and when he returned his gaze to the door, he found it smashed to pieces before him.

He moved through the doorway, stepping over shattered pieces of wood and bent pieces of metal to do so. Inside the room was as dimly lit as the hallway outside, but here the low light showed a huge table, laden with all of his favorite foods. Great mounds of roasted meat and ropes of spiced sausages. Baked mushrooms and glazed biscuits sat beside huge tankards of ale and bottles of rum. The table veritably groaned under the weight of it all, and Sveri's mouth watered at the sight of it. He stepped forward to take a taste.

Then there came the scream.

"NO! SVERI, PLEASE DON'T!" the voice cried, and Sveri realized that it was his mother's voice. It was odd, his mother had been a gentle soul. She had kept a level head and had been one of the only people who could calm his father down when the fury took him. She never shouted. Her voice was always sweet and patient. Sveri shook his head to ward off the confusion and again reached for the food.

"SVERI! GODS! WHY?!" His mother's voice grew even more shrill. Again Sveri backed away, but then he shook his head and forced his way forward to the table.

"STOP! Nononono! Stop! Augh!" The words devolved into a senseless scream that filled his ears and wouldn't let go. But Sveri pushed through the screams and pulled the food to his mouth. He knew that the only way to stop the screams was to feed. So he raised a knife that appeared in his hand and cut a slice of meat from the roast. He lifted a link of sausage and bit into it, snapping the skin between his teeth and gobbling it down.

The screams turned into a garbled mass of hysteria. He heard other voices now. That of his sister, Jaeina, and his childhood friend, Breuig. Their voices were mixed with sobs, and he looked around to see what the cause of their sadness was.

"Hello?!" he called out, but his words were only met with more terrified cries. "Jaeina! Come and eat! It's so good! You'll feel better once you've had some food." His invitations went unheeded, and the screaming did not abate.

In a moment of clarity, some part of him realized that he was dreaming, and with that realization came the thought that screams needed a source, they did not simply spring from the empty air. This thought terrified him, and he clapped his hands over his ears to block out the sound. He cast his eyes around for the source but could see nothing.

Something wet dribbled down the side of his face, and he squeezed his eyes closed, willing the dream to change. He felt the vision shift, and suddenly the screams stopped. He opened his eyes and found himself looking down at the table where all the food was still laid out from before, but now it was all half-eaten. Flies buzzed around the rotten remnants that looked as though they had been left out for days. His mouth tasted of chalk, and he tried to muster up the saliva to spit the taste of decay that permeated his mouth.

Then he looked up and spied his reflection in the mirror that had somehow appeared before him in a way that only made sense in a dream.

He stood in the same hall as before, but the table of food was not there. Instead, there were corpses strewn all about him. The bodies of his mother, his sister, his friend, and other dwarfs all lay strewn all around the room. Their blood was everywhere, and the only sound that registered to his ears was the ever-increasing noise of flies buzzing over the carnage.

In his reflection he was no longer the young child that he remembered. Now he saw himself as a grown dwarf. In his hands, he held Mortcwyl and Brydwr gripped firmly in his fists, and they seemed to have faces that sneered at him while the blood of his victims dripped from their edges.

Terror always gripped him, then, as he stared at himself in the mirror. But his reflection did not seem afraid. It looked back at him with a vicious grin on its face. It lifted its weapons above its head and roared, the sound rippling around the room and causing the mirror to shatter. But the reflection still hung there, suspended in the air.

That was when Sveri had awoken. He found that he was no longer in his bed. Instead, he had his small hands wrapped around the throat of the servant who had come in and tried to wake him from his nightmare, their eyes bulging with fear and pain as he squeezed harder, even though he had come fully awake now. He didn't want to stop.

He was hungry.

His father had flown into the room and struck him hard across the face, sending him sailing back onto the ground. Sveri had snarled, but before he could rise up, his father had been there with his foot on his chest, holding him down until the anger bled away and Sveri collapsed under the weight of his spent fury.

That was what it was like every time the Red Curse took hold of him. The fear. The lack of control. The fury.

Sveri could remember every detail from his dream because it was one that he had regularly, and it was getting worse. Times were that it used to be once every year or so. Then every other month. Now it was almost weekly that he had the same nightmare. The victims in the mirror changed. Now he saw the lifeless forms of Herneas and Banick laid out in the reflection. But he was always a helpless child until the animal in the silvered glass took him. Then he became rage incarnate.

When the dream came, it wasn't the anger that he felt. While rage was what his voice howled raggedly through his shredded throat, it was the fear of what he had done, and what he could do, that always stayed with him the longest.

He had almost killed Herneas several times when in one such fit as these. He had already maimed and wounded others who had tried to help him when he was taken by the Curse. He wasn't sure if he hadn't killed a friend or ally when the rage was upon him in the midst of a battle. He also wasn't sure that Herneas would tell him if he had. The thought of it all filled him with unease.

Rigid adherence to the warning signs, breathing techniques, and mental exercises had been drilled into him since he was a child, ever since that first episode had come upon him. Because of that, he was able to exercise some modicum of control. But if he strayed one way or the other, or if he ever allowed himself to relax... The very thought sent another shiver down his body.

Sveri was grateful that he lived in a society of dwarfs. The strict adherence to tradition, to tried and true methods, these things lent themselves to the kind of discipline that he needed to keep the beast at bay.

All of that tradition lay challenged in the valley below him. He felt the anger at this betrayal stirring within him. It made him angrier that Herneas had pushed for it. Herneas *knew* how important these values were to Sveri, not only from a traditional aspect, but from a perspective of control and security. Yet his friend had pushed for this plan.

Sveri felt his knuckles crack, and he looked down to see that his fists were gripped so hard that the fingertips had turned a bright white from the pressure.

"My lord, they are here," Myrgwyddn's voice cut through his thoughts. Sveri blinked, his vision was tinged scarlet, and he struggled to control the white-hot ball of fire in his chest. He took several deep breaths to try and regain dominance over his limbs. He wanted to rip out the stoneclaw rider's throat with his teeth. He wanted to feel the pleasant peals of his victims' cries as they died beneath his blows.

"Hold the line," he said in a strained whisper.

His fear had passed. Now he was simply hungry.

*****

Yorna strained as she tried to look further down the valley to where the bulk of her remaining forces were. At this distance, she couldn't see anything more than a few vague shadows on the valley floor that she assumed were them. She imagined that she saw the hulking form of Craggoth standing in the midst of them. Not for the first time, she cursed under her breath and muttered obscene curses aimed at Herneas. Why had she allowed him to talk her out of her original plan? It made sense logistically, but it still felt as though she was running away. How was it fair that she was asking the Ffionen warriors to risk their lives while she sat back, safe and sound with the cannons and the sharpshooters? The thought of it all made her stomach turn, but she pushed the sickening feeling in her gut down, trying to hold off the thoughts of all the ways that this plan could go sideways.

"Focus on what's right in front of you," she whispered to herself. She closed her eyes and took a deep breath.

Then there came the clarion trumpet signalling the approach of their enemy.

"It's time," Dig said beside her, hefting his rifle and taking aim. She was selfishly glad that he was there, and not down in the thick of the coming fight.

"Wait until they're closer before opening fire," Yorna tried to keep the tremor out of her voice as she spoke. She failed. Dig nodded and yelled the order out so that it would be carried on down the line. Most of the rest of the troops with them were rangers from Herneas's troops along with all of the artillery the clans had brought. Another sharp pang of guilt tugged at her as she considered the numbers that she had sent to act as bait for the ratkin. In total, along with the other volunteers from the other clans, there was only about a quarter of the entire army that Sveri had raised for their campaign. Yorna hoped that it would be enough.

She looked out across the distance between where she stood and where the rats were approaching. It wouldn't be long now, but there was nothing she could do but wait. She closed her eyes again and thought back to the conversation she'd had the previous night with the giant earth elemental.

"Hey there, big rock," she had said as she stepped up beside the elemental. The giant earth spirit looked down at her, and images of a gentle spring day filtered into her mind. She squinted at him and tilted her head to the side.

"Thanks, I think. At least I assume that those images were meant to be reassuring?" Craggoth nodded in response. Yorna took a shuddering sigh and leaned closer to him to whisper. "Don't tell anyone, but I'm terrified. I have no idea what I'm doing here. I have no right to be leading anyone."

More images flashed through her mind, this time they were images of what looked like the stone walls of Cwl Gen, then an image of a mighty dwarf shield standing before her. That image was easier to interpret.

"That makes me feel a lot better, knowing that you'll be watching out for me," Yorna said and was surprised at the lump she felt in her throat as she spoke. She coughed and sat down on a log, a strange sensation bubbling in her chest.

"There's something I've been meaning to ask you, Craggoth. I know this isn't the best time for this, but with the rats charging down on us and there being the chance that I might not be able to ask it if I wait, I figured no better time than now… But, um, why do you stay with me?"

This time it was several moments before the pictures came, but gradually the image formed of Yorna laughing, which was followed by an image of sunlight playing across rippling water. The image seemed to dance lightly across her mind's eye and caused her to smile. Then the image shifted and she saw Banick and her laughing together.

"You think that Banick and I would have gotten along together, huh?"

The image of her and Banick laughing together reappeared, then it shifted so that where Yorna had stood there was now a young dwarf with red hair. The image flickered so that Yorna and this new red-haired dwarf seemed to occupy the same space at the same time.

"I remind you of this girl?" Yorna asked. "She is somebody important to Banick?"

The image shifted again. Now it showed Banick crying while holding what looked like the body of the red-haired dwarf in his lap. Fire burned all around them.

She must have died. *Yorna thought to herself.* Banick obviously cared for her, and Craggoth cares for Banick. If he likens her to me, then I guess that makes sense.

She wanted to ask more questions, but she couldn't find the words to put to the questions that she had. Instead, they sat in silence as the night wore on into the gray hours of dawn.

"The enemy has engaged the decoys," Dig said beside her, and she opened her eyes to try and see the conflict.

That's when everything fell apart.

"Yorna! We have contacts on the right flank!" A voice bellowed, and she turned toward it.

"Are the rats trying to outmaneuver our decoys?" she asked, but before she could even focus on the speaker, her eyes lit on a swarming mass of fur boiling out from the rocks behind their position.

"Oh, Fulgria!" she said. "Turn the batteries around! We are under attack!"

*****

"*Uff'ran!*" Sveri swore as he goaded his mount into action. His Frostclaw riders had reported back that the war engines were being attacked. Somehow, the rats had found a way behind their position and were slaughtering the cannon crews even as they spoke. That was where the missing rats had been! How had they been able to get around their position?! It didn't matter, it was going to be a massacre! Beyond that, the plan that the treacherous elf had proposed wouldn't work, because without the artillery there to reign destruction down, the enemy would simply swarm over their forces unchallenged.

"Myrgwyddn!" he roared, venting his fury as the large badger beneath him stepped tentatively up to the edge of the steep decline before them. "Get word to Herneas and the elf! Tell them the plan has all gone to the Abyss! The artillery is surrounded and can't retreat. Tell them to send everything they can!"

Sveri lifted his hammer up and pointed toward the rear of the valley. The other berserkers on their brocks behind him looked on with a rabid ferocity that he knew was barely restrained. Sveri himself felt the hunger deep within his bones. His body ached for violence, and that need bubbled up into a crazed laugh that escaped his lips. He knew somewhere in the back of his mind that a child still sat cowering, scared at the laughing monster before him.

He didn't care. He was past the fear.

Now all that remained was the feasting.

"Jormyddwe the Cruel," he began his litany of ancestral names under his breath as Hellbrock threw them both down the narrow mountain path, toward his victims.

17
Fighting Dirty

The reason for the dwarfs' refusal to use what they deem as 'dishonorable' actions in battle is not born from a sense of superiority, although that has become an integral part of their reasoning at this point.

Rather, the origin of this resistance stems from a fear of falling. Remember that Abyssal Dwarfs are made, not born. No dwarf is born an Abyssal, even those conceived in the deadly courts of Tragar. It is through choice that one shackles oneself to the horrors of the pit, and this fear is what motivates this eschewal of underhanded tactics.

Because once you begin to take the easy path, it becomes all too easy to follow it down until you fall into the Abyss. It is better to choose the harder good than the convenient evil.

–Athro *Nythyl Goldspeak*
Stone Priest of Dolgarth from the Time of Winter

The pickaxe pulled free of the dwarf's skull with a wet crunching noise, and Krut Stonepaw laughed at the sound it made. He chittered and looked for his next victim. A dwarf directly in front of him cut down a smaller rat who squealed in pain as the axe bit deep into its soft belly flesh. Krut snarled and leaped forward, bringing his pick down in a vicious overhead chop. The dwarf spotted him and ducked backward, almost quickly enough to avoid the blow but not quite. The tip of the pickaxe caught his exposed arm and pierced it through so that the point exploded out the other side.

The dwarf screamed and dropped his axe. Krut did not waste time trying to free his own weapon and instead opened his mouth and clamped his sharp, yellow teeth into the dwarf's throat, cutting his scream short in a gurgled choking that dwindled away as Krut's tongue tasted the salty tang of blood. He spat bloody chunks out of his mouth and squealed with delight into the air above the battle.

The stonebeards knew fear! He could see it in their eyes! He could taste it in their blood! The looks that they gave him as they hid behind their shields and the weak way that they swung their weapons betrayed the terror that they felt! He looked around in triumph and saw Pratter and his shock troops causing murder among more of their scared enemy. His grin grew wider and he licked his chops, tasting the sticky salt of the blood that dribbled from his lips. He reached down and pulled his pick free.

"Make sure that we do not kill them all!" Krut chittered loudly at his lieutenant. "We need some of them alive to spread the fear of Krut Stonepaw!" Then he promptly ignored his own order and leaped toward another dwarf, his mining pick already above his head aiming at the stonebeard's chest.

*****

Everything was wrong. They were all going to die.

Yorna fired her pistol into the screaming maw of a heavily armored ratman and watched as the abomination fell to the earth. She then gripped her dagger in her other hand and looked around briefly. She was out of powder, and her pistol might as well be a club in her hand. She reversed her grip so that the barrel's warm metal rested against her palm, so that the weighted steel ball in the pommel of her weapon would be easier to swing. She now regretted not taking a more suitable weapon with her, but she had reasoned that their job was simply to hold the line and it wasn't likely that she would see much actual fighting.

Another rat lunged at her, and she swung wildly, her pistol clubbing the side of the creature's skull in a lucky shot that sent it crumpling to the ground in a boneless heap. She quickly dispatched it with her dagger that was held in an increasingly shaky hand.

All around her, bodies seethed in the crushing press of battle. One of the cannon crews tried to fire their shot even as the rats swarmed toward them. A small wretch of a creature leaped up to tackle the ignitions expert who was holding the flame to the wick and ripped a sizeable chunk out of the side of his neck. He fell with a bloody scream, casting his flame to the side in a panic.

A dwarf beside her cried out and fell back, clutching his stomach as blood bubbled out between his fingers. An armored rat stood over the fallen warrior with a rusty blade held over its head, and blood dripped from the weapon's tip. Yorna found herself staring blankly at the creature's sneering face as it advanced on her. She couldn't bring herself to move.

Her mind flashed back to previous battles. Images of goblins dancing among the corpses of cannon crews. The Teirhammers as they slaughtered Cerrig and his guard. In all of those situations, it had been the same. Yorna felt her fingers beginning to grow numb as she watched the beastman walking toward her. She didn't feel afraid. Her chest was gripped by another emotion that was far worse, at least to her.

She was ashamed.

Here she was, confronted by another horrifying creature of violence. The world was full of an endless supply of just such beings it seemed. She knew she should raise her weapon, she knew that the beast was going to kill her. But she couldn't command her arms to obey. Instead, she simply stared at her approaching death and screamed at herself internally.

You fool! Do something! Don't just stand there!

Why am I like this?

These thoughts skittered through her mind as the creature raised its weapon. Something that looked like a grin was spread across its face. Yorna tried to brace herself for the blow. The best that she was able to manage was a blink.

"*NO!*"

At first, Yorna thought that she had simply thought the word in her head, but she saw the beast flinch, and its features flickered from sneering cruelty to shocked surprise. Then it looked down, and Yorna followed its gaze.

Her dagger was buried up to the hilt in its chest.

The ratman looked at the weapon for a scant moment, then its eyes rolled into the back of its head and it fell to the ground. Yorna held on to the handle of her dagger as it slid free of the wound. She felt her breath coming in short gasps. She forced herself to swallow and took a step backward. Dwarfs closed in front of her and she took another series of breaths to try and calm her nerves. She swallowed the thrumming beat of her heart that was threatening to choke her and forced her knees to stop shaking.

"Hold the line!" she cried and was surprised at the steady sound of her own voice.

*****

Herneas sprinted across the rocky ground, his breath coming in ragged gasps as he pushed his sturdy legs to move faster. Ahead, he could see the lithe form of Inei and her elven Icekin far outstripping him and his fellow rangers.

The stoneclaw rider had brought them the news of the ratkin's deceit. Somehow they must have found a way through the underground caves that led them around Yorna's position, and now the artillery was surrounded and cut off from retreat. Everything had gone wrong so quickly!

The rider had also informed them that Sveri was engaging the enemy and had already broken cover – which meant that he had placed himself in a dangerous position as well. Herneas pushed the fear that either of his friends could be killed in the next few minutes from his mind with a sickening lurch and instead forced himself to focus on the burning sensation in his lungs as he struggled to push each foot to place itself with surety. He looked up and realized that he could see the battle ahead, and his heart leaped into his throat.

The rats were everywhere. His personal group of rangers was approaching from the side of the rats' position, but even here he could see how devastating their charge had been. Chaos swarmed all over the little plateau that had been the best position for the war engines to see all of the valley floor. Bodies of dwarf crewmen and their guards lay strewn across the edges, mingled with the corpses of vermin. The very air was tinged with the crimson mist of violence.

He made a quick calculation and ordered his rangers to hold march. He directed their gaze to several units of ratkin warriors at the back of the press of the battle, still waiting to get in at the fighting and completely unaware of the dwarf reinforcements behind them.

"Take aim!" he ordered breathlessly. He swung the Skewerer off of his back and fitted a strange-looking bolt into the channel. It had a bulbous tip that was made of glass and smelled of resin and chemicals. It was a gift from Yorna, and it had already saved him once before. Now he hoped it would do the same for her.

He raised the tightly-wound crossbow to his shoulder and sighted down the shaft toward his intended target.

"Aim for the back rank!" he yelled. "Don't worry about accuracy so much, we just want to get their attention so that they'll turn to face us." *Hopefully that'll give some relief to Yorna and the others.* He added to himself.

He took a deep breath and held it to steady himself, then he squeezed the trigger mechanism. The bolt shuddered and sent a forceful shock up through his shoulder as it flew free of the crossbow. He heard a myriad of twanging lines as several other rangers loosed their own missiles. He let out his breath in a steady stream as he watched his own bolt sail across the sky, but he lost sight of it before it hit its mark. He scanned the enemy ranks trying to determine if the shot had hit or not.

A sudden explosion blossomed amongst the tightly packed hordes of rats. A moment later, Herneas heard the thunder crack of the blast and felt the concussive force of the blow as it washed over him and made his teeth vibrate. His breath caught in his throat as he waited for the smoke to clear.

A stray breeze blew the tendrils of smoke and dust lazily away from the battle, and Herneas grimly surveyed his work. Scorched dirt and burnt bodies littered the ground where his shot had struck. He smiled grimly as he saw several nearby groups of ratkin warriors break and flee at the sudden display of raw destructive force. Others had turned now to face this new threat from behind. At least he had managed to get some of their attention. There were still many more, however, who fought on, barely even aware of the blast as they were too caught up in the thrill of the fight before them.

Herneas swung the Skewerer back onto his back. It was a shame that he only carried one of those bolts on his person at any given time. But it would be an even greater shame if the enemy ever got into close quarters and a stray blow wound up striking the bolt, blowing them all up. It didn't matter, though. He felt the need to close the distance now and ensure that he found Sveri and Yorna. To make sure that they were alive.

*****

Yorna ducked under another blow and brought her knife up to slice the exposed arm of her opponent with her dagger. The creature recoiled and hissed in pain. It wasn't a mortal blow, but it was enough that the creature was now wary of her. It wouldn't make the same mistake again of underestimating her.

She took no pride in this; it would have been better if she had been able to kill it outright, because the ratman had a bigger weapon and more reach than she did with her dagger and pistol.

She had heard the detonation at the rear of the enemy assaulting them on the flank and had even felt the concussive shockwave that had followed. But that was on the far end of the battle, practically the other side of the world from where she currently stood. She knew it was a long time before relief would reach her, if they arrived at all; and right now, she had the brute in front of her to deal with.

The rat lifted what looked like a cleaver with both of its clawed hands. A small part of Yorna noticed that blood dripped down its arm from her wound, and she took a small amount of satisfaction from that. The larger part was terrified of what was coming next. Her opponent watched her warily. Yorna cursed internally and gripped the barrel of her pistol. The weapon was useless as anything but a club at this point, and barely that. Its hammered metal was dented and bent beyond repair from all of the rat skulls it had been slammed against.

She had to wait. The battle swirled around them, but Yorna was a small target, and the other rats appeared focused on the bigger and more heavily armed dwarfs around her. Those dwarfs were in turn distracted by trying to stay alive themselves. No one interrupted their strange staring match.

A long moment stretched out between Yorna and her opponent. She watched and waited, feeling the creeping dread as it once again tried to steal over her limbs and paralyze her.

I need to act, she thought, *before the fear takes me again!*

Then the rat shifted its weight, and she couldn't wait any longer. As it took a step forward, Yorna hurled her broken pistol at its face. The creature flinched and tried to bat the thrown weapon away, and for a brief moment, its focus shifted to that task. Yorna threw herself forward, closing the gap between them, and tackled the rat onto the ground. She stabbed at its exposed belly again and again as they fell together into the dirt, and she felt the hot blood spill onto her hands with each wound she inflicted. The rat screeched and pawed at her weakly, but she pushed its arms away easily and stood while sucking breath through clenched teeth.

"Stand your ground!" she shouted, her voice was hoarse from the effort. Her chest burned from the exertion.

Then something slammed into her side and sent her sprawling. She hit the ground and rolled onto her knees. Her breath refused to enter her lungs, and she saw stars for several moments. She didn't stop moving, as to do so would be to die, she knew. She forced herself to her feet and took a few more steps back as her vision slowly and painfully cleared.

Standing before her was the biggest ratman she had seen in the battle yet. It towered over her and was clad in mismatched sets of dwarf armor and mining equipment. In its hand it held a heavy mining pick which it held above its head.

"A beardless stonebeard!" It chittered in a strange, screeching voice. "You are the pack chief, here?"

Yorna didn't respond; instead, she just stared at the creature with her mouth open. The big rat sneered and shook its head.

"This one does not speak well. It will not spread the fame of Krut Stonepaw. Better for it to die!"

*****

Herneas's axe split a rat's skull like it was made of rotten wood. The ranger even felt as though he were some kind of macabre lumberjack. His arms ached from raising and swinging his weapon. His blows lacked any form of grace or skill. They were butcher's strokes. But the rats were not great warriors, at least not the ones that he fought. The vermin threw themselves at him with almost reckless abandon, and he cut them down with almost careless ease. But they were worse than goblins, and for every creature he killed, three more sprung into being to take its place. Already his arms were a mass of small cuts, scrapes, and bite marks where the fangs and claws of the little devils had scored worrying little wounds on his skin.

He didn't care. His eyes scanned the battle for signs of his friends. They had yet to reach the beleaguered cannon crews, and all that stood before them was a seething mass of brown and gray bodies that screeched and squealed at him.

Then, abruptly, a dwarf appeared in the storm of fur; he held a battered rifle in one hand and was gasping for breath. It took Herneas a moment to recognize that it was Digaelion that stood before him. He gave a relieved sigh and motioned for his rangers to press forward and assist the sharpshooter.

He maneuvered until he was beside his fellow dwarf, and the rest of his fighters followed suit. They quickly set up a battle line that held implacably against the screeching ratmen.

"Dig!" Herneas shouted over the din of battle. "Where is Yorna?"

The older dwarf raised a shaking fist to point in the direction of the far side of the battle. Herneas shook his head, he wanted to ask more, but Dig's face was pale and he looked about ready to pass out.

"What's he saying?" A familiar voice called over the noise. Herneas turned and saw Brethod standing beside him. Blood trickled down the side of his head where a small gash had opened, the crimson stream tinged his sandy beard a pinkish color.

"They must have been separated by the battle!" Herneas shouted back. "Looks like we'll have to cut our way through!" He turned and barked a few orders to his remaining rangers beside him. They knelt down and offered their shoulders to the older sharpshooter before moving off and away from the battle.

"Yorna's resourceful! She'll be okay!" Brethod yelled over the battle, but Herneas just shook his head. He felt tendrils of anxiety worming their way through his stomach.

*****

The point of the pickaxe passed within inches of the female dwarf's head, and Krut sneered in frustration at the slippery movements of the beardless stonebeard.

"Why will you not fight?!" he howled as she backed further away.

"Are you a coward? Does fear already grip you?" Part of him enjoyed this idea, and his sneer turned into a cruel smile. "This is good, then! You are already prepared to spread Krut's legacy! You will keep your tongue and your life, I promise! But I must take your hands."

A look of horror passed over the she-dwarf's face, and Krut relished in it. He had her now, it was only a matter of time before she fell before him, just like all the other stonebeards had. He stepped forward and swung a casual blow aimed at her head again and laughed as she ducked under the blow.

His laughter cut off abruptly as a sharp, hot pain seared up his arm. He yelped and pulled back, clutching a wound that traveled almost all the way from his wrist to his elbow. The dwarf didn't hesitate, and like a demon, she launched herself at him with her small knife swinging toward his face. He tried to pull away, but couldn't quite get far enough. Blinding pain enveloped his face as the blade tore through his cheek and sliced into his left eye. He screamed and raised his hand to his face even as darkness took the vision from his ruined eye.

His foe moved to attack again, but she stepped wrong on a corpse at her feet and tumbled sideways. Krut did not hesitate. He leaped on top of her, placing all of his weight into his foot that he brought down on her hand that clasped the dagger. She grunted as he knelt on her stomach.

"You took my eye, you filthy stonebeard!" Krut screamed into her face, she flinched as blood and spittle sprayed across her cheeks and mouth from his exclamation. "You do not deserve to keep your tongue! I will mount your head on my flag to warn others what happens when you do not fear me enough!"

The dwarf tried to hit him with her free hand, but she couldn't get any leverage. Krut pushed his face closer to hers as an idea popped into his pain-addled brain.

"You took something from me, stonebeard! I will take it back before I take your life!" He cackled as he reached out with his uninjured arm and grabbed her face, squeezing it until she screamed in pain and bright beads of blood erupted under the edges of his claws where they lanced into the sides of her jaw.

But he wasn't finished, yet. Her pain was just beginning.

He raised his other hand and quickly sliced downward so that his claws cut through the left side of her face and eventually through her eye, just as he had intended. Krut laughed and lifted his bloody claw in triumph, releasing her mouth to let her howls of pain escape into the air. But nothing came. Krut looked down at her and saw that she had expired. He sneered. She hadn't suffered nearly enough for what she had done to him. He had tried to be careful and not cut too deeply. He'd only wanted her eye. At least at first. He shrugged and stood up.

Stepping over her body, he grabbed his pick and rejoined the battle.

****

Exhaustion was beginning to set in. The battle was mired, and all the forward momentum of their charge had been spent. Herneas's arms screamed in protest as he tried to lift his axe once more. A cramp in his shoulder forced him to step back and lower the weapon as he winced in pain.

There was blood and broken bodies all around him. The rats were a neverending tide of flesh and fur and fangs. It didn't seem possible that so many creatures could take so many casualties and still keep fighting until he considered there were still far more of them shrieking and clawing at the dwarfs than there were laid out on the ground.

"We can't keep this up much longer!" Brethod shouted at him breathlessly as he stepped back from the fighting. Another ranger took his place wearily to fill the hole in the line. "We haven't made a significant dent in them, and there's still more of them to go! They don't even look tired in some cases!"

"We can't just leave them to die!" Herneas protested, surprised by the growl that escaped his throat in response to Brethod's words.

"Look around! They're probably already dead! How does dying to try and rescue their corpses help anyone?!"

"What about Sveri? Our reports told us that he has already finished the fight on the valley floor and was charging here even as we speak. Do we abandon him, too?"

"Again, he'll be on the other side of the battle. Who knows how it will go for him? But we're doing nothing standing here and getting slaughtered." Brethod's face was pleading. Herneas glared at him, but he couldn't see any fear in the younger dwarf's face, only concern. His rangers fought all around him, pushing back against a mass of feral bodies that screamed and screeched at them, clawing for their blood.

"We can't..." Herneas started, but he couldn't finish his words. The battle had turned desperate. He knew that Brethod was telling him the truth, but he also knew that his friends were out there in the thick of this fighting. He knew that they needed him. He also knew that they might very well be dead, and he was spending the lives of his other friends to try and save them.

He opened his mouth to order the retreat, and then the detonations started. Sudden blooms of fire rose up in the middle of the tide of vermin before them. They were not massive explosions, but small blasts that sent geysers of dirt, blood, and smoke swirling into the air. Each concussive blast sent the rats scurrying away for a few small moments before scuttling back into their ranks, but it was obvious the effect that this new attack was having on their morale.

Herneas looked around in confusion. But then a shadow passed overhead and he shot his eyes up into the sky. Above him, a large raven passed overhead, its black wings beating against the air as it carried itself above the battle. Even as he watched, the old ranger saw a figure lean out over the side of the giant bird and drop something over the hordes of ratkin. Herneas tracked its progress until it landed.

At first, nothing happened, but then he saw the explosion that threw an unfortunate rat above the heads of his fellows. The creature's face was distorted with pain, and Herneas noticed that its arm was no longer attached to its shoulder, but rather it spun through the air heading in the opposite direction of its former owner.

The stonetalons had arrived! Herneas felt a surge of relief flood through him as he looked out over the battle once more. Dozens of ravens flew through the air, each one dropping its explosive payloads all around the seething masses of their enemy. Individually, the blasts wouldn't have made much of a difference, but together, the combined force of these attacks began to take its toll on the psychology of the craven rats.

Herneas could see it in the faces of the enemy directly before them as he watched them hesitate in their constant assault and glance nervously upward. Herneas groaned as he forced himself to his feet.

"Don't give them any respite! Press in for the kill! They're scared now! Don't stop until we've run out of corpses!"

The fighting renewed again, now with the aid of the stonetalons, and slowly the battle began to shift. Herneas found that he was stepping over more fallen ratkin than dwarfs as he pushed further toward the center of the battle. Then, just as gradually, he began to see other dwarf bodies underfoot – the light clothes of cannon crew members. He paused and looked about him, searching for a specific face.

"Yorna!" he tried to call out, but the sound of the battle swallowed her name as soon as it left his lips. He cast his eyes about, hoping to spy her somewhere, to know that she was alright.

Then he looked at his feet, and his blood ran cold.

Yorna's face stared up at him from underneath two more rat bodies. He barely recognized her, as the left side of her face was a bloody mess where three long, jagged gashes wept crimson. Herneas fell to the ground and pushed the enemy's bodies off of her and gathered her up into her arms. Her body felt cold, and her skin was waxen in appearance.

"Yorna!" he yelled her name and quickly felt at the base of her neck for a pulse. At first, there was nothing. Then, so softly that he had to wait for a second time to make sure he'd felt it at all, there was a gentle throb that pushed against his fingers.

She was alive! But only just, and she wouldn't last much longer without a healer. Herneas cast his eyes about. The fighting was still all around him, and his exhausted rangers were struggling to push the enemy back once again. The ratkin had become frantic for some reason that Herneas couldn't tell, but their ferocity had stopped the dwarf advance cold and now was even pushing them back once more.

One of his rangers fell to the ground in front of where he knelt, and Herneas looked up to see a large rat wearing ill-fitted dwarf armor. The beast looked down at him with a cruel smile and raised a bloody pick above his head.

"Was the beardless one your friend, dwarf?!" The rat's face was crazed, its one eye bulged from its socket while the other was just an empty hole that was covered in blood. "I will send you to join her!"

The rat lunged at Herneas, who could do nothing but cover Yorna's prone form with his own body. He tensed his shoulders and waited for the pick to pierce his back, anticipating the pain and the death that waited beyond it. But the blow never came. Herneas lifted his head and looked up to see Inei standing over him. She had blocked the incoming blow with her own blade and now stood pressed up next to the rat that had attacked him, pushing her sword against its pick.

The ice elf was a fearsome sight to behold. She was covered in blood, which was spattered across her pale skin in such vivid hues that she appeared to be glowing with the fruits of her violence. The furs on her armor and clothes were tinged a gory shade of pink, and her hair was a frazzled mess.

"Get your friend out of here, Hunter!" She yelled over her shoulder. Then she kicked out with her back foot and caught the ratkin warrior a blow to his side which caused him to screech and fall back.

Herneas didn't wait to see what happened next. He picked up Yorna and retreated to the rear of the fighting.

"I need a healer!" he yelled as he ran and tried not to trip over the bodies.

*****

Krut snarled at the tall, bloodstained creature before him. His ribs ached where she had hit him with her foot, and his ruined eye socket stung from a mixture of blood and sweat dripping into the fresh wound. The agony of the open sore was driving him to insanity, and he had found himself clawing at it from time to time just to try and lessen the pain. He'd already ripped the dead eyeball from its socket to try and find relief, but that only deepened his madness.

"I'll kill you first, Pale One!" he screeched and launched himself at this new foe. He swung his pickaxe, but his opponent danced nimbly to the left and swung her blade at his exposed ribs. He threw himself desperately in the opposite direction, and the blade missed him by the merest of inches. He landed and scrambled up to his knees just as the pale elf raised her blade high and brought it down, aiming for his head. Krut gripped his pick and lifted it to catch the blow with the haft of his own weapon.

The elf's sword bit deep into the wood of his pick, but the weapon held, and Krut snarled savagely at her as he pushed himself to his feet while still holding his foe at bay. She tried the same trick she had before and aimed a kick at his ribs, but this time he was ready for it and stepped into the blow, robbing it of its force. The motion took her off balance, and Krut pushed forward to throw her to the ground, her sword tumbling behind her.

Now he stood over top of her and smiled his mad grin down at her. She crawled backward slowly, her eyes fixed on the pick in his hands as he raised it above his head. He would savor her screams. He brought the pick down, aiming for her chest.

The elf reacted with blinding speed. She rolled to the side, and his pick embedded itself in the mud beneath where she had been moments before. Before he could do anything, she grabbed her discarded weapon and charged at him once more. He snarled and tried to bring his pick to bear, but it was stuck fast in the sucking mud. The elf swung her weapon, aiming for his head. He jerked back and instinctively raised his hand up to ward off the blow and felt a sudden sharp pain as he toppled backward to land on his back.

The elf stood over him now, her sword brought up into a defensive stance with the point toward him. Krut hesitated for a moment, looking up at her, and wondered if her blow had landed and he was dead but just didn't know it yet. But he didn't feel any pain in his chest; his breathing, though ragged, was coming normally. The only thing that felt odd was his hand.

He looked down and saw a confusing sight. His arm seemed to end just above his wrist, yet he could still see his hand lying a few inches to the side. Bright red blood was pouring from his arm, and the hand seemed to twitch as it settled into the gory mud. Then the pain hit him and he squealed a high-pitched scream that caused the elf to flinch. Krut gripped his bloodied stump to his chest and squeezed to try and stem the crimson flow.

He forced himself to his feet and snarled at the elf, who simply smiled coldly in return and took a step toward him. He felt his mouth go dry as he watched her, unsure of what to do next, and his mind was beginning to unfocus from the pain of his missing hand.

The elf's footing slipped on a corpse, and she staggered slightly to the side – not much, but it was enough for Krut to turn and flee. He didn't hesitate, nor did he look behind him. He simply ran. Bodies and fighters zoomed past him but did not try to stop him. Everyone was engaged in a fight for their lives at this point, and so none paid him any mind.

Krut finally risked a look over his shoulder to see if the elf was pursuing him and was relieved to see that she had not. Unfortunately, this meant that he wasn't watching what was in front of him and had the wind knocked out of him when he slammed full force into something big, heavy, and hairy that threw him to the ground. He wheezed and gasped for air as he struggled to look at his assailant, and what he saw chilled him to his bones.

The biggest dwarf, riding atop the largest badger that Krut had ever seen, towered over him. The nightmare being was covered in blood and was screaming obscenities at the sky; in one hand he held a massive hammer, in the other an equally large axe. He stared down at Krut, and then… he smiled.

Krut screamed. Then he watched as the dwarf raised his hammer almost comically slow. The ratkin leader did not wait for the dwarf to finish. Instead, he simply took off running again, pushing his way through metal, and fangs, and fur. Never stopping until he was out of sight of the demonic dwarf and the ice devil-elf that pursued him.

18
The Weight of Belonging

It seems as though guilt is as much a part of dwarf culture as rum.

–Lukmakra, ogre mercenary, when asked his impression of dwarf culture after fighting against them for seven years.

Ofn was growing impatient. He'd been chasing after Garrek and the rebels for days now, why would they not realize that they had been beaten and give up already? It was only a matter of time before the inevitable result came about, why did they feel the need to prolong it? He looked out over the ongoing battle and shook his head. Rordin was taking his troops across the river, but it was such a small bridge that there was no way for them to make it before Gruumen's forces fell on them. Garrek's troops, then, had been left as a rearguard to help ensure that the rest of their forces made it across.

Ofn stood at the back of his own forces which were pressed up against the foothills leading out of the mountains behind them and feeding onto the plains ahead of them. He could see that the majority of Rordin's forces were already across the river. It was a futile gesture, though. Even if Garrek managed to hold them off long enough, it would be a simple matter for Gruumen to follow them across and continue hounding them all the way to Dolgarth. Ofn knew that the enemy didn't have any blasting powder, and they wouldn't have time to demolish the bridge once they retreated across. So what was the point in all of this fighting? An enemy should know when they are beaten!

His stomach twisted in on itself as he thought about the whole situation. Gruumen had given an angry tirade this morning before leading the initial charge down toward the bridge. The Ashtel chieftain was angry, that much was evident. What should have been a quick and decisive strike to remove the threat of Rordin's meddling influence had transformed into a costly and difficult march.

"We must end this here and now! It is imperative that Rordin be removed from the board!" Gruumen had raged at his generals. *"If we do not take him out, then Golloch's opposition is left with a rallying cry. With our king distracted with the Freeloaders to the north, our resources are already spread thin. We cannot afford to have a long drawn out campaign against those who cannot understand the true meaning of loyalty! I shouldn't have to explain this to you all, but it seems as though the delicate nature of our position has been lost on the majority of you.*

If we fail, I will select one of you to personally deliver the message of our shortcomings to King Golloch!"

That last threat had proven more than effective. Every last general had been afraid to meet his gaze, and they had all scuttled off after Gruumen gave a sneering wave of his hand to dismiss them. Only Ofn had stayed.

"What will happen to Garrek and Banick?" he had asked when they were alone.

"What do you think?" came the snarling reply. Ofn had felt the weight clamp down on his chest. He had suspected that there wasn't much hope for his friends, but still, he had to try.

"Could I request that they not be killed, if possible?"

"Why would I agree to that?"

"There are better uses for them, I think. Rordin must die, obviously. But what if his staunchest supporter, Garrek, were to come over to our side? What if he were to renounce Rordin and pledge his full support to Golloch?"

"You must really not know Garrek if you think that is even a remote possibility," Gruumen snorted.

"Give me time with him, and I will bring him around. I helped Golloch see the light, didn't I?"

"Even if Garrek were to come over to Golloch's side, what would the aid of the Oathbreaker Clan do to help our cause?"

"If nothing else, he's a formidable fighter and general. We've seen that over the past few days at the very least. He could be an asset in that way. Perhaps he need not retain the moniker of Oathbreaker. Perhaps he could be reborn as someone new? It would be a fitting start to his conversion to Ariagful, would it not?"

This caused Gruumen to pause before he began to nod slowly.

"That could work," he said at length. "But I would require his conversion process to be long and… thorough in nature."

"Of course, I do not do things by half measures," Ofn responded, trying to hide his relief.

"That is assuming we can take Garrek alive, even. Banick must die, however. There is no question there." The sinking sensation in Ofn's gut returned.

"What if he were to convert and I were to take him to the Free Clans to try and convince them to join our side? Think of the dwarf blood that we could avoid shedding!" Ofn heard the edge of desperation in his voice, but he couldn't stop himself.

"No, the Freeloaders must be taught a lesson. Peace was never the plan for them. They are too proud and must be humbled. They have lingered too long on our Imperial teet and have grown fat off our hospitality, then they have the audacity to question us?!" Gruumen's

eyes fixed on Ofn then, and he could see the fires reflected in there. "The Halpi Mountains must be cleansed with fire so that they may be a more fitting gift to our king and to the Dark Mistress. Blood is a necessary sacrifice to appease her. I would rather that blood came from the Free Clans than from Imperial veins."

"But surely if we were to offer them up as bound captives rather than in bloody conflict…"

"Banick will die, and the so-called 'Free' Dwarfs will be the example that teaches the rest of the world a valuable lesson. We will kill our kin as ruthlessly as this, think what we will do to others who are not close to us if they do not also bend the knee when they are commanded?"

That had been the end of the discussion. Ofn knew that there was no argument that would sway Gruumen's decision, so he hadn't tried. He had spent the rest of the morning planning a deception as to how he might covertly capture Banick and keep him alive long enough to prove his worth as a convert rather than a corpse.

So far, no plan had shown any real promise.

Then there was the problem of overcoming Garrek and Banick's deep held convictions against the Abyss. They were far more altruistic than Golloch ever was. They were idealists. Part of that was what made them so endearing to Ofn, perhaps.

He snarled in frustration. How much longer would this fighting ensue! Every minute of violence made it more likely that Garrek would be slain! The thought of this tore at Ofn in strange and uncomfortable ways.

Why did he care so much?

It was times like this that he envied the stone priests, whose robes he had worn for the past several years. Many were the times that he had led prayers with the faithful when they had been troubled as he was now. He remembered the ashen taste in his mouth as he had spoken the farcical words of prayer to their 'Earth Mother,' thinking bitterly about how she had never answered any pleas for help that he had uttered.

But, even so, she was the Mother of the dwarfs. While his own mother was a horrible example of that role, he had seen what the traditional concept of a mother meant during his time in Caeryn Golloch and the families there. He was the very definition of a wayward child. His goals in life had been centered on spilling the blood of her children, his kin. He had been good at it, too. But shouldn't a mother still wish to help her dissident children, especially in this where his desires were different? Now he wanted to save lives. Even if it was at the cost of many more, surely that meant that his godly parent would be willing to hear him out?

This thought sat in his mind, festering like an infection in a wound. Ariagful would not be pleased with her servant praying to a rival, but he wasn't sure that he cared at that moment. She also praised seizing what one wanted using whatever means necessary. Was that not what Dianek would be in this moment? A means to an end?

There was only one way to find out.

Ofn turned and began walking, ignoring the looks of the other dwarfs as he passed them by, moving away from the battle. He didn't pay attention to how long he walked, but he didn't stop until he was alone, the sounds of the fighting an echo in the distance. He looked up into the deceptively calm sky and then back down at the earth.

"Oh... Mother..." The word twisted in his mouth like a writhing worm, and he grimaced at the sensation. He spat on the ground and tried again.

"Dianek... Dwarf Mother..." this didn't cause his gorge to rise, and so he continued. "I want to save some of your children. I know you have long since given me up for lost, and you are right to do so. I am not the one who I come to ask for your blessings..."

He was met with silence, but something pressed him to continue. He wasn't sure if it was something spiritual or if it was simply a relief to speak his thoughts aloud.

"You have a devout child, Banick, and one who serves Fulgria, a potential rival to your worship but a good dwarf nonetheless. These two have done more good than most for your children. More of their brothers and sisters draw breath today because of their actions than have been silenced by my own actions. I am not your follower, I am a vile depravity in your follower's eyes, yet still they were friends to me. They did not know my true nature, but they were kind to me when this world has been anything but that to me. If a lost child such as me can attest to their goodness, that should speak to their worth! But I also know that they are close to meeting their doom this day if things do not change."

Here he stopped to take a deep breath and was surprised to feel a catch in his chest that caused his breathing to stutter.

"I... don't want them to die..." he said simply, his throat constricting painfully around the words. He slumped to the ground. His emotions had been let off their leash, and now they swirled painfully in his chest and warred with his thoughts. The world seemed to spin uncomfortably beneath him. He felt as though he would choke.

His mind flitted back to the past, to his childhood. He remembered the welts that his mother's lover had left on his back from his belt. He felt the echoes of the bruises left by his fists, the ribs that had been cracked by his boots. He remembered his conversion to Ariagful and the promises of vengeance that he had been given as he had sacrificed captured slaves to her glory. He remembered the heat of his own fury as it had boiled out of him to consume his enemies. He thought over the countless faces of the victims that he had created with his countless acts of hatred and rage toward the dwarfs who had never once shown him an ounce of mercy or kindness. His gorge rose at the back of his throat, the heat of his anger kindling back to replace the pained emotions currently in his heart.

These were suddenly plunged into a cool iciness as images of the time he had spent in contemplative conversations with Garrek and Banick. The laughter that they had shared with him. His mind flitted to Rhosyn and her frequent visits to hear his counsel. How she had laughed at his minor blasphemies and had spoken with him at length about how much she was concerned for her husband and for her people. He felt the fleeting contentment of sitting with friends and the absence of the fear of how they might betray him. It boiled up inside him like a fire warming a cold cavern.

He was torn in two. He felt the heat of his vengeance, his anger at a world that had denied him all semblance of kindness in his childhood and much of his adult life. He also had the warmth of friendship and respect that he had thirsted for since the first time his mother had sneered at him, or her lover had struck him with the back of his hand.

Another thought wormed its way through the warring emotions in his mind. It sparked between the two sides of his inner turmoil and erupted in a flash of fire that ignited in his hand, channeling the energies of Ariagful to whom he had pledged himself. The ball of fire rippled in his palm, and he stared at it blankly as the idea took shape in his mind.

He could destroy the bridge.

He could save his friends. All it would cost him was an eternity of suffering. He could burn away the timbers and make the bridge unusable for Gruumen's forces to follow Rordin. It would save Banick and Garrek, but it would also prolong the war and would make enemies for him on both sides of the conflict. Nowhere would be safe. Everyone would seek his life, and death would not be the end of his suffering.

He would go back to the Abyss where his soul would writhe in pain until his masters of Tragar would pull him out and then give him new life, only to torture him in new ways. Perhaps twisting his flesh into the form of a Grotesque, whose every moment of existence was a new form of pain. Perhaps they would encase him in a soulless form of an Immortal, robbing him of his individuality while forcing him to continue existing. The numbers of nightmares that awaited such a betrayal were as infinite as the devils who abode in the fires of the Abyss. He would experience them all in excruciating detail for a betrayal of this magnitude.

This realization filled him with fear. But the thought of Banick's body torn and bloodied on the dirt caused an equal measure of dread to stir within him. An image of Garrek standing with the sightless eyes of an Immortal Guard, a soulless husk whose individual mind had been ripped from their body and replaced with the disposition of a fanatical servant, flashed through his mind. He flinched at the thought.

Could he live with either outcome?

He sat, staring despondently at the ground, his impossible choices swirling through his barely present conscience. He felt frozen, as if his limbs were made of stone and would not obey him if he tried to stand now. A distant part of him was afraid of what he would do if someone were to discover him in this state.

Then another question snaked its way through his thoughts.

Why?

Why was he considering this sacrifice for people who had discarded him and would not accept him even if he were to offer it up?

A memory of Garrek's sneering face floated to the front of Ofn's awareness.

"You are not my friend, Ofn! I don't know that you ever were! Get away from me!" The words seemed to slap Ofn across the face the same way that they had when Garrek had said it only a few days ago. By Ariagful! That seemed like forever ago at this point.

Garrek is not your friend. A voice seemed to say in his mind, he couldn't decide if it was his own or not. *He is no better than any other dwarf you have ever met! The memories you hold so dear of his comradery are already forgotten to him. He has many other memories and friends to replace yours with. You owe him nothing!*

"But I betrayed him! Of course he would hate me!" Ofn said aloud.

If you had been honest with him from the start, would he have acted any differently?

"Hello, I am Ofn, a follower of Ariagful masquerading as a stone priest, here to plot the overthrow of your way of life and to kill as many of you as I can..." Ofn said the words out loud ruefully and shook his head with a humorless chuckle. "No, that likely wouldn't have gone very well, either."

Your choices have led you to this point. You wanted this, did you not?

"I thought I did... but that was before..."

Before what? Before you got a taste of what they had been denying you since you were born? Comradery? Friendship? A place to belong? It was all a lie! You knew that from the start! You were the one who started the lies with them! They never cared about you! They liked the persona you presented them. As soon as you revealed the smallest portion of the real you, they rejected you out of hand.

Ofn flinched.

"No, that's not true..." he tried to protest, but the words rang hollow in his ears.

Yes it is. You have all the proof laid out before you. They will never accept you. You don't have a place among them, you never did. If you sacrifice your place among the Abyssals for them, then you will have no place and nowhere to go. Are these fair-weather friends worth that to you?

"I... I don't know..."

You'd better decide, and quickly. Your time is almost out before that choice is made for you...

Ofn stared down at his hand, the ball of fire still hovering over his palm, while his other hand gripped a handful of dirt that he had clawed from the ground.

"Master Ofn!" A voice cut into his reverie, causing him to start and the fire in his hand to extinguish. He turned to face the newcomer, who took a few cautious steps back when he met their gaze. It was a dwarf soldier, young by the look of him, bearing the Gruumen's livery.

"What is it?" he asked in a voice that was filled with gravel.

"Lord Ashtel is looking for you, and he doesn't look pleased."

"Very well," Ofn pushed himself wearily to his feet. "Go and tell him that I will be there momentarily."

The other dwarf hesitated for a moment, as if he planned to ask further questions, but something in Ofn's face must have convinced him of the folly of such a choice and he turned to walk away instead.

Ofn raised his other hand and let the handful of dirt tumble back to the ground. He watched it as it fell, a great emptiness welling inside of him.

19
Fulgria's Cleansing Fire

Bless me, Forge Mistress. Cleanse from me my impurities with thy constant flame, burn away the hate, the malice, and the guile. Make me straight and true like the steel of purest metal.

May I not be swayed by covetousness, lest the searing fires of greed consume my honor. Let my anger not be directed toward my clan and kin, leading me to commit vile acts of violence. May I not be tempted to allow impure things to dwell within my soul, poisoning me and corrupting my character.

Instead, let thy heat warm me as I press on into the cold hours of this mortality. Burn away my doubt and my fear and let thy light illuminate the way as I wander through the perilous dark.

So that on the day that I must finally journey through the fires of death, I might come across to the other side and look my ancestors in the eyes with my head held high.

–Prayer of Sanctification unto Fulgria
Song of the Forge, Chapter 3, verses 2-5

"Garrek! It's time!" Banick yelled from the mouth of the bridge. The older dwarf turned and looked behind him. The last of their forces were making their way onto the opposite bank of the river. He turned back to the remaining troops spread out before him and took a general stock of what was left. He groaned and wearily turned back to the battle, hefting his hammer which had grown progressively heavier as the day had worn on. A thousand small cuts and bruises screamed in protest at the motion.

The fighting had grown to a fevered pitch. He had kept only his most ardent Ironguard troops back to help him fend off the rest of the attackers, and they were now hard-pressed on all sides by the enemy. Blows were coming at such a frequency that even with their durable armor and thick shields, they couldn't stop them all. Garrek had ordered the vast bulk of his soldiers to begin their crossing after the other clans had completed moving across. The last handful of these were making their way across the river now. Of the nearly hundred warriors he had started this stage of the fight with, however, Garrek had lost about twenty soldiers. Besides that, all of the survivors, himself included, were exhausted and wounded from the fighting. Things were looking grim.

"Fall back!" he yelled over the din of battle. "Step!"

The combined forces of warriors took a single step backward in unison. The traitorous Ashtel soldiers were quick to follow up, and the move didn't even buy them even a breath's respite. Garrek grimaced as one of his Ironguard on the far left was pulled forward into the enemy ranks and disappeared beneath a hail of hammers and axes.

"Step!" he shouted again. The Ironguard obeyed, and more of them fell from the relentless onslaught that followed.

They would never make it at this rate, Garrek realized. He turned back to where Banick stood. His friend looked back with a worried expression on his face – he had come to the same realization. They were only a few feet from the bridge's mouth, it was so close! But if they turned and just retreated, they would be cut down before they could even take a few steps. Gruumen's forces were fighting as if a demon were at their backs, pushing them to reckless feats of strength. It was as if they were afraid of what might happen were they to allow Rordin to escape like this.

Garrek walked over to where Banick stood.

"Get across the bridge and tell Mimir to make sure that everything is prepared to blow the bridge. As soon as it is, do it. We can't risk it falling into Gruumen's hands and him being able to catch Rordin on the plains."

"We're not going to just leave you, Garrek," Banick responded, his eyes flashing defiantly.

"I appreciate the sentiment, but you might not have a choice in the matter." Garrek shook his head. "Once the bridge is destroyed, I will try to surrender, and maybe they'll take me hostage."

"Then they'll just kill you as a traitor!"

"That's better than letting them take the bridge and then Rordin. I'll die in that case, anyways, so what's the difference?"

"You really don't see it, do you, Garrek?" Banick gripped his friend's shoulder. "Rordin needs you! He relies on you and sees your friendship for what it is! Your forces need you as well! Most of your clan is on the other bank waiting for you. Without you there, where will they go? The Heavyhands are their home, their clan. The whole world knows you for your exploits, and whether or not they respect *you,* they must respect what you have accomplished. Rordin will need that connection, that strength, in the future. Right now, all of those Imperials who will come to Rordin's aid are just like the Heavyhand Clan. They will be outcast from Golloch's Empire. They will need your example!"

Garrek tried to protest, but Banick cut him off.

"No, you don't get to argue that!" Banick yelled. "I'm a Free Dwarf, I am an outsider to your politics, but even I can see your worth, Garrek. It is not meant for that value to be spent defending a bridge that no one will remember. Get your warriors across this river and bring yourself with them. We won't blow the bridge until you are safely across and can give the order yourself, understand?"

Garrek stared at Banick for a moment, his eyes flickering between his friend and the battle raging behind them.

"Fine!" he growled, but there was no heat in his voice. "Get yourself across and make sure things are ready. The moment you see me across, you light the fuses, do you understand?" Banick eyed him warily, but only for a moment before he took off running across the bridge. Garrek watched him go, then turned back to his troops.

He looked over his remaining warriors. It seemed as though another seven had fallen in the time that had elapsed during Banick's and his conversation. He felt the blood pounding in his ears. Mentally, he added them to the list in his head, the list of those that he'd have to mourn and remember. He felt his teeth grinding, and his fingers cracked as they gripped the Warp Hammer in his hand. Lifting his shield, he allowed the energies in the artefacts which he held to flow through him, feeling his muscles tighten and his vision grow sharper as he prepared for violence.

"Make a hole!" he yelled. Even in their exhausted state, his troops understood this order, and as one, the armored figures before him locked their shields together and pressed forward into the wall of enemy bodies. Using their shields as a wedge, they separated the foe and stepped in between. The rank behind them followed up with a secondary charge that opened the gap even wider. It wasn't much, but it was enough for Garrek to fit through.

Letting out a monstrous bellow of rage, the mighty warrior ran forward and slammed his heavy shield into the first dwarf face that appeared before him. The unfortunate soldier couldn't even look surprised as the edge of the metal lip caved his face in, crumpling his skull and shredding the skin there. He was dead before Garrek could even bring his next blow to bear.

Hoisting the Warp Hammer above his head, Garrek let out another warcry before bringing it down to crush the helmet of another dwarf warrior beside him. Gore splattered out like a rotten melon had just burst. The force of the blow sent ripples through the enemy ranks, and suddenly the overly eager Ashtel warriors staggered back in surprise.

Garrek didn't stop.

He whipped the hammer around his head and brought it down in a diagonal slash that crumpled the breastplate of another dwarf directly behind the one he had just killed. Another Ashtel dwarf rushed forward as Garrek lifted his hammer for another blow and aimed a shot at Garrek's face. The old dwarf flinched to the side and the strike sped past him, close enough to leave a streak of pain across his left cheek that seemed to bleed fire. Garrek roared and brought his shield up to slam against his attacker's wrist. He felt the bones there snap and grind as the heavy shield cracked the arm, and the axe that it had held toppled from nerveless fingers. He swung the shield back around and slammed it into the dwarf's face, silencing his howl of pain and throwing him to the ground.

An armband on Garrek's forearm began to glow, and he felt the pain from the cut on his cheek diminish. He didn't slow his attack. His arm rose and fell with the methodical carpentry of death that his hammer wrought among his enemy. Around him, his warriors renewed their assault, their spirits lifted and their resolve bolstered by their commander's show of force. Practically anyone the Warp Hammer touched, it killed instantly. The magical energies trapped within its deceptively small shape gave strength to each of Garrek's blows, making even a glancing blow lethal.

The armband, one of the recovered God Boons, crackled with arcane energy, and he knew that the soldiers around him would be feeling the effects of its magic as it healed their wounds and bolstered their vigor for battle. They renewed their assault, and in a heroic surge of motion they slammed their weapons into the enemy, cleaving shields and splitting helms. Garrek suddenly found himself standing in a lull within the battle; the unit he had been fighting was dead beneath his feet and those of his warriors' who were fighting beside him.

"Fall back to the bridge!" he yelled breathlessly. His dwarfs took several strides backward, keeping their shields up. Across the distance, another enemy regiment prepared to charge. Garrek glared at them, then turned his eyes back to his two remaining groups of warriors. The unit beside him had helped to finish off the enemy he'd been fighting, and the other had just finished off their own knot of foes. He barked an order at them.

"First group! Step to your right in unison, six paces! Now!"

They did not question his order. Instead, his Ironguard simply snapped their shields up in defiance of the obvious fatigue that they must have felt and stepped smartly to the side. This brought them almost directly in front of the retreating unit beside Garrek.

The enemy let out a bloody roar and charged across the corpse-strewn ground made uneven with the amount of bodies piled on top of one another. They staggered and tripped before slamming into the Ironguard's shield wall. Garrek was proud to see his own warriors hold firm against the onslaught, only losing a few of their number to lucky blows that managed to slip past their heavy armor and shields. Their commander called out orders, and the regimented guard struck back against their enemy, but it was here that their exhaustion began to show as most of their blows glanced off shields or missed entirely.

"Second group! Get across the bridge!" Garrek yelled. "Ordered march!"

The second group turned with regimented discipline so that each soldier was faced toward the bridge and then began to hurry across. Garrek turned back to look at his other soldiers and saw to his dismay that the countercharge from the Ashtel clansmen had finally won out over the fatigue of the Heavyhands. Six more of his warriors had fallen to the ground to be trodden underfoot by the enemy. Less than a dozen now stood to fend off their attackers.

They fought back, but their strength was spent, and the Ashtels easily deflected their tired blows. Garrek ran to try and assist them, but he knew he was already too late. Even as he charged, their foe surged forward and enveloped the last few remaining Ironguard, pulling them to the ground as weapons rose and fell above their prone forms.

"No!" Garrek snarled, and then he was upon them. The Warp Hammer glowed fiercely in his hand as it caved in helmets and breastplates with ease. Warriors tried to block his blows with their shields, but the hammer simply pulped the arms that held them and then continued on to do the same with their chests.

The enemy fought back, and Garrek felt a sharp pain in his side as an axe managed to rip through the mail links at his hip and tore a bloody gash there. He snarled and brought his shield down to break the offending wrist that held the axe. The dwarf howled in pain, but Garrek quickly silenced him with a backswing of his hammer. Another axe head flew through the swirl of enemy limbs around him and scored a glancing blow to Garrek's left shoulder, and he felt something give in the joint. He batted the axe away but then found that he couldn't raise his shield above his waist, as his shoulder refused to respond.

Garrek swung aimlessly with his weapon. He didn't need to aim, there were enemies all around him. Every blow landed and was rewarded with a scream. His cloak seemed to vibrate with energy, and he felt some of his more grievous wounds stitch themselves closed. His shoulder stopped hurting, although he still couldn't lift his shield above chest height. He deflected a blow that was aimed at his throat so that instead it only caught the side of his face and sent him staggering backward. He tasted blood in his mouth and spat, shaking his head to try and regain his senses.

Another blow flew at his face and he ducked under it, slamming his shield down on his attacker's exposed foot, and he felt the bone and cartilage there snap under the weight of the metal. His opponent fell back screaming. Garrek rose slowly to his full height and gazed at the remaining Ashtel warriors. There were more of them on the ground than were left standing, but Garrek knew that there was a sea of soldiers waiting to charge him after these were dispatched. Yet his current foes hesitated, hovering in indecision as to how they might attack him. He could see the fear in their eyes, they were close to breaking. But their trepidation gave Garrek a moment of space to think.

He glanced over his shoulder. His last few warriors were across the bridge. It was time to retreat. He turned and sprinted for the bridge. His feet twisted awkwardly underfoot as he ran across the bodies of the fallen beneath him.

His flight galvanized the waivered warriors behind and they charged, scrambling across the same difficult terrain of corpses over which he was struggling. Some of them proved more surefooted than he had been, and he was forced to turn and bring his shield up to block an attack from the first of his pursuers. He winced as his shoulder complained under the weight of the blow, but he brought his hammer up and slammed it into the other dwarf's face, turning it into bloody pulp. He brought the Warp Hammer around and brought it down on the shoulder of another dwarf who was preparing to swing at him. It crumpled his whole left side and he fell to the ground with a choked cry.

Garrek then stood and faced his opponents. But it seemed as though that had been enough to break their fragile resolve and they fled, pushing through the ranks of their fellow soldiers behind them. Garrek sighed and hefted his hammer deftly. He took a few steps back and found himself standing on the wooden planks of the bridge. The enemy pressed in close, preparing to charge him.

"Garrek! Hold!" a familiar voice called out, and the enemy stopped their advance. Their ranks parted, and an armored figure stepped forward and removed his helmet.

It was Ofn.

"You!" Garrek whispered, his breath coming in ragged gasps. A surge of anger and malice swept through him as he looked out at the dwarf who he had once considered his friend.

"Garrek! Let's stop this. You are already near to death, and our forces are close to overwhelming you and seizing the bridge. You cannot fight all of Gruumen's army, and you cannot stop him from getting to Rordin."

"You'd be surprised at what I can do!" Garrek growled.

Ofn frowned and began walking toward him, picking his way carefully through the littered dead on the ground.

"Garrek, please! Be reasonable! There is no reason for you to die!"

"Who says that I am the one who will be dying? Shouldn't you be worried about yourself?"

"I am always looking out for myself, don't you worry about that." Ofn stopped about a dozen yards from where Garrek stood.

"I am well aware of that, that's all you Abyssals do, isn't it?"

Ofn's face fell as he heard Garrek's words.

"Let's not throw insults at one another, Garrek. I don't want to do that."

He took another step closer, and Garrek took a corresponding step back. His breath was still wheezing in his chest, and his limbs felt like lead as the adrenaline faded from his system and was replaced by fatigue.

"I have nothing but insults for you. You are a traitor, and a coward! You treated me as a friend just so that you could manipulate me! I did nothing but treat you with respect and loved you as if you were family! You repaid my kindness with a knife in my back and spoiled memories of our time together!" he responded and watched as Ofn flinched after each word. He took a few more steps forward and then spoke in a tone that only Garrek would be able to hear.

"That's where you're wrong, Garrek. I never wanted to hurt you. You are my friend! I'm trying to save you now! If you surrender, I will make sure that Gruumen doesn't kill you. We can once again have our late night discussions! It can be just like how it was! And if you pledge yourself to Golloch, I might even be able to get him to restore your clan's honor! Think on that. You have done so much for both Free and Imperial Dwarfs, and yet you are only rewarded with scorn from both sides. 'Oathbreaker,' they label you, when you have done more than any other dwarf to try and restore the glory of former days upon our societies. I offer you a reprieve from that! Come to our side! Ariagful is just another side of Fulgria. She doesn't judge you like the followers of Dianek do! She will not shun you as the tenets of Fulgria demand because of your family's transgression. You will finally be free to forge your own legacy! You will no longer be constrained by a society that does not value you! That spits on your name and your deeds, all in the name of self-righteous 'tradition' that has never been free or fair. Ariagful may be cruel, but she is equally cruel to all who disappoint her, and she rewards those who please her just as equally. She is nothing if not fair. Wouldn't it be nice to have a fair judgment given to you, for once?"

Garrek took a few more steps back, and Ofn followed. Now they were both standing fully on the bridge, the sound of the rushing water beneath them as it crashed across rocks drifting up to muffle any other sounds.

"But that is not justice! You tell me that it is for the slaves' benefit that they are bound and whipped, simply because your god decrees it? That they deserve to be enslaved, to be killed? Justice is not always fair, and I think that your view on the subject is twisted beyond repair."

"You're not listening!" Ofn snarled, and a spark of fire erupted in his upturned palm. "You have the same choice as any of them! You can choose to die here today, or you can live on! There are secrets of immortality in the vaults of Tragar! You can spend an eternity forging the legacy that you want the world to see of the Heavyhand Clan! Or your story will end here, today, and the world will always only remember the Heavyhands as a family of Oathbreakers! That is your choice!"

Garrek glanced over his shoulder. Banick had said they wouldn't destroy the bridge until he was across. He was roughly about halfway now. He took another step back and Ofn tensed, raising the fire that was held over his palm.

"Garrek, stop!" he cried. "I know what you're doing. Don't take another step or I will be forced to stop you!"

Garrek sighed and brought his foot forward. He was tired. An exhaustion that went deeper than the fighting he had experienced permeated his very bones. It went deeper than the events of that day. Ofn's words hurt, not only because they came from the lips of someone he had once trusted, even respected, but because there was more than a little truth there. He thought back to Ddiangen's cruel words. The disdain that he had experienced from countless dwarf generals across the lands of Pannithor. He thought of the list of the dead whose names constantly cycled through his head of soldiers he'd sent to their deaths. All of these memories bore down on him at once with a crushing weight that threatened to drive him to his knees.

He was tired. So tired that anger couldn't even find purchase within his chest. The weariness wormed its way through his limbs and brought awareness to each and every wound and scar that he had on his body. Wounds from centuries of fighting at this point. Battles that had ranged the breadth of the world over. From the sands of the Cracked Lands, to the vast expanses of the Ardovikian Plain. He had been to the depths of the Forest of Galahir, and even to the edge of the Abyss. He had seen wonders and terrors and fought against both. He had names and monikers given to him by races who had only ever seen him from across the battlefield.

He had done so much.

Yet his memory kept lighting not on those moments of wonder and awe which he had experienced in his long decades in this world, but on the sideways glances whenever he was forced to walk the streets of Caeryn Golloch. The whispers of other clan leaders whenever he spoke in councils. The lack of recognition for his clan during the recitation of great deeds at every Claansvelt he had attended.

Then his hand brushed a small pouch tied to his belt, and something jarred within him. He reached down and pulled it free, noting with some surprise that it had somehow managed to not be torn free during the chaotic fighting.

"Garrek?" Ofn took a questing step forward, then paused.

Setting the Warp Hammer down, Garrek opened the pouch and poured its contents out into the palm of his hand.

A single piece of pyrite.

He smiled, his memory turning to the long conversations with Banick, the quiet council he had given Rordin. Their smiles and laughter drifted back to him. The chaotic energy of Mendeleev and Mimir flashed through his memory. Then the floodgate opened, and he remembered late night firesides with his warriors where drink and food had been plenty. It flashed to when the battles had gone well and spirits were high. Those rare occasions when a chieftain thanked him for his help. He even remembered several conversations with Ofn, before his betrayal. The laughter, the comforting words, the philosophical discussions, all of these things melted together into a single golden point in his memory that was reflected in the faint glimmer of this small piece of Fool's Gold.

"No," he whispered, lifting his gaze to meet Ofn.

"What?"

"No, I won't do it. You would have me throw away my honor out of spite. That is the difference between me and an Abyssal. You view honor as a form of currency, to be traded and sold in a way that gives you the maximum amount of benefit. I have not done the things that I have done in order to be praised by others of my society! Do their words and their disdain hurt? Of course they do, but only because they do not acknowledge the effort that I am putting in to make the world more just with my actions. But if my goal was ever to find fame in their eyes, do you not think that I would have given up by now? When it is obvious that I will never have their respect?"

"What is it that drives you then?" Ofn sneered. "Honor is a beautiful word, but it is hollow. What good is honor when you have nothing else?"

"I have friends," Garrek replied instantly. "I have people who rely on me and who need me. Friends who will be sad when I am gone and will remember my deeds fondly, even if only amongst themselves. I am loved. That is what honor brings me, and so long as I have it, my life is full." He stared hard at Ofn and took a challenging step toward him, ignoring the sharp pain in his joints as he moved.

"Tell me, Ofn. Who will sing your funeral dirges when you are gone? Who will lower you into the river of fire like you did for Rhosyn?

Is there anyone in this world who will mourn your passing? Or that is hoping and praying for your safe return?"

Ofn's chin dropped at this, and he stared into the slats of the bridge beneath his feet.

"I had hoped that you would be one such person, Garrek," he said at length.

"I have already mourned you, Ofn, or at least that version of you that I thought was my friend. Now I see only an abomination before me, and it is worse than the loss of a loved one, because I know what you could have been."

Ofn didn't respond to this, he didn't raise his eyes to meet Garrek's gaze, either. After several long moments which stretched out between them, Garrek shook his head and half turned away, picking up the Warp Hammer as he did.

"Goodbye, Ofn," he said over his shoulder. "I hope whatever it is that you have paid has been worth what you have lost." He began to walk slowly away, toward the far side of the bridge. His legs staggering wearily beneath him.

"Stop! Don't you turn your back on me! You're as bad as everyone else!" Ofn yelled, his voice cracking with emotion, but Garrek kept walking. He was almost there.

"I said STOP!" Ofn yelled, and suddenly fire engulfed Garrek from behind. At first his armor absorbed the worst of it, but the force of the blow pushed him to a knee. The flame continued to wash over him, and his armor began to turn red under the onslaught. He felt his skin beginning to scorch beneath.

"You would leave me, too?!" Ofn screamed from behind. "You abandon me when I offer you friendship? You! The one person that I thought would listen to me! That would understand me! You are an outcast! You live among those that hate you! I offered to take you away from this into a world that would fear and respect you! Surely that is better than sneers and disdain?!"

Garrek tried to push himself to his feet, but his legs refused to obey. He heard a sizzling sound, and now his armor glowed a bright orange. He clenched his jaw to keep from crying out. His cloak was burning away to ash under the weight of the magical fire, its healing properties disintegrating with it. Finally the pain grew too much, and he cried out before falling forward onto his chest. Abruptly, Ofn's fire cut off.

"Garrek?!" the other dwarf cried out. "Garrek?! Speak to me!"

He felt hands touching his shoulders that were still bright red with heat and heaving him over. Ofn's face hovered into view, barely seeming to register the pain in his hands from moving Garrek onto his back.

Garrek tried to speak, but all that escaped his lips was a strained groan that whistled between his cracked lips. Pain filled every one of his senses, and his vision swam in and out of focus.

"Garrek?!" Ofn shouted into his face, but he could barely hear him. He sounded like he was in a deep cavern and his voice was echoing off the walls. Garrek struggled to sit up, but his body refused to respond and instead he lay still and stared up at wooden beams that crisscrossed the awning across the bridge. His body felt numb, the pain in his back and limbs felt distant. Somewhere distant, he felt more than heard the sound of wind whistling through the rocks. It reminded him of home, somehow, even though he'd never really had anything that he could really remember as being worthy of that title. Yet as he closed his eyes, he could see it there, laid out before him.

A green landscape unrolled before him as he stood at the top of a mountain peak staring down into a sunlit valley. Gray mist rolled gently through the boulders as they stretched their stony fingers toward the soft sunlight that was muted behind the quiet fog that filled the whole vision with a dream-like quality. Garrek took it in, breathing deep as he felt something within his stomach uncoil. His shoulders and arms felt light, as if he'd just shed his armor after a long day of fighting.

Then he felt their gazes upon him, and in his mind's eye, he turned.

Dwarfs stood before him. There were hundreds of them, perhaps even thousands. They spread out as far as the mists would allow him to see. Some part of him recognized that it would be physically impossible for them all to stand at the summit of the mountain with him, and yet it did not feel crowded.

The closest one approached, and recognition dawned in Garrek's eyes.

"Braelwyr!" he breathed.

"Good to see you, my lord. It's been some time," the dead dwarf smiled. He had been one of several dozens of dwarfs that had fought with Garrek to reclaim the Warp Hammer and had not survived the battle. He was one of the litany of names that Garrek often found himself reciting in the bitter hours of the night when his nightmares were too strong.

"The others are here, too, ya know," Braelwyr said, gesturing at the extensive host behind him.

Garrek felt his throat tighten. He reached out to touch his friend, but the other dwarf paused just out of reach.

"There's a choice that you must make first," he said. Garrek hesitated.

"I'm so sorry for getting you killed," he said at last. Braelwyr shook his head.

"There's no need for that, my lord."

Garrek took a step toward him, but the movement caused his vision to tremble, and he stumbled.

"As I said, Lord Heavyhand, there's a choice that lies before you. One that you have to make before it's too late and the choice is taken from you."

"I don't understand."

"Sure you do. You know what this is. You know where you are."

"This is a dream," Garrek sighed.

"Might call it a dream, maybe a vision. It's possible that your injuries have finally driven you mad. But right now, you stand at the threshold, and just like my father used to say: 'there's no sense in just standing there with the door hanging open! In or out!'"

"You mean that I have a choice in the matter?"

"Of course you do! Everyone does to a certain extent, at least until they don't."

"What will happen if I go back?"

"You already know the answer to that. You pick up your hammer and you keep swinging."

Garrek looked behind him. The rolling landscape was gone now. In its place, Garrek could see the wooden crossbeams of the bridge. Small tongues of flame licked at the edges of his vision, and he could hear Ofn's voice speaking to him, but the sound still felt so far away.

"No no no no!" Ofn's words were so fast that they seemed to be tripping over each other, and Garrek could barely track them. "No, Garrek, don't die! You aren't supposed to die! We'll get you some healing and get you back to health. I'm sorry, Garrek! So so sorry! Here! I'll make it up to you! I'll burn the bridge! I'll do that for you, Garrek! Just don't die! Please?!"

The fire spread further, and some faraway sensation at the back of Garrek's mind could almost feel the heat as it washed over his body.

"You see, Garrek?! I'm helping you! Is this not honorable? You can save Rordin now, but you have to live in order to do that! GARREK!"

He turned his back on the flames and saw that Braelwyr now stood before a long rope bridge that stretched away into the fog. The far side was hidden from view. Garrek felt his hands growing heavy, they seemed to be dragging him down into the dirt.

"I can go back?" he asked quietly.

"If that's what you want."

"Is this real?"

"I think that's entirely up to you as to how real this is, Garrek."

He glanced behind him again. The fire was getting bigger. He sighed deeply and tried to take a step toward it. But he hesitated. The heaviness in his hands had grown to include his arms, and his chest grew cold as he stared into the flames.

"I don't want to," he whispered hoarsely. He turned back to look toward Braelwyr who gave him a sad smile.

"I don't want to," he said again. Braelwyr nodded.

"It's your choice, my lord. It always has been."

"But I haven't done what I set out to do. I haven't found the God Boons…"

"Few people ever really do everything that they set out to do with their lives. Those that do usually have small dreams and narrow visions of what they could be."

"But you gave your lives for my legacy. How can I leave that unfinished?"

"My lord, we gave our lives for you. It was never for your family's legacy. It was always you that we followed."

Garrek felt a shift in his chest as something gave way, and he fell to his knees, a sob ripping itself from his throat.

"I'm sorry," he rasped, his voice was small as it was swallowed by the mist. "I'm so sorry!" He couldn't stop the grief as it poured from him in waves that threatened to wash him away.

"I'm sorry for my weakness… I should have been better…" his words melted into the void around him.

"We never thought of you as weak, my lord. Only those who were blind would ever dare to call you that. The beauty of it all is that through that mist, once the gray veil parts and the light cuts through, we see the truth of it all…" Braelwyr broke off, and Garrek looked up to see him standing over him with his hand outstretched. Garrek took a deep, shuddering breath and took the extended hand, pulling himself to his feet.

"And what truth is that, Braelwyr?" he asked.

"That it was never for them to decide our worth."

"Then what is our measure, and how is it decided?"

"It's not as simple as all that, Lord Heavyhand. I don't know if I can explain it properly. The best example I can give is this: Our lives are like a veneer of rust that hides the true strength of the steel that lies beneath. It is only through the trials of use that the mettle of a life can be tested. You have been hammered, scalded, heated, and forged. Different things are crafted from different ingots of metal, and the value of a crown is not measured the same as that of a hammer, yet both have their uses. Who is to say which has proved to be more worthy: the beautiful ornament, or the faithful implement? To me, I would give this argument: how many houses has the crown been used to build?"

They stood now at the edge of the mist, the rope bridge spanning away into oblivion.

"All ready then?" Braelwyr asked. Garrek nodded and looked out into the mist. He imagined a single, solitary flame, and a prayer sprang to his lips.*Dearest Fulgria, I embrace your warmth. Let the light of your industry wash over me and guide me through the dark.Lead me not too deep that I fall to Ariagful, and bring me safely home to rest in my mother's bosom. Let not the fear of death make me shy away from my duty.Welcome me into your arms and convey me with sweet patience to the place of my fated doom.*

Let me not quail, but be a light unto others to show them the way.

Garrek sighed and began the recitation again. He could hear Ofn's voice pleading with him, but it was a long way away.

He stepped into the mist.

*****

"Garrek!" Ofn was screaming in his face now. He'd been screaming for what felt like hours, but he knew it could only have been minutes at most. He pressed his fingers to the prone dwarf's neck, searching for some small sign of life.

All around Ofn, the bridge was on fire. Gruumen would have his head for this, but he didn't care. Right now, all that mattered was helping Garrek.

"Help!" Ofn screamed, putting his arms around Garrek's chest he attempted to lift the armored dwarf off the ground, but he was only marginally successful. He fell heavily and pushed himself to his feet. He glanced behind him at his soldiers that stood on the other side of a wall of flames, backing away with their faces covered to avoid the heat as it washed over them.

"You cowards!" Ofn screamed at them through the roar of the inferno. "Can't you see that I need your help?!" He whirled back to Garrek and bent over, putting his face inches from the other dwarf's mouth. He couldn't feel a breath. He felt again for a pulse and felt nothing.

"Garrek! No!" He screamed. "Don't leave me! Please, Garrek! I'm sorry!" He grabbed Garrek's face with his hands, but the skin was waxen, and his head fell to the side with no reaction.

"Garrek?" Ofn whispered, his voice choking off into a sob as he placed his forehead so that it rested against that of the limp form before him.

It was at that moment that the world erupted in a searing whirlwind of fire and pain. Explosions ripped through the sturdy beams and shattered them into splinters.

Ofn felt himself lifted and thrown through the darkness and away from the light. Scalding air sucked the wind from his lungs and crisped the skin on his face and arms. He felt blisters form on his cheeks and hands, down his back, and across his chest.

He screamed in agony.

Then he felt the cooling sensation of water that lifted up to embrace him. The liquid buffeted him from all sides, and he struggled to stay conscious. He fought against the dark water as it spun him around, but it was futile. He felt his ability to focus falling away. The dark was closing in around him, and it was as if time slowed.

Then he felt something touching him. Hands grabbed his waist and hauled him up to the surface. He felt air kiss his burned skin, and he sucked in a great gulp of it. The next thing he knew, he was laying on his back, looking up into the sky. His vision was blurred, and something felt wrong about what he saw, but he couldn't tell what it was exactly.

"Get this bastard to Rordin," a voice said, it sounded familiar somehow; but it seemed to be coming from across the other side of a wide ravine, and Ofn couldn't focus enough to tell. "He'll want to talk to him."

Other hands were touching him now, lifting him. Ofn couldn't understand what came next, and instead, he abandoned himself to a world of swirling colors and pain that threatened to wash him away into oblivion.

20
The Best Laid Plans

Dwarf culture, to a human observer, can seem needlessly harsh. They are judgemental, critical, andhaveahardtimeforgivingpasttransgressions. This perspective is understandable; given our short lifespan and limited perspective that we have, it makes sense that we would think such about the dwarfs.

Older races, such as the elves, look at the dwarfs and see a race that is rude, lacking in refinement, and governed by hubris. The dwarfs view the elves as haughty, vain, and duplicitous. Both the dwarfs and the elves have similar views regarding humans in that they see us as overgrown children, easily excitable, and overly hopeful in their interactions.

The lesson that seems to be inherent from this is that the longer one lives, the more jaded they become in their view of others.

–Kielli Fittlespith
Professor of World Cultures
The College of Eowulf

The tent was silent. Nobody dared to move as Sveri glared at everyone present around the large wooden table. Herneas could feel his teeth grinding and had to force his jaw to unclench. He looked around at the other people present in order to avoid the berserker lord's gaze.

Inei stood furthest from him. The ice elf looked nonplussed at being present, but Herneas could see the tautness in her shoulders. She also kept bringing her hand up to inspect the bandage that was wrapped around her wrist, surreptitiously looking to see if the bindings were still tight, despite having checked it only moments before.

Standing next to her was the Ffionen sharpshooter, Digaelion, who spent most of his time supporting a tired-looking Yorna, who still wore a bandage wrapped around her head. Herneas winced internally as he looked at her. The ratkin general had nearly killed her. Healing magic had been her only saving grace. But only the most powerful of magics could replace an eye that had been sliced open, and none in their company possessed that level of talent. She had lain comatose for two nights before finally waking groggily in a state of panic. Herneas wondered how long it would be until the nightmares of what happened would subside in her mind, or if they ever would.

Myrgwyddn stood beside them. The stoneclaw rider was focusing his attention intently on the stitching in the roof of the tent, refusing to look down. Beyond that, several other of the major lords and chieftains that had led troops with them stood, waiting for Sveri to speak.

"What a mess," Sveri finally growled. The quiet of the tent punctuated his words so that they seemed to echo in Herneas's ears. "What a Mother forsaken mess we find ourselves in. I told you all that it was folly what you suggested. We set ourselves up as bait, and the damned rats outwitted us! Vermin were able to outmaneuver us!" His voice rose a few levels as he spoke, but he was not yet at the level of shouting. The cold violence inherent in his tone was far more chilling than any forcible tirade could ever be.

"That's not fair," Inei spoke up and stepped forward. Herneas looked at her sharply, mentally pleading with her to hold her peace, but she pushed on regardless. "We took a calculated risk. We didn't know that there were caverns behind Yorna's position. At least not ones that we knew would link to somewhere the rats could get! It was an unfortunate thing, but not anyone's fault. That is the way of battle, and you sitting here and trying to blame your warriors for failing to see every potential outcome indicates poor leadership!"

The tent seemed to grow colder as Sveri glared at her. At first, Inei met his gaze; but after a few moments, her eyes were forced down.

"Do not think to lecture me again in my own camp, frost-skin, or I will cut you down where you stand. Do I make myself clear?"

"Is this how you Free Dwarfs do business? Threaten those that speak against you into silence?" Inei tried to sound defiant, but her eyes did not rise to meet his, and it ruined the effect.

"It is today." Sveri continued to pierce her skull with his gaze for several long seconds of silence before turning back to the rest of the gathering.

"What an absolute disaster we have managed to find ourselves in. The plan that was proposed ended up costing us more casualties than an open, pitched battle would have done! What in Dianek's name were you all thinking?" Now his voice had risen, and the volume caused several of those present to flinch unconsciously.

"What's more! You have cuckolded our chances of confronting Golloch at Crag Hudd! With our dead and wounded, we are now little over two thirds of what we started this march with! Even without those casualties, we would have been hard-pressed to give fight to those backstabbing Imps, but now your clever trick to trap the rats has made any assault on the Rift impossible!"

His temper was rising, Herneas could tell by the way he was punctuating every word by stabbing an accusing finger at the audience. His tone was terse, and his eyes were beginning to bulge. If something wasn't done soon, it was possible that Sveri could work himself up to a frenzy which could result in him doing something regrettable that might alienate various lords or chieftains present.

Herneas looked at the faces in the gathering. Most were downcast in shadows of shame or anger, possibly a mixture of both. Sveri was somewhat justified in his anger. Their plan had failed, and there wasn't time for them to retreat to Eastport and gather reinforcements for another assault. They had been thwarted, and Golloch hadn't even had anything to do with it. He likely didn't even know of their existence. That in itself was frustrating, maddeningly so, and everyone in the room felt that frustration. Sveri likely most of all, but he was pushing things too far. Herneas needed to do something before it reached a breaking point.

"Perhaps we should disperse and come up with another plan, Lord Sveri?" Herneas used Sveri's honorific as a way of signalling to him that something was wrong. It was a system that they had used before to help cue the berserker without disrespecting him. "Something that we can put into play that will at least hinder Golloch's efforts? Perhaps we send saboteurs in to try and hinder his efforts while we go and seek out reinforcements? We can regroup and…"

"We don't have time for that!" Sveri snarled, and Herneas grimaced. "You said yourself that Golloch is likely only weeks away from having an army comprised almost entirely of golems! If we retreat, it could take us over a month to gather new troops, then another overland march that will take weeks! By that time, Golloch will be so far entrenched in Crag Hudd that we will never be able to pry him loose! This was our one chance and we lost it!"

It was then that Herneas caught something in Sveri's furious glare. It was well-disguised by anger, but Herneas had known him long enough to see past that. The ranger saw it in the downward turn of his mouth, and there was a fragile nature to the rage in his voice. Herneas knew what was caged behind those furious brows. It was despair. This realization filled Herneas with a cold sense of foreboding that felt like he had been dipped in icy water.

"We don't have to take the hold from Golloch to stop him," a small, rough voice said. Herneas was jolted from his thoughts as he turned to look at the voice's owner.

Yorna had risen to her feet, a little shakily, but she stood alone, waving off Digaelion's offers to support her. She looked tired, and for a moment, a vision flashed through Herneas's mind of her ashen-skinned face when he had carried her into the healer's tent only a few days prior. He shook his head and her much healthier, if still bandaged face, replaced the stark image.

"What do you mean?" Sveri asked. Her sudden remark seemed to have caught him off guard, Herneas noticed, because his words were quiet, but lacking the heat that had been previously building up in his speech.

"Our goal is to seal the Rift, right? Or at least make it inaccessible? We can do that without taking Crag Hudd."

"What do you propose?" Herneas asked quickly, before Sveri's anger could find its footing.

"The Rift is underground, right? Several levels below the surface? If I can get inside, I could find some way to rig the cavern to collapse, thus sealing it off, and potentially burying the golems with it. This would prevent Golloch from using it, at least for a while. It wouldn't be a permanent solution, as it doesn't close the portal, but it would buy us some time at the very least."

"More subterfuge?" Sveri growled, and Herneas winced internally as he spoke, sensing the heat in his tone. "Besides that most abhorrent aspect of your plan, there are so many other issues. How do you plan on getting inside the keep?"

"We have a way in," Herneas replied, turning to face him. "Grodgni and I, as well as others of my rangers, have already infiltrated the keep on several occasions."

"You've told me where your access point is, remember? Do you really think that she could make the climb necessary to reach the keep in the condition she's in currently?" Sveri waved a hand in Yorna's direction, and Herneas looked back to her as she stood on trembling legs, one hand held to her head where the bandages were. Herneas sighed.

"Perhaps someone else could go, then?"

"Do we have another someone in our company?" Sveri asked, but Herneas already knew the answer. They had a few lesser engineers to help run the artillery, but their specialty was munitions, not building architects or demolitions experts. All of Sveri's specialists in those areas were up in Cwl Gen rebuilding the broken keep, and none of their allies would have risked any such experts on such a dangerous mission as this.

"I can make it just fine," Yorna said before she swayed, and Digaelion was forced to catch her to steady her. "I just need a few days' rest."

"Even if that were true," Sveri said, "we don't have a few days to give you, except those that we will need to spend marching toward Crag Hudd."

"What if Craggoth were to carry me?" Yorna suggested.

"You would try to sneak a greater elemental into a fully defended keep? You're beginning to sound desperate."

"Isn't it worth trying it before you throw our lives away for a meaningless battle that you yourself said we can't win?"

"It is a battle that must be fought, but you would have me divert resources from our already depleted pool for a desperate mission that doesn't have a chance of success!" Sveri slammed his fist into the table. A deathly stillness followed his outburst. Yorna stared at the berserker lord with her one eye wide open. Herneas suspected not all of her trembling was being caused by her injuries.

"I have listened to your suggestions too much as it is," Sveri said at last, breaking the terrible silence. "I do not have time, nor patience to entertain them anymore." He turned his fierce gaze on Herneas, who took a deep breath in anticipation. "Send word throughout our host. If any of our allies are unwilling to march with us, I give them leave to depart and return to Eastport. Those who would stay by our side we would welcome, but they must know that there will be no shame given for those who would rescind their offers of aid. This is..."

"I can get into Crag Hudd without sneaking in." Yorna cut him off. Herneas felt his breath catch, and all of the air seemed to be pulled out of the tent as all eyes shifted back to the small warsmith.

"And how would you do that?" Sveri asked, and Herneas could practically hear his teeth grinding as he spoke. "Would you go up to the front door and ask for an audience?"

"Actually, yes," Yorna replied calmly. Herneas blinked in surprise, and there was an audible gasp from someone behind him. Sveri's knuckles were white from being clenched so hard at his sides.

"Do you mock me, girl?" Sveri said, red wisps of violence tinged his words, and Herneas braced himself for what he suspected was coming.

"Not at all, Lord Egilax. I am in earnest. Herneas has reported that they are trying to find ways to cultivate an army of golems but have thus far been unsuccessful. All of their creations have either failed completely or have been completely mad and ungovernable. But we have in our very camp a living embodiment of what they are trying to create. A construct that does not dissipate after a battle and will follow orders as needed."

"You are referring to Craggoth?" Herneas said before Sveri could respond. The berserker lord glared at him sharply.

"Exactly," Yorna replied, nodding. "I will approach them with Craggoth in tow, stating that I wish to defect, sensing that your cause is hopeless, and that I want to return to my family and my home back in the Imperial homeland. I plead clemency and offer Craggoth up as an offer for said mercy and as a token of goodwill. They take me inside, along with Craggoth, and then we break free from whatever cell they put us in, make our way to the Rift, and bring down the chamber around it before fleeing."

"So simple." Sveri snorted incredulously. "How do you plan to escape once you've done that? You would leave Craggoth in Golloch's possession?" Sveri almost snarled.

"No, because Golloch won't be there."

"How do you know that?"

"Because he will be fighting you." Yorna spoke in a matter-of-fact tone that caught Herneas off guard. By the sound of Sveri's voice when he responded, he wasn't the only one.

"What?" the berserker lord asked, a shocked look on his face.

"One of the other offerings I will give to show that I am earnest in my offer to Golloch will be knowledge of your whereabouts and your plan. Golloch is proud, he'll know he has a superior force to yours, and the idea of capturing or killing you will be too enticing for him. He won't allow you to lay siege to Crag Hudd, that would give you a chance to escape. Instead, he will march out to meet you, taking a significant amount of troops with him to do so. In the confusion of all this is when Craggoth and I will make our escape."

"What happens if you get caught or something else goes wrong? What if they just kill you and take Craggoth?"

"Then you will never have to listen to me again and are rid of a menace," Yorna replied bitterly. "Beyond that, the loss of a single elemental, even a greater one, will not change the outcome of the coming battle and you know it."

Herneas didn't dare move, it seemed as if all present were afraid to even breathe as the mighty berserker lord stared down at the injured warsmith. She did not flinch, she did not look away. But Herneas noted that her eye glistened with unshed tears, and that even with the sharpshooter standing near to support her, her legs were fiercely trembling. Sveri also trembled, but for an entirely different reason. When he opened his mouth, Herneas prepared for the outburst to come.

"No," was all he said and turned away.

Yorna stared after him for a few moments, then she fell back into her chair. Sveri turned his gaze on Herneas.

"Go and do as I told you. We will march first thing in the morning." Herneas did not move, something inside him telling him to wait. The moment stretched out for what felt like an eternity as he simply stared back at Sveri, unable to speak but unable to turn away either.

"Why?" Yorna's voice was small, but it filled the silence of the tent. Sveri turned slowly toward her.

"What?" he asked, a strange hitch in his voice that Herneas did not recognize.

"Why? Why won't you let me try?"

"Because your plan will not work, need I give another explanation?"

"But neither will yours!" Yorna yelled. Herneas took an involuntary step forward, readying to leap forward should Sveri lose his composure in response. Surprisingly, the berserker was stock-still, his face unreadable.

"Is it because I'm an Imp?!" Yorna continued. "Your prejudices prevent you from trusting me, is that it?! Need I remind you that I was the one who sabotaged the powder supply at the Battle of the Broken Peak! It was me who set the charges and provided a way for you to fight off an overwhelming Imperial attack! If it weren't for me, Cwl Gen would be under Golloch's control, and you likely would be dead! I lost my eye for you all! Why must I continuously have to prove my loyalty again and again for you?!"

"Because I will not be the one to cause the end of another clan!" Sveri shouted back, and it crumpled Yorna's remaining composure. She closed her eyes tightly, and the hot tears carved their way down her cheeks. But Sveri wasn't finished.

"I have already seen your chieftain's son dead while coming to our assistance! Then I learned that his father was killed and that their line was ended! I allowed you to put yourselves in the most dangerous position in order to better serve my own ends, and look how that ended for you!" Sveri gestured at the bandages that covered her face. "I will not sacrifice what is left of the Ffionen legacy on a hopeless attempt at a doomed outcome!"

A shattered stillness fell upon the gathering. Part of Herneas knew that they should not be having this conversation in front of all the other chieftains and leaders. But another part of him felt that something bigger than any of them was happening in that moment, and he was helpless to do anything. The stillness stretched out, filled only with the sound of Yorna's futile attempts to regain control of her emotions. Herneas didn't blame her. There were few who could weather the storm of Sveri's anger even as well as she had.

"You will take the remainder of your clan and you will return to Eastport. You will keep the Ffionen name alive as an example to the Free Clans that there is indeed honor amongst the Imperials. That there are those whom we can trust to the south and that there is at least some chance that we can overcome. We have suffered too much grief these past years. We have lost our home. We have lost so much of our identity. We have been betrayed by one who pretended to take us in and pledged to help us reclaim all of that. So many have already given so much and we are only just starting in this conflict. I cannot shoulder that burden… I will not."

Herneas felt something shift inside his chest. He hadn't been aware of this burden that Sveri was carrying. He had been so preoccupied with the march and the problems that had arisen, not to mention their own confrontation over the recent battle.

"But I am not a Ffionen," Yorna protested, but the heat had gone out of her voice. "They hired me just before coming north to help you. I am not bound to their clan, nor do they look to me as the heir to such."

"My dear Master Twilip," Sveri gave a sad chuckle, "if you think that, then why are you here, in this council of leadership for the gathered clans?" He gestured broadly to those who were assembled. Silence reigned in the tent, everyone present holding silent witness to this intimate exchange between them. Some at the back shuffled uncomfortably, but something pressed down on them, preventing them from interrupting or leaving. Herneas felt as though he were eavesdropping on a conversation that he shouldn't be, yet he couldn't stop himself. It felt like a long time before the silence was broken.

"Be that as it may, Lord Egilax," Yorna once again pushed herself to her feet, waving off Digaelion who moved to support her, "I would be remiss in my duties were I to follow your request. The last orders that were given to us by our chieftain was to assist you in the retaking of your homeland. I don't know what the future holds for the Ffionen Clan, but I would hope that it does endure, in whatever form that takes. But if it is to do so, it must have its honor intact. So I must insist that you accept our aid in this endeavor."

The two dwarfs stood staring at each other. A sad tension permeated the air, and Herneas barely dared to breath while he watched. Then, something happened that he had not expected.

Sveri sighed and stepped back.

"Let it never be said that an Imperial Dwarf is incapable of honor. Master Twilip, you have demonstrated that, and I will not have it forgotten. My lords!" He turned and addressed the whole of the gathered dwarfs. "A heavy battle is before us, and I fear it will not be one that we can win. Thus I am asking you to prepare messages to send back to your clans, to tell them to prepare for Golloch's inevitable attack that will be coming. Instruct them to begin gathering their strength. You have the testimonies of the ice elf and her warriors telling us of the fall of Crag Hudd, and you have the dedication of the Ffionen Clan to fighting against their fallen king. Take these back as evidence, along with my own avowal of their veracity. That will hopefully carry the necessary weight for the other lords to begin the necessary preparations.

"Master Twilip, there are many of your clan which are too wounded to fight. I would have you escort the rest of the wounded from our ranks back to Eastport, along with my own message to the remaining Free Clans."

"I will have our troops ready for that task, my lord." Yorna nodded her head.

"I thank you, and I will look forward to meeting you again, should we return from what lies ahead."

"I will not be going with them, though." Yorna spoke plainly, although Herneas still detected a slight tremble in her voice. "I have already told you that I will not abandon my chieftain's last command to us, and that is to help you in your struggle. I believe that my plan is still the best option that you have for success, and I know that I am the one who has the best chance of that plan working."

"That is not what I ordered, though," Sveri said, but the fight had gone out of him.

"Quite frankly, Lord Egilax, you are not my chief, so I do not take orders from you. If I have to enact my plan without your consent, I will. Although that would complicate things significantly."

Sveri opened his mouth to respond, but before he could, Herneas interrupted him.

"I will go with her," he said, and everyone in the tent turned their gaze on him. "I have already infiltrated the keep on several occasions, I can take a few rangers with me and we will be able to ensure that Yorna is able to escape and support her in her mission."

"I thank you for that, Master Hunter, but I cannot ask you to do that," Yorna said softly, although her face held a fragile smile as she spoke.

"Quite frankly, Yorna, you are not *my* chief, and so I do not take orders from you."

"I am cursed with brave, defiant fools, it seems," Sveri sighed. "My lords! I am marching on Crag Hudd for a desperate and ill-advised assault. I would welcome all those who will stand with me at this time. Any who feel that it is not in the best interest of their clan may depart without judgment."

"I think you already know our response to that, Sveri," a voice said behind Herneas. He turned to see that it was Ari Shatterpeak. "We'd be poor allies indeed if we left you now, when you needed us the most. Besides, this is shaping up to be a battle which they'll tell stories of for generations to come." There was a chorus of agreement that rippled through the other commanders.

"In that case, we'd best get started with the preparations." Sveri gave a slight smile and nodded toward the assembly. "Herneas, take

Yorna and hammer out your plan. Let us know what you need."

*****

The stars were bright, and the sliver of the moon was high by the time that the planning council adjourned. Herneas walked through the crisp night air with his thoughts whirling inside his head. The plan was desperate, and there were so many ways it could go wrong, but it was the best that they could conceive and so it would have to be enough. He prayed that it was.

He made his way to the outskirts of their camp; there was no way that he would be able to sleep at this point, so he might as well do something productive. It didn't take long until he reached the perimeter and began whistling to signal any nearby sentries.

"Couldn't sleep either, eh?" Grodgni appeared out of the shadows. Herneas was impressed, he hadn't been able to tell he was there until the former stone priest had spoken.

"No, it isn't likely to be a restful night for me. Any signs of trouble?"

"Nothing," Grodgni shook his head. "It's as quiet as I've seen it. The kind of quiet there is before a battle."

Herneas examined his friend. Grodgni's hair had grown out so that shaggy curls had begun to form, and his beard was tied simply with strips of cloth. He wore the same clothes that Herneas had given him all those months ago back in Cwl Gen before they had left. The dwarf bathed regularly and maintained his kit, but he wore absolutely no adornments. His face was not as hollow as it had been, but there was still a haunted quality to his gaze that made most dwarfs uncomfortable, even the other rangers.

"How are you holding up?" he asked. Grodgni shrugged.

"Same as always. I exist, although I don't know why."

"You lost your priesthood, not your life."

"Yeah, that's like telling a raven that it lost its wings, or a fish its fins. I lost the thing that I had built my life around. I'm not sure a building should still be standing when it has lost its foundation."

"I'm sorry, that was insensitive of me."

"It's fine. At least you'll actually talk to me, most of the others won't even do that."

"I'll talk to them about that."

"Don't bother. I get their discomfort, I'm a living reminder of what can happen when a dwarf puts their own desires first. I'm only a half step above an Abyssal in that regard."

"You sought to protect a friend."

"A friend who was harboring an Abyssal," Grodgni snorted, "and I like that you think I am that altruistic. I was scared for myself, too."

"Have you come to peace with it all?"

"No, not really." Grodgni sighed deeply. "Cwythn was a traitor. If someone as good and stalwart as him can fall, what am I capable of in comparison? I'm glad you gave me a place to be, even if I'll never belong here, because I don't know what I would have done otherwise. But even though I am grateful, I'm also bitter, too."

"At Sveri?"

"At myself, and at my situation. I recognize that it's entirely my own fault. But just because it's your own fault that you got caught in a rockslide doesn't mean you don't feel angry at the rocks for falling on you."

"What are you going to do?"

"Nothing. Everything I've done has led me to this point. So I will continue to follow orders and that's it. Until I decide to commit to a more permanent solution, maybe."

"That sounds… miserable," Herneas shifted uncomfortably, eyeing Grodgni sideways. The other dwarf shook his head bitterly.

"Thank you for not asking me what that might mean. I'm not planning on hurting anyone other than myself, I promise."

"Have you made a plan to do that?"

"Nothing specific. Just might let a sword cut me open in the next battle. Or try walking too close to the edge of the next cliff we come across. But up until now, I've been too much of a coward to actually do either of those things."

"I'm glad to hear that."

"Happy to oblige, any other ways my cowardice can make your day better?" Grodgni gave a humorless laugh. Herneas closed his eyes and shook his head. He was making a mess of this conversation, like he always did when his friend got like this. He opened his eyes and looked over at the former stone priest.

"Are you still able to work the stone?" he asked, hoping to change the subject. In response, Grodgni reached down and picked up a small rock which he gripped in his hand. Small flashes of flickering light glowed inside his fist for a few seconds, and when he opened it, there sat a figure of a small dog on his palm, perfectly formed to resemble the various mastiffs that were used to hunt tunnel rats.

"That answer your question?" he said, tossing the small sculpture away into the woods where it bounced off a tree with a hollow *thunk*.

"Grodgni, I'll be honest, I'm not sure how to help you," Herneas said, turning to face him directly.

"Me either. Not sure there is a way, unless you can find a way to go back in time."

"Would you do anything differently?"

There was a long pause before he answered.

"I don't know. I'd like to think I would, but I don't know what exactly. Wouldn't mind the chance, though. As things are now, my life has no purpose. I wander as your shadow, taking what scraps are offered to me from the other rangers, and I keep on breathing. That's my whole life, and I don't know that I want it to be a long one if that's all that I have to look forward to."

"You're still newly exiled. It hasn't even been a year yet."

"And it feels as though it's been ten," Grodgni growled.

"I'm just saying that you are still new to this way of life. Surely things will get better."

"Will they? I don't know that, and there's no evidence, yet, to suggest that it will."

"I like to think that they will, but that's easy coming from my position. That's likely small comfort for you. But I promise you this, I'm not going to just let you die, and I'm not going to leave you alone. You were a friend before all of this, and while what you did was bad, I can also understand why you did it, and I even somewhat agree with it. To me, that means that it isn't an unforgivable sin. There's got to be a reason for you to be here, Grodgni, even if that purpose isn't part of some grand design."

"Thank you for trying, my friend," Grogni said in a quiet voice, "but I fear that you are the only one who thinks that way. What will become of me should something happen to you?"

"My rangers have orders to ensure that you are cared for."

"That term has lots of different meanings depending on who you ask. You are the only one who talks to me beyond the bare minimum of curt nods and one word answers to my questions. I'm sure that they wouldn't allow me to starve, but food alone is not enough to make an existence less painful."

"I can't control that, Grodgni, I'm sorry."

"I know you can't. That's what scares me, honestly." Grodgni took a deep breath and let it out slowly. "You rush into battle, into dangerous scenarios, and you don't think of the bad consequences of your actions beyond what might happen if you *don't* rush in. You did it in this last battle and nearly got yourself killed trying to save Yorna. All the while you stuck me in another unit who didn't even see the battle until it was almost over!"

"I saw a friend who needed my help. What should I have done?"

"*I* am a friend who needs your help! Yet you left me by myself. Did you even think about that?" Grodgni snapped, his face suddenly twisted into a snarl. He brought himself up short and took a deep breath, his features uncoiling into a mask of stillness.

"I…" Herneas began, but couldn't think of what else to say.

"I know that I'm not your foremost consideration in these things. I also know that nothing will stop you from taking those risks, it's who you are and what you do. But Herneas, your fellowship is the last lifeline I have to my past self. If I lose that, then I have nothing left, and that thought terrifies me."

"So what is the point of bringing it up, then?"

"Because you are the only one I can talk to about it! Haven't you been listening?" Grodgni stared out into the shadows among the trees. "I just want you to promise me that if you ever plan on doing something reckless like that again, or if you know that you might be doing something like that in the future, I ask that you take me with you. That way I can try and keep you from getting killed, or if I fail at that, then I can die fighting alongside you. That kind of death is the least terrifying scenario of that type that I have been able to come up with."

The quiet stretched out between them for a long time. Herneas turned their conversation over in his head multiple times and tried to match it to the plan that he and Yorna had devised.

"Interesting timing for you to mention that," he said at length, "I think I have something that you can help me with."

21
Opportunity Knocks

The first and foremost need a dwarf has is a need for solidarity. This can be seen in our architecture: everything is constructed from stone and built to last for centuries. It can be seen in our societal constructs: clans and families work together to provide a firm foundation that is held up by a sense of trust and mutual respect. A dwarf knows that unless they do something blatantly wrong that their friends and family will support them. It can be seen in our religion: for what can be more assuring and solid than a mother's love?

This is also why the Abyssal Dwarfs of Tragar are insane, for they have forfeited the solidarity of their people in a desperate bid for power. They seek that firm foundation and know they will not find it among their evil brethren, and so they seek to create it by amassing power and wealth to act as a buffer between them and their inevitable betrayal.

But there is nothing more devious, or desperate, than a dwarf who is trying to hold on to ill-gotten power and authority, for they will do anything to ensure that it is not taken from them.

–Athro *Breggus the Stern*
Second High Athro *of Rhyn Dufaris in*
The Age of Winter

Argoll rubbed at his temples. It felt as though a red-hot ball of iron had wedged itself between his eyes and threatened to consume his entire body with its grinding heat. He felt the frayed edges of panic on the periphery of his conscious thoughts, always pressing in from the sides and never giving him a moment's peace. He did not sleep but for the occasional fitful nap that lasted only as long as his exhaustion managed to keep him unconscious. Every moment of his existence was filled with acidic fear that this would be the day that Golloch grew impatient and cut short his promised time to call him before the throne to answer for his failures.

The pens below Crag Hudd were full. There were hundreds, if not thousands, of feral lesser obsidian golems and dozens of greater constructs that were confined to the lower levels, writhing under the magical bonds that held them. So many failed experiments, and not one of them had shown any promise. They had all been mad as soon as they became aware of themselves. Several had even been crazed enough to tear themselves apart, seeming to prefer oblivion to the madness that assailed them.

He had tried every infernal incantation and theory that had been proposed. It was as if the golems were terrified and lashed out in their fear. This didn't make sense. Elemental spirits didn't feel fear, and any victim who had been thrust into the form of the golem would have been bound with dark power that should have prevented them from reacting like this. Yet these golems never showed the usual sense of disorientation that was typical of the average bindings. As soon as their eyes glowed to life, they immediately began swinging their limbs in a rage that chilled even Argoll's blood. Usually golems awoke like a child did from a deep slumber, but these creatures woke like a crazed lunatic waking from a nightmare only to realize that it was all real.

A shape passed across the wall to his left, and Argoll spasmed as he twisted to look at it, expecting to see someone standing there, but he was alone. The only movement was the shadows cast by the flickering torches on either side of the room where he sat. Although, he swore that he could hear echoing laughter as he took a few shuddering breaths to try and calm his nerves.

He was going insane, he decided. He'd been hearing voices and seeing phantoms for the past few weeks. All of this added to, or perhaps was caused by, the stress of his impossible task and Golloch's impending judgment for his failure.

You're not going crazy, a woman's voice seemed to whisper in his ear, and he froze, his breath catching in his throat.

"There's no one there," he muttered to himself, but his mouth was dry as he spoke. The laughter danced again in his ears, and he shook his head to try and clear it.

You keep saying that, but I don't think that you believe it... Argoll could hear the smile in the voice, even though he couldn't see a face to go with it.

You've seen my face! How could you forget it? Aquiline eyes and a fierce brow flickered across his mind's eye. He flinched at the memory.

Or would you rather I speak to you in a more familiar way? The voice shifted suddenly to some strange copy of his father's stern but gentle tones.

"Stop it!" he hissed.

Come, my son, why do you speak to me in such a harsh manner? I only wish to see you and help you!

"That dwarf is dead!" Argoll spat. "He died to me long before he was crushed by the side of a mountain falling on him."

And that fills you with the deepest regret, doesn't it?

"Silence! I... I won't..." Argoll felt something shift deep inside him, a deep emptiness like a gaping maw stretching wide to engulf him. He shied away from the feeling.

There it is! The voice changed back to its female form. *You know what that is. I know this feeling as well. It is called grief, little dwarf. Isn't it terrible?*

"Go away!" he yelled, and the voice retreated, its laugh ringing in his ears. There came a knock at the door to the chamber, and Argoll started violently.

"Are you alright in there, lord?" a muffled question came from the other side. Argoll cursed and walked over to fling the door open. A dwarf in armor stood there, his hand raised to knock again.

"What is it?" he growled. The other dwarf blinked and took a step back apprehensively.

"Someone has arrived at the gate. She says she wants to talk to you, asked for you by name, even," the dwarf stammered.

Argoll blinked a few times and then scrubbed his face briskly with his hands. A thousand ideas cascaded through his brain as to who this person could be, but nothing seemed to fit.

"Who is it? What do they want?"

"It's a Free Dwarf, that's the strange thing, and she came in riding atop an earth elemental. Says she has an offer for you."

Suddenly all weariness was gone and the memory of the voices was pushed to the back of his brain. Argoll blinked once more and then stepped back into the chamber to grab a long-handled hammer that he used for his rituals.

"Take me to her," he ordered, stepping back out into the hall and shutting the door behind him. They walked through the keep, climbing up toward the surface of the mountain, and as they did so, the whispers in the back of Argoll's mind seemed to recede.

They eventually emerged into the sunlight of what looked like midday. Argoll blinked against the sudden brightness. It had been weeks since his face had felt fresh air upon it, and the searing pain in his head worsened at the sudden white light of the sun overhead. The other dwarf then led him a bit further, guiding him up a set of stairs until they stood on a battlement looking down into the entry courtyard.

Standing in the open with several weapons pointed at her stood a short but wide dwarf with bandages wrapped around her head and obscuring one eye. She looked gaunt and drawn out. She leaned heavily against a large earth elemental that was bent down on four monstrous limbs like some kind of strange ape. On its back, among several blue crystals that glowed eerily, the elemental housed some kind of strange metal apparatus that glowed a faint orange. Argoll couldn't tell if it was because of his eyes still straining against the sunlight, or if it was because the metal was heated to a high temperature.

"Who is she?" he asked his guide.

"She says her name is Yorna Twilip, and she's come to parlay with you. She said she had something to trade, but would only talk to you."

"Yorna?!" Argoll exclaimed in spite of himself. He hadn't recognized her with the bandages. *This* was the dwarf who had sabotaged Gwrthod's powder supplies back at Cwl Gen? He found himself sneering and quickly smoothed his features. He remembered the anger that Golloch had leveled at him when he had reported their defeat and Gwrthod's death several months ago. He cleared his throat.

"I am here, as you asked. What have you to say? Quickly now, before I have you gutted and your entrails sent back to your friends as a warning."

Yorna looked up at him; her face was pinched with exhaustion, and she blinked several times before responding. When she did, her voice was hoarse and breathless, as if it took all of her effort to force the words out.

"I hear that you have been having problems with your golems," she rasped. Argoll lifted an eyebrow. How did she know about that?

"What do you mean?" he asked.

"No need to play coy," Yorna said between breaths. "You took a Free Dwarf hold and expected Sveri not to know how to sneak around it? You think he didn't send spies after you tucked tailed and ran from him at Cwl Gen?" She coughed and lifted a hand to her head.

"He knows all about your feral golems," she continued after a pause. "It's why he's on his way here to try and deal with you. At least, that's his plan. Not working out too good for him."

Argoll bit back a curse at her words. The Free Dwarfs knew what they were planning?! He looked away for a moment to clear his thoughts. This was a minor thing at present. If Sveri or any of the other Free Dwarfs showed up at their doorstep, they could just unleash the feral golems on them. Rounding up the leftovers would be a chore, however. No, this changed nothing, but he was still a dead dwarf if he couldn't figure out how to tame the mad constructs.

"I fail to see how any of this has anything to do with you, or why you came here," he said at length. "What do you want? I'll warn you in advance, my temper is running extremely short at present, and you are trying what little patience I have left. I urge you to be brief and concise with your response."

"I have the answer to your problems right here," Yorna replied, motioning toward the elemental beside her. Argoll looked it up and down. Something tickled in the back of his mind, stories from battles several years old now. Something about a certain elemental, one that kept showing up alongside... Banick Kholearm!

"Explain yourself," he commanded, but the wheels were already turning in his head.

"This is Craggoth. He's an elemental that has been bound to this corporeal form for over a decade now, with no signs of degradation or madness. He is just as strong today as he was when he first approached Banick before the Halpi Mountains fell to you lot." Yorna stopped and looked up at the giant stone creature with something that looked like sadness. "Now that Banick is dead, it seems that I've inherited his caretaking. Which means I can explain to you how it is done so that you can fix your feral golems."

The world seemed to stand still. The pain in Argoll's head faded away, and he stared down at Yorna. She turned to face him, her face red with the effort of speaking. His eyes moved hungrily over to Craggoth, scouring the creature for some hidden detail that might reveal this secret that had evaded him for so long. A hunger stirred from deep within him, and without thinking, he lifted a hand as if reaching out to grasp the knowledge that lay before him. But he stopped himself and pulled back.

Something was wrong. It was too convenient. Here he was, struggling to find an answer, when the solution to his problem simply stumbled into his lap? The universe had never been this kind to him. In fact, it had often times done the exact opposite. Everything he had, he'd needed to fight, kill, and bleed for it. Warning bells were going off in his head, and the pain of his headache returned.

"Why would you do this? Why would you betray your people?" he finally asked.

"The Free Dwarfs aren't my people," she responded. Had she been a little too quick with that response? "If you'll recall, I am an Imperial Dwarf, and I have a bounty on my head issued by the crown for my part in the battle of Cwl Gen. As it stands, I can never go home. I can never see my parents, or any of my friends back there. And because I'm an *Imp*, I'm treated with suspicion and doubt in Sveri's camp. That's a fine reward for all that I've done for them. To me, it isn't worth it."

Had she prepared that speech? Possibly. But was it meant to deceive him? He wasn't sure. He wanted so desperately for it to be true, which is why he knew that it likely wasn't.

"Why should I believe you? Furthermore, why shouldn't I just kill you and take the elemental myself for my own study?"

"You could," she responded. He strained to see if any trace of fear or desperation betrayed her voice, but she only sounded exhausted. "But Craggoth here is rather fond of me, I don't imagine he'd react well if you did kill me. You could probably take him down, but a greater elemental inside your walls will likely do a number on your defenses. Then, once you've killed him, you won't be able to study what keeps him alive. I can instruct you on the process, tell you how it all works and how we do it. Keeping me alive is just more economical for you. Basically, I have something that you want, which is why I'm betting that you won't kill me." She shook her head and sighed heavily.

"Secondly," she continued, "as a sign of good faith, I can tell you where Sveri is right now. He was coming to storm this very keep, but we ran into a horde of ratkin. That's who's responsible for my new face." She waved a hand over the bandages covering her head. "If you couldn't tell, it didn't go well for him. Now he's licking his wounds and preparing to retreat, but he's got a bunch of injured he's gotta take with him. If you hurry, you can still catch him. Taking Sveri out this early in the fight with the Free Dwarfs could very well end the war before it even starts. But I don't have to tell you that."

Argoll contemplated all of this silently, knowing that the silence was stretching out and those around him were beginning to fidget. He didn't care.

The warning bells were still going off in his head. Everything about this was too good to be true. She must be playing at something. Why would a dwarf who risked her life to destroy their powder supplies at Cwl Gen suddenly turn against and betray those whom she had defended? As far as deceptions went, this was a poor one. It was obviously a trick of some sort. He should kill her and be done with it.

Except for one thing. He was desperate. He didn't know if the elemental actually held the answer to his dilemma, but he had exhausted all of his other avenues of research, and Golloch was demanding answers. If he killed her now, he would never know and was likely to follow her into death when Golloch found that he was no closer to solving the issue with the golems. Perhaps that was the solution? She did have information that he wanted, and she was willing to walk into her own torture chamber where he could have her answer all of his questions. After she was subdued, it wouldn't matter if she had some devious plan, she would be trapped. He could tear his answers out of her and feed her corpse to his ratkin slaves when he was finished with it.

"Very well, I accept. Where is Sveri?"

"Not until I have your word that I will be granted amnesty and the bounty on my head will be removed." Yorna shook her head. "I want to be able to go home after all of this is over."

"You have it. I will even pay for passage for your trip there," Argoll responded, perhaps a little too eagerly, for he saw her hesitate. Then, she looked at her feet, closed her eyes, and nodded.

"Sveri is half a day's march to the southeast of here. Follow the mountain stream and you won't be able to miss his host." Yorna's voice was cracked and raw at this point, and she didn't look up after she spoke. Argoll had to fight to keep the smile off his face. He turned to the dwarf beside him.

"Send word to dispatch a clutch of gargoyles to verify what she said is true. Have her taken below and separated from her elemental. Bind it in the pens with the other golems and with the same restraints. Take her to a different cell and make sure her wounds are taken care of. I don't want her dying before I can interrogate her." He turned back to the courtyard.

"You've made the right choice," he said, unable to hide his smile any more. "Soon enough, all of this will be behind you and you will be on your way home."

*****

The sun was beginning to graze the tops of the mountain peaks around them. Herneas stared out at the walls of Crag Hudd from between the branches of a few scrub-like trees that he and his other rangers were using for cover.

"She's been in there a long time," Grodgni said beside him.

"I know."

"Think they figured out it was a trick?"

"I certainly hope not, for everyone's sake."

"How much longer do you want to wait before we send the message back to Sveri that it's a bust?"

"Not for a bit, yet, at least."

"Certainly hopeful, aren't you?"

"One of us has to be," Herneas grunted, unable to keep the irritation out of his voice.

"Life has been a bit too real for me to acknowledge hope that readily. I'm far too pragmatic."

Herneas turned to glare at him, opening his mouth to say a few choice words when Brethod on his other side suddenly grabbed his shoulder and pointed.

"Look, there!" the younger dwarf exclaimed. Herneas looked to where he was pointing and strained his eyes. What looked like a flock of birds had begun circling above the ramparts of Crag Hudd, but then Inei, the ice-elf hissed.

"Get down!"

The flock of birds drew closer, their squawking getting louder until Herneas realized that they were more like tortured screams torn from a human mouth. Their shapes took on better definition to show the skeletal forms of women with horrible, horn-like protrusions from their head and gray, scaly skin covering their bodies. Leathery wings beat the air around them, propelling them through the sky.

The gargoyles sped over the copse where Herneas and the others were hiding and then swung further south, their silhouettes getting lost in the dying light of the day.

"That answers that question," Herneas grunted after a good amount of time had elapsed since he lost sight of them.

"Indeed." Grodgni shrugged. "And now we wait."

22
The Painful Truth

I am reminded of the parable of the wayward fisherman:

A beggar was plying his trade down by the docks one day when a lost fisherman came by... He asked the beggar where to find somewhere to sleep that night, and the beggar directed the fisherman down a nearby alley where the beggar promptly stabbed him through the heart and robbed him...

The moral of the story was that the fisherman never trusted another soul ever again after the beggar lied to him about his true profession.

–Caius Brasser
Representative of the Basilean Duma
when asked about the events of the
Dwarf Civil War

Darkness engulfed Ofn on all sides. He had a vague memory of fire wrapping its fingers around him and then a sensation of flying. Then water had poured into his mouth and nose, and he had almost choked on it.

He remembered hands pulling at him and then air kissing his lips as he sucked in great gulps of it that strained against his scorched lungs. Somewhere a voice had said something like:

"Get this one to Rordin, he'll want to talk to him..."

After that, he'd had flashes of visions snagged from the fever dreams of his existence. Flashes of sunlight filtered through the slats of a wagon. The sensation of someone standing over him. The rough and painful staggering movements as the ground rumbled and bumped underneath his tortured body, every jolt a stab of pain that ran through his body from temple to toenails. In between each sensation was a lifetime of darkness, and what little he could piece together was disjointed and filtered through a red haze of agony that prevented any rational thought.

Where is Garrek? He found himself thinking, but something stopped that thought from taking hold, and it slid across his mind like water across ice. Instead, it jittered and sparked in his brain before sprinting off into the darkness.

"You've done it now," someone said from the shadows, and Ofn thought it sounded like Banick's voice.

"Banick?!" Ofn called out, but it hurt his lips to speak.

"Like he would listen to you, after what you did," another voice, this one belonged to Garrek.

"Garrek?!" Ofn cried his name, ignoring the pain in his lips as a deeper ache ignited in his chest.

"How can you think to speak to me after all of this?" Garrek's tone was accusing, it dripped with anger and malice.

"No! I... I... never..." Ofn's words trailed off, and he found he was slurring his words as if his tongue was swollen.

"You took what you had and you threw it away. Burned it like it was trash!" The voice switched back to Banick.

"You've even thrown away what I offered you, too." Now it was Gruumen's angry tone that echoed up out of the darkness.

"I don't care..." Ofn slurred, his lips felt like they were breaking apart as he spoke. "Was gonna kill you anyways..."

He tried to lift his hand to wave off Gruumen's presence, but his hand refused to obey him, and his arm stung from the effort as though his skin was being dragged across hot stones. He realized at that moment that it was true, too. He'd never given voice to that thought out loud or officially planned anything, but the thought of placing his hands around Gruumen's throat and squeezing his life out of his eyes filled him with a sense of satisfaction. He'd just wait until Gruumen had won the fight against the rest of the dwarfs, then he'd kill him and be seen as a hero by Free and Imperial Dwarfs alike!

"Is that all we meant to you?" Banick asked, still standing somewhere out in the darkness. "Were we just stepping stones to you? Tools to get you more power? I guess I shouldn't be surprised by that. Still hurts, though."

"No...! Friends..." Ofn managed to mutter.

"The honesty is good. Although some part of me had hoped that you would have held some value in our interactions back in Caeryn Golloch. Too much to hope for someone like you, I suppose."

Ofn frowned and then grimaced at the effort. Something felt off in Banick's voice. He sounded more solid than the other voices had, more real. Gruumen and Garrek had sounded far away, as though they were speaking on the other side of a large chamber and it was only their echoes that reached him. Banick, on the other hand, sounded as though he were sitting right next to him, although Ofn couldn't see him.

Part of Ofn realized that he was dreaming. This part of him dredged up the images of a burning bridge and Garrek's slumped form amongst the flames. The other part of Ofn, the side that just wanted to continue sleeping, immediately threw those images away. But the damage was done, and control of the dream spiraled away from him.

"You killed me!" Garrek's voice growled.

"Didn't… want… that…" Ofn rasped.

"What you want and what is before you are often two different things. Your lack of resolve and dedication are what led you to this point," Gruumen's voice chastised him.

"Maybe I did want to be friends with you," Banick's quieter voice cut through the other whispers. "Maybe I just needed a friend, but I trusted you, and you betrayed that trust."

"Banick!... Why?" Ofn tried to turn his head to look for him, but his muscles screamed in protest to the motion.

"Because you acted the part so well. But you were willing to kill me, and you did kill Garrek. I see what friendship gets you amongst the Abyssals."

"Didn't… mean to…"

"That makes it better? You still did it!"

"S-sss-...orry…" Ofn grimaced.

"What does that even mean?" Gruumen's voice took over again. "You're sorry? Is there anything in your life that you haven't betrayed? Anything that you've cared about enough to not destroy it?" Ofn flinched internally at Gruumen's mocking tone.

"Stop it!" he cried. The effort of the outburst burned his throat, and he felt something salty and wet on his lips.

"Fine," Banick said, "I'll leave you be. You have a reckoning coming, though."

"Wait! Don't go!"

Ofn woke up.

He was looking up into a stone ceiling. A candle or some other open flame flickered, casting its stuttering shadows across the only wall that he could see. The dream still circled in his brain, giving him a sense of vertigo. The room looked strange, and it took him a moment to realize it was because he was looking through only one eye. The other one was swollen shut, it refused to open no matter how hard he tried.

His body hurt everywhere, especially his head, and he tried to lift a hand to his throbbing temples, but it wouldn't respond. He tried to move his neck to look down at the limb, but he only managed to get a few inches off of his pillow before it caused his vision to blur with pain, causing him to grunt before allowing his head to fall back.

"I wouldn't try to move, were I you," a familiar voice said to his right. Ofn forced his head to turn, the effort causing him to stifle a moan. Banick's face appeared in his vision. His features were stern, his beard poorly disguising a deep scowl that creased his brows.

"Wha… What happened?" Ofn rasped.

"You blew the bridge for us, while you and Garrek were both still on it."

"Garrek? Did he…?" Ofn trailed off. Banick's scowl seemed to deepen, and it was a long time before he responded.

"You killed him. At least that is the assumption. We weren't able to find his body, but we saw how the fight between you had gone. You might have killed him before the explosives ignited for all we know."

"I… I'm sorry." Ofn couldn't think of anything else to say. His body tensed as something heavy slammed into the bed in which he lay. He blinked as he realized that Banick was leaning directly over him now, his face a red mask of fury.

"You're sorry?!" Banick yelled, the sound was so intense that it made Ofn flinch. "Who gives a rat's ass that you are sorry?! Garrek is dead! You killed him! Nothing is going to change that! Least of all your pathetic apology!" His words echoed against the stone, pounding themselves into Ofn's skull like blows from a hammer. The silence that followed as Banick simply sat and stared at Ofn was even more terrifying.

"Where are we?" Ofn asked lamely, his voice was growing stronger the more he spoke, but words failed him. He didn't know what else to say, and his heart ached at the thought of Garrek's demise. Banick gave him a look of surprise, then closed his eyes and took a deep breath before responding.

"We're in Dolgarth. We managed to make it in no small part because of you. When you blew the bridge up, you forced Gruumen to make the long trek to an easier crossing, at which point we had over a week's headway over him. Our scouts last reported that he was retreating back to Caeryn Golloch to consolidate his forces. You are alone, and no one is coming to rescue you."

"I don't think you understand how displeased he likely is with me. If he were to 'rescue' me, it would likely be to simply give me a more painful death." Ofn felt a tickle in the back of his throat which triggered a violent spasm of coughs that filled his body with agony from the exertion.

"How did I get here?" he asked when the coughing subsided.

"I found you while I was walking the riverbanks trying to find some sign of Garrek. The only reason you're not dead already is because I think that you might have some useful information that you might trade for your life."

"Glad to know that you still care," Ofn chuckled painfully.

"You don't get it, do you?" Banick shook his head and leaned back.

"What's that?"

"I am not your friend! I didn't put a knife to your throat because you are more useful alive than dead. At least for the time being."

"Guess that means I should prove useful, then, huh?" Ofn tried to smile, but Banick's frown only deepened.

"Why?" he asked at length.

"Why what?"

"Why did you do it all? Why did you pretend to be my friend? Why go through all that effort? There surely was another way that you could have done it. Was it just to be more cruel? Is that your Abyssal nature showing through?"

"I..." Ofn opened his mouth to answer but quickly shut it again. He took a deep, shuddering breath and tried again. "I never lied to you about being your friend, Banick."

"Bullocks."

"Believe what you will, but I always considered you someone that I would trust with my life. It seems as though I was right, considering my present circumstances."

"You're burned over half of your body. It's a wonder that you've lived this long."

"Not my first time being burned like this, I promise you," Ofn winced. "Though this might be my last... I wouldn't recommend it."

Banick didn't respond. Ofn closed his eyes as a wave of nausea rolled over him and he was forced to swallow a wad of spit that threatened to evolve into vomit in his mouth.

"I wish things had been different between the two of us, Banick. I think we could have been great friends if circumstances had been changed ever so slightly."

"I don't care, Ofn. You betrayed me. Left me to die. You threatened my friends and have killed several of them."

"I never wanted Garrek to die. I tried to prevent it."

"How?! By burning him alive?"

"That was... an ill-thought-out decision on my part."

"Oh? Is that all? You murdered him when his back was turned on you. What kind of 'friend' does that?"

"I am not saying that I have been a good friend, but you have to remember that where I come from, friendship can get you killed. It is seen as a weakness. That world is nearly all that I have ever known until I met you and Garrek."

"I don't care about your tragic history, Ofn! You knew that Garrek and I would have helped you break away from all of that had you but asked!"

"I suppose some part of me might have thought that," Ofn sighed, coughing a little as he fought to fill his lungs again. "But all I have ever known is betrayal. I have had people use me in the past who pretended to care for me. My mother, for instance, should have been the one stalwart in my memories, but all she did was bring a parade of her lovers through my life, each one worse than the last, each one leaving lasting injuries on my flesh and my psyche until I could bear it no longer and I killed her with my bare hands. Since then, I have sought to be the user, always, rather than the used. You expected me to throw a lifetime of habits away after a few months of knowing you?"

"But you weren't in Tragar!"

"No, but I had brought all of that with me, hadn't I? Now your homeland burns because of what I and a few others were able to do without raising a hand of our own for the violence!" He gave a bitter laugh.

"You've done plenty of violence at this point, though."

"I've done what I needed to do in order to survive. Something you should know about, Banick."

"I have never betrayed a friend before."

"What about a lover? A wife? A fellow soldier? Who are those ghosts that haunt you, Banick?"

"I never…" Banick sputtered, but his words died on his lips.

"You forget that I was your priest for a time. I know what dwells in your heart. And I know that you and I are not so different, really."

"I am nothing like you!" Banick spat.

"You are a survivor, like me. You're an outsider to a society that only cares for you when you are useful. Otherwise, you are considered dead weight and expendable."

"That isn't true."

"Isn't it?" Ofn growled as another bout of pain bounced up from his feet to the top of his head. It felt as though his skin was ready to slough off his bones. "Look what happened to you once you were disgraced! Your wife left you, just in time to be killed by the goblins who raided her settlement. You went into exile, to be forgotten in the mines when the ratkin came storming into your tunnels, and suddenly you became valuable once more. You helped retake Cwl Gen, and in return, you were rewarded with a mission to be thrown before the wolves of Caeryn Golloch. When will you be honored for your accomplishments rather than used as a tool for them?"

"I chose that, though. Every part of it. I chose my exile. I was the one who pushed my wife away. I got my friends killed through my poor choices, and I have chosen to weather that regret rather than justify it. That is the difference between us. I chose to come to terms with my choices, and you have chosen to become a victim of yours!"

"You think that I have been a passive vehicle in all of this? That I have not chosen the best outcomes that I could have with what I was given?" Ofn snarled. "You think that wearing your transgressions as a badge of pride, like some kind of martyr, makes your actions more justified than mine? At the end of all this, Banick, your friends are still dead, and your home is still burning. The only difference is that in my case, it is my enemies who lay at my feet. Do your ends justify your pious indignation? Do you think that I wanted to grow up in Tragar? That I wanted to feel my mother's beatings rather than her tender embraces? That I didn't wish that I had felt the warmth of a hearth fire rather than the blistering heat of the slave pits? I have sought my whole life to be free from suffering. While you are so oblivious to what suffering truly is that you seek it out in the name of misguided self-righteousness. The mockery of the hurt that you have felt in your life is the only thing that has separated you from me. Had you been through what I have, you would have made the same choices!"

"Is that how you turned Gruumen? You used his abusive father against him?"

"Gruumen was turned long before I met him. I was just part of the push that made it official. There's a better example of what I am talking about. Gruumen grew up in your society, or one more similar to yours than mine was, yet he knew what suffering truly was. To have a parent wear so many different masks that you don't know which one will be waiting for you at home each night? Will it be the happy drunk or the angry belt that waits for you? No one in your dwarf society offered to help him, even though it was the worst-kept secret in his community. It wasn't any of their business, they reasoned. So they left him to his father's whims. Gruumen recognized the teachings for what they were!"

"What is that?"

"They are the truth! Ariagful doesn't hide behind deceitful promises or beautiful lies! She's a spiteful bitch, but at least she is honest about it. She doesn't lie about how suffering is part of life, but that there is a true purpose behind that suffering. It sharpens the edge of our anger like a whetstone. It purifies our fury like a crucible, and it hardens our resolve so that only the strongest emerge from our suffering. We are not burdened with family, and our vision is clear as a result. This is why your king 'fell.' It was because he recognized that truth: that each individual is responsible for their own fate, and that only the strong have the power to seize true greatness!"

"Golloch is alive, then?"

"Of course he is! And he is coming for you! I wanted to try and save you, Banick, you and Garrek, I wanted to try this friendship that you say we had between us. But I see now that all it took was a slight betrayal to undermine those bonds that are supposedly unbreakable by your standards! I'm tired of you and Garrek's judgemental stares and harsh words simply because I chose to save my own life! If that is what constitutes friendship, then I want nothing of it!"

Banick stared down at him, his face carved from stone as Ofn snarled his angry words. They sat in silence for a long span of seconds that caused Ofn's stomach to churn. He felt something breaking inside him. He wanted to recall those words, to summon them back, but it was too late, they were out. But perhaps it wasn't too late. Forgiveness was a part of friendship, wasn't it? He had to try.

"Banick, I'm sorry… I shouldn't have said those words," Ofn started to say. "Can you forgive…"

"Is that sufficient evidence for you?" Banick cut him off. He wasn't speaking to Ofn, though, his gaze was fixed on someone on Ofn's other side.

"More than enough, I think," Rordin's voice answered. Ofn twisted sharply, his body screaming in protest at the sudden movement. Rordin stood there, a few paces from the bed where Ofn lay. Several other dwarfs stood beside him, some of whom Ofn recognized from the meeting of the clans that seemed so long ago now. He hadn't been able to see them with his eye swollen shut when he'd first awoken. He blinked and gave a soulless chuckle.

"Very clever, Banick," he grimaced, forcing his aching head back around to stare at the other dwarf. "You would have made an excellent Abyssal."

Banick ignored him and continued talking to the other dwarfs.

"Do you believe my story now?" he asked without looking down at Ofn.

"You're asking a lot of us, *Free* Dwarf," an unfamiliar voice responded.

"No more than we've already given to try and keep your lands safe, *Imp*." Banick's voice dripped with barely contained anger and frustration.

"That will be enough of that," Rordin's words cut across the conversation. "Will you join us, Balchder?"

"The bastard killed my father and made the Afalans look like fools. Even if Golloch weren't an Abyssal, I'd join you at this point."

"What about the rest of you?" Rordin said, and he must have turned further away because his voice became more muffled.

"We are with you." Other voices joined in the affirmative.

"The Crydwe Clan will join with you."

"The Sandroots stand with you, too."

"The traitor has a lot to answer for!"

Various other dwarfs joined in. Ofn tried to count their numbers, but a wave of pain caused him to screw his eyes shut and clench his jaw so that he wouldn't call out.

"Looks like it was all for naught with you," Banick said. Ofn opened his eyes and saw the other dwarf staring down at him.

"What do you mean?" he spoke through gritted teeth as the pain began to slowly recede.

"The Imperial clans are uniting against Golloch. Soon, they will march on him, and then his tyranny will end."

Ofn gave a humorless chuckle and winced as it sent ripples of agony through his skull.

"You have, what, a score of clans here? I didn't keep track, but even if I'm off by a few, that still doesn't account for even a tithe of the clans in the empire. You don't know which ones will side with Gruumen and Golloch, and which will follow your Rordin, still. Worse, you don't know which ones are also Abyssals in disguise. For all you know, I might have allies in this very room." He watched as Banick's jaw clenched, he could practically hear his teeth grinding.

"It doesn't matter. Golloch's secret is out. There is no putting that badger back in its hole. He won't be able to subjugate the clans unwittingly now."

"Then he is back to the original plan of doing it by force. That's all that you have changed. Instead of an easy transition, you have forced the way of bloodshed and pain. Is that what you wanted?"

"Better to die fighting for our freedom than live in abject slavery."

"That is a lie!" Ofn snarled, ignoring the pain. "Dead is dead! Once you cross that threshold, there is nothing else that can be done! The final page in your story is written, and there is no chance to change anything. Don't feed me this bravado of 'death before surrender!' Who are you trying to convince? I have seen stronger dwarfs than you break, their whimpering pleas for the pain to stop still ring in my ears at night! Their morals didn't save them! Didn't protect them! Their bravery did nothing to ease the torment of my blades on their skin! In the end, they died with gratitude in their eyes as I slid my steel deep into their bellies! Do not tell me that you do not fear the storm that you have brokered with this revelation. Your words are as hollow as your friendship ever was!"

"I could never be friends with a monster like you," Banick replied.

"You forget that you have confessed your sins to me," Ofn chuckled, but his eyes were hard as they stared back at him. "I know what kind of monster you are, too. I know what haunts you, and I hope you are ready for an entire host of spectres to visit you for your part in the death that is coming for them."

A wave of coughing wracked its way through his chest, and Ofn spasmed with pain as his breathing came in between shuddering hacking fits. The world turned red in his vision, and bright spots flickered on his periphery.

When he finally regained control of himself, he saw that he was alone. Banick was nowhere to be seen. A hollow ache filled his stomach, twisting itself up into his chest and constricting his throat. Outside the room where he was, he thought he could hear a lonely wind whistling among the stones, a haunting melody that filtered through the cracks in his soul.

"I'm sorry!" he choked on the words and they tumbled from his lips as a whisper that seemed to echo in the emptiness around him. The ache was deep within his bones. His heart beat dully in his chest, the painful rhythm uneven and halting as it tried to match the wind's howling aria.

He willed it to stop. It slowed as if in answer. The room grew darker. Ghosts moved in the shadows, waiting for him.

They wouldn't have to wait long, he thought.

He only wanted silence now. He took a breath and squeezed his eyes shut, surrendering himself to the dark and the hopeful isolation of oblivion.

23
The Subtle Art of Deception

Elementals do not understand the concept of lying. It is not in their nature to deceive, for they have no basis around which to form such a thing. They can comprehend danger, they understand pain, and they know when a stone priest calls them that such is a chosen vessel of Dianek and so will do the Athro's *bidding.*

However, deception requires subtlety, and there is nothing subtle about stone. It does not seek to hide its motives, it simply is, and the world around it must either force it to move or retreat.

That is the argument of stone.

–Athro *Crudwych of Rhyn Dufaris*

"It looks like they're sending almost everyone," Brethod whispered beside Herneas as they stared down at the column of abominations marching out of the gates of Crag Hudd.

"One can only hope," Herneas replied. He slid back from the edge of the hill where they lay surveying the keep. The rest of their group was kneeling a few yards down from the crest. There were about twelve of them, including himself and Brethod. Inei knelt beside Grodgni, who had a sour expression on his face as he toyed with the satchels that Yorna had left with them. They housed the explosives that would be needed to seal off the cavern where the portal lay. The others looked at him expectantly as he approached.

"It's time," Herneas said simply. "You all know the plan. We go in through our private entrance, free Yorna and Craggoth, and set the cavern where the Rift is to blow before fleeing ourselves. Try not to make any more noise than we have to. The keep is mostly empty, but there are still more of them in there than there are of us."

"How do we know where Yorna and Craggoth will be?" Inei asked with a raised eyebrow.

"They've built containment pens to house their failed experiments in. Grodgni and I saw them the last time we snuck in. I doubt that they would just willingly trust Yorna. They would likely take her and Craggoth there, as it's the only place they could be sure would hold him."

"And how do we get them out of there? Are there keys we need to steal?"

"It uses magical power that it siphons off the Rift. There's a device that's located next to the cavern that funnels the excess energy and uses it to create the barriers which the feral golems can't cross, strange crackling bolts of red lightning. We take it out and it should lower those."

"What does the device look like?"

"Like some strange, crystal pillar. It's hard to miss, all of the red lightning streams from it like it's a piece of metal in the middle of a thundercloud."

"If we destroy that, won't it let all of the golems out, too?"

"I imagine it will." Herneas grinned wickedly. "I sure hope that it does in any case. Let the bastards deal with the horrors that they have created. Admittedly, it may make things a bit more difficult for us. We'll have to move quickly, but the golems could also cause a major distraction that will help us escape."

"Sounds like there is a lot in your plan that could go wrong." Inei frowned.

"All the best plans do that, from what I understand." Herneas shrugged. "Any other questions? If not, let's go."

They moved as one. The sky above was turning dark with storm clouds as if they saw what was happening and were participating in a dark play that was unfolding beneath them. The warriors made their way around to the base of the rise where the keep's main entrance stood and began the perilous climb to the entrance of the cave where they could infiltrate the lower halls.

When they finally did pass from the natural stone passages into the carved corridors of the keep itself, Herneas felt his pulse quicken as he glanced up and down the hallway. There was no movement besides the flickering of the torches in their sconces. He motioned his rangers forward, indicating that the elf should scout ahead. She nodded and melted into the shadows. She reappeared before every junction to guide their steps. Occasionally she would hold up a hand or urge them back while the armored figures of guards stomped past, but her familiarity with the keep helped them to avoid detection.

Finally, they came to a door that they couldn't bypass, and sneaking past the guards was out of the question. A group of four heavily armored dwarfs stood with spears and thick shields facing the only approach to the large double doors that led down toward the cavern that held the Rift.

"I'll take aim with my bow at the ones on the left," Herneas whispered. "The rest of you sweep in on the ones on the right and cut them down as quickly as you're able. Guard your rear and I will take out the other guard once I've reloaded before joining the fight if you haven't finished the other two off by then."

There was no argument, and the other rangers spread out against the opposite wall to him, preparing to spring once he pulled the trigger on his Skewerer.

Herneas placed the butt of the crossbow against his shoulder and took several deep breaths, raising the weapon to take aim. Time stood still for a long moment. He took a final deep breath and held it. He could feel his heartbeat hammering at his temples. He squeezed the trigger and felt the shock of the bolt's release reverberate against his shoulder.

The world seemed to freeze at that moment as the projectile flew through the air. His aim was good, and he knew he would hit his target. Even so, it seemed to take hours for the bolt to slam into the chest of the dwarf closest to the door. As soon as it connected, though, time seemed to run to catch up. The guard was thrown backward by the force of the hit, and he toppled back into the door with a loud crash and slid to the ground. The other three dwarfs stared at their fallen comrade for only the briefest of moments before their instincts kicked in.

"Intruders!" the closest to the already dead dwarf bellowed, banging his fist against the door. The other two dwarfs raised their shields and rested their spears against them in a defensive posture. Herneas cursed as they covered the other dwarf's back so that he couldn't get a second shot off now. His rangers rushed forward silently, their axes raised as they closed with the enemy. The defenders stabbed out with their spears, causing the impetus of the charge to falter as the first few rangers struggled to dodge the attacks in the confines of the corridor.

Herneas wound the string of his heavy crossbow back so that he could place another bolt in the groove. Once that was in place, he raised it to his shoulder again and released the safety. He felt the tension in the trigger and tried to steady his breathing so that he could take another shot, but the enemy was taking no chances. They hid behind their shields and only poked the top of their heads out when they were about to attack. It wasn't the most effective or deadly strategy if they wanted to kill any of Herneas's rangers, but it kept them from being overwhelmed.

The old ranger grunted in frustration as he tried to line up another shot but couldn't find a good target, or if he did, the chaos of battle pushed one of his own warriors in the path of his shot. Then to his dismay, the doors behind them opened, and two more armored dwarfs rushed out to stand beside the others, while the one who had been yelling ducked away into the passages behind his comrades and disappeared out of sight.

Cursing, Herneas loosed the bolt in his crossbow and it sailed through the air to embed itself in the knee of one of the defenders, who screamed and twisted sideways. The rangers were upon him in an instant. Brethod charged forward and brought his axe down on the exposed arm of the wounded dwarf, cutting through the crease in his elbow and nearly severing the arm in one fell cut. The other dwarf turned and thrust his spear half-heartedly at the young ranger, but Inei was quick to lunge forward and drove her sword down and through the distracted fighter's throat, sliding underneath the edge of his helm.

The last dwarf, seeing the bloody demise of his two comrades, threw down his spear and turned to run, but another ranger rushed forward and cut him down from behind before he could take two steps.

Herneas rushed forward and surveyed the damage. The door was open, but one of the guards had escaped. He would likely be sounding the alarm at this point.

"We need to go. Quickly!" he growled, and they ran through the door, not bothering to clean up the site of their skirmish.

They rushed down the hallways, finally reaching a set of stairs that descended until they came to another door. This one opened up into a more hastily constructed passageway that wound downward even further. They continued following it until at last they spilled out into the cavern where the swirling energies of the Rift cast purple light all across the walls. The air seemed to grow stale, and the scent of blood and other bodily fluids filled their nostrils. Herneas grimaced.

"Spread out. The device for the cages should be in the next room. We need to hurry before…" he cut off as the sounds of boots on stone caused him to turn and look behind him.

"They are coming!" Inei hissed.

"*Uff'ran!*" Herneas swore. How had they reacted so quickly? "Quickly! Hide, we will ambush them as they come into the cavern!"

The rangers scattered to either side of the entrance. The sound of stamping boots drew closer. Herneas glanced across the way and locked eyes with Grodgni, who was shaking his head sadly.

What is he planning? Herneas thought to himself. But he didn't have time to consider anything else as at that moment a group of guards charged into the chamber. Herneas hesitated for a moment before charging them from the side as they stormed past him.

The first dwarf in his path died without ever seeing him. The second turned to face the oncoming threat but was unable to do anything as Herneas's axe caved in his helm and cut deep into his face, killing him instantly. The other rangers fell viciously on their foes all around him, but there were too many for them to slay before they were able to react. Graedle, an older ranger, went down with a spear to his gut just to the side of Herneas. He cursed and grabbed the haft of the spear; running his axe up the length of the weapon, he connected with his opponent's hand, severing the fingers. The dwarf fell back, screaming, and Herneas turned his attention to the next fighter in line.

All around them was chaos and blood. Herneas wasn't sure how many of the Imps there were, but even after the violent start to their encounter, it looked like they still outnumbered his own soldiers. He swung his axe at another of the armored traitors, but it glanced off his pauldron, and Herneas staggered back in order to avoid the counterattack that immediately followed. In the process of doing so, his foot slipped on a corpse, and he found himself tumbling onto the blood-slicked ground.

His foe was on top of him in moments, and Herneas was forced to raise the haft of his axe to ward off several blows, twisting this way and that to avoid the stabbing point of a spear aimed at his ribs. On one such motion, he wasn't quite fast enough and felt a searing pain as the point pierced his side deeply. Black blood welled up from the wound, and he snarled as he reached up to grab the Imp by his beard. He pulled down hard and brought his axe up to meet the other dwarf's face as it came toward him with a crunching sound of bone and cartilage breaking. The dwarf fell back, blood fountaining from his nose, and Herneas quickly wrenched the spear from his side and reversed his grip on it to ram it back into its owner's exposed belly.

He staggered to his feet, pressing a hand to his side and feeling the hot wetness there as blood boiled through his fingers. His head spun, and he found that it was hard to focus his eyesight.

"Herneas!" Grodgni's voice shouted in his ear, and he winced at the sound. The former stone priest was beside him suddenly. He pressed a hand against Herneas's wound, and a faint glow began to emanate from his palm. Herneas gasped as a cold shiver ran through his body. He felt the puncture in his side knitting closed. His vision began to focus once more. He looked down at Grodgni, who was wincing as he continued to chant prayers under his breath. It seemed that even though dwarf society had ostracized him, the Earth Mother still heard his pleas.

Grodgni coughed, and a glob of bloody phlegm spilled from his lips. Herneas forced his hand away from the wound, which had stitched itself closed now, although it was still raw and tender beneath his tunic.

"That's enough! Any more and you'll kill yourself!" he growled at the former stone priest, who grinned a red smile at him.

"You say that like it's a bad thing. At least it'd be a noble death," Grodgni wheezed.

"Stop talking like that. Don't you dare," Herneas snarled and pushed himself to his feet to survey the fight. His rangers were fighting well. They'd killed almost twice their number, but the enemy still outnumbered them. Besides Graedle, there was another ranger, Faedra, with her red hair, who lay in a pool of her own blood. Other rangers were wounded, but all were still fighting tooth and nail. But it was not a fight that they could win.

"You've got to get out of here!" Grodgni called out.

"I'm not abandoning anyone."

"I don't think you have a choice! The mission is more important!" Grodgni took Yorna's satchels from where they hung around his shoulders and thrust them at Herneas, who shook his head. But even as he watched, one of the Imps managed to pass his spear through the lines and skewer Brethod's foot. The young ranger cried out and cleaved the offending dwarf's skull in two with a mighty heft of his axe. On the other opposite flank, another ranger screamed in pain and staggered back, clutching his shoulder as a spear punched through it. Grodgni stepped closer to him and whispered fervently.

"Leave me a few of the wounded who would only slow you down and go find Yorna! She needs to shut this portal down to stop all of this madness!"

Herneas looked over at him. He felt empty inside as if he had been hollowed out with a knife.

"I can't..." he started to say, but he stopped himself. He closed his eyes and took a shuddering breath. He reached out and snatched the satchels from Grodgni.

"Brethod! Kyleah! Goshen!" he bellowed. "You will stay with Grodgni and guard our retreat!"

Even as he called out, he saw the faces of those whose names he'd said flinch, but then a grim determination came over their faces and they formed up together. Goshen with his wounded shoulder picked up a light spear and braced it against his foot. Kyleah and Brethod held onto each other and limped over to join him. Grodgni walked over and placed his hands on their shoulders. The same blue light that had healed Herneas's wounds flickered into existence as he began to move his lips in silent prayer.

"Rangers!" Herneas growled, forcing his constricting throat to obey him. "Pull back! Make for deeper into the caverns!"

With the drilled precision that the Master Hunter expected of his handpicked troop, the rangers each took three sweeping steps forward and took a swing with their axes with each step. It had the desired effect of forcing the enemy onto their back foot, allowing the rangers to retreat. The four dwarfs that Herneas had ordered to stay behind took up defensive positions. Herneas looked at them for as long as he dared before turning and sprinting into the darkness of the deeper chambers.

Silently, he added each of their names to his ever-growing list. Each one felt like a cut across his flesh.

*****

Yorna sat in her cell, slowly losing her mind. They had separated her from Craggoth hours ago. She had no way of knowing how long she had sat in this windowless cell and stared at the stones in the near pitch-black darkness. Her only illumination, and the only way to mark the passage of time, was a single candle.

Her ruined eye still ached, and it itched something terrible. She didn't know if she would ever get used to its absence, and at night, she was still haunted by visions of the ratman standing over her, his face filled with the glee of battle. She felt the hot lines across her face as his claws carved her eye from her skull again and again, her mind replaying the scene over and over. Then she would wake, a muffled scream on her lips. Most nights when this happened, Dig had been there to help talk her through the nightmare so that she could relax and return to sleep. She wished he was here now.

She wished a lot of things at this point. She wished now that she had never left the university. All of the aggravation, the snide comments about a girl doing a male's job. The passive-aggressive ways in which she was shunned. All of that seemed paltry compared to where she found herself now. Her face scarred and her dreams haunted. She wondered if her leg would ever heal properly. It still hurt to put too much weight on it. She was banished from her home and would likely never see it again. She had volunteered for what was quite likely a suicide mission and was even now waiting for an Abyssal Dwarf to decide her fate, which may be that death was the most pleasant of outcomes that she could hope for.

Then her mind drifted to the faces of her friends. Wynn's eager grin flashed before her eyes, causing her to smile in spite of herself. He'd never balked at her words. He'd always respected her and followed her instructions. Dig, with his warm, caring smile and his kind words. Herneas, who was a bit of a conundrum to Yorna. She didn't know what to think about the hunter, but she knew that she was always glad when she saw him. She was always relieved when he returned from a patrol. It had been him that had been sitting by her bed when she first woke after the battle. It was confusing. He was much older than her, but he never treated her as anything less than an equal.

She shook her head to clear it of where her thoughts were leading. She looked at the dim outlines of the stone masonry surrounding her. This brought to mind another of her friends, the most unexpected one. Craggoth was being held in some pen down below, like some kind of animal. The very thought made her face want to curl up into a snarl. She thought back to the conversation that she'd had trying to explain their deception to him, but the elemental hadn't grasped the base concept of lying. She had to laugh now, it came out as a grim chuckle, but she couldn't hide the warmth that lay within it.

She remembered what he'd finally said to her. He'd sent her images of a vault closing around a heart, or something to that effect. Then he had pointed to her.

"Thanks, Crag, love you, too?" she had responded quizzically. The elemental had shook its head and then more images entered her mind. This time of a sleeping babe in a cradle, but in her mind's eye she saw that the baby resembled Craggoth in some way that she couldn't quite describe. Then she saw an image of her standing over the cradle, she was in armor and held a hammer that was almost twice her size. Her face was resolute like she was watching over the cradle.

"Yes, ya big rock! Of course I will watch out for you!" she had laughed. Craggoth had nodded at this, and she felt the relief washing off of him in waves at that. More images appeared, this time of Yorna walking down a trail and Craggoth following close behind.

"Yeah, just follow my lead, will ya?" she had grinned up at the giant elemental.

Something wet fell on her hand, and she lifted it to her face and felt her cheeks were damp. She wiped the tears from her face and stared hard at the stone prison in which she sat.

She missed her friends.

There came a rattling at the door, the sound of a key turning in the lock, and then a stream of light as the door was opened. A figure stepped inside. She wiped her face one more time before looking up.

"There's been a complication for your conversion to our side." She heard Argoll's voice even as she squinted into the sudden light, trying to will her remaining eye to adjust.

"What might that be?"

"Follow me," he said, turning and walking out, leaving the door open. Yorna hesitated for a moment before hurrying to catch up. They walked deeper into the keep, descending down until the stone hallways gave way to more natural cave-like architecture.

Yorna gasped as they entered the cavern where she spied the Rift. Its swirling surface reflected purple lights all across the cave in shimmering dots and waves that looked like light dancing across the water. It would be almost beautiful if it wasn't so terrifying.

Argoll didn't stop there, though, and continued on to the entrance to a series of passages that wound for long enough that Yorna began to worry about getting lost.

"Is this where you house your golems?" she asked as they passed several branches in the path. Red light flickered down each of them, sending eerie shadows along the walls of the cave. Argoll said nothing in response. Then they emerged into another large cavern.

The first thing that she saw was something that looked like a giant glass column standing in the middle of the space. Red lightning flickered across its surface before crackling out through a separate entrance that she could only assume ran deeper into the caves. This had to be the device that Herneas had told her about, the one that maintained the power necessary to hold the feral golems. Her mind began to race as she imagined ideas for how she would destroy it.

Then she saw the prone figures forced to kneel on the ground before it, and her heart sank.

She recognized Brethod first. The young ranger was in Herneas's troop of rangers. His face was bloody, and one of his eyes was swollen shut. Beside him sat the dour-looking priest who had been excommunicated. Grodgni was his name, she thought. He didn't look much better than Brethod. Blood caked his beard, and his nose was bent in an unnatural way that caused her stomach to turn as she looked at it. Standing on either side of them were two massive dwarfs covered in black armor. Their faces stared silently out from beneath great winged helmets, and their eyes were dead as they looked at her. Further beyond them stood two more dwarfs. These ones looked worse for wear. Several were covered in spots of blood and seemed to be favoring a certain leg, or holding an arm protectively.

"You followed me, did you?" she said quickly, trying to keep up with the pace of events. Grodgni raised an eyebrow at her but didn't say anything, Brethod didn't even look up.

"We found these fools trying to sneak into the lower halls," Argoll said from behind her, and she could hear the sneer in his voice. "They haven't told us anything, but we have suspicions as to what they were looking for. We think that one of the things they are looking for is the device you see in the center of this room. So we've come here hoping to catch them when they make their move. I think that's not their only goal, though. They're after something else, too."

"What's that?" Yorna asked without turning around.

"Why, you, of course." His voice was suddenly right in her ear, and she felt cold metal at her throat.

"Wait! You don't know what I know, yet!" she pleaded.

"Hmmm... yes, your secret for controlling the golems. It does seem awfully convenient that you turn up with the exact solution to my problem right when I am at my wit's end. Then, shortly after you arrive, we find rats sneaking into our larder. You can understand my trepidation in believing you, can't you?"

"I know it looks bad," Yorna scrambled for something to say, but the edge of the blade made it hard to focus.

"Bad doesn't begin to describe it. I'm tempted to take you into the next room and wrench your secrets out of your body with a set of pliers. I think I'd start with your teeth. It's amazing how losing a few of those manages to loosen a person's tongue."

"You promised me that I would be safe!"

"Yes, and it seems that we both lied as to our true intentions, now didn't we?"

"Please!" she gasped.

"You have one chance, and only one, to prove to me that you had nothing to do with these dwarfs you see lying before you," Argoll snarled, spittle spraying onto Yorna's ear, causing her to flinch. He reached a hand out and snapped his fingers. One of the dead-eyed dwarfs stepped forward and grabbed Brethod by the collar of his cloak, yanking him to his feet. The blond-haired ranger staggered dazedly toward her.

Argoll removed the knife from Yorna's throat, and she took a shuddering breath. Then she felt his hand on hers. He twisted sharply, forcing her palm up, and slapped the handle of the blade into her grip before closing his fingers around hers. Slowly, deliberately, he guided her hand up so that the point of the knife lay at the base of Brethod's throat.

"Kill him." His voice was flat, and yet it carried a finality in it that made it echo in her ears.

"What?" she replied, dazed.

"Kill him, and I will believe you when you say that you had nothing to do with them being here."

"I..." she stammered.

"The alternative is that I start carving bits off of you until you wish that you had."

"No... I... can't..." Yorna whimpered, but Argoll's grip tightened, and he pushed the point forward.

"Shhh!" he hissed. "It only takes a slight amount of pressure. That's it!" A dark red jewel of blood blossomed at the base of Brethod's throat. He started at the sudden pain, his eyes focusing on Yorna. She could see the confusion in his gaze. Behind her, Argoll continued to make soothing sounds. She tried to pull back, but his grip was too strong.

"Stop!" she cried, but he only laughed.

Then something whizzed out of the dark passageways in the direction that the red lightning went. It flew through the air and connected with the dead-eyed dwarf's head, snapping it to the side. Argoll's grip loosened, and Yorna stared for only a brief moment as she realized that it was a crossbow bolt that was sticking out of the dwarf's head as he fell to the ground. Then she twisted sharply, wrenching the knife free of

Argoll's hand. She turned, wincing as her leg tried to give out on her, but she managed to stay standing and drove the point of the dagger toward her captor's chest. He tried to move out of the way, but the tip of the blade slammed into his shoulder, and she felt it slide into the flesh underneath his tunic.

He roared in pain, and his hand lashed out to slam into the side of Yorna's face, sending her sprawling onto the ground. She stared up at the ceiling above her, her vision swimming in and out of focus. She thought she saw someone kneeling over her and shouting her name, but she couldn't bring herself to respond. Then she felt something pressed into her hand before the person's outline disappeared from her view. After a few moments, she finally managed to push herself into a sitting position, and then she saw that the room was an ocean of violence.

All around her, she saw dwarfs fighting one another. She recognized the green cloaks of Herneas's rangers, and she spied the lithe form of Inei dancing among the shorter figures in armor. Each of them was dealing death all around them while red lightning flashed around the cavern.

Herneas himself was squaring off against Argoll. The Abyssal Dwarf had grabbed the large cudgel that his dead-eyed guard had been holding and was using it to fend off the hunter's blows. Yorna again felt something in her hand and looked down. It was some kind of canvas-wrapped package that was familiar somehow. She shook her head, trying to clear away the fog.

Then everything shifted into focus. She recognized that it was one of the satchel charges that she had left with Herneas to bring to her. She wasn't sure where the others were, but that was a problem that she would have to solve later. Right now, she realized that she was sitting at the base of the giant glass pillar and no one was paying any attention to her.

"This seems familiar!" Argoll's voice rang out, and Yorna froze for a moment, terrified that he had seen her. But when she turned to look at him, she saw that he was taunting Herneas. The fight between them had shifted, and now the ranger was on the defensive. His axe moved to counter the powerful blows of the red-haired Abyssal.

"It seems the last time that you and I danced like this that it didn't go well for you, Hunter!" Argoll snarled.

"You're right," Herneas agreed, wheezing from the effort. "But I'm not fighting you to win right now."

"Seems like a poor choice. What was the point of all this then?"

"I'm just trying to distract you," Herneas retorted, smiling as he glanced over the Abyssal's shoulder at Yorna. Argoll stiffened and risked a glance back.

Yorna stood with a vicious smile on her lips. She pointed to the pillar and the charge that was fizzling at its base. Argoll's eyes went wide, and he turned to point at the satchel. His mouth opened to shout an order, but whatever he was going to say never left his mouth.

The cavern lit up with the force of the explosion. It threw Yorna and everyone else to the ground, and she rolled in the dirt. The glass pillar shattered at its base and began to collapse while flashes of red energy flickered and pulsed. The great clear pylon toppled sideways and crashed into the floor. Shards of crystal and crimson lightning shattered into the air as a wave of magical power washed over the cavern in a wave that forced Yorna to put her hand up to shield her face.

When she lowered her hand again, she couldn't see Argoll anywhere. *The coward must have fled*, she thought to herself. She struggled to her feet and walked over to where Herneas was leaning, still panting. She saw Grodgni kneeling over the prone form of Brethod, blue light emanating from his hands. She watched as what looked like a cut seemed to blossom on the former stone priest's cheek as he muttered under his breath. Brethod gave a gasp of air and sat up sharply. His gaze focused on Yorna, and she smiled at him; his eyes simply widened incredulously in response.

"We don't have much time now. The feral golems will realize that their prisons have been opened shortly," Herneas groaned as he pushed himself forward.

"What about Craggoth?" Yorna asked.

"What about him? Isn't he with you?" Herneas replied.

"Do you see him here?" she snapped, then took a deep breath and tried again. "They separated us. They said they were bringing him down here to lock him in one of the golem pens. I'm not sure which one."

"You have a job to do…" Herneas began.

"We can't just leave him down here! They'll tear him apart!" Yorna cried angrily.

"Let me finish!" he barked, and Yorna glared at him. "I am not suggesting that we leave Craggoth. You take the remaining charges and head back to the cavern where the Rift is and start prepping it to blow. Grodgni and I will go and search the pens for Craggoth."

"But there are so many of them! How will you find him in all of this?"

"I don't think he's in the deeper holdings, those were nearly full when we were last here, and that was several weeks ago. I would wager they put him in one of the pens closer to the entrance. We'll start our search there. Once we find him, we'll meet you in the Rift cavern and we'll make our escape. Understood?"

"Yes," Yorna replied, although something writhed in her stomach and wormed itself into her limbs.

Something inhuman shrieked in the darkness behind them. Something that was deeper into the passageways. It sounded like metal being dragged across glass. It set Yorna's teeth to buzzing and made the air in her lungs burn uncomfortably. She felt a desperate need to relieve herself suddenly. She glanced around and saw the same feelings reflected in the others' eyes.

"We don't have much time," Inei said, cutting through the silence. "I will take Yorna to the cavern. Meet us there when you are finished looking for the elemental."

She reached forward and grabbed Yorna's arm, pulling her forward. Behind her, Yorna could hear the sound of heavy steps grinding their way against the stone of the caves. The sound was laborious and slow, but it was getting closer and closer.

They ran.

24
The Folly of Tradition

Not all greed is bent toward riches or power. Our greed can extend to things like wanting the best for our own children at the expense of others. It can be a desire to lift one's self above the rigor of the world and glorify their ancestors, even if it means we have to bend a few rules in order to do that. Perhaps the most deadly is the desire for glory that forbids us from using tools that we see as beneath us, even if those tools could save us or our loved ones from harm.

The worst, most insidious type of greed is the kind that worms itself deep into one's heart and calls itself a noble attribute.

–Athro *Korbus Ironbrow*
High Stone Priest of the Arceus Clan

"We've lost the left flank!" Myrgwyddn yelled as he leaped from his giant bird onto the ground before Sveri. The berserker lord cursed. The red strained at the edge of his vision, the bloodlust screaming to be let loose.

"How bad is it? How many have we lost?" he bellowed in return.

"About five regiments of Ironclad. There's a large group of spear levies that is surprisingly holding out, but they won't for much longer."

"*Uff'ran!*" Sveri swore again, this time much louder. "Can your ravens help them regroup? We have to hold!"

"We can try, but we are outnumbered almost three to one. We can't beat them in an open fight."

"I know that!" Sveri bellowed. "Have everyone form up on me. We'll circle our spears and prepare a fighting retreat. But I don't want to leave until we've spied the snake himself. If we can take Golloch out, then maybe this fight will have been worth the sacrifice."

"Why would he risk showing himself? He doesn't need to. He can sit back and let his minions come for us."

"Because he's a prideful ass, that's why. I'm going to give him a challenge he can't ignore, not without looking like a coward in front of his warriors."

Myrgwyddn shook his head and blew out a long breath.

"Are we falling back to the hill, then?" he asked after a moment's pause.

Sveri could feel his teeth grinding and forced his jaw to relax.

"That's right," he growled, then he turned his head. "Hetar!" he yelled. Hetar Mrawd turned his head and walked over to him.

"Yes, Lord Sveri?"

"We're falling back to the hill that we agreed upon before the battle began. It looks like the damned Imps are more bloodthirsty than we gave them credit for. It's time to make our stand."

The hill in question was a small rise that was nestled up against the side of the rocky cliffs of a giant peak that rose up into the sky. Sveri had seen it on the march toward Crag Hudd and had made note of it for a desperate defense. Because of its placement, it cut off two avenues that the enemy could come at them from. The mountain at their backs meant that they couldn't be charged from the rear, and the hill provided a natural shelter that cut off assault to their right side as well. Of course, this also meant that they would be cut off from any form of retreat, too. But the way the battle was going, that wasn't likely to be an option in any case.

"Sound the retreat." Sveri shook his head as he looked out over the fighting. Hetar nodded and walked away, bellowing his lord's orders. The sounds of the horns were heard over the din of clashing steel and the screams of the dying. The sound rippled down his lines, and as one, the lines began to shift.

"Why are you still here?" Sveri growled at Myrgwyddn. The stoneclaw rider stared at him for a moment, weighing the dangers of speaking what was obviously on his mind.

"If we fall back to that hill, a large number of our warriors won't survive. A good number of us will die, and you might be included in that number, my lord."

"I know. But we will take a number of these traitors with us."

"But is that enough of a reason to risk that? Without you, Lord Sveri, will the Free Clans be united enough to stand against the Imps *and* the Abyssals?"

"What else can we do? Do you really think Golloch will let us simply walk away from this fight? So that we can come back stronger?"

"We can get you away, my lord. We can deny him the trophy of your head. A trophy that he would wave over the other clans and use to subjugate them in turn."

"Or it would be a strong rallying cry for justice. Do not underestimate the clans. Besides, I won't leave my Hellbrock." The giant badger had been injured earlier in the battle, a spear piercing its shoulder so that it couldn't support its own weight, much less with him riding it. So he had sent it to the back of the ranks where healers were working to calm the raging creature enough that they could use their magics on it to treat the wound.

"I think you have given them too much credit. Do you not think that the past decade of injustices should have been enough to instigate an uprising? Yet there are talks from some of the chieftains of *joining* the Imps!"

"What do you want from me?!" Sveri roared and turned to face the other dwarf head-on. "I have nothing else to give! I have fought with my blood and sweat to free our home! After a year of fighting, what do we have to show for it?! A broken mountain in Cwl Gen and a decimated army that has known nothing but pyrrhic victories! What about my leadership do you think is so essential that it cannot be replaced?! None of us are that important in the grand scheme of things! But if by my death I can serve as a rallying cry, then perhaps it will have meant something!"

The two dwarfs stared at each other while the sounds of battle rang out all around them. Then, Myrgwyddn turned his gaze to look out over the breaking lines of the Free Dwarfs. He raised his hands to his mouth and called out.

"ALL HAIL THE BROKEN PEAK!"

The words rang out, rising above the cacophony of death. At first, it seemed as though the chaos would simply swallow the cry. But then came the return.

"HAIL THE BROKEN PEAK!"

At first it was only a few voices, but then a chant began to rise among the ranks that rippled out. Lines were shorn up. Frightened backward glances from warriors on the edge of fleeing turned to grim scowls of determination.

"FOR CWL GEN! HANNER BRIG!" Myrgwyddn yelled, and the chant took on a more solid cadence. Now Sveri could more fully make out what they were saying.

"HANNER BRIG! HANNER BRIG! HANNER BRIG!"

The cheers grew to a feverous crescendo that echoed out among the beleaguered dwarfs, and Sveri watched as the impossible happened. The Free Dwarfs pushed back against the Imperial traitors, and the line shifted. It was imperceptible at first, but another round of battle-cries brought about another surge of vigor, and this time it was undeniable. The Imps were pushed back one step, then another. Caught off guard by this sudden wave of anger, Golloch's forces struggled to regroup, and a few of the more worn out groups even turned and fled. Myrgwyddn turned back to Sveri.

"Do you still think that all you have won is a broken peak and a defeated army? You've given the clans hope. Before I joined this march, Lord Sveri, I did not think I would ever see my beloved Halpi Mountains ever again. Yet here I am, standing on my homeland's soil. Your legend is growing. You and others like you who have struck back against the Abyssals and now the bastard Golloch, too – you are leading the charge that others will follow. Do not throw that away because despair is a lighter load to carry than hope."

Sveri stared at him for a long moment, thoughts racing through his head. He felt something that sent ripples through the red mists that clung to the edges of his vision. It was something that cleared away the fog in his brain like sunshine cutting through the mist on a cold morning.

"Who are you to speak to your lord like this?" he said out loud, but his voice was strained as he fought to get the words through a throat that had become uncomfortably tight.

"I am nobody, my lord. History will not remember my name. That is not a burden that I can hold. I am just someone who loves my people and my home. I see some semblance of hope that I will see both of those restored in the way that you fight. I could not stand the sadness that your words brought me, so I thought I would remind you of what your victories truly mean." The stoneclaw rider smiled and looked away sheepishly. Sveri stared at him for a moment longer before reaching out to clap a hand on his shoulder.

"I do not know about history, but I do know that I will not forget your name, Myrgwyddn Tallpeak."

"That only means something if you live beyond this battle, my lord." The raven rider gave a weary smile.

"I can make no promises, other than that I will do what I can," Sveri replied.

"Then that will have to do." Myrgwyddn turned and strode back to his mount, climbing up to the platform on the large bird's back. With a furious beating of wings, the Stoneclaw rose into the air and flew off to aid the faltering flank. Sveri watched him go for a moment and then glanced back at the battle, his anger once again kindling in the depths of his chest.

"Form up! We make for the rendezvous point! Fighting retreat! Make them pay for every backward step we take!"

He lifted Mortcwyl and bellowed a warcry.

*****

Things were not going well. The battle raged for what felt like hours, but time had lost all relevance as Sveri's arm rose and fell tirelessly. The mindless violence that spread all about him as he killed, and killed, and killed again was numbing to his senses. The anger in his chest had dimmed to a seething boil that sustained him for now, but he felt the edges of exhaustion pushing into the fringes of his stamina.

They couldn't get enough of a reprieve to fully retreat to the designated spot. The Imps were persistent in their attacks, and they had the weight of numbers on their side. As a result, the threat of being overwhelmed prevented Sveri's troops from truly committing to the withdrawal. The crumbling flank that Myrgwyddn had reported on had completely collapsed now, and the enemy was pressing in on two sides.

It was all looking desperate. Sveri was vaguely aware that death loomed over their heads, but he couldn't find space to breathe to allow his senses to fully process this danger.

An axe blade passed too close to the front of his face, and he jerked back to avoid it; the edge of the weapon scored only a glancing blow across his forehead. Blood poured down into his eyes, and he staggered back to try and recover. Even as he did so, the warriors to either side of him closed the space so that the line remained intact. He felt hands pulling him backward, and he dazedly looked back to see two dwarfs yelling over his head.

"Hold the line!" one of them shouted. "Give Lord Egilax a chance to catch his breath!"

They deposited him on the ground, and Sveri found that his body felt like it was made of lead. His limbs were heavy and he found his hands were shaking, whether from exhaustion or fear, he couldn't tell.

He looked out over the figures before him. He couldn't see past the backs of the battle line ahead, but he could see that the ground was wet with blood beneath their feet and there were several bodies strewn across the ground.

"What is happening?" he mumbled through a mouth that ached. His words came out slurred, and he blinked to try and clear his vision. Someone was kneeling beside him, and he felt something being wrapped around his head. Sharp pain from the bandage being drawn tight brought the world back into focus.

"We are fighting, my lord," the figure said as they finished tying off his head wound.

"I can tell that, but why? Why are dwarfs killing one another? Why is this happening?"

"Are you well, my lord?" The voice asked, and the face of a young dwarf appeared in his view, a concerned look on his face.

"No, I'm not, and I don't know that I ever will be again." Sveri winced and closed his eyes, reaching a hand up to feel the bandages around his temples. "The world is not well. There is a sickness that is spreading, and it has infected us all. I am sick to my heart for what has become of us."

Part of him knew that he shouldn't be speaking this way. He opened his eyes and saw that the expression of the young dwarf before him had turned from concern to something far worse. His eyes mirrored the fear and regret that he himself was feeling.

"What can we do, then, Lord Egilax?" the warrior asked him. Sveri took a deep breath and considered what lay before them carefully. He thought back to his memories of his childhood, to those nights he had lain awake for fear of the cursed nightmare that haunted his dreams. Visions of his dead family members with their accusing, vacant stares etched into his brain. He remembered his mother sitting beside him, holding him close. The fear had paralyzed him in his youth, but how had he overcome it?

A slow, sad smile crept across his face as he remembered his mother's presence. She had never tried to talk him out of his fear. Instead, she had taught him how to confront it.

"Fear only has what power we allow it. It will take what we will not deny, and it is a greedy thing. This is why I think the Abyssals are cowards, they give all of themselves to their fear and it makes them angry and hateful toward those who do not give into that greed."

"How do we stop it from taking everything, Mama?" he had remembered asking.

"We remind ourselves of the important things in our lives, and we show it that we are the ones in control," she replied.

"How do we do that?" he asked. His mother sat in silence for a long time the first time he had asked that question.

"I suppose everyone has their own ways of doing it," she said slowly at length. "Your father practices his battle poems. I remember that your grandfather had recited poetry as he went into battle, or even when he found himself unable to sleep in the long nights."

"I would never have thought them to feel scared," Sveri said despairingly. His father and grandfather had been fearless in his eyes.

"Don't you remember Grandfather's favorite rhyme?"

"The badger's in the barrow, he got there chasing a squirrel. He fell down flat, and couldn't get back, and every curse his tongue unfurled," Sveri cracked a grin at his grandfather's awful poem, the image of an angry badger swearing up a storm as it tried to get itself unstuck.

"Well, he came up with that one for me when I was younger than you. I had walked in on him when he was having a nightmare and he had awoken with such fear in his eyes. When he saw me sitting at the edge of his bed, he called out to me and scooped me up into his arms. He composed that little poem with me there and it made me giggle uncontrollably.

"At the time, I had thought it odd that he did it with tears in his eyes, but much later when I was older, he told me about that night. He'd dreamed that I had been lost in the dark and he couldn't find me. He'd looked and looked for me in his dream, but in a way that

only makes sense while you're asleep or just waking, he'd known that I was gone forever. Then he'd woken up and seen me at the edge of his bed, he'd been so relieved that he couldn't contain himself. He said that the rhyme had sprung unbidden into his mind, and he'd said it without thought. He said it was my laughter that was the key that finally dispelled the horrible spell that the dream had cast on him. After that, he'd begun composing poems that he could use to remind him of that relief and to help him keep in mind what he had to protect. He said it helped him to deal with his greatest fear of losing my mother or me."

"Is that why he calls you his 'little squirrel,' Mama?"

"I think so," she said thoughtfully. "Maybe he saw himself as the grumpy badger who went chasing after the squirrel and got stuck in a dark place when he thought he'd lost me."

"So Grandad gets scared, too?"

"Yes, he does. I don't know anyone who doesn't get scared at least sometimes. But we all have different ways of dealing with it."

"How do you deal with it, Mama?"

She smiled at that question. It was a small smile, but it touched her whole face so that it seemed to light up as she considered her answer.

"I sing," she said, and Sveri had understood something about her. His mother was always humming, or singing softly to herself as she walked around. She bobbed her head to an invisible beat whenever she sat at court with his father. She always had musicians perform for the family and was always generous in hiring minstrels to play at feasts. Many nights he had heard her singing softly to herself as she put him to bed.

"Are you scared all of the time?" he asked with wide eyes. This time, his mother laughed.

"No, not all of the time. Sometimes I sing because I am happy, too. But when I am scared, it is music that helps me to be brave."

"What song do you sing?"

In response, she simply began to hum. This went on for a few seconds until she broke into the first verse of a song. She had never possessed what others would call a beautiful singing voice, but her music had been a honeyed balm to his weary child's mind at the time. He'd heard traveling minstrels and bardic troupes sing their culture's version of the song – it seemed to exist in one form or another throughout Pannithor. The most memorable one had been a wandering ogre warlock who had shared his tribe's version. However, It wouldn't be for a few years later that he had bothered to ask his mother for the name of the song as she knew it. Then he, too, had sung the song on the long nights when the Red Curse had weighed heavily on his dream-addled mind.

Flashing back to the present, he looked down at the fearful dwarf warrior who looked up so expectantly at him.

"Do you know the tune to *The Ballad of Circe Daloon*?" he asked. The young warrior gave him a quizzical look, but Sveri rose to his feet and began to belt out the first verse. Like his mother, his voice was not the most melodic, but what he lacked in skill he made up for in gusto.

There once was a maiden
Called Circe Daloon
Who fell for a young dwarf
And married too soon.

Her father, he raged,
And her mother, she scorned,
She went to her child
And these words she did warn,

"I've loved you for one day
I've loved you for two,
I'll love you a lifetime
Despite what you'll do.

"You'll grow and you'll learn
And you'll leave our fair home
To find another
And forget where you're from."

He felt a little foolish at first, but then he heard the other dwarf beside him join in, and slowly other voices could be heard. Soon, the whole Free Dwarf line was singing as they fought, and the Imps stared back at them with confused expressions on their faces. Some of them even hesitated in their fighting.

The wedding was honey
The night, it was sweet,
And soon she did carry
A child born of heat.

She held him and smiled
At her new baby boy,
And spoke these words to him
This new source of her joy,

"I've loved you for one day

I've loved you for two,
I'll love you a lifetime
Despite what you'll do.

"You'll grow and you'll learn
And you'll leave our fair home
To find another
And forget where you're from."

The tune was simple, the lyrics were sentimental. Yet it fit with a profundity that Sveri felt catch in his throat. He looked around him at the towering peaks that surrounded them. Even as they were beset by their enemies, the Halpi Mountains rose above them like silent witnesses. They *were* home. Even if they died here, it would be in the land of their ancestors. He launched into the third verse with those around him.

Well the years wore on
And the child grew and grew,
But time was not kind
To Miss Circe Daloon.

She passed in her sleep
While her son moved away,
He came to her wake
And these words he did say,

"You've loved me for one day
You've loved me for two,
You've loved me for always
Despite all I do.

"I've grown and I've learned
And at last I've come home,
I'll never forget
That you are where I'm from."

"Enough!" A voice bellowed out over the din of battle and singing, and as if directed by the voice of a deity. Silence suddenly reigned in a way that sent shivers down Sveri's spine.

A figure strode through the ranks of the Imperials, head held high and a long flowing cape covered most of him. He stood a good head and shoulders taller than any other dwarf whom he passed by, and an aura of malice accompanied his shadow.

"Golloch!" Sveri snarled.

"Your rightful king," the figure snarled back, drawing close enough that the berserker lord could make out his face. He wore a large helm that towered above him and held embossed quillons that crept up each side of the metal, giving the impression of horns.

"You are no king of mine. You are a tyrant!"

"Regardless of what you may call me, I am the one who has given your people a place to stay. I am the one who has collected your taxes and has come to Halpi to ensure its recovery. It is because of me that your people are even still alive. Even now, you only live because I have not ordered the full might of our forces to descend on you. You are at my mercy."

"That seems a costly mistake to have made. Either that, or you are bluffing."

"Take a look around, berserker, does it look like I lack the strength to end you?"

"Then why haven't you?"

"Because," the Imperial king laughed, "you would make a much better trophy for me to display were you to be kept alive and brought back in chains, where you can face your judgment."

"Just like Banick did, eh?"

"Banick got what he deserved. You would support a murderer and an assassin? I suppose that means that you were the one who ordered him to kill me?"

"You've drunk too deep of your own lies, traitor, that you've begun to believe them yourself."

"You have no idea the things that I believe. The things that I *know*!" Golloch raised a fist in a heavily mailed gauntlet and clenched it before his face.

"I know that you are a traitor and a liar. That is all that I need."

"Is that right? Then will you not surrender and spare your warriors' lives, such as they are, from being slaughtered here and now?"

"I think that they would rather die than submit to you."

"That is the likely outcome should we continue, yes."

The anger was back, pulsing like a red storm on the edge of Sveri's vision. His heart was pounding in his ears, and it drowned out the words that the traitor king was saying. All he could think of was how it would feel to pulp this pretentious king's skull with his hammer or take his head with his axe.

"Enough talk!" Sveri growled and stalked forward. "I'll end you here and now!"

He broke into a charge, raising both of his weapons overhead as he ran toward Golloch. The traitor didn't even try to move. Instead, two other dwarfs leaped in front of Sveri's path. He cut down the first one easily with his axe, Brydwr, the blade cleaving through his neck and sending a spray of crimson gore onto the ground. The second dwarf raised his shield to defend himself, but Mortcwyl fell with the weight of a mountain; Sveri heard the dwarf's arm snap under the blow, and he fell back howling. Now nothing stood between him and his target. He lifted his hammer again to deliver a crushing blow.

Golloch smiled as Mortcwyl sped toward his face. Sveri felt a moment of triumph as he braced for the blow to land. At the last second, Golloch threw back the cloak that had been covering his chest, and something glinted in the dull light as it flashed out to arrest the movement of Sveri's heavy weapon.

The berserker lord grunted as the hammer stopped midswing, the suddenness of it sending jarring vibrations up his arm and into his shoulder. He looked up and saw an armored claw extending out from under Golloch's cloak, the fingers wrapping themselves around Mortcwyl's haft.

"So very predictable," Golloch sneered and twisted his arm sharply. The hammer was wrenched from Sveri's hand in a single pull, and he watched as the Abyssal tyrant held it up as if to inspect it. "An outdated relic of your people's unworthy history."

Golloch pivoted and threw the heavy mallet at Sveri, who just managed to duck to the side as it flew past to connect with another dwarf standing beside him, killing the soldier almost instantly.

Before Sveri could recover, Golloch was upon him. The cloak had fallen away completely now to reveal a massive suit of armor. Tubes and pistons connected the joints, and the sound of steam escaping with every movement punctuated every blow that he threw at him. In one of his mailed fists, Golloch held a wickedly flanged mace that had flaming wings spanning each side. As Sveri dodged a blow, it connected with the stony ground and sent a shower of shrapnel from broken rocks flying up as if there had been a small explosion.

"How good of you to live up to your reputation, Lord Egilax! It is said that your fury in battle is matched only by your quick temper beforehand. A dwarf who is quick to anger is easy to control!"

Sveri snarled and lunged toward him, bringing Brydwr around for a sideways strike. Golloch blocked the blow with his forearm and pushed it aside before slamming the front of his helm into Sveri's face. He felt bone and cartilage pop, and for a moment, he was blinded as he staggered back from the unexpected strike. Golloch laughed, and Sveri felt something heavy slam into his chest, throwing him back onto the ground.

The air whooshed out of his lungs and refused to come back. Sveri gasped desperately, but his throat seemed to be filled with molten iron. His vision was returning, and he saw Golloch standing over him with his mace raised for a killing blow. Sveri rolled, narrowly avoiding the weapon as it once again cracked the ground where he had lain only moments before.

At last, his throat opened, and he sucked in a huge gasp of air. He became dimly aware that the fighting had resumed around him and bodies were throwing themselves at each other in the macabre dance of battle. He turned his head just in time to see Golloch's metal-clad foot slam into his stomach, lifting him off the ground and sending him tumbling onto his back.

"Your little experiment is over," Golloch sneered while standing over him. "The Free Clans were a mistake, something that should have never been allowed to happen. We are the descendants of a goddess! Our cousins to the north have bonded with immortality! We should be the kings of this world! But we spit and squabble amongst ourselves, and all for the scraps left over from the rest of the world."

"You're insane!" Sveri spat, he tasted blood in his mouth. "You really think the Abyssals will embrace us? That they will do anything other than enslave us?!"

"The weak must be separated from the strong. That has always been the way of the world, has it not?"

"That's what you desire for your people?"

"Better that we fight for our privilege than give in to our sloth. We have grown indolent and soft. Our aspirations have become wasteful and lazy. You Freeloaders are a prime example of this! You take and take and give us nothing for our charity! I will no longer allow this, and neither will those who follow me!"

"What a bleak future you must see," Sveri coughed, feeling his ribs shift uncomfortably as he did so.

"There is no future for the Free Clans." Golloch shook his head and raised his mace high. "You will be my sacrifice that will unite the Abyssals and the Imperials under a single banner that will march across the world!"

Time seemed to slow almost to a standstill as Sveri looked up at his approaching death. His senses had never felt so alive. The anger was so strong in his head that he could practically taste it in his mouth. The dirt beneath him felt gritty and damp with the blood of the slain all around him. He snarled his defiance, but he couldn't bring his limbs to move. The sounds of the world faded away, and he felt as if he were laying at the bottom of a well; the only light he could make out was fixed on Golloch and his massive cudgel as it fell toward his skull.

Sometimes we have different ideals that come into conflict with each other, and when that happens, we have to decide which of those ideals is more important. Sveri could almost hear Herneas's voice as the memory came back to him. It all seemed so long ago, their argument felt so futile now in comparison to the fate that was speeding toward him. Funny that this was the memory that triggered in his final moments.

You want to see your clan restored to its homeland and your family and friends established for future generations. You also want to win all of your fights honorably so that songs may be sung of your achievements and you will be remembered as an unblemished hero of our people. When the time comes that you must choose between these two strong desires, which of them will win out?

Another voice seemed to enter his head, speaking at the speed of thought. *What will it be, berserker lord? Will you die an honorable and pointless death? Or will you fight tooth and nail, honor be damned, to save yourself and your people?*

"No!" Sveri yelled. His hands clenched the dirt beneath him, and he threw himself back. He threw the gravel and earth up so that the spray hit Golloch full in the face. The imposter king sputtered and brought one hand to his face, causing his swing to go wide and narrowly missing Sveri as he rolled back and away.

Golloch coughed and spat, scrubbing one hand at his eyes while the other swung his mace widely to try and ward off any potential blows. Sveri made to rise but slipped in the blood-slicked mud beneath him, which caused him to topple onto his side. As he raised his free hand to push himself up, his fingers closed around a familiar handle. He looked up to see Mortcwyl lying in the mud.

He slowly rose, both of his ancestral weapons again in his hands. He glared defiantly across the way at Golloch, who had finally managed to scrub the dirt from his eyes.

"You are beneath my contempt!" Sveri spat. "You do not deserve my respect, and I will not fight you as an equal! You are filth! A vermin that is not worth the weight of my conscience. I will kill you and set my people free from your tyranny!"

"Pretty words for a dwarf who was inches from death only moments ago."

"Someone once counseled me that I should dispatch the threats to my people as I would a wolf that was stalking my livestock. I thought them a fool and a coward. But now I am beginning to see the truth of their words. You are not worthy of any honor that I would bestow upon you. You are the embodiment of trickery and deceit. So I will treat you as the creature that you are, and kill you like the rabid beast that you have become!"

"Let's get on with it, then! Let's see who kills who!" Golloch snarled. He raised his mace, and Sveri raised his weapons in defiance of him before charging forward.

The Red Curse swarmed his vision, and he let it take him away in a wave of crimson fury.

25
Unto Darkness

Sacrifice is always in the back of a dwarf's mind. It is not that we ask for martyrs, nor should any seek for such a dubious distinction. But at any given time, should the need arise, we must all be willing to step up and give everything of ourselves in order to protect that which we love.

Beware the dwarf who actively tries to 'attain' this hallowed status, however. For theirs is the mind of the zealot, the fanatic, and in their hearts lie the seeds of the Abyss, for such a sacrifice is not motivated by selflessness, but by the greed of accolades and the praises of mortals. This desire will lead to damnation as surely as the lust of gold has ever done.

–Athro *Degrinne Thundersledge*
Stone Priest of Caeryn Golloch
circa 3660 in the Current Age

Something was stalking them in the dark.

Herneas could sense it almost better than he could hear it. The sensation of a thousand sightless eyes staring at him out of the depths of the pitch-black shadows in the tunnels. He could hear the grating sounds of their volcanic glass feet being dragged across the stone floor as they shuffled toward him. Some part of him recalled Grodgni's description of the spirits that inhabited the possessed golems, and in his mind's eye, he could almost hear their tortured screams as they fought to escape their soul-bound coffins.

Each step became a feat of bravery as he descended deeper into the pens of the crazed obsidian creatures. Grodgni was beside him, and though they exchanged fearful glances with each other, they didn't dare speak aloud, lest even a whisper be enough to break the silence and bring the monsters down on them.

They rounded a bend and peaked down a long passageway that had likely held several of the pens used to house the creatures. The darkness of the tunnel was imposing, but Herneas couldn't hear anything moving. He turned and motioned to Grodgni, and the pair stepped quietly down the passage, the only light a fleeting echo of the torches in the passageway beyond. Herneas's mouth was dry as he walked, but he kept glancing about dutifully, looking for signs of Craggoth and where they might find the giant earth elemental. They quickly reached the end of the tunnel and were met with disappointment. The cells that had been used to hold the golems were empty, their occupants having vacated them to wander the tunnels beyond.

Herneas shook his head and motioned for them to return, and they began the laborious process of walking back. As they approached the main passageway again, there came the sound of heavy steps that crackled with the sounds of shattered rock crunching underfoot. Herneas pressed himself back into the shadows to try and obscure himself from view, but as he did so, a dwarf-sized figure staggered around the corner and ran right into him.

Unwittingly, the ranger toppled to the ground, a gasp of surprise escaping his mouth as he fell. His unknown assailant tumbled against him for a few moments before Herneas kicked out and they separated.

It was only then that he recognized the other dwarf. Argoll stared back at him, a look of surprise and terror washing over his face in waves. As the Abyssal's eye focused on him, though, the look on his face passed from fear into anger.

"You!" he snarled. Herneas leaped to his feet, pulling his axe free. Argoll also pushed himself up and held out a hand, a small bundle of flame forming there.

"Where is Craggoth?" Herneas growled.

"Your pet rock?" Argoll snorted bitterly, taking a step sideways, his eyes flickered to Grodgni who stood off to the side, his own weapon raised to strike. "How should I know? I'm sure he's around here somewhere if the other golems haven't torn him apart in their madness."

"Why are you down here, still? Your pride not letting you admit defeat and flee?"

"We're all going to die down here, I hope you know," Argoll spat. "What you have done is catastrophic for this area, but anything's better than letting Golloch rule, isn't it?"

"What happened to you, Anobreth?" Grodgni asked from behind Herneas. "What made you this angry? This bitter?"

"What happened?" Argoll laughed, it was a hollow sound. "By the look of you, you know exactly what happened to me. It seems you are on the same path. The people I claimed as my own, the people I swore to protect, abandoned me when I did something that they didn't like! When I acted in a way that I thought would offer the most protection!"

"But you found a home in Sveri's hold! Why is your anger directed at him?"

"I was just a lesser pariah at Cwl Gen, you know that. People whispered behind my back, and I was never trusted to be alone."

"That's not true at all! No one ever said anything untoward about you! You imagined that they did because you carried the bitterness of your former clan on your shoulder like a badge of honor!"

"So you say, but I saw the looks on people's faces. It was either disgust or pity! Neither of which I was willing to allow!"

"Sveri himself oversaw your funeral that we held when we thought you died!"

"How noble we all are in death, aren't we? The great absolver of all sins! That was far too little, and much too late, to be of any use to me."

"And your father? What about Cwythn? He loved you! Enough that he willingly followed you into exile!"

"He was a fool! He saw a wayward son that he thought he could save. He saw me as his own failure and thought that if he could bring me back, it might bring him his own redemption for having failed to bring up a worthy heir to his name!"

"Is that what you really think?! Has your anger and your own bitterness turned you so much against what you used to love?"

"It merely opened my eyes to what was always there. Life among the Abyssals is hard, and dangerous, but at least I know what to expect there. Everyone is at least honest about their intentions. They don't hide behind societal niceties, and they don't act as if they are morally superior to you. There may be a thousand daggers aimed at your back at any given time, but at least it is obvious that they are there and aren't hidden underneath a cloak of traditions and cultural obligations. We don't go to sermons to feel better about our shortcomings, we simply embrace them!"

Herneas listened to the exchange with half an ear, the rest of his mind was watching for an opening the entire time. As Argoll said this last part, his hand dipped slightly, and his focus shifted to fixate entirely on Grodgni. The ranger saw his chance and leaped forward, swinging his axe in an underhanded cut that would have sliced across Argoll's belly, had he not suddenly pivoted to the side. Herneas's weapon passed within inches of his body and cleaved only air.

"Nice try, hunter!" Argoll snarled and shot a blast of fire that singed Herneas's shoulder as he ducked under the flames.

"Anobreth! Stop!" Grodgni cried out.

"That isn't my name anymore!" Argoll retorted and fired another stream of heat that shot out to slam into the disgraced stone priest's chest, throwing him back onto the ground. Herneas leaped up and took another swing at the Abyssal while his attention was diverted. Argoll again danced out of the way and this time leaned forward to slam his fist into Herneas's jaw, causing him to stagger back in pain while his vision swam with sparks of light. Argoll followed it up with a series of other blows that connected with the center of Herneas's chest, forcing the air out of his lungs and making his vision begin to grow dim.

Herneas was barely aware as the shadow of Grodgni's form crashed into Argoll's side and they fell to the ground in a tangled heap. He took a few gasps of air and tried to clear his vision, but every breath hurt and he wondered, vaguely, if Argoll had broken one of his ribs. He glanced at the struggle on the floor and saw the two combatants locked together, but Grodgni had the upper hand. Herneas tried to push himself to his feet and winced as pain washed up from his side. He felt the urgency of Grodgni's plight, though, and so pulled the Skewerer from his back and shakily placed a bolt in the groove of the weapon. He cranked on the wheel to pull the string back and locked it into place.

"Augh!" Grodgni cried out in pain, and Herneas lifted his gaze to see that Argoll had managed to find his feet again and had produced a wickedly curved dagger from somewhere. The edge of the blade was dripping dark red droplets of blood onto the ground. Grodgni knelt before his attacker, his hands clutched his stomach and his fingers were red where the wound was pushing his lifeblood through them.

Herneas didn't hesitate. He lifted his crossbow and took aim in one swift motion. His vision was still fuzzy from the beating he had taken, but he took a single intake of breath to calm his shaking and squeezed the trigger. The Skewerer shuddered as the heavy metal arms pushed the projectile free and it sped across the distance toward his target.

The bolt slammed into Argoll's hip, and the force of the blow threw him back. The one-eyed dwarf glared his murderous intent at Herneas, but then his face cracked with a painful wince and he turned to flee back up the passageway. Herneas lowered the crossbow and ran over to Grodgni.

"Are you alright?" he asked, kneeling beside his friend.

"Well... I don't think I'll have to worry about exile much longer," the disgraced priest laughed humorlessly.

"Keep pressure on the wound." Herneas looked toward where Argoll had fled and saw a series of blood splatters that made a trail leading around the mouth of the corridor into the greater passageway beyond. Herneas could hear the sounds of grinding rocks coming from that direction, and they were getting louder, too.

"Don't worry about me," Grodgni said through gritted teeth. "Go after him!"

"Let the golems have him," Herneas said, turning back to him. "We have a mission to complete. Let me get you back to Yorna and the others, and I'll come back and look for Craggoth after."

"We don't have time for that!" Grodgni tried to argue, but his words cut off abruptly with a grimace of pain.

"Can you do anything to heal the wound?" Herneas asked.

"That's not how the benediction works," Grodgni wheezed, shaking his head. "I can take other's pain and wounds and make it my own, but that doesn't do much good when I try to do it to myself."

"Guess we're stuck with the more traditional method, then." Herneas leaned Grodgni back and tore away his tunic around where the wound was. His friend hissed in pain at the movement but relented. The ranger produced a wad of bandages from his pouch at his belt and a small jar of ointment. It was a strange blue paste that was made from a weed that grew in these parts of the mountains and was used to dye clothes blue. It also had the side effect of causing the blood to thicken and scab faster. It seemed like a wonder plant, but there was also the mild hallucinogenic effect it had on anyone who touched it with bare skin before the paste dried. He spread it on the wound with a scrap of fabric, taking care not to touch it directly with his own hands.

"This should help to stop the bleeding, although I'm afraid it's likely to cause you to start seeing things." Herneas smiled.

"Oh good, I love being trapped in a set of nightmare tunnels, in the dark, and the inability to trust my own eyes as an added bonus." Grodgni chuckled, and then winced as he did so.

"Better than just bleeding out, isn't it?" Herneas sighed and began wrapping the bandage around Grodgni's torso.

"I'll let you know if we get out of here if it is, in fact, the better alternative."

Herneas grunted at this instead of replying and put Grodgni's arm over his shoulder to help him stand. Together they staggered back toward the cavern where the Rift portal was located. Every so often, Herneas risked a glance over his shoulder and could just make out massive shapes shifting and staggering in the darkness behind them.

*****

Yorna felt along the wall, her one eye closed as she did so. In the darkness, she could sense the layers of the rock. It was disconcerting the way the stone seemed to speak to her, and she couldn't fully explain how it worked. She'd never had this happen to her while she had lived in Caeryn Golloch. Her whole life had gone by without having the mountainside reach out to her and try to communicate. It had all begun when she had witnessed Cerrig cut down in front of her, it had been the same time that Craggoth had found her.

She had spoken a bit with the grizzled former stone priest Grodgni about it during their march, and he had proposed a theory to her.

"That actually makes sense, and yours isn't the first story that I've heard like that. I have a theory as to how this works," he'd said. Yorna had looked at him quizzically, quietly urging him to continue.

"Well, there have been many stone priests who didn't begin to manifest their connection to the earth until after they had suffered some kind of loss or grief. Usually the death of a loved one, or the fall of a friend or family member from grace. After going through something like that, it was as if the stone started to talk to them. Some of them thought they were going crazy, others leaned into it. My theory is a simple one, but I think it fits. Dianek's grief is what gave birth to our very race. Her tears formed the first dwarfs, after all. So, it makes sense that she would reach out to her children when they are experiencing that same level of grief and loss that she would have known so much about. When you watched Cerrig die, that was the first time that you had ever lost someone that you truly cared about, and in that moment of grief and fear, something inside you called out, and the Earth Mother answered you. Maybe that's what called Craggoth to your side."

Yorna had stared at him for an uncomfortably long time after he said that. So much so that he had coughed and excused himself before she could find words to respond. Yet it had fit. Since Cerrig's death, she'd been left with a series of events that had seen countless numbers of dwarfs die, many of them at her own hands. Her nightmares were getting worse at night, yet she'd always awoken next to the still form of Craggoth, and that had made the long, dark hours more bearable.

She wanted to believe that it was true. But if it *was* true, that brought with it a terrifying realization. This meant that all the old stories were true, and that Yorna was stone-touched. She was used to the ostracization that such a label would bring, being a female warsmith in a college that was dominated by rather chauvinistic males almost made the isolation comforting. The real fear came from the accountability of what she had been gifted. Her achievements in the war colleges of Caeryn Golloch had been accomplished by her own skills and intelligence; she didn't owe anyone any kind of debt for the skills she had acquired there. Yet this was different, this was a divine gift. She felt somehow as if she was now obligated to do something with this power. The thought of such a weight of responsibility was terrifying to her, especially since it was such a nebulous and undefined debt.

Her hands touched an invisible seam that ran deep into the mountain's roots, the resonance of the fault echoing through her fingers like a series of pinpricks that ran up her arm. She opened her eye and tapped the spot with her knuckles.

"Put one here," she called out. One of Herneas's rangers ran up with one of the satchel explosives and secured it to the place she'd indicated. She then turned and walked over to where Craggoth was leaning against a wall; his hand was extended, and Yorna gingerly stepped into the giant earth elemental's palm.

"Where in the Abyss did he come from?!" she heard Herneas's voice and turned to see him staggering in from one of the entrances to a series of tunnels leading deeper into the mountain, Grodgni had his arm over his shoulders and his face was pale. Bandages were wound around the former stone priest's midsection, and his gaze seemed far away.

"He appeared shortly after you two left to try and find him," she said with a concerned look on her face. She hurried over to them as Herneas lowered Grodgni carefully onto the ground. "What happened?"

"We ran into Argoll, he looked like he was trying to avoid the golems that were loose."

"Craggoth said that the tortured ones were everywhere down here. He said he put down a few of them when he came looking for us. He was sad about that," Yorna said absently as she glanced at Grodgni's bandages. They were already showing spots where the blood was soaking through.

"How did he know to come here?" Herneas asked.

"He said he felt something calling him, or at least, I think that's what he said. While Craggoth can be very eloquent, we're still working on our ability for concrete conversation."

"Could've saved us a lot of heartache had we known he was going to show up here on his own," Herneas grumbled. Yorna ignored that and turned back to Craggoth. The greater elemental lifted her up so that she was three-quarters of the way toward the cavern's ceiling. She closed her one good eye again and began feeling along the wall.

"How much longer do you need?" Herneas called up to her.

"I don't know, we only have five satchels, so I have to put them where they'll do the most damage. I'm trying to hurry, but I'll need several more minutes."

"From the sounds of things down the passage, we don't have very long. The golems are awake and they're very angry."

"I know! I'm working on it!" Yorna snapped, then took a few deep breaths to try and calm herself. It didn't work very well.

Meanwhile, the sounds of the crazed golems in the tunnels were growing louder and louder. She couldn't tell if it was because they were getting closer or if more of them were starting to gather together. Either way, she knew that time was running out.

*****

Argoll gritted his teeth as he took another step up the ramp. He'd managed to sneak by the Free Dwarf saboteurs as they milled around the cavern where the Rift was held. They'd been too occupied to notice him as they scurried around the chamber, trying to attach what he could only assume were explosives. His anger flared when he thought about what they were trying to do, but the bolt in his hip grated against his hip bones with every step that he took. He was in no position to try and stop them in his current state.

He kept imagining the sounds of heavy obsidian blocks being dragged across the stone behind him, and for a few moments, he thought that the feral golems had caught up to him. His heart pounded in his ears as he stopped to listen and realized that the sounds weren't in his mind, nor were they behind him – but rather they were coming from the passageway ahead of him!

He limped forward to investigate and peeked around the bend to see a group of five golems with their backs to him. He could just make out beyond their massive shapes that there were a handful of dwarfs shouting and stabbing with their spears at the tainted constructs. He quickly ducked back around the corner.

How had they gotten ahead of him?! he thought with a sense of panic rising in his chest. He knew that he'd taken a detour down a side set of passages to try and throw the Free Dwarfs off his trail after they'd destroyed the pylon that had powered the cages. That had been where he'd run into that damnable Herneas and Grodgni again, and he'd been rewarded with the shaft of wood that even now protruded from his side. It must have been while he was occupied with that when the golems from other parts of the keep had made their way up.

The real question was how many of them had already made their way to the surface?

"Hold them back!" one of the dwarfs from the passage cried out. Moments later, there was a thunderous crack followed closely by the wet sound of something slapping against the wall.

"To the Abyss with all of this!" another voice cried out. "They can have this place!"

"No, you fool! Don't break ranks!" a third dwarf yelled, but another series of thuds happened in a frighteningly rapid succession. More sickly squelching noises, this time accompanied by several screams of pain that were then cut violently short as the sound of something heavy being dragged across the stone resumed.

Argoll risked another quick glance around the corner. The golems were making their way across the bloody remains of the dwarfen defenders. Chunks of what looked like skin clung to the appendages of the victors, and their bodies were splashed with gore that dripped from the sharp edges of their obsidian limbs.

Argoll shuddered as he watched them move. They walked with staggering steps that were completely at odds with the typical motions of a regular golem or even an elemental. Each step was a shaky mess, and their heads twisted at unnatural angles. He saw that the spirits that were housed in some of the creatures had formed faces that were screwed up to look like they were howling in agony, but no sound escaped their tortured mouths.

The creatures staggered forward toward the surface, and Argoll watched them go with a sense of foreboding. After they departed, he limped forward to survey the carnage. He was used to the slave pits of Tragar, so viscera and gore did little to upset him. But even he had to admit that the scene before him was extreme in its violence. Bodies had been crushed flat, the worst were those who had partially avoided the blows so that only their lower extremities had been pulped into a gory mess. These corpses displayed faces that wore death masks of agony that Argoll could almost still hear their screams of pain as they died.

There came a sound of coughing, and Argoll spun around to face it. A single dwarf lay propped up against the wall. His legs and one arm ended in bloody stumps that trailed broken pieces of bone and torn flesh and clothing.

"Oh, gods!" the dwarf rasped, a wet sound in his words. Argoll staggered over toward him.

"What has happened here?" Argoll asked, trying to sound commanding even as the terror ripped at the back of his mind.

"Please!" the dwarf begged. "You have to help me!"

"Look at yourself," Argoll sneered, "there isn't anything short of a miracle that could save you at this point! The best you can hope for is that someone will end it quickly for you so that the pain will finally end. If you answer my questions I will do that for you."

"I don't want to die!" the dwarf sobbed.

"That's not a choice you get to make, I'm afraid. Now, stop sniveling unless you want me to leave you here to suffer!"

"No! Please don't leave me alone!" His words were starting to slur.

"Answer my questions, then!" Argoll snapped. "What are things like higher up in the keep?"

"I don't know! We were called down into the caverns because there was word of intruders, but as we went, we were attacked by those monsters! They… smashed through our lines, and my group got separated in the chaos. We… we were trying to make our way back up to the surface when we found the golems were blocking our way out of here. Our commander ordered us to attack and force our way through to the surface."

"I see how well that turned out for you. How big was the first group?"

"Wha… what?" the dying dwarf blinked.

"The first group! The one that sent you running in the first place!"

"Didn't… really stop… t-to count… must have been dozens of them, though… m-maybe more…" Blood was starting to drip from his lips now, and his eyes were beginning to glaze over.

"Blasted Imp! Speak up!"

"They… were… everywhere…" The dwarf's voice was a raspy whisper before a choking rattle, almost like a cough, bubbled out of his mouth. His eyes were completely unfocused now, and bloody spit drooled over his beard and dripped onto his chest.

Argoll cursed and slammed his fist into the ground. The corpse of the other dwarf began sliding slowly across the wall. Argoll looked anxiously upward to the keep itself and felt a cold nagging anticipation. Could he hear the sounds of battle up there? Or was that just his imagination? Were those screams coming from the upper halls? What was happening? He felt the gorge rising in the back of his throat.

"What in all the levels of the Abyss do I do now?" he wondered aloud.

Come back, little dwarf! a familiar voice whispered in his ear, and suddenly the panic in his chest disappeared. He shook himself and tried to stand, wincing at the crossbow bolt still embedded in his hip.

Do you want to die here? In the mountain halls of your enemy? The voice was louder this time, more insistent.

"No," he found himself answering out loud.

Then come back to me!

He felt his feet moving beneath him. Part of his mind screamed at him to stop, to pull back, but the larger part of him only felt a strange sense of relief. His steps brought him back down, toward where he had fled.

That's it. Come back to me and I will ease your burdens. I will give you terrible purpose! The voice cooed in his ear as he continued to stagger onward. He was vaguely aware of shapes shuffling around in the dark just ahead of him. Great hulking things that moved to the side as he approached and did not move to stop him. Instead, they lumbered past with their own sense of purpose, and as they passed, Argoll could swear that he heard what sounded like whispered conversations. They sounded like the mad rasp of cracked lips as they muttered crazed prophecies. He felt that if he wanted to, he could listen and make out what the whispers were saying, but something warned him that if he did, he would never recover the broken shards of his sanity.

Instead, he gave in to fate and continued his downward descent towards the Rift and the voice that called out to him from its depths.

*****

"There are too many of them!" Herneas called back as he ran back down the passageway toward the cavern where the rest of his team was. "There are at least a dozen of those golems in the passageway ahead. I can't see any way around them."

"But the fuses are already lit! We have maybe ten minutes to get as far away as we can!" Yorna exclaimed, ignoring the worried glances that the rest of the party shot at her. "How did they get around us?"

"There must be other passageways that we were unaware of. Maybe the Imps dug them to hold more of the cursed golems," Herneas replied. Grodgni groaned from where he lay propped up against the wall of the cavern, and Herneas moved to stand beside him.

"It's alright, we'll figure out something," the ranger lied.

"I'm sorry, Cwythnn!" the disgraced priest sighed. "I couldn't save him!" Herneas bent down and checked his forehead. His skin was cold to the touch, and sweat made him clammy and damp. Neither of those things was a good sign.

"Hang in there, you damned fool!" he muttered under his breath. He glanced to the side and saw the swirling depths of the Rift glitter and pulse. It seemed to be mocking him, gloating that he was trapped there as it, too, soon would be. He had often wondered how his death would come, but being trapped under a falling mountain was not what he had envisioned.

"You've just given up, haven't you?" Yorna said from behind him. Herneas sighed and turned to face her.

"What else is there that we can do? Even if we had the ability to fight through the golems that are in our way, we wouldn't have time to get far enough away from the blast before the explosives detonated. We aren't going to disarm the satchels just to save ourselves. This was the whole purpose of our coming here, and we won't risk another chance of coming back. I haven't given up, I've accepted that our time has come, and I take comfort that at least we were successful in our mission."

"But this can't be it!" Yorna cried. "There has to be more to it than this!"

"I'm sorry…" Herneas began, but he found that he couldn't think of anything to finish his sentence.

"No!" Yorna growled. "No! I refuse to believe that this is everything. When I woke up with half of my face torn away, with my eye gouged out, I could have given up then. Fulgria knows that I wanted to! I thought that I would never be able to do the things that I wanted because I had a maimed sense of sight, and my hands now shake for no apparent reason! I have nightmares that follow me every night! But I forced myself out of bed. I pushed myself to move! To think! To create! I have seen others in similar situations to my own who have still gone on to accomplish great things! I won't let the things that have happened to me break me, nor will I let a plan gone awry be the end of me!"

"I don't think we have much say in that anymore." Herneas sighed and shook his head.

"Why not?!"

"Because that's not how life works! Things don't always work out like they do in the songs! Sometimes people die with unfinished dreams! Sometimes they are cut down in the prime of their lives with all of their potential ahead of them, like you! Many of us die of old age having never accomplished the things we wanted from our years! I have fought, and scrapped, and bled, just like you, and I know that it isn't fair! But what else is there?! What else can we do?!"

Herneas hadn't realized that he'd been shouting, but as his voice reverberated off the walls, a shocked silence hung over the rest of his companions that stood in the cavern. Yorna stared at him, hot tears brimming in her one eye. Herneas felt a tightness in his chest that mirrored her expression, and he turned so that he wouldn't be forced to face the despair in her gaze.

"I thought you were unbreakable," Yorna replied, her voice was thick as if she was being choked.

"I'm sorry..." Herneas squeezed his eyes shut. "Nobody is unbreakable, though."

"Don't quit on me!" her voice was small. "There has to be a way out of..." she suddenly cut off mid-sentence. Herneas opened his eyes and looked back at her. She was staring at the swirling patterns of light as they played across the walls. The lights caused by the shimmering Rift.

"We have not explored every possible outcome," she said at last. Herneas's eyes widened in surprise.

"You would have us go through there? Into a place where Dianek only knows what awaits us?"

"Well, we know what awaits us here," Yorna replied. "Would you rather wait for certain death? Or a chance that we might find some way to live and the possibility of finding our way home again?"

"I..." Herneas couldn't find the words. She was right. Death was the only thing that awaited them here, but was that better than what awaited them beyond those swirling depths?

"The time for deliberation is over. I know my course, and while I hope you will follow me, I will not force anyone to do so." Yorna took a deep, quivering breath and blew it out again. Then she began making her way toward the Rift. Craggoth immediately followed, and Herneas found the rest of the team watching him to see how he would react. He stared at Yorna as she limped forward and put a hand out to the vortex.

He turned and looked at the doorway leading up to the surface, the one he knew was hiding a horde of golems waiting to grind their bodies into pulp, and that was only if they beat the explosives to it.

He sighed and shook his head. There was nothing for it.

"Fall in! We don't know what will be waiting for us on the other side!" He pointed at the Rift and started walking toward it before his nerves could fail him again.

*****

Sveri staggered back under the force of another blow, his wrists ached from the impact, and his shoulders burned with the strain of the ongoing fight. Golloch didn't even appear winded as he stepped forward and swung his massive cudgel toward Sveri's head. The berserker lord danced backward, just out of reach, and sprang forward after the strike flew past him. Golloch didn't even bother altering the trajectory of his weapon, instead he simply raised his armored forearm and caught the edge of Sveri's axe with the heavy plates that encased his limb. Meanwhile, the traitor king's weapon swung around in his other hand and slammed into Sveri's side. But he had anticipated the strike and had stepped inside his opponent's strike zone which robbed the hit of any power.

"Do you give up? Little berserker?!" Golloch sneered, his voice betrayed no weariness, his eyes showed no signs of tiring. Sveri could feel his heart pulsing in his eyes, and his vision swam with every beat.

"You can bathe with the Wicked Ones, you forsaken traitor!" he managed to yell, but there was a ragged edge to his words. He couldn't keep this up much longer. Panic was beginning to replace the anger in his belly, his hunger for violence had turned to ash in his mouth.

"Such eloquence in your insults, Lord Egilax. But perhaps you need to sit down? You sound tired." Golloch's leering smile broadened as he spoke, and a flicker of red trickled into Sveri's vision. It was quickly smothered, though, when he tried to lift the heavy Mortcwyl by his side and his arm screamed in protest.

"It's over for you and the rest of your separatists!" Golloch bellowed, shaking his head. "You haven't been able to rally the clans to reclaim the Halpis in ten years! I have accomplished more in that time than your whole conglomerate put together! What makes you think that you can stand up to me?!"

"We will not bow down before a tyrant," Sveri growled, willing his tiredness away. "It's in our very name! We are Free Dwarfs! Our clans will never be fooled by the likes of you! Have you no shame?! You have sold your soul! And for what? For power?! For pride?! What?!"

"You wouldn't understand! I tried to teach you about this when you first came under my protection! I tried showing you how we could unite! Heal the breaches in our people and welcome our lost brothers and sisters home! How, together, we could unite and dominate all of the other races of Pannithor! The dwarfs! The rightful and faithful children of Dianek! Ruling over the whole of her domain! Can you not imagine it?"

"I cannot! You paint a picture of such majesty, but then you forget the flames which dog your every step of conquest! What price would you pay to put the world under your thumb? How many of our people are you willing to sacrifice in the name of your ambition?" Sveri flexed his hands, trying to work some feeling back into his fingers. Golloch stared at him for a moment, then blinked and looked at the ground. If it weren't for his exhaustion, Sveri would have struck at that moment. But the moment passed, and Golloch raised his eyes to stare into Sveri's.

"I would sacrifice everything at that altar," he said after a long pause.

"Then there is nothing else for us to discuss," Sveri replied. "You are past saving, Golloch! Your soul is black, your honor is beyond tarnished! You have succeeded in securing a legacy that will live on in the stories of our children, but it will be a story of your madness, not your victories, that will be passed from one generation to the next. Golloch the Traitor will be your title! The Mad Tyrant! The Elf-Witted Ruler! Take your pick among those rotten accolades and wear your shame with what pride you can!"

"You dare?!" Golloch growled and launched himself forward. Sveri braced for the coming impact.

But it never came.

Instead, the ground began to shake as Sveri looked up into the distance where he saw a bright red light shoot straight up into the sky. The crimson pillar shone for several seconds before the sound of shattered thunder ripped across the battlefield. It was so loud that all of the combatants were forced to hold their hands over their ears, and the fighting immediately stopped as the torrent of sound assailed them like shards of glass being thrust through their skulls. As Sveri fell to his knees, his own hands trying to block out the noise, a cloud of dust blew through the air and covered the battlefield in a dirty typhoon. The dust forced his eyes shut even as the screeching assault on his senses threatened to overwhelm him.

It felt as though the cacophony would never quiet, but after several moments, it began to fade as the echo of its passing reverberated off of the other mountains. The dust cloud receded, and an eerie silence remained. Sveri's ears rang in the sudden quiet.

"What in the name of the Abyss was that?" he whispered, his voice sounding distant and muffled even to himself. He shook his head and looked around frantically, remembering that he was on the field of battle. But Golloch was nowhere to be seen. All around him, the fighting had stopped and both sides were now shifting back to form proper battle lines again after the forced pause. Exhaustion filled everyone's movements, and the abrupt storm seemed to have shaken their resolve, both Golloch's warriors as well as his own.

A shrill horn rang out, and it sounded muffled to Sveri's ears. It was not one of his own. Then there came noises from the enemy lines. It took him several moments to recognize that they were voices, and several more before he made out what was being shouted.

"Fall back! Make for the keep! We are betrayed!" they said.

The enemy Imps reluctantly began shifting away, some staggered over the corpses that now littered the ground. Sveri couldn't believe what he was seeing. Part of him wanted to press the assault, but he could feel the absolute exhaustion gnawing at his limbs, and he knew that his army had been devastated to the point that pursuing the fight would be suicide. He didn't fully comprehend why Golloch was retreating when his victory had been so close at hand, but he also lacked the strength to question it.

"My lord?" a voice spoke from behind. Sveri turned slowly to see Myrgwyddn standing there, his face crusted with dirt and blood, a vicious cut ran from his right ear down to his jaw.

"Sound the retreat as well," Sveri muttered, his tongue tripping over his words so that he had to repeat himself a few times before the other dwarf seemed to understand. The stoneclaw rider nodded and walked off, yelling out what Sveri could only assume were the orders he had given.

The world seemed to be shifting under his feet, and he struggled to stay upright. He sank shakily to one knee and waited for the dizziness to stop. Meanwhile, the sounds of the dead and dying all around him began to seep through the wall of buzzing that currently assailed his ears.

26
Tentative Trust

The topic of kingship is a touchy subject among the dwarfs. Even before the civil war between them. Thankfully, there has been but one ascension since they were forced to set aside their prejudices, or rather, there has only been one that has been acknowledged. But there is always the fear of what the future holds, because Golloch showed them that tradition can be as much a tool for manipulation as it can be for guidance, and it is difficult to tell which way a new monarch will steer them.

It is hard for a race of people that has built itself upon a foundation as immovable as stone to find their way forward when that same stone has been known to rise up and crush them under its weight.

This is why anyone who wishes to rule must demonstrate how they mean to wield their own traditions, and which they will break.

–Jouer Brodenshod
Professor of Military History
College of Eowulf

Rain was falling outside, filtering the gray light of dawn through a curtain of tears. Rordin stared out of his window over the ruins of Dolgarth, the former capital of the dwarf empire. His mind played back to when he'd first received the order to come here. It had been a mandate from Golloch himself, but Rordin had felt as though he were being banished. The ruined hold had been overrun with monsters and beasts, abandoned to rot on the outskirts of Golloch's domain. Rordin could not help but make comparisons to how he had been treated similarly under his uncle's reign.

He lifted an armored bracer that he held up to reflect the dim light of the melancholy morning sun. It was inscribed with the mark of the Heavyhand Clan sigil, that of a fist clenched beneath a mountain's outline. It was remarkably similar to the Ashtel heraldry, and the irony of that was not lost on Rordin. He sighed and looked once more out onto the ruins of the city that he had fought to reclaim. He had not been the only dwarf to be forgotten under Golloch's ambitious rule.

There came a knock at the door, startling him out of his thoughts. He took a deep breath and turned to face it.

"Enter," he commanded. Banick opened the door and stepped inside. Rordin shot him a sad smile. The Free Dwarf had been with them over the past month since they had arrived at Dolgarth, but he had been more reserved and quiet than before. It was obvious that he was hurting from Garrek's death as much as Rordin was, perhaps even more so. Even now he wore a stoic expression on his face.

"Your nobles are ready for you," Banick said at length.

"Thank you..." Rordin replied, and his voice caught in his throat. He coughed and shook his head. "I apologize, perhaps I am not yet ready for them."

Banick's features softened and he nodded, turning toward the door.

"Just a moment," Rordin called after him. Banick paused, his hand hovering over the handle. He shifted his head to look back at the younger dwarf.

"Should I not inform them that you will be with them shortly? Is it not rude to keep them waiting?"

"I don't know that I care so much, honestly. I'm not sure what to tell them, anyways." Rordin sighed and walked over to his chair, which he promptly sat on. Banick eyed him for a moment and then turned to face him again.

"Tell them the truth," he said simply. Rordin laughed, but it was not an amused sound.

"The truth?" he mused. "The truth is that we are at war with ourselves. Battles have erupted all along the Abkhazla Mountains, no one is sure who to believe. Ofn's confession bought us some solidarity, but with only a few chieftains to corroborate his story, it leaves a lot of room to sow seeds of doubt, and plenty of ways that the story can be twisted as it is projected across the realm."

"I apologize that Ofn can no longer bear witness for you," Banick said in a flat, unreadable tone. Rordin shot him a suspicious look.

"Why apologize? His wounds were grievous, I'm surprised he lived long enough to give us what he did. You had nothing to do with his..." Rordin stopped mid-sentence as something flashed across Banick's face so fast that he could almost believe that he imagined it. Rordin paused for a moment before continuing.

"Don't tell me anything," he growled, closing his eyes and leaning back in his chair. "I don't want to have to lie about any confession you might make. I wouldn't blame you if you had finished him off. Not sure if that would have been considered mercy or vengeance."

"Perhaps both?" Banick suggested. Rordin sighed, opening his eyes and fixing the other dwarf with a stern glare. Banick shrugged and looked out the window as he spoke.

"Part of me still considered Ofn a friend. He helped me out in a difficult time of my life. The fact that he was manipulating me doesn't change the fact that his words and counsel were uplifting at the time." Banick paused before continuing. "That was definitely the smaller part of my mind, though. The majority was hurt and confused by his betrayal, but then that only confirms that he had been someone that I cared for, or else the hurt would not have followed his treachery. Perhaps it was the idea of who I thought he was that I mourned, and the traitor who died in his cell was the one who killed that version of Ofn. With that death, perhaps some healing can finally occur."

"We could definitely do with some healing," Rordin said. A moment hung in the air between them. As if prompted by fate, the rain outside ceased, and a single shaft of crimson light from the sunrise pierced the gloom through the window where Rordin had been standing.

"Gods but I miss him," Rordin breathed a deep sigh, looking out through the window.

"Garrek was a rare breed," Banick agreed. "I fear we won't see his like for generations to come."

"I should hope that we won't have to see someone in his kind of situation. Our society already failed Garrek, it would be a shame were it to do the same to another poor soul."

"That's the problem, isn't it? I am a follower of Dianek, and therefore a minority among your people, but there is a strong sense of tradition that binds all of us together. Whether a disciple of stone or fire, dwarfs cling to the past as a way of seeing into the future. This is the source of our strength, isn't it? If it has worked in the past, then surely it can help in our way forward! But with that comes a glaring weakness that Golloch was able to exploit. He's still using it today to tear us apart. Old grudges between clans, personal vendettas against rivals, feuds that date back so far that there are none living amongst us who can say where they began… All of them are being laid bare right now, and Golloch has turned us against each other through doubt, suspicion, and fear. Meanwhile, those same things are what unite our enemy against us, because they hate us more than they hate each other."

"You paint a grim picture, Master Kholearm," Rordin spoke in a whisper, but he didn't contradict anything that Banick said.

"I'm sorry, I do not mean to despair." Banick shook his head.

"You are not wrong, though." Silence crept into the space between them, filling the room with an emptiness that caused Rordin's stomach to knot.

"Can I share a secret with you?" Rordin spoke just to end the quiet. Banick shifted to look at him more directly, then nodded for Rordin to continue.

"I don't know what to do..." Rordin didn't know how to finish his thought, the silence returned, and with it, the anxious hammering in his stomach.

"I don't envy you your position. You have a shattered people to lead. You have received a broken crown from Golloch that..."

"I am not their king," Rordin interrupted.

"Only because you refuse to acknowledge it," Banick replied.

"I am no example for anyone to follow. I am directly tied to Golloch. I was his appointed heir. I should not lead the empire."

"You are perhaps the one thing that Golloch did that may actually serve your people. And if you do not step up to unify the Imperial Clans, then who else will?"

"There are so many noble clans that could fill that space."

"And what will that do with their rivals? Will they just fall into place behind their former antagonists?"

"In time, arrangements can be made to ensure that everyone will accept the choice of whoever is appointed."

"Do you really think that you have that luxury? There are Abyssals at our very gates, within our halls, even. If this were a perfect world, then you could make that argument. But your people need a leader now. They cannot wait until one is debated and chosen. If they do that, then Golloch will only drive the wedge deeper between the clans, and his plan will succeed in subjugating us all! If it bothers you that much, then abdicate after the war is over and let whoever is left decide who should be king. But at this point, action needs to be taken."

"That is all the more reason that someone should be properly chosen to lead. Suspicion and doubt will plague my leadership."

"Garrek believed in you, and he was the best dwarf I have ever known. Trust in his judgment if not in your own."

"And look where that got him!" Rordin snapped, his voice was filled with venom. That same silence stole back into the room, only this time it was filled with something more fragile, more hollow. Something clutched at Rordin's chest like a dagger was searching for his heart. Banick was quiet for a long time before speaking.

"Garrek and I were on opposite sides of the religious spectrum within our societies," he said at length. "We would have the most fascinating discussions because of that difference at times. We were both outcasts, and we both had shame associated with our names, but we each chose to face that in different ways."

Banick took a shaky breath, and the icy stillness of the room began to crack.

"Garrek had always admonished that the fires of Fulgria were a source of purification, meant to burn away the flaws of past mistakes and sins so that a follower could emerge a new creature. This new being would be stronger, and better able to accomplish those tasks for which they had been created," Banick sighed before continuing.

"The argument of stone, I countered, was that we were meant to be that object of permanence upon which a life could be built. We were meant to represent the steadfastness of Dianek's love for her children, our brothers and sisters as it were. Yet I never felt that love more than among those who found their purpose outside the narrow confines of our society. Garrek in particular was the very embodiment of that. He accepted me with my flaws and all. He didn't try to burn away the impurities of my shame and the instability I represented to the society of which he was a part. He moved to make room for me. He believed in me when everyone else was content to ignore me, and in doing that, he gave me the confidence to change my approach. I was able to confront my impurities, at least some of them, and come out stronger because of it."

"A beautiful sentiment and a better memorial speech," Rordin replied bitterly, "but I don't see how it applies to me. Garrek is still dead, and he died because I ordered him to be our rearguard."

"He died because he was willing to fight for what he believed in," Banick replied. "You did not send our enemies against us, and you did not ignite that bridge while he was still on it. But that is not the point that I am trying to make."

"Then what is the point?"

"Garrek affected a change in me, not with the intense heat of insistence, nor on the heavy pressures of tradition, both of which are the casual interpretations of our personal faiths. But rather with the consistent warmth of his presence and acceptance, he forged in me the will to continue fighting even when I thought all was lost. It was there, in the balance of our two faiths: steadfast in his regard for those who stumbled, yet unwilling to allow us to remain in our flawed state. I am not the only one, either! The entirety of the Heavyhand Clan is built of individuals who have fallen from grace but who needed another chance to prove their worth! Garrek took the impurities of our society and refined them into stalwart pillars that defended our homes and gave their lives in defense of a people who would have preferred to forget them! He took that part of his identity over which he had no say and turned it into his legacy. He knew quality when he saw it, even if it was hidden under a veil of flaws.

"When you look at yourself, all you see are those flaws. I think that is what most dwarfs see about themselves, it is in our nature and the nature of our various faiths. It is beaten into us by our society from an early age. But Garrek looked at you, and he saw a king!"

A moment of time seemed to freeze as silence coalesced around Rordin's vision like a jewel made out of ice. He didn't dare speak, lest he shatter what lay before him. Banick's eyes bore into him, and he saw the desperate grief that lay behind them. It was the Free Dwarf that spoke first, but he didn't break the spell.

"We take ore from the stones beneath our feet, and then we use fire to pull those minerals out of the rocks that forge our armor that is steadfast and strong in our protection. It is both fire and stone that crafts our people, and you can be that for the Imperial Clans! Right now, things are broken, but with that comes an opportunity. When reforging a blade or a shield, we are afforded the ability to correct previously unseen flaws in the design and temperance of our materials. Do that with the clans now, and reforge them stronger and sharper than they were before. Garrek, I think, saw that strength in you."

Banick then did something that caused Rordin's vision to tilt slightly as a wave of vertigo threatened to overtake him. He knelt and bowed his head.

"I see it as well, and even though I am a Free Dwarf, I would be proud to have you as a king."

Banick lifted his gaze to stare meaningfully at Rordin, who did not respond. The silence returned, but now it was different once more. Banick smiled a strange smile and rose to his feet. He bowed again and turned to walk out the door without saying another word.

Rordin watched him go and then looked down at the Heavyhand sigil on the bracer which he held. An idea began to form in his mind.

"Transforming fires to burn away the impurities, eh?" he muttered to himself.

*****

Banick looked around the spacious hall that was filled with dwarfs wearing expensive clothing, jewelry, and armor. He wasn't sure how he had been afforded a seat at this meeting among the chieftains and nobles of the clans who had responded to Rordin's invitation to meet and discuss Golloch's betrayal. Rordin had said it was so that he could stand as a witness that the Free Clans were willing to stand against Golloch as well, but he wasn't confident that he could be all that convincing.

The door opened, and Rordin entered the hall. Immediately all side conversations and speculative chatter died away as the red-haired dwarf walked through the crowd toward the front of the room where a raised platform stood. The other dwarfs parted to make way for him, and Banick noticed that Rordin was wearing the bracer that he had been holding during their conversation earlier. It bore Garrek's sigil. Whispers followed along behind Rordin, and Banick realized that he wasn't the only one to notice the bracer.

When he reached the platform, he stepped up and turned to face the gathered assembly. Silence reigned for what felt like an eternity as Rordin swept his gaze across the faces before him. He took a deep breath before speaking, and when he did, his voice resonated from the stone walls.

"My brothers and sisters! We are gathered for an auspicious meeting. By now you have been given reports of Golloch's betrayal, spoken by one who was close to our fallen king. I assure you that I have done my utmost to ensure that this accusation has not been embellished or altered in any way. The confession was simple: Golloch murdered his wife and has been plotting to deliver us up to our Abyssal counterparts further north in Tragar. His plan was to kill me and any others who would have stood against his insane desires. Those who would not have opposed him would have been given up as slaves."

Here, Rordin paused and looked around the room.

"This is something that we cannot allow. If you are here, it is because you will not allow this to simply come to pass and are willing to fight to ensure the future both for yourselves, as well as those who stand beside you. This is a noble trait, and one that I hope that other clans, not yet present among us, will emulate."

Here, Rordin's eyes met with Banick's, and the younger dwarf smiled a broken smile and nodded.

"But that is not enough, I fear," he continued. "For we can no longer hold to the petty feuds we have held for the past generations. Golloch has pitted us against each other using these old rivalries that we have borne from parent to child, all for the sake of supposed honor and societal demands. Yet those demands, that code of conduct, caused us to exclude those who would have been our greatest allies out of a sense of misguided propriety and gave Golloch the space to develop the festering rot which now threatens to destroy our way of life. If we are to overcome this sickness that has infested our homeland, then we must change how we view our siblings under Dianek."

With that, Rordin raised his arm which bore the bracer into the air.

"I will be the first to do this. Garrek Heavyhand was known by many names among many peoples. But among us, his own society, he was known primarily as an oathbreaker. Because of the sins of generations past, he was held accountable for deeds he did not commit and was passed over the honors that his own actions were warranted. With his passing, his clan's fate stands in the balance. Without having a worthy successor, they stand at a crossroads and may even face being disbanded, their fellowship broken and their found family scattered. I can only speak for myself, but I for one will not stand for such an affront. The Heavyhands have always been stalwart defenders of all things good and right. Whereas my family name should be seen as tainted with its connection to Golloch and his betrayal of everything we stand for. As such, he will be known henceforth as Golloch the Faithless."

This caused a ripple of whispers in the crowd and a few shocked gasps at the implications of Rordin's declaration.

"As for myself, I can no longer hold with the name that I have been given. Its legacy is tainted, its glory cast in shadow by its association with that traitor. I will take a more honorable name which I will carry forward." Rordin brought the bracer close and stared at it for a moment, his other hand touching the sigil reverently. "From this day forward, however, I will wear the name Heavyhand, and bear it proudly into the coming conflict!"

The hall erupted into a series of shouts and angry yells. Rordin's hammer appeared in his hand, and he slammed it down into the stone beneath his feet. The rock cracked with a deafening sound that quieted the dissenting voices. Silence reigned in the hall as the red-haired dwarf stared at the others who were present. Even Banick found it hard to meet his flinty gaze.

"I understand if what I say sounds too extreme and as a departure from what you hold dear. I do not require anyone to follow me who does not wish to do so. I do this not as your king, nor as the heir-apparent that is the title that has followed me for much of my life. I do this simply as a fellow dwarf who is concerned for his homeland. I abdicate my station as Golloch's heir, I want nothing from that traitor. I do not seek to be king, but I cannot stand by and watch the injustices of our past overwhelm the possibilities of our future." Rordin lifted the bracer, and his gaze lingered on the device it bore.

"As I said, if we are to have any hope of defeating Golloch, then there are certain things that we must look at changing. We can no longer hold to the grudges of our past. We cannot afford to be divided over the wrongs we have suffered and the slights we have borne. We must come together in spite of our past differences! Tradition is a wonderful guide when it is not holding you back from potential strength. Tradition ceases to be worthy when it binds us instead of freeing us. The tradition of shame, of ostracization, of guilt… those things must end if we are to face our foe. For Golloch represents all of those things: He is our shame, for we allowed him to seize power and did nothing to stop him. He is our guilt, for we should have been better at seeing him for what he was, but instead, we allowed him to grow because to face him was to admit that there was something wrong with our way of life. He will be ostracized because he encouraged us to abandon those of our families who did not conform to his shallow vision of what we represented. I refuse to hold on to those shameful practices! To do so would make me burn with embarrassment at what we have become. I wish to feel the fire of pride within that we all long for! The pride that makes our mountain holds home to all who are brave enough to seek it, and strong enough to defend it. How long has it been since we have truly stood proudly against the storms of the outside world? How long since we have felt secure in our keeps and known that our loved ones are around us, safe against the storms of this world? How long since we could call ourselves truly the keepers of Dianek's children?"

No one dared to meet Rordin's eyes as he cast his gaze around the hall. Even Banick felt the weight of his accusations as he remembered his own self-imposed exile back home. Had he not found it easier to run from his failures than to own them and continue in his duties to protect his home?

"Think on that and be honest with yourselves! And if it has been some time since you can sincerely say that you have lived up to that potential, then I invite you now, at this time, to let the fires that Golloch has made of our homes transform you. Swear new oaths: To protect our home! To give shelter to those who mourn! To lift up those who stumble and not send them away in their time of need! The dwarfs are builders, we should not be tearing our Earth Mother's children away from her!"

Murmurs began arising in the crowd, whispers that grew into shouts of approval. Banick felt something stir in his chest and found his throat constricting as he looked around.

"That is my oath, and my way forward." Rordin's voice grew quiet, and Banick leaned in to hear it. "I do not begin to deny that such is a difficult path, but it is one that I will walk. I do not require anyone to join me on it, but I hope that I will not walk alone."

The murmuring in the crowd died away, as if unsure how to respond. Then a single dwarf stood and approached the platform. Banick looked and saw that he was dressed in the blue and white of the Afalans Clan. He recognized him as Balchder, Ddiangen's son, and he stepped up to stand beside Rordin before speaking.

"What are your intentions, then? You say you are abdicating the throne, but what does that mean? You also speak of upsetting tradition and change, but how are we to know that these are good things?"

"I will not lead anyone against their will, but I will not follow Golloch's tradition of manipulation and fear. Things cannot keep going the way that they are. Golloch knows how we have operated for the past centuries, and he knows how to manipulate us if we keep to those paths. Something has to change in order for us to overcome him."

"And you think that you are the dwarf to do this?" Balchder's voice lacked the challenging sneer that his father's usually held, but even so, Banick held his breath. This was a precarious moment, and he knew that he was witnessing history unfold before him. Rordin paused for a handful of seconds before responding.

"I am only *one* dwarf. I cannot say for certain what the future will hold. I have a vision, one that I inherited from someone for whom I shared a deep respect. I do not wish to be king, if that is what you are asking. I only know that I love my people, but I must also follow my conscience, and I feel as though this vision that I have is a worthwhile one. If the people want it, then they are free to follow. I have no ambition to rule, but the way ahead is dark and unknown, and if there are any who wish to undertake the voyage ahead together, then I would welcome them."

"Those are pretty words that you have practiced for us, and I think that Golloch likely made similar ones when he was rising to power," Balchder said and sighed. "The Faithless is your kin, that cannot be denied. You speak of a world where we may be judged by the weight of our deeds instead of the weight of our names, yet that undermines our very way of life that we have established over millennia of tradition. This is convenient for you, as your name has recently become tainted. Under your leadership, my father was killed, and you have suffered only defeats at the hands of our enemy."

"Your father died exactly because he did not follow the plan that we had agreed upon," Rordin spoke through gritted teeth but did not go further. Balchder nodded before continuing.

"You are bold to accuse the recent dead, the mourning period has not yet passed for my father," Balchder spoke with raised eyebrows.

"I would do away with speaking falsely simply in order to maintain appearances. Your father was a powerful dwarf. But his pride caused him to be blind to the realities of the situation. He would not bend to someone he deemed below him, he ended up paying with his life, and many other dwarfs paid the price for his inability to see past social standings."

"Again, that is a bold statement," the new Afalans chieftain said. His voice was flat and lacking emotion. Banick couldn't tell if he was furious or bored. "There are many troublesome aspects of your past that could also qualify as discrediting indiscretions, too. You have spent time among the Basileans, have been known to associate with elves and barbarians in your past, and have gone on adventures all the while shirking your responsibilities as Golloch's heir. Would you have had similar words delivered as your eulogy that you have gifted my father?"

"What you say is true. I do not deny it. Your father also suspected Golloch and proudly stood beside me even when faced with the potential disgrace of being labeled a traitor. He was brave, and he held a strong sense of justice. He had good qualities that should be praised along with his follies which should also be justly scrutinized."

"And the Oathbreaker was not a participant in those sins of which you accuse my father?"

"You misunderstand me. Comparison is the sin upon which our society has based itself, and it is the flaw that I will no longer tolerate. Garrek had his failings, I assure you. One of those being that he believed it when told to him that he was less than the other members of society. Because of that, he did not stand up against the injustices that were dealt to him and to others, and he eventually ended up sacrificing himself because of this perceived inequality. He held himself as being below the lowest station of clans, and he did not realize his true potential. Your father fell to the same sin of comparison by lifting himself above those with whom he had entered into an alliance, which allowed him to be drawn into a foolish charge that cost him his life. Garrek died because he felt he wasn't good enough, your father died because he held himself above another. It is an apt metaphor for our society."

A collective gasp rippled through the gathered assembly.

"This is how you mean to rule? Through insults and disrespect to those who have given their lives for your cause?"

"I have already told you that I do not mean to rule. I have a path ahead that I will tread, but it is not an easy one, and I cannot allow pleasant lies to distract from what reality dictates."

"This is ridiculous! You would divide us even further with your audacious words?"

"I would have us restored to the glory for which we have formerly striven. Golloch's tricks involved flattering egos and catering to your prejudices to his own advantage. All we do by ignoring reality for the sake of tradition is play directly into his hands. I will not have this be my legacy. If you wish to cling to those ideas, then I will not stop you."

"Is this what we could expect from your reign if you were to be king?" Balchder's tone was careful, but it lacked the heat of accusation. Rordin did not falter in his response.

"Yes."

"So you do not deny that this is your ambition? To be king?"

"No, I do not want that responsibility," Rordin replied. "But I will not subjugate myself to anyone who is unwilling to be honest with me, either. Nor will I bow to one who would hide behind a cloak of tradition as justification for their actions."

A long silence greeted his words. No stunned whispers disturbed the quiet that followed as the entire hall held its collective breath. Banick felt a war inside his chest as frustration fought with an unknown fire that had ignited at Rordin's words. The moment stretched out for what felt like an eternity before Balchder broke it.

"Dianek help me," Balchder sighed, "but I believe you."

He held out his hand to Rordin, who stared in barely contained surprise before reaching out to grasp it.

"My father was a great dwarf, but I have grown weary with those who have offered me sweet falsehoods as to the magnanimous nature of his character. He was brave and bold, but he was also stingy and vain. I admired him, but he was not the paragon that his funeral painted him to be. I speak only for the Afalans Clan, but Golloch and his Ashtel allies are targets for my vengeance, and I feel that you are the best chance I have at that. I do not know what waits for us on the other side of this coming war, but I feel that you may be our best chance of seeing that come to pass. The Heavyhand name fits you well, for you do not shy away from the harsh truths that lie heavily at our doorstep, and you deal them with a steady hand."

Balchder broke their grip and turned to face the assembly.

"Word has already spread of Rordin's boldness with Ashtel at the meeting of the clans. He has shown that he does not bandy words, nor will he jockey for political position like a cowardly elf. That speaks highly of him. With a smaller force, he was able to keep the Traitor's army at bay until my father went against his orders. This also speaks to his military acumen. I believe him when he says that he will not bow before Golloch. There are many unknown things in the dark days ahead, and we will need someone to lead us through it. After that, we shall see who shall wear the Imperial crown, but I see wisdom in the decision to postpone that decision until that time, when we are less rushed and better prepared to discuss such weighty matters.

"I move that we declare Rordin Heavyhand as our reigning War Marshal until such time as we have defeated the Betrayer's forces and restored our empire to its proper order. Are there any that disagree with this action?"

The entire hall was silent as if none even dared breathe.

"All those who agree?"

Again, the silence was absolute, and Banick could feel the weight of that moment. Then there came, from the back of the hall, a heavy sound of something striking metal. The sound repeated rhythmically, and then it began to multiply. Banick looked around and saw that the gathered assembly had begun striking their chests with clenched fists in something akin to a salute. More and more dwarfs began to take up the beat, and soon the hall was filled with the sound.

"Glory to Lord Rordin! Dianek guide you!" and the cry was taken up by others. Sporadically at first, but then growing in unity and strength until it filled the grand chamber.

"Hail Marshal Heavyhand!"

27
The Aftermath

Where does it all end?
When does conflict cease?
Is it in this life? Or do we continue waging war in the aether of the afterlife as well?

Is there any rest to be had, in this world of ours? Or do we toil until our spirits are spent and we collapse to be tilled into the bloody soil of the gods' fields?

Where is there respite in Pannithor? Is it in Galahir? Or do we seek it in the Mountains of Abkhazla? Are we doomed to struggle in every corner of our world?

The only rest is in the arms of a friend, the only reprieve is the embrace of a loved one. What then becomes of us when we have lost those?

Therein lies the path to madness.
–Khiobar the Philosopher
circa 3804 CE

Sveri sat alone in his chambers. There were no windows and only a single candle to combat the gloom. Several bottles of spent rum littered the table and floor, and yet still he could not feel anything other than numb as he stared at the sputtering flame on that solitary candle.

"It would be so easy…" he muttered to himself, contemplating whether to blow out his light source or not. "Why does the light never last?"

On the table was the written report from the scouts he had sent to investigate the ruins of the former Crag Hudd. It lay half-read as he had begun drinking soon after receiving it, and the words had begun to run together.

Essentially it painted a grim picture. The hold had collapsed into a pile of rubble, the explosion had effectively sealed the Rift, although there was no way to tell if it was gone forever or simply buried under tons and tons of rock and stone. The feral golems that they had been constructing seemed undaunted by this change, and roving packs of them wandered the surrounding area. Sometimes they attacked each other, sometimes they stood in place for days at a time, swaying back and forth. More of them seemed to claw themselves free of the debris every day, so it was unknown as to how many there actually were. Estimates placed the numbers in the hundreds if not thousands, but it was impossible to give an accurate number. They did not travel far from the ruins of Crag Hudd, no more than a few miles, but it made the area dangerous for any traveller, and impassable for any army.

Of Herneas and Yorna's party, there was absolutely no sign. They hadn't found any bodies in the wilderness mauled by the roaming packs of wild golems to indicate that they had run into them. It was most likely that they had been caught in the explosion or the subsequent collapse of the keep, which meant that there would never be any bodies found, nor closure given on the matter.

Perhaps it was the drink, but Sveri felt like eyes were watching him from the flickering shadows of the room. He was not afraid of the invisible watchers, he was far too weary to feel that. Besides, his drunken madness was tinged with sorrow, and so the specters took on the guises of his friends. Herneas and Banick in particular seemed to stare out of the gloom in his periphery, their gaunt faces sad and concerned.

"What do you expect of me?" Sveri growled at them. "Everything is a mess! I've managed to get both of you killed! And for what?! For what?! I have a cracked mountain hold, and a destroyed one! Golloch is still out there with his armies, and we are no closer to securing our homeland than we were before!" He gritted his teeth and slammed his clenched fist against the table, causing several of the empty bottles to rattle from the impact.

The candle remained steadfast, only flickering a little.

"What more can we do?" Sveri questioned. "What more can *I* do?" He lowered his head onto the wooden surface and closed his eyes. It felt as though something was trying to squeeze his heart. He could feel his pulse pounding in his temples.

"Mother Dianek!" he pleaded. "What can we do? I have lost so many friends in this conflict! I do not know if I can stand to stomach more in the coming battles. What would you have me do?"

These words tumbled unbidden from his lips, and he blinked in surprise. He had never been one to call on the Earth Mother for solace. If anything, he had always felt a bit jaded toward his faith. With his childhood being dominated by visions of his nightmares and learning to control his Red Curse, he had never felt as though he were blessed enough to be seen as favored by her. To be truthful, he'd always resented her for giving him that burden, as it was easier to blame her than his father for passing it on to him.

But at this moment, the question hung in the air, and he did not call it back. If ever there was a time for her to speak, it was now. Another dead friend's face appeared, that of Grodgni, his former spiritual advisor.

"You always took her side in these arguments," Sveri jokingly accused this newcome ghost, who simply stood in silence with sadness in his eyes.

"She's got to have *some* answers!" he yelled this time, but the shadows swallowed his ire. "She can't always sit as some passive presence! She needs to actually help her children somehow!" Sveri's jaw trembled, and he clenched his teeth to still it, swallowing the tightness in his throat. He felt as if he were a child once more, having just awoken from the terrifying throes of his nightmares. Only this time, his mother wasn't there to comfort him. He was alone in the dark with his ghosts.

"What do I do?!" he wanted to scream the words, but he found himself out of breath, and so it came out in a wheezing gasp. In all his years, he had watched warriors succumb to the Red Curse, it was a horrible thing to witness. Normally when a warrior first had the curse come upon him, he became an angry, frothing mess, eager for violence. They would growl and snarl, and they would charge headlong into battle, their eyes bloodshot and scanning for their next target. It was a horrifying vision to behold. Older berserkers, though, were even more terrifying. The ones who had decided that they had had enough. They did not yell their bloodlust to the sky, they did not move quickly; their steps were resolute and their gaze fixed on the object of their bloodlust. They were quiet and resigned. Once the killing began, it did not stop until they were dead. Even if they ran out of enemies to kill and had to be put down by their friends.

Sveri had never understood what pushed a berserker to those levels. He had danced dangerously close on several occasions but had always managed to claw his way back for the sake of his friends and to return to those he cared for. Now, however, he felt as though he was beginning to understand. The draw of oblivion and an end to all of the nightmares sang a sweet song of invitation as he sat in his dark room and contemplated horrible things.

A knock at the door pulled him back to the present. At first, he ignored it and attempted to sink back into his comforting, awful thoughts. But then the knock came again, this time more insistent, and he growled under his breath.

"Enter!" he barked. The door opened to reveal a younger dwarf. He held a stack of parchments in his hands.

"What do you want?" Sveri snapped.

"Several messages have arrived for you, my lord," the young dwarf replied. "Responses from various clans within the alliance."

"Put them on the table, I will look at them eventually." The young dwarf hesitated, something on his face causing him to look as if he were in pain. "What else, beardling?"

"There is another message, my lord. This one is from Rordin of the Imperials, or at least it bears his seal."

"Rordin? You mean Golloch's heir? What could he have to say?"

"I don't know, my lord, but I thought you should know." The other dwarf walked over and placed the stack of letters on the table, carefully avoiding the puddles of spilled rum. Rordin's letter was on top, and it seemed to glow in the light of the guttering candle.

The messenger departed, leaving Sveri once more alone in the dark staring at the pile of letters. The solitary candle flickered and danced. He leaned forward and took the first message off the pile, some unknown force pulling at him from its contents. Breaking the seal, he pulled it open and read, then re-read, the short paragraph that it contained. He sat back and lifted his gaze to the ceiling overhead as a choked laugh escaped his throat.

The contents of the letter were simple and straightforward:

My friend Sveri,

I am so sorry that I have not contacted you sooner. Time and circumstances have not permitted me to do so. I was sworn to secrecy for my own survival, as well as to prevent our enemies from knowing of my location. But the time for secrecy has ended, Rordin has seen to it that all secrets have been brought to light. So I thought it was time that I did the same.

I am coming home, my friend. I look forward to seeing you and the others upon my return. There is much for us to discuss. I will be bringing news from Rordin, the new War Marshall of the Imperials, as well as a proposal of truce that I think bears examining. Look for me in the coming days. I have missed you all.

Most sincerely,
Banick

Sveri closed his eyes. A different pressure now squeezed his chest, and he felt as though some weight had shifted. It was still there, but now it was more bearable. He shook his head and looked back at the short letter.

"Thank you," he whispered into the dark. The candle flickered in response.

28
Shadows and Whispers

Our perception of the world is so very limited. Magic is proof of how much we do not know or see. Invisible energies permeate the very air around us, elemental spirits move through solid rock and molten lava alike. It is both wondrous and awe-inspiring to consider.

Yet with that awe comes a sense of trepidation. For all these wonders of which we are vaguely aware, how many dangers lurk beneath the surface of our perceptions? What monstrosities are waiting behind the veil of sleep, for instance? What entities would be willing to feast upon us if only they were conscious of us, and it is only by their unawareness that we continue to live on in blissful ignorance?

–Je'efra Gildentur
Scholar of Magical Physics.
Quote given a week before his disappearance.

"Anobreth! It's time to wake up!"

A hand on Argoll's shoulder shook him gently, and he forced his eyes blearily to open. He found himself in a room. Sturdy stone walls surrounded him, and a window above where he lay glittered as moonbeams pierced the glass and gave the room and its occupants an ethereal glow. He realized he was lying in a bed, and he felt warm and comfortable. His limbs protested his stirring as he pushed himself up on an elbow. He was alone, but he felt a chill as he looked around the room. At first, it was something below his waking thoughts, but as he continued to stare, he realized what was causing his stomach to churn uncomfortably.

The room was wrong.

Initially, he hadn't realized what it was that was upsetting him, but then he began to notice that the walls, though made of stone, seemed to be carved out of smoke. They looked sturdy, but as he leaned in closer, he realized that they rippled like the surface of a pond. The moonlight felt odd as well, the light hurt his eyes for some reason, as if it made them harder to focus rather than illuminating the room. The biggest clue that something was wrong, however, was the last thing that he noticed.

There was no door to the room.

"Are you finally awake, sleepy head?" a familiar voice said at his elbow. Argoll leaped back as he turned to face it. His father sat on the edge of the bed, a smile on his face that caused the wrinkles at the edge of his eyes to crease. The amused look on his face flickered, and for a horrifying moment, his face wore no features at all, just smooth skin. Then Argoll blinked and the smiling visage was back.

"What are you?" Argoll whispered.

"Don't you recognize your own father?" the being said, the smile not faltering at all. The kind eyes seemed to be staring at something just behind Argoll, and he had to fight the urge to turn and look.

"You are not him."

"You are in a strange mood this morning."

"The moon is high, morning is hours away," Argoll replied to this with a sense of anxiety creeping into his gut.

"Very clever," the creature wearing Cwythn's face continued to smile.

"Plus my father is dead."

"How do you know? Did you see his body?"

"No, but..."

"Then how do you know?" The voice was slipping into a sibilant jumble of slithering noises. It was a chorus of snakeskins rubbing together to form words from the sounds they produced.

"Besides, this whole room screams its lies at me." Argoll felt his back press against the wall behind him, but he seemed to sink into it as if it were a mattress or a cushion. Suddenly, a blood-red beam of light shafted through the window, and the room turned a sickly shade of crimson.

"There is the sunrise, now!" the creature hissed. "It is morning, and you are still just getting out of bed?"

"Is that your idea of a sunrise?" Argoll put fire into his voice, because anything else and it would dissolve into a piteous wail. "Have you ever even seen one?"

The smiling mask cracked, and the creature stood. Even though it still wore his father's skin, the other dwarf towered over him.

"Not for a long time," it admitted, shrugging. "One tends to forget those insignificant details after a while."

Argoll watched in abject horror as the skin of his father's face sloughed off, revealing a grinning skull with bloodshot eyeballs spinning in their socket.

"What are you?" he sneered, trying to keep the quaver out of his voice. The grinning skull took a step back as flesh seemed to materialize out of its bones. It did not suddenly appear, but rather it blossomed like a sickly flower reaching for the sun. Blood, tissue, and skin matured and stretched to cover the sickly face. Gradually, features began to appear. A sharp, aquiline nose, gaunt cheeks, and finally, pointed ears that swept back through glossy hair that cascaded from a freshly-covered scalp. A beautiful elven maiden stood before him now, which only caused Argoll's sneer to deepen.

"I am that which called to you from the other side," the elf said in a voice that somehow managed to be melodic and jarring at the same time.

"This isn't you," Argoll growled, though in truth, his stomach was threatening to betray him. How long would the visage of a skull being covered in flesh haunt his nightmares? "You are no elf! Nothing mortal that I could ever imagine could change their flesh like a change of clothes!"

"This is what I once was, you might say… or perhaps it is what I will be again? It is not set in such ways that one of your understanding could comprehend."

"You talk in riddles, at least you make a better elf than a dwarf."

"Would you prefer a different face?" the maid asked and raised her hand to the side of her jaw to pinch the skin there.

"No!" The word ripped itself from Argoll's throat, and he felt his brow dampen at the thought of watching another horrific transformation. He took a deep breath to steady himself and let it out shakily. "No. You said you summoned me here, to what end?"

The elf smiled and wagged a finger at him.

"Not just yet. Such a revelation would surely break you, son of Ariagful."

"What do you mean?"

"I mean exactly that. I could tell you that I summoned you here so that I could break free, but that is not how things work here. Some part of me will always be free, just like another part will always be trapped. But you will help me to escape with more than what I had before, and we will visit horrors upon the world as we do so."

"I do not understand you."

"Of course you don't, you haven't been properly prepared to do so. But we will come to that soon enough. Suffice it to say that I do have a purpose for you to be here, for all of you to be here. Your purpose is to find your way back to the realm from which you came."

"Can't I just go back the way I came?"

"No, that way is shut. There are others who will likely open it again at some point, but they are nasty creatures, and ones that you likely wouldn't want to meet."

"What do you mean?"

"Your dwarf sapper friend blew up the mountain and brought it down on top of the Rift. I have found ways to bypass many laws of the natural world, but even I cannot move a thousand tons of rock on my own."

"She is not my friend," Argoll growled.

"Oh, but she must be if you are to fulfill your purpose in coming here."

"She lives?"

"No… or maybe yes… it is hard to speak to that exactly. Do you mean currently or in your linear future?"

"I mean now!"

"She won't be, at least if the shadows that I have seen prove accurate."

"I have had enough of your damn nonsense!" Argoll snapped and took a step toward her. He reached out to grab the front of her dress, but as he did so, a slit opened up from her right shoulder to her left hip, and a massive eye appeared across her chest. He staggered backward in surprise.

"What are you?!" he yelled.

"I told you, didn't I? Or maybe I told you now…? The particulars of events become difficult to maintain without a proper order, and I haven't taken the appropriate time to organize our talks just yet. I will do it sometime before you arrive, and you will soon see a more sensical conversationalist from me. I promise."

Argoll simply stared at her.

"I am that which called you forth to here, the Void. It is a negative space where creatures of madness lay. All things are broken here: spirits, minds, time, hope, sadness… if it can be broken, it will be in this place."

"Why have you done this?"

"We have a place to go, and important appointments to keep, little dwarf."

"Who are you to speak to me like that?! I have helped topple Golloch's empire! I have been through hell and back! I will not stand for your patronizing words."

The elf stared at him for a moment, and he swore that her eyes grew bigger. Then she took three slow steps toward him. The giant eye on her chest blinked.

"I have gazed into the darkest parts of the timeless Void, *young* dwarf," the elf spoke slowly, and softly, but the words had an edge like a knife. "And do you know what I found there? Even darker places that I dared not go. There are leviathans in those depths that could consume our world with a passing glance and not even be aware of what they had done. I have clawed my way back through the tides of madness and the lonely spaces of the dark. You speak of knowing torment and having traversed its depths, but I assure you that you have only witnessed mortal suffering, and you know nothing of the horrors of eternity."

By the end of this, her face had filled his vision, and he felt as though her eyes were trying to devour him. He cleared his throat.

"What do you know of my suffering?" he whispered. The elf smiled and stepped back.

"I know that it isn't finished."

Silence hung in the air for what felt like an eternity before she turned and started walking away from him.

"Come along then, little dwarf," she beckoned over her shoulder.

"Why would I go anywhere with you?!" Argoll gaped at her.

"Because you don't want to be left alone in this place." She snapped her fingers and the walls of the stone bedroom melted away. Argoll found himself standing on a vast plain that seemed tinged with purple moonlight. There was nothing visible for miles. The crushing isolation of what he beheld fell on him like the collapsing mountain he had just escaped.

"Wait!" he called as the elf turned away from him. She stopped and looked over her shoulder at him with an arched eyebrow. "You still haven't answered my question! Who are you?"

She smiled then, and it turned into a wicked grin. For a moment, her whole being seemed to flicker and shatter. Argoll thought he saw something with elongated limbs that bent at unnatural angles, but then he blinked and the elf was back again.

"In the world of sunlight, I was called La'thael Bleakheart."

End of Book 2

About the Author

Ben lives in the wilds of Idaho, the land of potatoes, with his lovely wife and their kids. Ben is an English teacher who doesn't care enough about grammar to judge yours and teaches for the Department of Juvenile Corrections. He is an avid tabletop gamer and storyteller and has had a love of fantasy and adventure for as long as he can remember. He is always more than happy to share this passion with as many people as are willing to endure his ramblings.

Look for more books from Winged Hussar Publishing, LLC – E-books, paperbacks and Limited-Edition hardcovers. The best in history, science fiction and fantasy at:

https://www.WHPSupplyroom.com
Instagram: WingedHussarPublishing
Facebook: Winged Hussar Publishing LLC

For information and upcoming publications

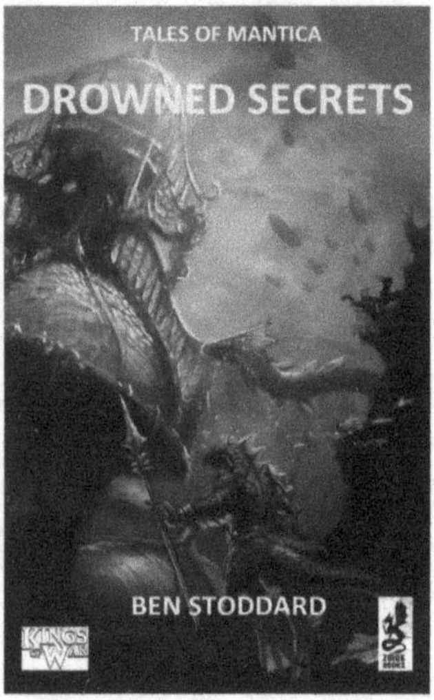